honesty

seth king

To my first real love.

For loving me,

leaving me,

and giving me this book

.

Based on a true story

"I love unmade beds. I love when people are drunk and crying and cannot be anything but honest in that moment. I love the look in people's eyes when they realize they are in love. I love the way people look when they first wake up and have forgotten their surroundings. I love the gasp people make when a favorite character dies. I love when people close their eyes and drift to somewhere in the clouds. I fall in love with people and their honest moments all the time, with their breakdowns and their smeared makeup. Honesty is just too beautiful to ever put into words."

-Unknown

~

"Speak your truth even if your voice shakes. Live your truth even if your body breaks. Spirit survives."

-Katheryn Hudson

~

"Man is free the instance he decides to be."

-Voltaire, *Brutus*

1

If my life was one of those quirky novels for teens, it would have an orange cover. Bright, though – think tangerine, not pumpkin. The title, something cheeky and hipster-cool like *I'd Fall Through the Clouds For You* or *I'd Give You the Universe* or *Every Last Star in the Sky*, would be splashed across that tangerine cover in a large and very loud handwritten font, and all the characters inside those pages (recycled, organic paper from a progressive Portland publisher, of course) would have improbably trendy names like Finn or Sienna or Agnes. Each of those characters would be quick to crack a joke and make suspiciously eloquent conversation and fall into deep love, and no matter how messy their pasts may have been, their futures would be picnics in July. But my life is not a quirky teen novel, because everyone knows those stories always have happy endings. The kids in those books always find their way back to each other in the final frame, and whoever is supposed to end up together, ends up together. Finn and Agnes always get over their differences and skip off to some cutesy college hand in hand, and nothing else is ever an option.

But yeah, no, none of that ever happened for me. My story was real, and it happened, and no matter how hard I try to forget it, I will never be able to make it unhappen. There were no witty comebacks to soften the blows that fate lurched my way, no sparkling plot twists to set everything right and send me off to a lifetime of bliss with the one I loved. The world took that from me, and I will probably never get over it. Nobody would ever want to read my story, anyway. Nobody would ever want to read about how this life introduced two kids to each other over one messy year, remade their worlds and taught them what glory tasted like, and then yanked them apart again. Nobody would ever want to read about how I met a boy who felt like he was made for me, the boy who grew me up, and then let him slip through my fingers like an idiot. Nobody would ever want to read the story of how I let Nicky Flores get away. But just in case you do, here it is.

11

This is how I lost him.

~

The day after I turned nineteen, I let my father bully me into signing up for an exercise program called FitTrax. Regardless of how many times he had walked in on me reading novels with pink covers and binge-watching episodes of *Real Housewives* over the years, he'd still spent the better part of my life laboring under the delusion that I was simply one *aha* moment away from realizing I was actually a crazed womanizer. Since pushing me in the direction of every serviceably-attractive female within a two-hour drive of my house had ended each time in a general series of *mehs*, he was pulling out his next trick. FitTrax, it seemed, was his latest cog in his evil machine meant to transform me into George Clooney 2.0, and so it was with a heavy heart and a half-erect penis that I shoved my Kindle into my drawer, walked into the giant gym full of sweaty college guys on Third Street, and tried to figure out how to pretend like I wasn't two seconds away from orgasming into my new workout shorts.

I went through the motions as best I could, but it didn't take long for trouble to erupt. In the beginning the jock squad was only laughing at Patty, an overweight girl in the corner. I heard them murmuring and laughing in those bro-ish voices of theirs, and that's what sounded the alarms in me – so I was eternally relieved when I looked over and saw they were only laughing at her. My relief at this made me hate myself for a second – sometimes I didn't even know how I lived with me. The Bro Pack was calling Patty a Sea World attraction or something – I didn't really notice exact details, since all jocks' lame and unimaginative insults seemed to melt together after a while – and so I laughed to blend in. This was my first mistake. My laugh was more of a girlish cackle than an actual, traditional male's laugh, which was something my dad never let me forget. My face went numb the instant I heard the sound leave my mouth, betraying me. The jock spotlight fell on me immediately.

"Faggotsaywhat?" one of them coughed into his hand, followed by some snickering. Our workout coach looked up a little from his chart, then shrugged it off, meaning I was officially on my own. As the panic set in, cold and sharp and biting, I tried to do what I always did during the assaults: I tried to turn my face away. I tried to stay stone cold. I tried not to let them know I was sliding into a hole at the bottom of myself. I'd been called the F word before, of course, and it hurt just as badly every time. Because it was not a word people said, it was a word they *hurled*: when they used it, their teeth turned to fangs and they threw it out like a grenade. It was a quick, hot little burst of a word: not faggot, but *faggot*! It reminded me of bubbling anger, bared teeth, deep-seeded hatred – all of those things and more.

The leader glanced at his friends, and then the Bro Pack did that thing all alpha males did where they laughed and then looked around to make sure everyone else was laughing, too, because anyone who – gasp – emphasized with, or even *defended*, a suspected gay guy was clearly a gay guy, too, so pounce on him before he could somehow reproduce and populate the world with more faggoty creatures! I focused even harder on a chip of mulch that had somehow been kicked into the gym. It didn't belong in that place any more than I did, and I suspected we both knew it. Stupid mulch.

"He's a *faggot*," the ringleader said. "Tell him, Nicky."

"Huh?" asked Nicky, a fringe member of the goon squad who was standing apart from the rest, with no particular interest. For one too-short moment, I prayed this boy Nicky would be my savior. I wanted him to throw me a life raft, to step in and break it up like they did in books in movies. No such rescue came.

"I said, *faggot*," the leader cackled, and some of the other goons laughed a little too hard than was called for. Except Nicky, who just stared at me not with pity or anger or disgust or anything, just…curiosity. And for the first time I really looked at him. He seemed like that one kid in every cool crowd who wasn't really actively interested in being popular, but his empirical beauty just guaranteed him a spot at the cool

13

table anyway. He was tall and curly-haired and sparkly-eyed, and in his deep blue workout shirt with the black piping, he looked like the good kind of trouble. He was the kind of boy that kept me up at night, and always had. Yes, I steered very clear of boys like Nicky.

The guys laughed again, and the leader gave me one final, hateful glare and waddled away. Burning up under their magnifying glass, I finally made my escape, sort of limping over to the water fountain and contemplating drowning myself in it. I got so mad I started to cry a little, these Hot Tears of Rage that squeezed out of my eyes and betrayed me all over again. The leader said something else then, but in my state of panic it was more of a metallic blur than a word, and I swayed a bit as I stood. I bent down to the fountain and wiped my forehead, throwing my stupid headband to the floor. What was I even doing here, pretending to be this thing I was not? I was too gay for this crap, and everyone knew it, apparently.

As I tried to make my final escape, though, I walked directly into a metal bar and sort of staggered backward a bit, knocking over a medicine ball in the process. I guess I never *could* win at this game of grace. A few girls giggled by the far wall. The whole thing was a mess, and I had never been more embarrassed. (Well, okay, I was a slightly effeminate guy from the South – I'm sure I'd been more embarrassed at some point, but you get the point.) Soon I was stumbling down the sidewalk toward the bike stand, wishing I could shrink into myself and become nothing and nowhere. And as I pumped my bike home the despair soon turned to anger, then white rage. Before long something snapped in me, like someone had pulled a lever in my chest I hadn't even known existed. That's when I knew I was done.

You know, I would've just taken this abuse in the past. Hell, I'd taken it this time like a total doormat. But this was the *last* time. I'd been swallowing up the poison I'd been fed for far too long. When I got home I yanked my phone off the charger and threw myself on the couch, feeling like boiling tomato soup was sloshing around inside me instead of blood. The idiot jock's voice knocked around in my head, and then

14

my mom's joined in, and then my dad's, and then my Sunday School teacher's, and soon a whole chorus was in my ears, hating me, and encouraging me to hate *myself*, stamping out all the traits they found undesirable in me. But I wasn't going to listen anymore. I was so sick of telling myself I was content with this life, with going to sleep restless and waking up sad, that there was freedom in the lonely nights, comfort in my long weekends with my books and my dog and my hand. I wasn't free, not by a million miles. I was suffocating here in this society that had supposedly set me free, and this wasn't a road I was going to let them drag me down again. This time I would kick and scream, even if I screamed like a girl. This time I would fight.

I guess the gist of my issue was this: my whole life, my world had told me who to be. And suddenly I wanted to talk back. I didn't want to buy into the lie that I needed to hate myself just because of who I was. Screw society for trying to make my gayness into A Thing – it wasn't A Thing, it was just a detail about me. I was just a kid with the dreamer's disease who spent too much time on his phone and read too many books and maybe even wanted a hot boyfriend to go to the farmer's market with on Saturday mornings sometimes. I never wanted to feel like I had back at that stupid gym again. Hating yourself sucked, and it was the worst feeling in the world, short of that three-second state of panic when you drop your phone on a sidewalk and think you've shattered your screen. I didn't want to ever let myself believe that I was somehow less of a person, somehow not a whole human, because I maybe liked penis and most other dudes didn't. The jocks were about to find out just how much of a *faggot* I was – it was as if I'd been sleepwalking all my life, and one six-letter word had just jolted me awake.

With a mushroom cloud of jock-stoked fire burning in my belly, I downloaded a dating app called Mixr and then did the craziest thing I had ever done in my nineteen years and one day of being alive, something the Me of two years ago would have been scared shitless of doing: I selected *"Interested in: Men"* instead of women and got going trying to

15

find a match. Every iota of me was rioting and throwing warning bursts of confetti into my bloodstream, but I didn't care: I was on a mission.

I got to work sifting through the collection of half-dressed male bodies on the app, since this was still the South and none of them would show their faces because that could possibly result in societal excommunication and/or death, and then I paused and felt my jaw drop out of its socket a little. Because at 8:11 on a windy evening in May, I found myself staring at the unmistakable workout shirt of the boy called Nicky.

2

Hi, I said before I could stop myself. I heard a ringing in my ears and suddenly I couldn't believe I'd *actually messaged a guy*. Masturbatory fantasies in the safety of my room were one thing, but actually *acting* on this urge? Whoa. When I was younger this would've pulled up a white, paralyzing, almost sickening terror in me, terror that I was Different. Terror that someone would find out and expose me, terror that everyone in the world would point and laugh at me, terror that the secret that I was not worth loving would be exposed to the world. All of it together brought up a very specific and urgent fear in me, a fear that simply said: *everyone will hate you. Everyone will look at you. Everyone will talk about you. Nobody will want you.*

But suddenly I didn't really care. Not enough to stop, at least. I just waited. And waited. And waited...

Hot guys always took longer to respond than regular people. I'd always noticed that, just from texting my few straight friends. It was the same with pretty girls – I guessed they were all just busy being hot. It took up more time than being ugly did. But I didn't think they'd take *this* much time.

Hey, he finally said, and suddenly I was without a chill. I was rendered chill-less. Goosebumps spread over my arms like breeze on grass: Nicky, he of the glorious hair and beautiful eyes and goon squad, was talking to me. This was a thing that was happening. Nobody like this had ever even acknowledged me, much less messaged me. I had no idea what I was doing, but all I knew for sure was that I couldn't stop.

What's up? I responded. Then my mind went insane – all of the lights in me flashed at once. What the hell was Nicky, certified member of the bro pack, doing on a gay messaging app in the first place? It was too delicious to be true. I hadn't really wondered about him earlier, mostly since he'd appeared to be a beautiful pipe dream, but now that I knew he was...well, possibly *like me,* I wanted to toss over every stone, investigate every avenue. Had he searched for men on accident? Or was he just getting home from the gym, too, and was now tossing his sweaty shirt on the ground, chugging some water, and wishing for someone to love? Was he exploring a long-suppressed urge, or was he a philanderer who came on every night to get sexy times from dudes and somehow just managed to keep it hush-hush? Soon a whole hurricane of questions erupted in me: who was Nick, really? What did his life entail? Was he lonely like me, or did he have someone? What beautiful guy, or girl, was lounging by his side this very minute, feeding him grapes or charging his phone for him or something? For some reason I became instantly jealous of these hypothetical people for hypothetically getting to hangout with him. Hypothetically, of course.

But then I told myself to chill the hell out. This also could've been some kind of trap – maybe the jocks weren't satisfied with not getting to beat me down, and now they were trying to bait me into showing myself to confirm their suspicions and take me to pound town. But then again, why would Nicky hide his face? What were the odds that he knew I was me?

Not much, he finally said. **You?**

Same, I said, and then the conversation went dead for a minute. Okay, so he was a boring texter. There were worse issues, like a having a raging cocaine habit or being one of those kids who posted eighteen thousand Snapchat stories a day or something. But the conversation was fizzling, and I had to push it along – so I pulled out the one card I knew would blow things up in his face.

Could I get a face picture?

My throat seemed to shrivel into my stomach as I sent the message. This was *the big one*: I was asking him to "out" himself, basically. I knew who he was, of course, but

18

obviously I couldn't admit that. But would he even show me? How "in the closet" was he? Was I crazy to be asking him this?

I waited. My stomach disappeared into itself, reminding me of those YouTube clips of office buildings being detonated into dust. This was it: the point of no return.

Yeah, he said, **after you.**

I froze. I couldn't possibly show myself after that scene back at the gym. How could I tell him that his own friends had just gay-bashed me half an hour ago, while he'd stood there letting it happen? This was a Macarena in a minefield, and it was getting messier by the second.

You first, I said out of a sheer inability to come up with anything else.

Ugh, fine, whatever.

He sent a photo. It was grainy, but it was him, really him. And he was so beautiful. I tried to recover from the moment of paralysis that came from corresponding with a hot boy, but it never came.

Oh, I said. **I kind of know you.**

I regretted sending this message instantly, though. I'd never used an app, but I'd still trolled enough message boards to know the basics of how this all worked. Talking on these apps required a degree of trust, because in the South, all of this had to be conducted under the radar. You had to know the other person wouldn't talk to people about seeing you, and a good way to ensure that was to talk to a total stranger, since they wouldn't give a shit about who you were or what the world knew about you.

A tangy metallic taste erupted in my mouth, and my vision seemed to melt together in a weird way. The tone between Nicky and I seemed to change, as if I could actually pick up such things over a phone. But for some reason, something told me I could.

You do? he asked. **From where?**

Do you really want to know?

Yes.

FitTrax, I said.

Who are you? he asked after a long pause. **Show me.**

I didn't say anything. My heart was beating too loudly, and in my ears. Was he daring me to show myself so he could beat my ass back to Sweden, or did he really want to know? I'd never even talked to a guy like this before, and it made me want to do a bunch of very filthy things to myself in my shower immediately. My neighbor's cat was mewing on the porch and pawing my door, but all I could think about was this beautiful boy and the unexplainable fact that he was messaging me.

Show me, he said again. Breathless, I sent the most attractive photo of myself I could find. From my graduation, it was framed in my parents' living room. My father had once remarked that my head was skewed to the side in it, and that only "gay, feminine" men tilted their heads, as if there were any correlation between head angle and sexual preference. I didn't care, though, and actually I thought I looked pretty hot in it for once, thanks very much, pops.

The conversation flat lined. For one minute, and then two, and finally three, he said nothing.

…? Is there a problem? I asked. His next response came directly after:

First of all, I'm sorry about today. About everything. I really am. There's a lot you don't know about me.

And suddenly nothing in the world made sense anymore.

Okay? And? I said, but my message didn't go through. He'd already blocked me and signed off.

I spent the next day trying not to shit myself about going to FitTrax. Not about the goons – I'd be sure to stay clear out of their sights – but about Nicky. His words – *there's a lot you don't know about me* – would not exit my head. What was I possibly going to do when I saw him? Would he know who I was? If he did, did he think I would "out" him? That's the last thing I wanted, mostly because it would ruin my chances with him, and I was nothing if not narcissistic and self-motivated. There were so many variables, and soon I decided I had three options: one, walk up to him and talk to him. That was out of the question immediately, since I was such a pussy. Two: try to go about it some sideways way, and allude to the app, but not *really*. And three: do absolutely nothing and try to pretend the conversation had never happened.

Soon I got *so* overwhelmed with all of it. Liking dudes was *so* rude and frustrating. I couldn't even manage my own debit account without bouncing it all the time, so how was I supposed to figure all *this* out? Everything was still so backwards. For all the "progress" society claims to have made, it still only seemed to want to accept gay men who either hated themselves, or were willing and eager to become the butt of the joke, become the monkey dancing for laughs and approval. Gay guys in movies were always either quietly depressed closet cases who moped around for decades before dying alone in a trailer somewhere, or exuberant fashion queens named Nigel with bitchy dispositions and vague European accents who were delegated to lispy sideshow status while Kate Hudson (or whoever) got center stage. Society's acceptance came with an asterisk: *oh, sure, we'll accept you! But here's your box we've created for you – fit into it, or get thrown back out again.* Either be the clown who did tricks for laughs, or the recluse. I wanted neither of those things – I just wanted a normal life. I wanted kids and an SUV and a hot husband, or maybe none of that at all. But I still wanted to choose, for myself. I wanted love, with nobody watching – or worse yet, laughing. I wanted to be a guy, and not just a *gay* guy. But I didn't get to choose. Society chose for me. And how was I going to choose to talk to Nicky with the peanut gallery watching?

Nineteen was already *such* a confusing age, for so many reasons. I had one year of college under my belt pursuing some vague communications degree, and I had nothing to show for it. I was like a nineteen-year-old toddler. I wanted to do something that came from my soul, but I didn't know my soul wanted. I was stuck in something I couldn't even name or describe, wishing for something I couldn't even pinpoint – nostalgia in reverse. I knew I had to let go, but I didn't know what I needed to let go of. I knew I needed to move on, but I didn't really know what I wanted to move on to. I was perpetually in the middle, nobody's child and nobody's parent, feeling too much like a kid while thinking too deeply like an adult, wanting to jettison my past and hug it at the same time, wanting to run from the future and embrace it with big open arms all at once.

Everyone I knew was just as clueless as I was, too. Nobody even had a job, but their social media profiles still read "dreamer/dancer/visionary/consultant/artist" under their work descriptions anyway. Their dream was to do nothing, and they wanted everyone to watch them while they did it. And so they all just danced forward, spinning in circles to avoid the crushing student debts and the blown-out job market and the sense of resigned doom that had messed with us ever since the towers fell on the news and made us stop looking to tomorrow. They drank to forget, they snorted to go numb, they went to sleep and remembered. But I was nothing and nowhere, neither on the outside looking in nor on the inside wanting out. I was perpetually on the bubble, within and without, staring at my reflection in a golden window, alone…

I did not see Nicky in class that day until I smelled him. His scent jumped right out at me for some reason – it was this crisp, cool thing that invaded my nostrils and made me feel cold. Not chilly, but *cold*. Downright freezing. I looked up, and there he was – all six feet whatever of him. I knew it was a rule of humanity that being tall made people hotter automatically, but he was almost *too* tall. And he was looking down at me. He didn't really look furious or nervous or anything like I'd expected, he just looked…curious again. And it was such a relief. I felt something bloom within me then, something I'd forgotten a long time ago: I think it was hope. I guess I'd never really noticed the point when I'd stopped looking forward to the future – I'd gotten so wrapped up in everything, I'd gone numb, become content with a life in the middle of the road. What a terrible, reckless thing to do. And I'd done it.

But here he was – new hope. He was back. And he was staring at me like I was burning. Everyone should get to feel like this, I thought as I savored him, and try to hold onto it with everything in them.

But then I became Cole Furman again. Knocked senseless by the force of his stupid eyes, I sort of staggered backwards like I'd been punched. Something in his face changed, and he pulled his eyes away. But he didn't say anything, and everything he hadn't said, and *could've* said, seemed to scream at me as he walked away.

As class went on I licked him up from across the room as he bro'd out with his friends. You know those people who were just heart-stoppingly beautiful? Those people who made you stop and stare, who made you want to congratulate their parents and high-five the universe for assembling such a well-formed collection of molecules? Yeah, well, Nicky wasn't really like that. Not at first, at least. But upon further inspection…

He was magnificent, really. As I pretended to stretch, I admired the curve of his shoulder muscles and his shortish, curly hair, which was medium-brown, but touched by the sun on top. I noticed the thoughtful expression he always took, like he was figuring out a math problem that was just out of reach. I studied his nose, which was just the right amount of strong. The most noticeable thing about him, though, was how he seemed to sparkle in a way that most people our age did not sparkle, not after the realities of this sucky new world had set in. College tuition, rent, electricity bills: that world hadn't gotten to him yet. Not to mention whatever flopped around under his gym shorts whenever he jumped or ran... (By the way, could we all agree to high-five whoever had invented gym shorts? They were like push-up bras for dudes.)

I also liked his eyes. As a wannabe photographer, I'd always been into eyes. They really did say so much about a person, and they could always surprise you. And Nicky's eyes were surprises. They were such a cool color – I was so sick of seeing boring eyes. Brown, blue: so many were the same. But his were different. Most people would probably just call them hazel, actually, but to me they were everything. A strangely vibrant yellow on the inside, a seafoamy green on the outside, with darker green/brown flecks throughout: they were like two galaxies swirling in his face. What must it be like, I wondered, to look out at the world through galaxies every day instead of eyes?

All my life I'd trained myself not to notice these things. I'd learned very early on that if someone caught you checking out another guy, you were done, instant kryptonite. If you got caught staring too much, the whispers would start and soon you'd be radioactive. It had happened to boys at school, at church, everywhere. I could even remember this kid, Dinesh, who'd get caught staring at other guys sometimes in freshman year. He even did it to me once, and I noticed that he was hard *down there*, even though I never said a word about it. But once he stared at the wrong kid, and word got out. Soon there would be a literal gulf in the crowds whenever he passed in the hall. He tried to come to a field party out near the football stadium one night, and he ended up getting his faced kicked in. He needed jaw surgery and stitches in his eyebrow, and yet he never revealed his attackers. Snitching would've just made it worse, and everyone knew it. So he withdrew and finished out high school from home. Hatred ruined his life, and in the end *he* was the one who had to apologize for his own downfall. (I heard his parents got wind of the rumors and sent him to some creepily religious "pray away the gay" type camp in the California desert, but that was a different issue altogether.)

Taking all this into account, I'd put on the mask and try to blend in. And if I *did* check anyone out, I'd do it slowly, inconspicuously. I'd track my eyes across a room, pretending to scan for friends, but really lingering on a torso or ass before continuing, my dormant mind twitching with possibilities. If I had a dollar for every time I'd been caught staring at a guy's ass and had then unconvincingly pretended I was casually in the middle of a yawn, my last name would be Hilton.

Now that I studied Nicky, though, I guess there were *some* markers that he was gay, some things I should've noticed. It really did take one to know one, and I *knew* him. His voice was…soft somehow, with maybe a *bit* of a lisp. It wasn't effeminate in any way, it was just…gentle, rolling over on itself, maybe a little high-pitched for someone of his height. His walk was delicate, almost bird-like, too, his heels only kissing the floor. And there was a softness in his eyes, a sort of misery that perhaps spoke of a self-hatred that looked suspiciously like mine. Not all gay guys were "girly," but some were. As for me, my father and my classmates had spent my life mocking me for my rail-thin frame, my not-entirely-deep-voice, my unaggressive body language, and my complete lack of interest in anything sports-related. What if Nicky really was the same as me?

I knew I needed to slow my roll, but I couldn't. I could not pull my thoughts away from him. I felt like my mom's slutty chef friend Karen who would drunkenly attack me at block parties and then try to take me home for the night "to try out this new cookie recipe on me." I felt my deadly eyes pulling to him all class long, those insidious revealers, betraying me. I had to stop this. For good. So I simply started rubbing my chin whenever I wanted to look at Nicky, to satisfy the tic. But it didn't take long to let myself slip. I glanced at him while he jump roped, and some spark jumped from me to him. He just made me feel…hot. He looked back, and some mysterious factor told me that he knew – he'd felt it, too. I knew he did. I don't know how, I just…*knew*.

26

In the end I only tripped twice during the group workout, which was probably some kind of record for me. As I got water towards the end of class, though, I caught Nicky staring at me again. Something in me flipped over and then got all flimsy or something, like when you caught a fish and then tried to hold onto it. My face went white, then red, then numb again. In his presence, what was air? What was life? None of it added up anymore.

But then I second-guessed myself again. Why was I such a creep? And why was everything I did so weird and awkward? I needed to stop. I was in too deep, and maybe he wasn't in at all. Nobody felt this much emotion in the world, and I needed to become anybody but me. I'd had a taste for straight guys (or "straight" guys, anyway) all my life, and each time it had ended in slash-and-burn devastation. I'd imagined guys like Nicky being into me a million times, thinking I saw a habit or noticed a little tic that pointed to Gay Town, and then I'd fall desperately in love with them only to come to school the following Monday and watch them make out with a cheerleader named Christine while I stood alone by the Coke machine. Maybe I had to quit this bad religion – I just didn't know how

But then again, if Nicky *wasn't* into me, then why did he check me out as I walked out of the gym with a look in his eyes like I was the Hope Diamond?

"So how are you?" my dad asked me on the phone that night. "What's going on?" I had zilch in common with my father and had no idea what to tell him, so I said nothing. "What about FitTrax, then?" he asked. "How's that going?"

Part of me wanted to tell him the truth: *Oh, it's splendid! I'm getting kicked around by a bunch of dumb jocks because you're forcing me to go to a gym every day and act like somebody I'm not, and worse than that, I'm actually letting it all happen. How about them Atlanta Braves?*

"Oh, it's just dandy!" I said instead. "You know me – I'm Mr. Olympia, basically. If I got any better at all this stuff,

27

I'd be walking around with a gold medal and a steroid dependency."

"Oh, hush. Stick with it – it'll do you good to be around some other guys your age, and not just those girls you go around with. Furman men stick things out, that's what we do." I tried to keep my shoulders from falling, but they still did. The words still hurt. My dad wasn't outwardly mean or anything, he was just careless and casual with his comments, which was worse in my eyes. The casual kind of cruelty hurt the worst, as it usually rolled off the lips of the ones we loved most. Sometimes we let our loved ones pick and pick and pick at us until suddenly there was nothing left to save. "Or should I cancel the subscription to the gym?" he asked after a moment. "It's so expensive, you know…"

"NO!" I shouted, shocking myself, as galaxy eyes swirled in my mind. "I mean, uh, no, no – I'm fine. I was kidding. I love it."

"I knew it! That's amazing. And what's going on with Drea?"

I made a face and rolled my eyes. Drea was my cousin's roommate who happened to be – and God bless her little heart – uglier than a newborn Rottweiler. "*Dad*. It's the same as last time you asked. I don't even know her. She's…nice, I guess?"

"Well she's looking much better ever since she got that goiter removed, or whatever it was. And she's really matured and filled out in the chest area, if you know what I mean."

I cringed. I didn't want to talk about boobs at all, but *especially* not with my own father. I'd always been horrified by this whole thing he did where he tried to be a meat-eating, all-American male with me, and it made me squirm on my couch. "Can we talk about something else?"

"Sure."

I listened to the sea for a minute. The sea didn't ask you questions. The sea didn't care about who you loved.

"Oh, I heard about Naomi and Ruth," he said, who were the sixty-something ladies who lived in the unit directly under me and were clearly partners, even though they called

28

themselves "roommates." If I passed them on their porch and saw them holding hands, they'd cough and pull away from each other as quickly as they could. It killed me inside and embarrassed me in equal measure. I didn't know why they thought I cared, or why they thought they had to hide at this point in their lives. Wasn't it a little late in the game for the whole "closeted" charade? But deep down I still sort of *understood* the reflex to hide, and it made me fear for my future with everything in me. "Two old ladies shacking up together?" he said, disgust in his voice. "It's gross, if you ask me. Nasty. That's what it is."

"Dad, wasn't your own *cousin* gay?" I asked him. I froze as soon as it left my mouth, though. What was with me and spitting out highly regrettable statements, anyway? My father's first cousin had been closeted her whole life, and had only started opening up to my family six months ago – which also happened to have been her last days on Earth. She'd drank herself to death at the age of forty-nine, and this was a subject my family would not touch with a ten-foot pole.

"*Maybe she was,*" my dad hissed, "but Kathy's no longer with us, and I won't allow you to insult her memory like that."

I was silent. I wanted to tell him so many things, but I couldn't.

"Yeah," I finally said. Technically he didn't know a thing about who I was. He didn't know anything about me at *all*, really. He'd never asked. "I don't even…yeah. Whatever."

He huffed and puffed with all the power of a Southerner with decades of well-practiced ignorance under his belt. "Well I'll tell you, the thing with your neighbors is *unacceptable*. If anyone did that kind of business under *my* roof, they wouldn't be under my roof for very long, if you know what I'm saying. Might have to talk to someone who knows someone, and see what that someone could do about it, if you catch my drift. It's just not natural."

I inhaled. "Oh, so that Juvederm you get injected into your face every six months *is* natural?" I said before I could stop myself.

"Hmm?" he asked, and I slapped a hand over my mouth. "What was that? I was flipping channels."

"Nothing!" I said, so relieved I could die. "Yeah, let's get back to what you were saying. Guns! Religion! Birth control! Jesus! Yay!"

"That's the ticket," he said proudly. "I swear, the world these days…if only we could clone Reagan and make America great again…"

Suddenly I realized I was biting my nail so hard, it hurt. *Make it great by getting back to* what, *exactly?* I wanted to ask him. *What are these hallowed treasures of American history you're always referring to? Slavery? Homophobia? The KKK?*

"Anyway," he said after a minute, "gotta run. Jodi-" who was his heinous bitch of a wife who hated me for absolutely no reason – "needs some stuff for her tennis tournament tomorrow. I love you, Coley."

The silence filled up with all the things I wasn't telling him, all the things I'd *never* told him, all the things I still had *no idea* how to tell him. Like how my over two-hundred viewings of *Titanic* over the years had had much more to do with Billy Zane's blue eyes than my "admiration for the special effects supervisors," and like how I'd bought all of Hilary Duff's albums as a kid for reasons that had nothing to do with the "huge crush" I'd claimed to have had on her. Even sitting here tonight, I could feel the weight of who he wanted me to be pulling down at my shoulders. And I knew my dad loved me – more than anything, probably. I was his only kid. That love just came with strings attached, and I didn't know how much longer I could play this game without reaching up and snipping myself free, no matter where it made me fall. I wanted to say it back, too, but I couldn't, so I hung up. I reminded myself to keep him in mind, no matter how much I wanted to be who my soul told me I was. I couldn't forget that the South was an island of ignorance in this new world. I wanted to believe we were changing, with Pride marches and all the gays in the media and everything, but yeah, none of that stuff was really happening down here. We were a thousand miles away from New York, and we were stuck. I was stuck, too.

I swore I could still hear my father's voice knocking around in my head until well past midnight. Would he still love me when he knew the truth about me, or did he just love who he *wanted* me to be?

And I could see two other things, too, shining at me from the blackness of my mind…

Those damn galaxy eyes.

The next day I saw Nicky, my forbidden fruit. He dropped his head, licked his lip, stared at me with all the intensity in the world, and then walked away. He still wouldn't talk to me, but for now, this was enough.

And soon I was starting to suspect he wanted me, too. Ever-so-slowly, he seemed to be warming up to me. It was like he was testing the wall between us, dancing up to it and then jumping back again. Sure, we didn't talk or anything, but he was avoiding me less and less, and each day a little more of the angst would leave his face whenever he looked at me. And every time his eyes would hit me like a shot of whiskey, golden and warm and shimmering. The following week went like this, snapshots of a deepening obsession:

Monday: I was getting some water at the fountain, trying not to think about him, when he brushed by me. Except he didn't really brush me at all: he *bumped* me in a way that could not have possibly been accidental, then turned back and looked me right in my eye. And somehow, it made me remember that I was alive.

"What's up, buddy?" he asked me, his voice somehow overpowering like a techno song at full blast. He slapped me on the shoulder, and I realized how high it could make someone fly, just to be touched for the first time by the one that took up all the space in their brain. Then he was gone.

But a second later, I felt eyes on me again. He was watching me, burning me, and I was his. All he had to do was say the word.

31

Tuesday: He put my things away for me after the workout, my exercise band and my medicine ball and all that. He didn't make any fuss about it or whatever, he just did it, quietly and dutifully. His presence made me panic and made me feel like I was floating on air all at once. I watched him, this sensation running over me like I'd just jumped into a cold pool, and I had no Earthly idea what to say.

When he finished, I looked over. "Oh, thanks," I pushed out, like it was the most difficult sentence ever produced. He smiled until he realized someone was watching, then jerked his head away. But I held onto that memory all day, and when I went to sleep, it still burned inside of me. His eyes – they were just too beautiful.

Wednesday: Before the class leader took roll call, I stood by the front door for what seemed like centuries but was probably only three or four minutes. He never came.

Thursday: a new sighting. New life in my veins.

Friday: Nothing much had happened over the last few days, so I didn't have very high expectations when I came into the gym. (*Him*: I was starting to realize I only ever thought of him as being "him." I once read an article a pop star who was so megafamous, all her employees only referred to her as "she" because they were so afraid of her – I assumed this was something like that. I was pudding in his presence.) So I slumped to the gym only to have Nicky get a bar and put it down in front me. I looked up at him as my nerves started feeling more like nerves, clueless of what to say. He was too good looking and I was blinded. That was so cliché, but I didn't know how else to describe it: when he looked at me, he was all I saw. The rest of the world became a fuzzy, inconsequential silence. The coach was prattling on about some local jump rope legend who had completed thousands of jumps in an hour or something, but I didn't even pretend to pay attention as I stared at Nicky. In my eyes, he was the only legend.

Sure, I wanted to be around him as much as possible, but weirdly, I almost started to treasure the scarcity of our run-ins, too, or whatever you wanted to call them. Because love and infatuation fell apart – my parents' marriage had proved that – but I was getting the best of him, every day. He was like a song you loved immediately, but stopped listening to for a while so you wouldn't ruin it. You could savor the best things for later, and Nicky was the best. I wasn't being defeatist – just honest. Everyone in my life had walked away, but as long as he stayed ten feet away, I couldn't mess things up and make him fully leave. He was mine to admire, just from a distance.

Of course, I spent most of my free time stalking the living hell out of his profiles online, and soon I learned more about Nicky Flores than any stranger should ever know about anyone. (What was it about infatuation that made you abandon all logic and become a total psycho stalker?) Soon I knew all kinds of things I would never publicly admit: he was born the day before Valentine's Day. He was kind to his mother. He seemed depressed. He had zero female friends. And he seemed imprisoned in the way society imprisoned all dudes who liked dudes, even if he buried it deep in his eyes. But the most shocking thing was this: I could not find a fault in him. He was flaw-free. Dangerously so. I was so used to forming crushes on people until I stalked them, only to find they were gross losers or something. But that didn't happen with Nicky. There were no embarrassing bathroom selfies with a dirty toilet in the background; no ill-advised, grammatically incorrect political rants to let me know he was an idiot or – even worse – one of those self-loathing gay Republicans. I couldn't find anything wrong with him, and it was a revelation. And not only that, but he also followed a few accounts that no straight guy would ever follow – pages for male models, fashion blogs, and so on. So maybe this wasn't an impossibility – maybe he was waiting, watching, ready to stick a toe out of the closet and date me. There was so much I

33

wanted to investigate further, and it drove me even crazier than I already was.

After class on Friday, though, I forced myself to press pause on the Nicky thing and hit the streets for work. If I didn't post anything soon, my boss would hit the roof again, and I couldn't afford to abandon my life any more than I already had the last few days. My photo blog *Honesty* was mine, technically, but I'd joined the masthead at *Void*, an online network of local zines and blogs, and *Honesty* had somehow become the most popular part of the empire. It wasn't really a *job*, per se, but I figured I'd ride it out for as long as I could and see where it took me. Basically I roamed the sidewalks, passing cafes and bars and bookstores like the stalker I was, and when I saw someone who looked like they had a story in their eyes, I'd ask them a few questions. I'd gradually get more and more serious until I'd hit rock bottom and dig down to their most basic truth, then I'd snap their photo and post it along with the best quote I could get from them. It didn't always work, and sometimes people clammed up or even got offended when I tried to talk to them, but sometimes I struck gold. In the past two years I'd uncovered shocking and heartbreaking and mind-blowing bits of honesty, all from total strangers. Check out my last post, from a hollow-eyed guy in his forties who'd told me about the death of his best friend while he sold hot dogs outside a Lowe's home store:

I wish I was strong enough to give my brother Eddie a hug the last night I saw him, but now he's dead and I'll never get the chance. I wasted so much of my life being strong for everyone else that now I'm all broken.

I know, I know – heavy shit. It surprisingly wasn't that hard to get people to spill, though, because I guess something about me had always been disarming. I could still remember when one of my best friends, Quinn, lost her dad on my seventeenth birthday. It was awful: he'd had a stroke and died while she was getting ready for school one morning. Brush your teeth,

34

fix your hair, watch your dad collapse on the floor of the kitchen and pass away: what a morning. She left school for a week or two, and when I saw her for the first time, I smiled and hugged her and asked her if everything was good – and I never thought of it again. When I saw her months later, though, she came up to me and hugged me hard.

"Whoa, what's up?" I asked, and she looked me in the eye and told me I'd saved her.

"What?"

"You saved me," she said. "That day I came back, I was famous for five minutes, and everyone wanted to gawk at the girl whose dad had been in the newspaper, treat me like I was wounded or something. But you were the only person who treated me like I was normal and asked me if I needed anything and…made me feel like the girl I was when I had a dad. I don't think I'll ever forget that."

That was the day I realized I could really, truly make people happy just by making them feel comfortable, by making them feel heard, making them feel witnessed, like they mattered. Our generation was nothing until our pain was in lights, after all, so that's what I did: I was the lights. Maybe because my life had been so messed up, I never judged anyone else when they told me about their problems – mostly because I had *absolutely no room* to judge them. My mother said that if my heart were any closer to my sleeve, I'd drop it on the ground. Strangers loved to spill their guts to me: drunk girls in bars cried to me about their exes, old women at the supermarket shared dreams they'd had about their dead husbands, a gruff construction guy at McDonald's once told me his wife was dying from cirrhosis of the liver and he was so guilty about getting her hooked on alcohol, he'd taken a mistress in his own wife's final days. All I'd done was turn this into a blog. I was freeze-framing shame or pride or terror and broadcasting it. Some magazine had just called me "the storyteller of the South," and I had thirty-three thousand fans, a number that grew by hundreds a week. Each of my posts got around seven hundred likes and a few dozen comments. My guess was that since we were so used to being assaulted by lies all day – by the media, by your parents telling you everything was going to be alright, by your ex's well-lit bikini selfie that made her look like a nine when she was really a six and a half – that when confronted by truth, people lost their minds. We didn't know how to handle honesty, and that was proved every time I posted a truthbomb of a post and got a thousand likes. I made *some* money from it, and I didn't really have to work because of that combined with the measly allowance my parents direct-deposited every month, but the blog was still local, and I was restless. Was this it for me? Wasn't there something else out there? This couldn't be all, right? A teenaged zombie, nineteen and dead inside?

On Monday afternoon I found myself watching Nicky, once again, while simultaneously trying not to think about how good at everything he was. He wasn't the strongest in the room – that honorable distinction went to the other members of the goon squad – but he *was* the most naturally athletic. Anything he tried, he excelled at, while I stood in the corner trying to master the extremely complicated art of the jump rope. I'd always despised and admired people like him, people who could charm the world just by being themselves. I still didn't even know who "myself" was, but I *did* know that person didn't charm anyone. It was like he was some other species, and it wasn't even fair for us to be on the same playing field. How could he do himself to me? I was burning up for him, feverstruck, and barely seemed to care that I was alive.

At the end of class, he walked slowly by me on the way to the water fountain. I felt every inch of his closeness to me: his orbit alone pulled me even closer. He looked even better up close, too. He was just as good as the dream of him had been. I was so sick of being let down by the real world: "freedom" had turned out to mean paying my own electric bill and having to figure out how to get my own medical insurance. But here in this gym, the reality of Nicky Flores was every bit as magnificent as the fantasy had been.

"Good lifting today, Nick," some girl said in a voice that sounded like ice cream on a hot day, and he blushed. *Slut,* I thought as my thoughts turned red. Girls would never understand how much easier they had it, how they could wake up in the morning and like boys and not be conflicted to the bone about it. And not only that, but they could get those boys to actually *like them back*, too. They had it so easy and they had no idea – straight people lived in a luxury they didn't even know existed. I also hated Nicky in that moment, too – he obviously loved the attention. *Whore.*

"Not as good as you," he said with a goofy smile that made the concrete under me feel like it had been liquefied. The girl made a kissy sound and got on her bike, and all the while I wished it would crash. I enjoyed the effect of his perfection on *me*, sure, but when wielded on someone *else*, it made me want to burn myself. *Both whores.*

But then he turned to me, and a blue planet stopped spinning. I swear I could even hear that *dun-dun-dunnn* sound from the movies. Was that normal? Was *anything* normal? Why did he make my body react like this? Why were humans and their bodies so effing weird, anyway? As he stood there I wondered more and more about him. What did he go home to? Did he love his father? Did his father love him? Who exactly was this alien? And did he know how happy he made me simply by existing? I also wondered what it was like to be him. He was the guy I'd always wanted to be, the guy my parents had always reminded me I *wasn't*. A few details aside, he was strong and masculine and dark and handsome in a classically male way, and it didn't matter what he was deep down, because he was "normal" enough to blend in. He didn't have to hide at all.

Meanwhile I was none of those things: I was skinny and blue-eyed and had wild hair that had once been strawberry blonde but was now more of a burnt coppery color, and I more closely resembled a middle-school art class kid than someone who was two years away from being legally able to buy alcohol. If someone wanted a hot bod and all that, I wasn't exactly the best place to start. I guess I wasn't *totally* fugly –

37

actually, I'd been the unqualified hottie of the Episcopal High School Literary Lovers Club, thanks very much – I was just galaxies away from Nicky's orbit, and that was totally apparent.

He came closer. Caught by something foreign and *whoosh*-y, I let my defenses fall and smiled at him. Even though I was sure I was acting like a psycho, the sparkle didn't leave his eye. He seemed to look around – *to see if anyone was watching, maybe?* – then licked his lip in that way that only *he* could make look natural.

"Hi, Cole."

And all the oxygen in the world disappeared. Everything was a black, empty vacuum. Nicky had turned off all the lights.

"Wh…hi?" I said, then I inched backward a bit, overcome by the sudden energy the air had taken on. It was like the atmosphere was thicker and heavier than it had been thirty seconds before. Nobody had ever made me feel like this, and I didn't know how to process it. Didn't he know I was off limits? Didn't he know I was that *faggot*, social kryptonite, not to be messed with? Didn't he know how reckless this was – for him, at least?

His eyes sucked me in and pushed me away all at the same time. *This could all be so beautiful,* I thought, *if we let it be.* We were right in front of the door and the coach was starting to look, so I knew I had to say something, as impossible as the act of forming words seemed to be. The goons could look over at us any minute and see him talking to me, and it could all come tumbling down just like that. The phrase "playing with fire" came to mind, but we were playing with the whole atomic bomb.

"Aren't you gonna run with the class?" I whispered, fully under his trance, since we were supposed to do a cool-down lap after every workout and everyone else had already left.

He threw his eyes over to the coach, then looked back. "No," he said softly. "I might be done running, anyway. From a lot of things…"

In the end, I was the one who had to tear my eyes away and run around the stupid block.

Sure, I was disappointed that he hadn't said or done any more, but it was short-lived. Just as sleep started to take me that night, my phone pinged. I picked it up, and the words Nicholas Flores stared up at me. The boy with the galaxy eyes had added me on Facebook.

Finally.

4

You win, he messaged after I accepted him, and of the lights in my mind flashed at once.

I win what? I asked.

I tried, but I just can't NOT talk to you.

And I could swear the sun had found a home in my throat.

Well, hi, I responded. **Took you long enough.**

What do you mean?

You know what I mean. Why not just talk to me in workout class?

He didn't respond.

You're a bit of a strange one, aren't you? I asked to move things along.

All the best of us are. So what's up?

I didn't know what to say. He'd basically ignored me just a few hours before, and here he was, wanting in. I had *no idea* what he wanted from me, actually.

Can we talk? he asked after I didn't say anything.

About what?

You.

Okay? Why?

Because I'm curious about you

And your life.

And my mind filled with fireworks and explosions and laughing babies and everything good and happy in this world. Who *was* I?

Okay, I said. **Fine. Ask away.**

Soon he asked me a bunch of really banal questions – where I went to school, how long I'd done FitTrax, where I was from. I could tell he wanted to dig deeper, but he was dancing around it.

What do I need to know about YOU? I asked during a lull.

There's not much to know.

Try me, I said.

Well…
I have a pet snail named Tammy. I love my mother like I love Nilla wafers, my dad doesn't exist to me, and…
I'm kinda/maybe/definitely sick of being the dude the world wants me to be.
Hence the messages.

In that moment I was sure that somewhere in the world, violins were playing. I could hear them.

There's something else… he said.

Yes?

Well…
I wanna keep getting to know you, but right now…it can just be on our phones.
Is that okay?
Please say yes

41

I said nothing. The violins faded.

I don't know how to talk to you in person yet, he continued.
But I want to.
Eventually.
Is that cool?

Why? I asked. **Is it because I'm now a known "faggot" and you can't be seen with me?**

Wait, what?

I waited for him to say more. He did.

Hold up, I think I know what you're talking about – it's not that serious. The guys call everyone a faggot. I'm pretty sure it's a blanket term meaning "we don't like this kid." It doesn't necessarily mean…what you think it does. I just…I need time to figure this out.

Whatever, I said. **I would never be able to live with myself if I had friends like yours.**

So you've met Ryan? he asked, and for some reason I could swear I could hear him laughing. (By the way, Ryan, Matt, Josh: why did meat-head types always have the same names? Why couldn't a bully be called Alastair or Melvin or something?) **He doesn't exactly have the highest brain cell count,** Nicky said.

Haha. Yeah.
Why do you even want to talk to me, anyway?

Well, isn't it obvious? he asked.

…No?

Well, for one…have you SEEN your ass?

I knew I shouldn't have been flattered, but I was. It *was* true: he liked guys. At least enough to look at their butts, anyway.

Oh, um…
I come from a family of athletes, I said. **But trust me, that line of athletes ended with me. As you've already noticed…**

You weren't that bad, he told me. **So…do we have a deal?**

Yep, I said as something in me wished I had the strength and self-respect to say no instead.

Ahh, awesome! I've got a ton of stuff to do, so I'll message you the same time tomorrow, okay?

Wait…
What about FitTrax?
Are we still "strangers" there? I asked.

I'm getting this all straightened out in my head, I swear.
Until then…
Work with me here, Furman.

I signed off before I could let myself become any more desperate.

The next day bled together, and at nine that evening I found myself sitting on the edge of my bed, waiting for Nicky and trying to remember how to breathe. He signed on twenty minutes late.

Where were you at FitTrax today? he asked in lieu of a greeting.

Work, I said, even though I was lying – I'd just been too nervous to face him. I'd biked up to the building, caught a

43

glimpse of him with his bro friends, and turned away. **Why? Were you disappointed?**

Yes. To be honest I was.

I smiled bigger than I had for a long time, and the conversation continued. We talked again, on and off, for a week or two. He would pepper me with questions some nights, and other nights he'd just fall off the grid, and I'd sit there waiting until I wanted to punch myself. He'd make no mentions of his disappearances the next time we talked – he'd just launch back into the questions. He was strangely mercurial, zipping in and out of different moods, hot and cold and up and down, and I couldn't even keep track of him half the time. All I knew was that I never wanted to stop trying.

As the heart of the summer started to unfurl itself in front of me, Nicky became one of my good friends on the phone, and pretty much ignored me in public. I embarrassed myself by how high I let myself soar whenever I waited for roll call, and by how hard I fell whenever I'd realize he still wouldn't talk to me. Now that I knew he was a slim possibility instead of a pipe dream, I was addicted to thinking about him. Oh, God – I was obsessed. But I knew this song and dance, but I couldn't handle it forever. I had to do something. I had to let him know he could trust me with the secret we both shared. But how?

During our talks, he started opening up to me more and more. But it was the weirdest thing: the more he opened up on the phone, telling me about his life and his hobbies and his fears, the harder he'd yank himself away in the gym. If the air had felt electric around him that first day, it was veering extremely close to bursting-into-flames status now. Sometimes I'd get hard just by being around him, and I knew he felt something, too. How could he not? I'd catch him staring at me from time to time, doing that weird lip-licking thing he sometimes did, and it confused me to no end…

One night he messaged me, right on time. But after a few minutes I got so sick of everything I sort of snapped a little.

You should just call me. I'm so sick of typing.

But I wasn't. I would type to that boy forever.

Okay, fine, he said. I sent him my number, and he called. I held my breath and answered the phone.

"…Hello?"

"Hi." There was a smile in his voice. A rush of something white and terrifying, in the best kind of way, took hold of me, left me reeling in its wake. "What are you up to this fine evening?"

"Oh, you know…reading, doing dishes, that sort of thing," I said, taking my phone to the couch and diving headfirst into ColeyAndNickyVille, our safe little world that only existed inside our phones.

"And here I thought you were the type to be into doing black tar heroin on a weekday night."

"Nah, I'm afraid the heroin is only for weekends."

Who was I? Who was this person who was talking to Nicky Flores and keeping it together?

"What were *you* doing? I asked. "And…what was up with today?"

"What do you mean?"

"When you stared at me."

"Oh." He paused. "I was mad."

"Mad?"

"Yeah. You were staring right at some other guy."

Suddenly my face felt all hot and weird. "I was?"

"Unless there was something stuck to his ass, you were checking him out."

I swallowed. "Okay, but, if I was…what would that have to do with *you*?"

45

I heard him suck in some air. "Because I was…jealous, okay? I didn't like it, and beyond that, I didn't know *why* I didn't like it."

"Oh."

"Yeah."

"So…do you go on the app a lot?" I asked to change the subject and save myself from Death by Boner.

"Um. No."

"How often?"

"Well…that night you saw me was my second time ever. The first time, I got scared and deleted it after a few minutes." He paused. "You?"

"First time. Why were you on it *that day*?"

He sighed. "You're lucky I just had a few beers with the guys tonight, so I'm feeling open. The thing is…I don't know why I went online that night. Seeing what Ryan did to you, it made me…mad. But I didn't know what to do. It also got me started thinking about guys, and…yeah. My 'mad' cells are very close to my 'horny' ones in my brain, if you know what I mean. So I downloaded it, and then you messaged me, and…"

"Okay," I breathed. "Gotcha. And why'd you flip out and block me?"

I tried to stop asking him things, but I couldn't. I'd always had the tendency to say too much, reveal too much, let too many words tumble out of my mouth like water from a gurgling hose. But I felt safe here, between this black noise, inside his silence. Nobody was watching. Nobody cared. And I could tell he felt it, too.

"I'm sorry," he said, "I just…I got scared. When I found out who you were, I had to think about things. I didn't know your motives. You have to understand, I thought you hated me after that whole 'faggot' thing, and I was sure you were gonna tell everyone you saw me. I just needed some time to think, and process everything. I'm sorry again, by the way. You didn't deserve that. Nobody does. Honestly speaking, I hate myself so much sometimes for standing by and letting my friends do the things they do…"

46

I was silent for a second. I didn't know how to say how much I appreciated him for saying that.

"And what did you think," I asked soon, so quietly I wondered if he could hear, "when you found out who I was? That I was from class?"

"I was kinda stoked," he murmured back, and my heart threw itself around in my chest. "Let's confess," he continued, a bit louder. "What all do you know about me?"

"Too much," I sighed.

"Like what?"

"Don't ask."

"I am right now."

All the blood in my body rushed to my head. I wished I could disappear, but I started whispering instead. "Well, I know people call you Nicky, and not Nick…"

I waited for the recoil. The hang-up. It didn't come. "Yep. Call me that. Everyone calls me that but my dad. The name 'Nick' makes me think of him. I'm the baby of the family, anyway, so it works."

"Me too!"

"Yeah, I'm a lot younger than my sister."

"And I was the only child, the baby by default, so I was Coley. Even though my dad used to yell at my mom every time she called me that, and say it wasn't *manly* enough…"

"Well *I* like it," he said. "Coley and Nicky…it certainly has a ring to it."

I smiled – he was lighting up my world and he didn't even know it. Then I thought about what that meant for us, that we were both considered eternal babies by the people who loved us most.

"And I know you're close with your big sister," I said.

"How?"

"Instagram."

"Yeah, well…pictures can deceive. She's very Catholic, so you know how that goes. I love her a lot, but…if she knew anything about…certain things, she'd disown me."

"Oh. I'm sorry to hear that."

"It's cool. Anything else you don't know, but want to know?"

Oh, God. Where would I start? *Do you know you're extraterrestrial? Do you know you fell to Earth from some other realm to visit humanity and show us what real bone structure looked like? Do you know how hard it is for me to breathe in and out right now?*

"Never mind," he said, "*I* have a question. What is being…gay like?" he asked, his voice soft and inquisitive like a child's.

"Um…"

He caught himself. "Oh, you know what I mean – I'm asking about, like, a *real* gay guy. Do you think it's wrong, like, deep down?"

I winced, then thought about the question. For a second I just stared at the TV. I was raised in the South, and my family was Methodist. I might as well have been born into a nunnery. People who weren't from here, they just didn't understand – we were decades behind the rest of the nation. I loved the South, but it was a beautiful place with hatred baked into its crust, like arsenic apple pie. If you were different – and by "different" I mean anything other than a straight, white, khaki-wearing adult – you were never allowed to forget your differentness for one second. And I was *different*. I was the minority, and I felt it all day. My childhood had been a horror show of what could happen to children raised under the wing of the religious right, and I'd had hatred and bigotry pounded into me from inception like a butcher beating a pork chop. My Sunday school teachers had preached fire and brimstone to anyone who ever considered straying from the flock, and even my own schoolteachers had regularly made shockingly off-color comments about gays and lesbians. One of my teachers Mr. Stubbs actually *was* gay, and after word got out that he lived with another man, a group of parents had sent around some weird petition to get him fired for "morality issues."

And the craziest part of it was that the rest of the country had no idea how bad it still was down here. Everyone thought of Florida and pictured white-sand beaches, crystalline waters, and transplanted Yankees, but my city was eight hours and a whole world away from the relatively progressive Miami area. It was the deepest of the Deep South, and Georgia was twenty minutes up the road. Our high schools were named after Ku Klux Klan heroes, our highways were named for Confederate generals, even our population was still basically racially segregated from east to west, north to south. I'd once had an entire car full of people (male *and* female) slow down to angrily scream "*faggot!*" at me for daring to wear skinny jeans on the sidewalk, and when I'd gotten my driver's license at sixteen, I'd found that the courthouse downtown had two sets of bathrooms for each sex – they hadn't updated since the days of racial segregation, and the plaque that had clearly once said "coloreds" had simply been painted over. That's what I was dealing with down here. The South was burning, and the rest of the country was turning a blind eye.

But don't get me wrong – not *everyone* was awful. Some of the best, most compassionate people I'd ever met had come from my church, for example. (I wasn't one of those religion-haters who sat and angrily blamed God for all my problems, I just found it to be an uncontestable fact that the majority of Christianity was indoctrinating an entire generation into a mindset of hatred and intolerance that had its roots in a book written thousands of years ago.) Realistically I would guess that twenty percent of people were supportive and accepting, sixty percent were indifferent, and another twenty percent were gun-toting, Bible-carrying types. But that last group was embedded everywhere – they infested law enforcement, courthouses, churches, the state Capitol. You couldn't escape them.

"I don't know," I began. "Whatever my issues with certain things are, they're not religious. God is not real. Or at least the God they talk about, the one who reigns from on high just to sentence teenaged boys to eternal hell for kissing their male neighbors and falling in love with them, that guy does not exist. Jesus was a long-haired preacher of free love who hung out with prostitutes and outcasts, and using the Bible to

49

defend social intolerance makes about as much sense as using *Mein Kampf* to spread peace and goodwill."

He laughed, then mentioned how I sometimes wore a church T-shirt to the gym. I did a double take, unaware that he even cared enough to notice details like this.

"Well, things change," I said. "Sure, my childhood made *Little House on the Prairie* look progressive – church three times a week, being forced to watch every Republican debate, being dragged to gun shows, bla bla bla. And a few years ago I would've said yeah, I hate myself for all this. Because of church, I was totally disgusted and ashamed and all those other things that religious types are raised to be. But…as I got older I broadened my scope and realized that this same book that disavowed homosexuality also gave you tips on how to treat your slaves, and said women should be servants to their husbands, and gave husbands permission to cut off their wives' hands if they stepped out of line...so much of the Bible is senseless, weird, outdated gibberish. And now I don't care anymore." I paused. "But, like, do I feel gross *sometimes*? Do I feel dirty on occasion? Yeah, and I guess that'll never really go away. Those are just the side effects of being force-fed poison your while life. But generally, I don't really give a damn anymore. What about you?"

He didn't say anything.

"Come on," I said. "I'd never repeat any of this."

"Let's focus on you. Do you watch all the girly reality shows? Like, *Housewives* and stuff?"

"Um…when I want to." Translation: *every single night*, but I didn't want to tell him that and look like a stereotype.

"Do you have...mostly female friends?" he asked.

"Um, I guess."

"Do you go shopping a lot?"

Come *on* – was he really this ignorant? "I hate shopping. I don't care about clothes." Which was sort of a lie, but who was counting?

"Do you hate sports, too?"

I couldn't help it: I laughed. "I guess *that* stereotype is accurate. I would rather make out with my grandma than throw a ball."

"Ew."

"Ew at sports," I said. "Why do you wanna know all this, anyway?"

"Because I do. And sorry if I'm trading in stereotypes, but I don't know anything about all this. Don't you realize it's hard for me, too?"

"What do you mean?"

His voice lowered, even though there was nobody except me to hear it. "Well, I had a buddy, Joel. I used to party with him and whatnot. Soon, whispers started going around about how he was staring a little too intently at other guys in the showers after football practice, and…let's just say I never saw him at another party again. That was that."

"Oh."

I heard him sigh, and I wanted so badly to be next to him, touching him, enjoying him. For a moment my brain tried to tell me I was an unlovable garbage can who didn't deserve him, but I shut it out. "Ugh, why am I saying this? I don't even know why I'm telling you any of this, Coley Furman."

"Oh, speaking of that, how did you know my last name to add me on Facebook?"

"Do you really want to know?"

And the walls seemed closer than they had a few seconds before. "Yes."

"Okay," he said. "I look over your shoulder every time you sign in at the computer in gym class. You also wear the same green shoes every day, and you hate doing push-ups."

"How do you know?"

"I don't know, I guess you told me."

I shook my head, then remembered I was on the phone. "I did?"

"Yeah. One day, it was really humid in the gym, and I said that it was gross. I guess I was trying to make conversation. You said something like, *at least we're not doing push-ups.*"

I still drew a blank. I was sure he was telling the truth, I just had no idea he'd even want to store something away like that. "You remember that?"

"I remember everything you've ever said in that gym, Coley."

And my insides sort of fell away.

"So that's what you meant by, you were sorry? That you couldn't talk to me there?" I asked him.

"Yes. And for the…the fact that it has to be this way. I don't like how my friends act, and how the world is, and sometimes I wish I could change things."

I laughed a little.

"What?"

"You're just being sort of a hypocrite. Why are you friends with those douche-heads?"

"Okay, look, I know they can be a little ignorant, and-"

"So why are you friends with them?"

He scoffed. "Like you wouldn't be, if they offered?"

I didn't know what to say. He was probably right. We were both just trying to fit in.

"Ugh, it's midnight," I finally said. "On a weeknight."

"Hang up, then."

I waited. The silence was warm, fuzzy, generous, inviting. "I kind of don't want to," I said. "Is that weird?"

He sighed, but I thought I could hear happiness in it. "I'm afraid I feel the same way, Mr. Furman. And I kind of have no idea what to do about it…"

I sat in his silence until he finally hung up and made the night close in.

At our eye contact the next day, the rest of the world became white noise again. I thought he was going to talk to me, finally acknowledge me, but he didn't. Instead he motioned an "I'll call you" sign. He turned away, but I stood taller. I had to do something. I wasn't going to let him stay away from me. Here I was, alone again, accompanied by nothing except some dust on the rubber mat, another speck of mulch, Nicky's hat…

Nicky's hat, I thought. He'd left his hat under the water fountain. I snatched it up and followed him.

"Hey," I said, my adrenaline sprinting away from me, Serena Williams at the net. "Hey. You forgot this."

"Mhmm?" he said, turning. Suddenly I was aware of every freckle on my face, every inch of unnecessary flab around my butt. When he saw that it was me, he seemed to hold onto my gaze for a second longer than was necessary. I grasped onto every second of it, of course, as the colors exploded. He was neon purple, blazing orange, vivid yellow, burning red. That's what I saw when I looked at that boy: all of the colors.

"Thanks," he said, reaching for it, although something in me questioned how accidental this had really been. Our hands grazed each other, just like in the movies, but instead of shocking or electrocuting me it made me feel ice-cold, like he'd sucked all the heat out of my body with one touch. I turned away a little, feeling inferior again. Ugh. He was so dumb for being so perfect. He pulled eyeballs toward him just by breathing, absorbed light just by living. He couldn't help himself, but still it drove me crazy.

Finally, *he* spoke instead of me. "You in the business of staring, or do you do it for free?"

Oh my God. So I *hadn't* been hiding it. I was such a creeper. But even then, I couldn't stop. It was like he swam in the air, shimmered like he might slip away at any moment if I didn't drink him in quickly enough. Everything he did thrilled me.

"Oh, um…" I didn't know what to say. God, I didn't even know who I was. This creature, this Coley, was alien. "Sorry. I guess I…zone out a lot. But you probably know that by now."

He smiled, and it sparkled. He was constantly jumping, shifting, morphing to the point where sometimes he was somewhere else altogether. "It's okay," he said. "I was just starting to wonder if I had a rash or something."

I stared at him. My tongue retreated down my throat. "A rash?"

53

"Oh, it was…I was just joking…never mind."

He looked away. I was such a screw-up. Why was I always screwing everything up? Why did I have to be me? I usually sucked at human interaction anyway due to a debilitating case of social awkwardness that usually came off as arrogance, but Nicky made me a hundred times worse at person-ing.

"Wow, I killed that vibe pretty quickly, didn't I?" I asked, regaining some semblance of composure. I looked down and noticed that his leg was positioned in the same exact way as mine. Maybe we were two different people, meant to live different lives, in different places. Or maybe we really were the same.

An idea came to me. I reached into my bag and took out my phone to look like I had some authority and wasn't just another idiot.

"Hey, let me start over. I'm…um, I'm on assignment, and I'm supposed to ask some people a few questions today. For my blog."

"Blog?" he said, vaguely interested, since every asshole and their mom had a blog. I didn't realize I hadn't told him about this yet.

"Yeah. *Honesty*."

Those pretty eyes flashed. "Ah. I know who you are. Or, I mean, I didn't know you were…*you*, though. Wow."

"You know about *Honesty*?"

"I'm pretty sure my baby cousins know about *Honesty*," he laughed. "That's awesome. You're like Peter Parker – normal kid by day, super-famous blogger by night. I'll do it, no problem. Just don't show my face."

I took out my Polaroid and my phone from my gym bag. He breathed and got going.

"Every night," he said, his voice starting to shake a bit, "I dream that my dad is dead. And every morning I am disappointed when I wake up and realize it was just a dream."

I just stared at him, dumbfounded. I'd imagined the fiery death of my father more times than I would ever admit.

"Coley?" he asked after a second, something dangerous sparking in his eyes.

"Yeah?"

"Leaving my hat wasn't an accident."

Suddenly I forgot how to be alive. I studied him, my lips parting, and for the first time I understood the phrase "star struck:" I was tossed down the vortex, into his cortex, and stars were flying through me, piercing me, lighting me up, and I was one with the cosmos. Or something. I didn't really know. I'd never felt like this and had nothing to go by. But I was just swallowed by him. No one had ever had this effect on me. Ever. I felt like I'd just downed eight cups of coffee, or maybe done heroin, and then gone on the craziest rollercoaster at Six Flags, while wasted. He was everything, and all of my nothing didn't know how to handle it.

"Why's that?" was all I could get out. He didn't respond. Instead he placed his hand on top of mine, and I felt like I'd been zapped, electrocuted. He looked me right in the eye, which was *so weird*, you know? Because it was a new century and iPhones existed and nobody even talked on the phone anymore, *much less looked each other in the eye*, and geez, eye contact usually felt more aggressive than getting slammed against a wall. But with him it just felt soft and beautiful. Some moment flowed between us – it was blue, beautiful, flowing, fluttering. I was the power line and he was the electricity.

"I just want you to know that I don't like the rules, either," he said.

"The rules?"

He swallowed something down. It looked large and painful. "Hey, there's a teen night thing at this bar, the Pier...wanna go?"

"With you?"

"Uh...yes, with me."

"Oh. Sure. Yeah. I'll be there."

Just as quickly as he'd touched me, he turned and disappeared down the alley on his bike, retracting himself in a whir of silvery metal and inhuman beauty. After he left I stood

55

there in the aftermath of him, not moving, not talking, just breathing. Suddenly the streetlights burned clear, the horizon cut a sharper line into the ocean. It was a Friday evening in the dead of summer, and my world was rearranging itself.

5

After FitTrax I retreated into the shelves of the library a few blocks from my house, my own little safe haven, as I always did when I was going crazy and needed to scrape out my brain. Basically I'd always been a bit of a nerd. Books had saved me. My childhood had been borderline awful, and I'd escaped into *Harry Potter*. I insulated myself in a false world, comforted by the fact that even though my life sucked, I could slip away and fall into a world that didn't, even if it wasn't real. Because the things you created in your mind were real, too. They just wouldn't protect you from distant mothers and silent fathers and boys who saw you glancing at other boys on the playground.

And it's not like I had I many other options as I grew up: although I liked beer, my stomach couldn't handle taking shots, and I didn't know how to smoke weed without turning into a white-hot ball of social anxiety. I was more likely to overdose on books on my Kindle app than Ecstasy, I didn't have a #squad, and my social life was mainly limited to whatever fictional characters I happened to be speaking to in my head that week. But I was fine with it, because you were never alone with books. They would never publicly deny you and try to act straight around their bro-friend before sending you a million mixed signals. They would never paint you a roaring sunset and then blow all the clouds away again. Book lovers were also fools, in a way. Everyone knew they could never find love, because all they did was compare real life to life within the page. And spoiler alert: the page always won. A lifetime of believing in books and their boyfriends had me chasing people that didn't even exist. (Before Nicky, at least.)

All I wanted was to find *one* real-life book boyfriend like they described in the stories – you know, the flippy-haired, preppily-dressed, English-accented, just-the-right-amount-of-cocky dreamboy who would swagger into my life with a few witty jokes and a come-on that was just forward enough to be charming without crossing into creeper territory. I'd catch him staring at me from over his iced latte in some trendy coffee shop with books on the shelves, and then he'd come at me with some improbably-witty comment, and we'd be in love two weeks later. He'd be dead soon, of course, from a dramatic sledding accident or a sudden car wreck or something else that would keep him looking like a Balenciaga model until the very end, but it wouldn't matter: we would've already forged eternal love by then, and he would've already rescued me and taught me how to love myself and made me feel All The Feels within my previously feel-less soul. But try as I may, that boy would never walk off the page. The book boyfriend never materialized. And still I slept alone, with my books safely by my side, perpetuating this cycle that both fueled the fires in my soul and made me wish I lived another life, all at once…

But today my bookthirst went unquenched. I just couldn't find anything. All the books for teens were out of the question for me at this point, because they were quite frankly extremely annoying. It was like someone had snapped their fingers and decided to make all the books the same. All the characters' names were, like, Maude or Gertrude or something, which was just…no. Nobody named their kids those things except Gwyneth Paltrow, and even she looked like an asshole for doing it. These teen books were full of twee hipster characters with fantastically improbable and adorkable character traits – *they all have the same birthday! they have a rare disorder that makes them allergic to love! they're obsessed with death and attempt suicide every single day only to adorably evade death at the last minute!* – and the book covers made them all look like they were set in cupcake bakeries. These books would take on life-or-death subjects like depression or bipolar disorder or self-mutilation and treat them like jokes, tackling them with the flirty, ironic, light-handed air of an episode of *Modern Family*. And even if they *weren't* suffering from Adorkable Overload, they were one of the parade of romances that, judging by their covers, were all titled "straight white couples embracing on a Southern beachscape at sunset." I was tired of hearing about blonde heroines falling for tattooed, motorcycle-riding heroes – that had nothing to do with my life. I loved reading, don't get me wrong, but when was something different going to come along?

And this was the "something different" I wanted – I wanted a gay book. I wanted to explore the world I was falling into, but the "gay novels" were even worse than the straight ones. They all featured phrases like "turgid member" and "throbbing tool" and showed two muscled torsos wrapped across each other on their covers, with campy titles like *GETTING BENT* or *ROCK HARD STEAMY SUMMER: SAN FRANCISCO EDITION*. Straight romances were allowed to be deep and thoughtful and at least halfway poetic; most gay novels seemed to look like sex-fests with a few weightlifting sessions on the side. (And if they weren't literary gay porn, they were about two closet cases who lived in silent misery and then died alone. Go figure.) They were also filed in their own category called "male/male romance," which was just essentially not okay. "Gay romance" was just romance, and separating the gays from the straights was like separating books starring blonde heroines from brunette ones. After I watched *Brokeback Mountain* with my friend Katherine one time, she'd remarked that it "felt almost like a straight romance movie!" and I could remember wanting to shank her. The movie featured two humans falling in love – what else was it supposed to feel like?

I just wanted a realistic, accurate, measured depiction of what it was like to have a crush on dudes in today's world, with some hot gay boning as a side dish, maybe, but never the main course. And all I seemed to have were six-pack-abbed dudes staring into each other's eyes under a sexy waterfall. The gay experience was hard as *shit*, and for women to take all that and reduce it to two jocks boning each other on a book cover – it just felt cheap to me. I guess I just wanted a gay book that was – *gasp* – allowed to act just like a straight one! I wanted something real, and beyond that, I wanted to know that it could get better for me, not "get better" in the sense of the messages offered by cheesy YouTube video or ad campaign on the side of the bus. I wanted to know I would be able to talk down a street one day and see it for what it was – a street – instead of imagining a million different faces that might disapprove of me, a million little opportunities for people to hate me and tell me I wasn't good enough. I was alone, and I wanted to not be alone anymore. I just didn't know how to get out of alone-ville. Maybe books could do all that for me.

As I browsed, I spotted a gorgeous, golden-haired boy writing at a table alone by the computers. I snuck half a peek at him from behind a bookshelf, my cheeks flushing, until a rich-looking blonde sat across from him and smiled. "What's going on, Cooper?" she asked as I turned away. Ugh – *of course* he was straight. All the good ones were.

I steered clear of the section condescendingly called "homosexual issues," but as I passed a certain shelf on the way out, I spotted something featuring two guys together that sparked my interest. Just as I reached for it, though, a helpful clerk came out of nowhere and threw a smile at me. "Hey, that shelf is super high, would you like some help with that?"

I blushed and shook my head as I stumbled away. No matter how badly I wanted the stupid book, I was still more afraid of being seen with it in my hand. I could not even buy a "gay book" in public without being choked by fear – what was wrong with me? Forget my father's insanity he called conservatism – I was my own biggest enemy. Wasn't I supposed to be part of the solution, and not another facet of the problem? How was I ever going to even get *close* to dating a guy when I was this terrified of my own feelings? Was this whole "gay" thing even something I could really, truly, honestly even *do*?

I biked to the bar that night, out of my mind with nerves and panic and something tickly that felt like butterflies in my throat. I'd saved Nicky's Polaroid and put it on my bedside table – I knew I'd never tell anyone about him, as he was my little secret – and the picture had stayed in my mind all day. So I ordered a Fireball and Cream Soda, my trademark drink, and then turned around and saw Nicky Flores standing in the middle of a pile of girls. And he was staring right at me with a look in his eyes that could've disarmed an entire squadron of assassins.

He burned me. It was that simple. I sped back around so quickly, the bartender gave me a weird look as she dried some glasses. Oh, God. I turned away and, of course, found myself looking into a mirror. Only now was I noticing my not-quite-strong chin, my pinkish complexion, my flaws. Would being around him get any easier? I was fully aware of him, even from across a room. Did he feel the same? Or was I back in high school, falling for the straight linebacker again, one eager blonde away from heartbreak?

Soon I glanced back again. The various girls were looking at him like he was a freshly-roasted turkey on the counter and they were hound dogs on the kitchen floor. It made me want to punch something.

Ten minutes after I got there, he bumped into me, and it made me feel like I was losing control on a dark highway at 200 MPH. I had no brakes. He'd taken them from me. Seeing him in regular clothes, and not workout crap, was…too much. He was in black jeans and a grey shirt made of some thin, expensive-looking material, and very quickly I realized I could not even look at him. Not directly, at least. He was making my insides scream, and I didn't want it to show on my skin.

But still, this was the safest public space we'd found yet, lost in a crowd of chattering strangers. Nobody from FitTrax was here to beat me up or catch onto him for talking to me. As far as anybody knew, we were two friends saying hello. I didn't know him from Adam.

"What's up?" he asked, and I could instantly tell he was drunk, because he was talking to me in public without a shred of angst. I didn't know how to take it, but still, his galaxy eyes hurt like heaven. This was just another side effect of him: he made me feel like I was being murdered by joy.

"Not much! I'm, just, um – waiting on a friend."

He laughed, and it sounded somehow like when you pop open a Coke and hear that soul-warming fizzing sound fill your ears. He had a laugh fit for the commercials. "You're alone, aren't you?"

I angled my lower body away. Oh, God – something was happening. In my pants. I had to sort of cross my legs and angle away in a weird way. "I guess."

A glob of people migrated closer to the DJ's stage, and we were suddenly alone.

"Sorry we never really got a chance to talk in person before," he said, and again things lapsed into awkwardness.

"So why'd you invite me here?" I asked before I could shut my stupid mouth. "Considering the jock squad and everything…"

"They don't own me," he whispered, his mood turning black on a dime. Then he exhaled. "They also don't come to this particular bar, so that's part of it, too, I guess."

"Oh. Yeah."

He made eye contact with a goon, who shot up an eyebrow. Then he leaned in closer to me, making me feel like I was soaring somehow. "Look…I can't do this. I thought I could, but I can't. I don't want to talk to you here."

I pretty much gave up then. This was pointless. I had no idea why I'd even come.

"So I'm ditching the boys," he said. "A sudden stomach cramp has come up, it seems, so I'll meet you around back. By the bike rack. In ten minutes or so."

And suddenly, hope flowed back into my soul. I tore him apart with my pupils, trying to see past his angel eyes to the ghost inside. He looked back at me. All that boy did was look at me, and yet I can still feel the glory. Finally I nodded, my eyes popping out of their sockets. *Oh, God.* I had to stop doing that. The structural integrity of my facial bones depended on it. Ryan could be anywhere, and his fists were horny for my face.

I told Nicky I'd see him soon and then watched him disappear into the crowd. And twenty-five minutes later, he kept his word. He met me. In person. When I saw his face it looked pleasantly surprised, like when you come home from a long trip and find that your dog is super excited to see you. I was so giddy I didn't know what to do with myself.

"You must've waited for me a long time," he said, and I blushed, because God knows I would've waited forever for that boy. I can still remember the way his eyes looked that night: they looked the way music sounds. "Sorry, they wouldn't let me leave. But let's walk."

We walked over to the end of the alley that opened up to an empty street. Beyond that rolled the black Atlantic. I felt like I was having an out-of-body experience – I was alone on the street with Nicky Flores. The world wasn't the world anymore.

An older man walked by, turning to stare at us like we were hoodlums up to no good. And we were, according to the vast swath of humanity. I saw the accusation in the dude's angry eyes: *what kind of boys walk closely together in alleys at night?* Or maybe I'd just imagined it. But the way Nicky and I both jerked out heads away and motioned our bodies away from one another proved I wasn't the only one who thought we were doing bad things. We'd both been brainwashed, and maybe it would never get any better.

"So…what was so important that you had to rush me out of the bar to tell me?"

"I don't know," he said. "Nothing in particular."

"Okay." The liquor tickled my stomach, urging me on. "Well…can I say something you might not like?"

"Mhmm?"

"There was no need to avoid me in the gym for so long. There was never any danger of anyone finding out about you, anyway. You're much better at…hiding it than I am."

"Yeah," he said, and looked away. "I don't know about all that."

Shit. I'd said too much again. Being around him felt like being around myself, like he was my reflection in the mirror, and I was letting my mouth say way too much. *Coy, Furman – be coy!*

"Actually, can I say something *you* might not like?" he asked soon, his voice cracking the silence, fireworks.

"Sure."

"There's a reason I…did what I did. Came back to you after I swore I'd stay away, I mean. I could just…tell. That you, you know…were who you were."

"Oh. Yeah." I swallowed. "I guess I've never been like you. I never really had much of a father, so I never got around to learning the whole *macho* thing."

"Trust me, it doesn't take a father to teach you how to be a man," he said. "Actually, mine taught me everything *not* to be. Don't even get me started on the dad issue."

His nostrils widened.

"You should've just talked to me in gym class," I said a minute later. I could feel our time together coming to an end, and I was already mourning every second. "It's not like I would ever say anything. You can trust me."

He kicked a curb. "It's not that. I just have more to lose than you do."

"Like what?"

"Everything. My friends, my family…everything."

We walked by a man speaking in a loud, animated voice to a group of biker dudes outside Lynch's Irish Pub. His voice drifted to us on the breeze as we passed. "…And I told him, I said, I would never let a coupla damn *queers* into my party…"

We both winced. Oh, the South.

Nicky stepped a little further away, creating a safer space. I did the same, too. I don't know which hurt more: his distance, or my distancing of myself. I wasn't any stronger than he was. They both reinforced a basic truth: we may have been built for this, but our world wasn't.

And then I realized just how foolish I'd been to think I could just throw a hand in the air and let some stupid rainbow flag ripple in the wind. This was so much more complicated than that – I'd jumped out of a plane without a parachute. We were thousands of miles from New York, and CNN and all it stood for just didn't matter down here. Liking dudes in These Modern Times of Ours™ was such a funny thing. People acted like it had all become an endless carnival of cupcakes and tank tops and Ariana Grande songs. Equality! Equal opportunity laws! Supreme Court decisions! The continued fame of Lady Gaga! Hold the streamers, though, because most of that was bullshit. I knew what could happen if I "came out" officially, no matter what the MTV specials said. I heard the things my friends and family said in private, when they weren't being forced to say the right thing and be progressive with a capital P. If I became more open, many people I knew would distance themselves from me immediately. My number would be magically deleted from dozens of phones. Family friends would stop inviting me to Thanksgiving (since my own father rarely invited me to his own house), acquaintances would stare at me on the sidewalk, I'd be hated by a vast number of strangers simply for the act of being me. All this would happen and more. My life as I knew it would be virtually over. It sucked ass, but it was an unavoidable fact of living down here, like hurricanes or humidity, and I didn't know what to do about it. Because everyone wanted to be accepted at the floor of themselves. Nobody wanted to be shunned. Especially me. How much shunning could one dude even take?

"Look," Nicky sighed. "Suppose you were a boy. A boy the world believed in. You were big and strong and you lifted a lot of weight and the girls liked you. Then suppose that boy was a lie. He didn't exist. How hard do you think that boy would cling to that lie? How quickly do you think his life would fall apart if the lie went away? How quickly do you think all those other boys would step away if they knew the truth?" He gulped. "That lie was the best chance I had for survival. You don't know hard it was – you don't know my father..."

"I know mine," I said, "and sometimes I think that's enough. But you hate those guys, anyway. You're miserable with them. My grandma would be able to tell, and she's blind."

"Whatever. That lie is the only identity I have. And if it breaks...who would I be?"

He sounded like he didn't know the answer to the question he was asking. Who would we be, with a little honesty?

"And I almost feel bad for them," he said. "I was a lie that I let my family believe. What if they knew that every time they set me up with a girl, every time I'd pretended to have a crush on Heidi Klum to fit in with my football-playing cousins at Thanksgiving dinner…all those times were…lies? The person they know…he's not real. They'd have to get to know me all over again, as a totally different person."

I listened to the waves. "Well maybe that's their problem," I said, and it was just dawning on me that maybe I was right. "Maybe the world forced you into the lie, and your truth is nobody's issue but your own. Don't ever let anyone make you feel bad about being who you are," I said, my voice slipping into the night, unsure of even itself.

"So…does that mean you like who I am?"

I turned the color of roses. As Nicky walked, he glowed like a meteorite – he was the boy who fell from the sky. So I looked up at the stars, his home. He needed to stop all this before I fell in love with him.

"Perhaps." I took out my phone, and he stared at the screen, like he wanted to grab it. I felt panic climb into my throat, because everyone knew the act of people stealing phones was specifically designed by an evil universe intent on exposing closeted gay boys and their screen-shot paparazzi photos of Zac Efron doing pushups on the beach in Santa Monica or whatever. But then I remembered: I didn't have to hide with Nicky. He was the same as me. He knew. And that felt like walking into the sun after a lifetime of prison.

I slid my phone back into my pocket and looked over at him with wide eyes. The world got blurry, and then there became two worlds. And there he was, in between. The air itself seemed to bend around him, as if his presence melted gravity and all sorts of other laws. I was alone, watching him from a safe distance the world made us keep, but for now, that was okay.

He swerved a little to avoid a bench, and we found ourselves at the end of the boardwalk. We were close now. Very close. His breath smelled like whiskey and something else, some human smell. Pheromones, maybe. It was crazy-delicious and addictive and somehow otherworldly, whatever it was.

His arm fidgeted in an awkward way that matched his awkward words, and he was lit at the edges like he was standing in front of headlights. This enthralled me. Everything about him enthralled me. Even his faint floral smell was blooming in my skull and activating long-dormant nerve endings and reminding me I was alive. Sure, my epidermis had encased a set of functioning human organs before him, but post-him, I was *alive*. I had lived far too long without anything burning in my belly, and I was only just now realizing this. Was *this* what all the authors were writing about, with all their lovey-dovey shit? Lovey-dovey had never seemed real before, but here it was, in screaming color.

A shutdown restaurant was on one side, a vast windowless brick wall on the other. It was the two of us, alone in an alley that smelled like wet dirt, in a rude world full of unsayable truths. And he looked at me then, in that way of his, that dazzling sparkling dangerous way that said he knew things about me I didn't even know about myself. It was terrifying and overwhelming and undeniable. *I literally could not deny him.* In the distance, I could swear I heard sirens.

"Coley?" he asked, and suddenly I was absolutely sure he was going to kiss me. The funny thing was, I had never done this before, this flirty, walking-together-at-night thing. Not really. I'd never been *allowed* to. I'd been closeted my whole life, and while everyone else had been getting dating and kissing and breaking up out of their systems in middle school, I'd been going home alone and reading my books. So I didn't know how to tell him that I heard thunder when I looked at him. I didn't know how to tell him that he dominated my thoughts and lorded over my dreams. I didn't know how to tell him that when I was around him I felt like when I'd had a near-fatal reaction to a piece of popcorn shrimp at a gun show and then been strapped into a Life Flight helicopter, like my stomach was disintegrating and the rest of the world was falling away. I didn't know how to tell him I was burning up for him and he didn't even really care that I was alive.

"Yeah?" I asked. His posture fell, and he looked at the ocean.

"When I was ten, my mom found a body."

"A body?"

He bit his lip, but it wasn't sexy. It was scary. He looked conflicted, terrified. "Yeah. She was walking the dog, and the dog ran into the neighbor's garage through a side door, and she followed. She…smelled him before she saw him. It was our neighbor. He was dead, in his car."

"Oh. Yikes."

"Yikes is right. He was…I guess he was *gay*," he said, rushing through the word as I did, too, "and one day he found out he had HIV. Instead of sticking around and finding out if his wife had gotten it, too – they'd just separated – he drove home and killed himself. My mom found him four days later."

I shivered. I had no idea his self-loathing went this deep. There it was – the HIV subject. Every gay or questioning kid of the '90s grew up terrified of the disease, and was sure they'd die of it one day.

"Wow. Did the wife get it?"

He breathed deeper than I knew anyone could breathe. "No. She had a meltdown, of course, and had every test known to humanity. Healthy as a marathon runner. But he never knew that, though. He didn't stick around to find out. He let the…the guilt take him. The fear." He stared off at something I couldn't see, something I didn't *want* to see. "But you wanna know the thing I'll never forget? The thing I still see in my dreams? You want to know what my dad said before my mom pushed him out of the room?"

I swallowed. "I don't know. Do I?"

He ignored me and took on an acid, bitter tone. "He said something like, 'serves him right, for being such a *deviant* and diddling with guys, and all.' Honestly, if they hadn't done a full suicide investigation on the body and confirmed my neighbor had done it himself, I wouldn't be surprised if my dad had pushed him along."

I sucked in some air through my teeth. This all made me feel so dirty, I itched at my arm. Nicky swallowed hard, and I know right then that this thing was going to harder than I'd ever expected. He hated himself far more than I ever had.

"I've had the same dream ever since then," Nicky said. There were tears in his voice, but his eyes were dry. "This ghoulish, awful, ridiculous thing. I discover the body, and he's dead, but he's still staring right at me. He knows I'm like him. And then he opens his mouth and tells me I'm next."

"Jesus."

"I know. So, if it's gonna be like this," he said to nobody at all, "if we're gonna hangout, it's gotta be...friendly."

"Oh," I said, as all the fires within me extinguished themselves.

"Yeah. You're super cool and everything, and I would like to be around you more and stuff – I would probably *love* it, actually – but it's gotta...it can't be like that."

I felt my shoulders slump. Ugh. So much for stepping out of the closet – he wasn't even going to stick out a toe. And things kept in the dark could not grow. Just ask any gardener or closeted preteen.

"Is that cool? Are you okay with that?"

As he spoke, he looked sort of nervous. Or did he? How much of what I was seeing was just what I *wanted* to see? How much of Nicky was I wishing into a tenuous reality?

I tore my eyes away. He didn't deserve my gaze. He was making me an offer any sane person would refuse: have him in my life, but in the last way I wanted. I knew I could refuse him. I could tell him I didn't want to play this game, that we weren't in middle school, that we could do whatever we wanted, and that he was crazy and cowardly for being so scared of being seen with me, even as a friend. This was the last thing I needed in the world: a beautiful, intelligent, galaxy-eyed boy who was ashamed of me.

Or I could be real and acknowledge that he had to be careful. He operated in a different world than I did. But it wasn't just because of the goon squad. Our lives weren't just about us. We weren't on our own any more than our dogs were when we walked them down the block. We were playing by the rules of our parents, and their money and acceptance were our leashes. Maybe we'd never be free. Not really. Or maybe we could break free of this. That was the thought that kept me going.

I *could* just take the leap and see what happened. I guess I didn't how to hang out with a guy in public anymore than he did. In my nineteen years, I'd never gone out alone with someone who had a penis. And ultimately I supposed this was the saddest thing: I would take any amount of Nicky that he gave me, and we probably both knew it.

"Okay," I said. "Yeah."

"Yeah?"

"Yeah. Of course. But relax. Friends hang out in dark alleys at night, you know."

He smirked, and it made the whole world shine. Maybe my chances hadn't totally been smashed to bits. "That right?"

I nodded.

"Okay, well…I'm glad to have made a new friend."

My face collapsed again. I couldn't help it. *Friend*…the word suddenly felt so hollow, as if it had been carved out like a turkey.

I sat on the sidewalk and put my back against the brick wall. "Me too, Nicky Flores."

He smiled this too-big smile and sat next to me, and all he did was put his hand next to mine. But that was enough. That one gesture made everything in my life up until tonight – all the deleting of web histories, all the rolling up of car window at stoplights so nobody would hear my Britney Spears songs, all the concealment and shame and evasiveness – it made all that nonsense suddenly seem worth it. This was all I wanted for now, anyway, and now that I had it, I suddenly felt like I could rise into my own giddiness and hit the sky. Because the clichés were all so suddenly true now: Nicky

70

Flores was almost holding my hand. It felt sweet like the purr of a sleeping kitten, or triumphant like the Fourth of July. I couldn't tell which one. Basically it just felt like everything.

6

Romantic movie dates. Sunny afternoons spent crisscrossing the trails of state parks. Occasional trips to gay bars to chat up friends. Shopping excursions to malls and outlet centers. Put-putting. These were the things I thought I would do with Nicky. These were also the things I did *not* do with him, not by a million miles. They were the ignorant, slightly silly fantasies I'd once had of what two boys would do, how they would act, in a world that let them in instead of locking them out. This what my relationship with Nicky *really* looked like:

The day after the hand-holding event started out as a dream and a half. After FitTrax he met me in the alley behind the gym, in real life. The workout class had been a disaster, but seeing Nicky alone made it all okay. It was one of those cool summer evenings when the winds rushed in and rinsed away the bored restlessness of the day, and I was floating.

"Do you want to come over?" he blurted out, like he was still deciding if it was worth saying.

"To your house?"

"No, to the teepee I live in, out in the fields. Yes, to my house."

"Why?"

"Because we should be friends?"

"Oh," I breathed.

"What?"

"You…want to be *friends*…with me?"

He was breathing so hard, I could feel it on my face. "You say it like I offered you cancer."

"Both are equally plausible in my mind," I said under my breath. "And yeah, I'd love to. Sure. I mean, why not. I can cancel my plans. That I had. Because I definitely had plans. With my friends. That I have."

Nicky smiled and got up close to me as we walked with our bikes towards the sidewalk, the breeze ruffling his hair so beautifully, his scent cold and crisp in my nostrils, and in that moment I could swear the world had been invented just for us.

But then he stopped, peering over his shoulder again. A girl was watching, but nobody else. "And Cole?"

"Yeah?"

"Could you maybe ride behind me?"

"Oh. Sure."

"Maybe, like…a block behind?"

And so we rode to his house…separately. I kept my distance, as requested, and when I saw him turn off the street, towards the ocean, my panic grew with every foot closer I got to his house. I learned he lived on the ocean, too, but his apartment building was much more run-down than mine, and was set further away from the beach. We parked our bikes and walked up two flights of stairs, and there we were – in his house.

I blinked and then drank it in like a cold Miller Lite. I didn't know what to expect, but it wasn't this. It was…chic, almost. "So…you live here alone?"

"Yep. I'm gonna change shirts, hold on."

He went into the bedroom…and closed the door behind him. *Okay then.* I looked towards the sea, and that's when I saw it: two pairs of shoes. His dirty tennis shoes were next to a pair of women's embellished flip-flops. Then I looked at the key pegs and saw two sets of keys. In the refrigerator, everything was divided in half. Someone else lived here with him.

"Sup," he said, stepping back into the room in a glorious blue tee. "Are you down for some video games or something?"

"Um…video games…yeah. Great. I love, um, video games."

"Yeah? Which ones?"

"Uh, I love that one…*World of Battle Fighting*, and um…*Fast Racing Cars*. Those are my faves." He hesitated, and I cringed. Ask me about which singer was dating which movie star, and I'd tell you the location of their last date. But toss me a question about "boy" stuff like Fantasy Football or video games, and my motherboard was scrambled like a pan of eggs.

73

He looked down, and suddenly he was cringing, too. Then he smiled. "Um…pocket banana? Or excitement?"

I looked down and wanted to end myself right there. I wasn't hard, per se, but I was *getting* hard, and because my filmy gym shorts were so wet with sweat, you could clearly see the outline of what was going on down there.

"Ugh, sorry, forgot to wear underwear," I said as I turned around and reached down to fix things. I had no idea how to act around him, and it was so obvious. When I faced him again, his face cracked, and for one second his mask fell off. Longing slid into his eyes and took hold of him, and I could see it so clearly: he wanted me. So much was compressed into that look, a lightning bug in a beer bottle, and for just a second, his face was on fire.

"I didn't say it was a bad thing," he murmured. And the room caught fire.

He turned away, heat still radiating off him. "Yeah. So. Anyway. Video games it is." He breathed so deeply his shoulders trembled. "By the way, will you be there tomorrow?"

"Where?"

"FitTrax."

"Oh. I mean, sure. Probably." Obviously I'd go anywhere he was, and it made me feel pathetic and breathless, and also a little giddy.

"Okay. Meet me after class, then, at the same place. Same time. And maybe the day after that, too?"

He couldn't see me, but my eyes were as big as the sea. "You got it."

He sat on the couch, and I used the opportunity to scan the room. For some reason I wanted to remember every detail, inspect everything I could. I saw a tank with what looked like a large snail inside. "Why snails?" I asked him.

"I just like them. They're cool. Nobody can ever mess with them. They're too…protected."

I glanced at his blinds, which were shut in the middle of the day. Then the curtains on the back door, which were closed. And I think I understood him a bit more. He was so weird, but I liked it. I was so used to being bored by people. Even interesting people were interesting in all the same ways, like those quirky teen novels that tried so hard to be unique, they all ended up sounding the same. But not Nicky.

He saw my eyes, and what they were noticing. "Don't look at me like that," he said. "You don't know me yet."

"What do you do for fun," I asked, "when nobody's watching?"

He hesitated, then pointed to the magazines on his table. *Architectural Digest, Modern Kitchen*, all the big design magazines were there. "Really?" I asked. I was memorizing every fact about him that I could gather on the phone – his favorite song was *Closer* by Kings of Leon, he hated green beans, he was terrified of big dogs – but this had never been mentioned.

"Really. I love for things to look clean, orderly, for everything to be in the right place."

"That's not your major, is it?"

He looked away. "Nah. I'm in more of a general art program – my family says interior design isn't 'suitable' for me, in their words."

"Oh. Gotcha."

I stared at him for a second.

"Maybe this is just me," he asked soon, "but does the world ever feel like a-"

"Prison?" I asked, and he licked his top lip as I thought about the wars we kept inside ourselves, the secrets that killed us. And suddenly all of the feelings I'd never let myself feel before exploded inside me at once.

~

As the world slipped into the summer, Nicky and I started hanging out in person more and more – as "friends," though. First we went to the dog park, then we went to the beach, finally we went to a matinee. He kept me at an arm's length most of the time – Michael Jordan's arm length, actually, avoiding anywhere his friends frequented like the plague multiplied by the bird flu. That didn't leave many places for us to go, of course, so the red-rose dates were out of the question. He'd come over and then follow me straight through the dunes to the beach, always looking over his shoulder, always maintaining an almost bizarrely wide berth. If we went back inside to eat or something, I'd keep the curtains drawn at his request, and sometimes he wouldn't even walk into the bathroom without peering through the window first, since it faced the walkway. I knew I was being a kept a filthy little secret, but I didn't care enough to try to change it. The pros were massively outweighing the cons. Because something was happening. Something was sparking. He was letting me into his world, and it was reinventing mine – even if I needed a heavy dose of wine and Adele every night to forget how bad it made me feel every time he denied me.

Suddenly I was falling in love with my dumb little town, and felt like I hadn't seen nearly enough of it. I'd never seen *any* of it, really. He made the world seem like a whole new place. We'd bike down the avenues, so beautiful in their rundown-ness, and get froyo at a cheap place with rickety, falling-apart picnic tables. We'd sit at hipster bars and drink gross beers and make fun of how shitty the local magazines were, and all the while I'd be drowning in him and be totally unable to mention it. We'd bodysurf, never touching or cavorting, just riding the waves, drowning in what was possibly deepening between us. But my favorite thing was to get on his golf cart with him and just ride. It was one of those expensive gas-powered ones, and sometimes it went so fast it made me dizzy. Nicky made me sit in the back, of course, and he usually wouldn't bring it out until the sun was about to go down, to ensure nobody would stare. "Two dicks on one vehicle is just out of the question," my dad used to say, and I assumed Nicky's father was the same. But on that golf cart, we didn't have to worry, didn't have to look around, didn't have to think about anything. We could just ride.

The hangouts continued. Before long he became the highlight of my being alive, his light shining into every corner my life. I didn't know how else to put it. I waited all day to see

76

those galaxy eyes. For someone whose solo "Netflix and chill" sessions usually devolved into "overanalyzing my life choices and quietly slipping into a state of vague panic on my couch while not chilling" sessions, having a friend around all the time was sort of maverick to me. I never had to be alone anymore. I even started waking up to texts from him, and it felt like an explosion in my chest every time. He'd rant about his obnoxious neighbor or maybe complain about his mother, but I didn't really care what he was saying, just that he was saying it. He was confiding in me, *only* me, and that made all the difference. One strange thing was that we did not talk about "the gay subject" one more time. Not directly, at least. But it was enough for me. *He* was enough. For now. He was undoing everything everyone else had ever done to me, and I never wanted it to end.

I still had no idea how to conduct myself around him, though. Not a clue. I'd never been so self-conscious. When I acted like a friend it felt all stiff and wrong, and on the other hand, if I ever tried to get flirty, I'd scare him off. I'd never really had a close male friend before, and sometimes even *I* had to laugh at how awkward I was at the whole back-slapping, high-fiving, burping-in-public part of Being A Dudebro. We came across some of his guy friends once or twice, and when I attempted to slap hands with them, I usually missed and hit empty air. This was usually followed by several seconds of dead silence. Every time I tried to act like Nicky, or like Nicky's *boyfriend*, I felt like I was trying to stick a laptop charger into an iPhone. It was like trying to read a book by a bad writer. Writing was a born skill, something you either could or couldn't do, and the reader picked up on this immediately. The harder a non-writer tried to write, and sound like some artist or master, the more awkward and forced the reading experience became. *Trying* to figure out how to act just made everything worse. The most frustrating thing was that all I wanted was to act like *myself*. I was falling for him, and he was just a friend. Or was he a friend? What was he? What was *this*?

I started looking forward to our hangouts with everything in me. Stepping into his world was like being inside a firework. He was the most spontaneous person I'd ever known, and he seemed to enjoy being alive more than everyone else did. So many people went through life half-asleep. I'd tried living once, and it sucked, so I'd gone back to my books and my photography. But he was different. If he wanted to do something, he'd do it. If he wanted to go hiking, he'd go. If he wanted a frozen coffee drink, he'd get up and get one. And I was just lucky to be along on the ride. During our days together, a lifetime of aloneness just melted away – I finally felt like I didn't have to go through the world alone anymore.

Onc random Saturday, we rode bikes from my house to Atlantic Beach, talking about all the different houses we liked. He liked traditional and I liked contemporary, but I was willing to overlook this in the sake of how sexy his hair looked in the sun. On Sunday he drove us to Lemon Bar, this outdoor bar on the beach, to use our fake IDs to get some beers. Drinking around him terrified and thrilled me, but so far he hadn't really let the friend thing drop, *even* when he was drunk.

In the meantime I was doing everything I could to make myself more desirable. I got layers in my hair, I stopped eating candy, I tried to grow out my facial hair a little to look mysterious. None of it worked. I knew exactly what I wanted, and had no idea how to get there. Still Nicky called me "dude" and "bro" and sometimes talked about girls he thought were hot. There was a strange airiness to him when he talked about females, his eyes looking like the vacant apartment buildings downtown. If he was an actor, he'd win worst performance of the year during these speeches. I didn't say anything, though. We were all allowed to have our delusions, and also, what if *I* was actually the delusional one? What if he really *was* intent on being straight, and this was all a massive dose of wishful thinking on my part, just like usual?

At night, when I was alone, I would lie on my couch in the light of the TV and imagine what our love would look like, if it were allowed to bloom. If I couldn't have him, I would have the Him of my fantasies, and for a book nerd that was almost as good. I was good at it imagining, after all, as the only real relationships I'd ever been in had occurred exclusively within my head.

"Oh, Nicky," I'd say as we snuggled together in my daydreams. "You're such a softie. The real version of you is so much better than that bro-ish hologram the world created of you." He'd say nothing, nuzzling my neck instead, healing ancient wounds, as we settled into an all-night marathon of *Will & Grace*. We'd laugh at every joke, not feeling dirty or sinful for it at all, like when my dad had walked in on me watching the show after his divorce and called me a "queer" and turned off the TV. And some nights – okay, most nights – I would dream of Nicky, and it was always the same. I'd be driving along a random road on a stormy day, and a tornado would storm into my rearview mirror. It would chase me to the ocean, and then I'd have to ditch my car and swim away from the twister as it chased me down. Each time, I'd reach an island of safety, and the only person on that island would be Nicky. Only Nicky.

And okay, maybe he *wasn't* totally straight. Soon some cracks started showing in his resolve, however small they were. I was skeptical at first, but before long it became almost undeniable. At first it was just looks, like when I'd catch him checking out a guy in a restaurant, or even checking *me* out as I walked to the bathroom. A few times I'd catch him singing along to a "girl song" until he'd notice me and pretend like he didn't know the words. But soon the *big* thing happened. After he biked over one night, we jumped around on my neighbor's trampoline she kept by the sand dunes for her grandkids who visited maybe once a year. Soon we fell down in the middle of the net and started talking, and before I knew it, we were yawning.

Was this normal? I wondered, fully aware that we were in plain view of all my neighbors. I had no idea what that word "normal" even meant anymore. Before this, my life had existed in terms of black and white, right and wrong, gay and straight, faggot and jock. But now we were sliding into the grey, whatever it contained. Every time we touched I felt an earthquake, every time he accidentally bumped into me, my knees wanted to buckle. I don't know when or how we got sleepy that night, all I know is that I had never felt more comfortable, easier, than I did with him on that net. My old life suddenly seemed a million years ago – here I was, wonderstruck, lying around in my dead-end town with a kid I liked more than anything in the world. Who was this dream person I was becoming?

"Nicky?" I asked when it became clear we were crashing outside for the night.

"Hmm?"

"Why'd you take so long to talk to me? After the app, and everything?"

He was silent for a while. I was getting so bad at hiding my affection for him, and I knew I had to at least pretend to play the game, but I couldn't.

When he did speak, his voice was gruff and muffled and a million miles away. "Because I didn't want to admit I was me yet."

I tried to creep closer, overcome by some deep and unexplored yearning for him. He felt like nothing I'd ever felt before.

"Don't touch me," he groaned, rolling away.

"What? Oh, I was just…finding a more comfortable spot. That's all."

"Well please don't." For a minute I just heard the wind, but then he took a breath, his back to me. "Sorry, I know I'm weird about that. My father never touched me or hugged me growing up – not once, *ever* – and so touching is still, like, 'a thing' for me."

"*Okay*," I said, turning and facing the sea. "Okay. Fine."

He put his head up, and I could tell he was half-asleep. "You're not leaving, though, right?"

I smiled, and suddenly I felt like I was not tethered to the ground anymore. Gravity was gone. "Nah. I'll be right here."

As he fell asleep, he relaxed, even rolling a bit closer to me again. And everything in me unclenched just a little bit more.

That night I dreamed about swimming to strange blue islands in pink oceans. I woke abruptly at five in the morning, still on the trampoline. A thin blue line on the horizon spoke of a sunrise that was about to break, but the world was still grey and muted. I looked around then, at this scene I'd woken up to a hundred other times, the grass giving way to the rolling dunes and the ocean beyond, but suddenly I felt like I'd been transported somewhere else. Suddenly everything looked different. Everything felt better. The grass was greener and crisper, the dunes were glowing with the light from the stars, the ocean was no longer this featureless black puddle but a living, teeming ecosystem full of animals and shells and boats and hurricanes. Even this early, my body felt jumpy and electric and revived. It didn't matter if Nicky was keeping himself away from me in every way possible – I was so used to waking up and staring a muted world with dead eyes. Nicky was making my life feel new.

And I knew I was being stupid. I knew that a boy who wouldn't acknowledge me, who treated me like just another friend, who was terrified of what I felt for him, was the last thing I needed on this green planet. But still I was powerless. Under a violet July dawn, love grabbed me and ran away with me. Because beauty like Nicky didn't just stumble into your life – you had to chase it. And something told me I was going to chase him until we faded to black and white.

As I lay there I felt something on my hip, and I reached around to find that Nicky was snuggled up behind me, his arm resting on my side, like how married couples slept. I froze and listened to the wind, simultaneously burning up and melting all at once. This was the first time he'd ever *really* touched me.

81

Nicky finally woke up at about seven, and by this time he'd rolled away, ensuring he never had any idea he'd spooned with me. But as he jumped up and ran to his bike, mortified that my neighbors might wake up and see two dudes sleeping together, I smiled for what felt like forever. I knew I was a fool for liking him, but I didn't care. He was my pair of brand new eyes, and that was the end of it. Something was happening, something I could feel but not name – something that felt like speeding down a country road on a Saturday morning and realizing you were happier than you'd been in a while. Maybe forever. Here are some other things that made me think Nicky and I were becoming more than just friends:

- He started paying for everything. Not just meals, but ice cream, drinks, parking fees, *everything*. I never questioned it or mentioned anything, but each time, it made me feel something I'd never felt before: special.

- One rainy night we went to the movies. I sat one seat away from him, keeping my distance, like I assumed he wanted me to. As the lights darkened, though, he looked over and motioned for me to move closer and sit next to him. I did, and he sat back, smiling. I could feel electricity radiating off his legs all night long.

- One day at FitTrax, some dude came up to me and told me he liked my technique at a certain lift we were learning. He was pretty "straight," but I was still super flattered, mostly because no one had ever talked to me there. It seemed that Nicky's approval had made me, if not accepted, than at least *tolerated*. But when I looked over after the dude left, Nicky was murdering me with his eyes. We never talked about it, but we didn't have to. He was furious.

- One thing I noticed was that Nicky was a planet, and I was a nervous little ball of energy darting around him, like a moon bouncing around his gravitational field.

Every now and then I'd catch him looking at me, maybe stealing a glimpse at my thighs, or even checking out my ass, his eyes large and curious and confused. So I started touching him. I'd graze his elbow or brush past his legs, all the while feeling like my insides had caught on fire. At first he would freeze up or even brush me off, but soon he started giving in. Before long he didn't even acknowledge me.

- None of this was to say that he was an easy person to be around. He was catnip to every girl we ever came across. Seeing how much he was wanted by other people made me want him a hundred times more. Girls would flock to him by the bucketful, and I hated every minute of it. And there was nothing I could do about it, since we were just "friends." I was never allowed to forget that he was valuable, wanted, desired. And okay, I kind of loved it in a sense, too, because I had a hot dude who wanted to hangout with me, and these bitches didn't. Nicky would do nothing to discourage all this attention, and most of the time he flirted back while I stood off to the side, silently fuming. It infuriated me and also turned me on, because he was so smooth and charming and *goodness*, he was just magic. Lightning in a bottle, that boy. From his smirk, which always seemed to tease you, to his eyes, which danced and glittered with all the colors of the rolling green Atlantic – he was art brought to life, the Mona Lisa in motion.

- Best of all: on a Saturday afternoon we biked to Publix for some buffalo chicken subs. Some asshole in an SUV cut Nicky off and made him swerve, and he lurched into me and knocked me over. He landed on top of me on a patch of grass, our bikes clattering to the side, and after we stopped laughing he froze and stared into my eyes. I stared back, and I could swear in that moment, we were the only two people on the

83

planet. Other people were alive out there, of course, but not like us. Not like this. His laugh made me want to smile. His sadness made me want to die. I wanted more than anything in the world to cross this bridge and become his boy, the one he called his own, and not just his friend. But I didn't know how. "Sometimes I explode for you," I whispered on the grass before I could stop myself, lost in his galaxy eyes, but he didn't say anything. We stayed in that position until a car drove by and every single member of the family inside watched us with open mouths. He jumped up and muttered that we could never do that again, but still: my body stayed alive for hours.

Of course, I know *I* was awful at pretending to keep up the whole "friend" act. He was all I wanted to think about, all I wanted to talk about. I was probably getting so annoying, but I didn't care. Everything reminded me of him, everything circled back to him. He became the beginning and the end of all I knew. Soon I realized we were even starting to dress the same – I subconsciously adopted some of his darker colors, and his clothes got a bit tighter. Once I even noticed he'd bought Birkenstocks, which I wore all the time because of my flat feet. As I got tanner and my hair darkened to a coppery color, we started to look the same, as well. But I couldn't help any of it – he skittered across my brain all day. One afternoon my neighbor asked me why I kept smiling as I helped her move boxes, and before I could stop myself I said "Nicky." She smiled and said she was sure Nicky was a beautiful girl. I smiled back, sick to my stomach with giddiness. For the first time I was starting to understand the term "lovesick:" all day long I was full of a helpless kind of longing that made me feel heavy and lethargic and useless and starry-eyed, like I was bogged down by an unbearable joy that made my bones feel like they were breaking inside me and flying out of my body all at once. Nicky was an exquisite pain, a luxurious heartache. I had been smart at one time, but that boy was making me so stupid.

All this glory at the hands of Nicky Flores was accompanied by another emotion: panic. He was the best person I had ever met, even counting his pretty serious flaws. He knew all kinds of facts about the weather, he made me feel like I mattered, and he could sit and talk about useless shit all day. He was a nerd like me, except he wasn't ashamed – he was proud. He was kind and good and smart and fun and he made everyone and everything else look like vanilla pudding. But before him, everyone and everything good in my life had left, disappeared. What would happen if we tumbled off this razor-thin wire we were balancing on, and it all went to hell? What would happen if I lost him? Where would I be without Nicky?

He wasn't just the desire of the deepest parts of myself – he was my best friend. All my time with him was spent trying to cling onto that time and remember it while it was happening, catalog it and store it away, like reaching up and trying to grab the whistling wind. All my time away from him was spent inside those memories, treasuring them, turning over every little detail in my mind, wondering why he'd laughed a certain way during a movie, or asking myself why he'd looked at a certain person with such disdain in his eyes, or trying not to acknowledge the time the waitress had asked if we were together and he'd shaken his head no, unaware that I was watching. Because he didn't speak much – usually he was as silent as a phone on vibrate. So I had to look for language in other forms. One look, one gesture, one sigh, could leave me reeling and deciphering for hours. And regardless of it all, I knew he craved my presence, too. I noticed he was starting to make room for me in his life, ditching hangout sessions with the bros to go to the beach with me, or blowing off his mom's phone calls to sit and do nothing with me on my living room floor. He never admitted or acknowledged what he was doing, but he didn't need to. Nothing outside our little bubble mattered when we were within it. He was the still point in my turning world. Alone, we were lost. Together, we were on fire.

In any case, for me the month of July was like when you started reading a book and realized, *Oh shit, this is it. This is a special one.* The words crackled, the story clicked, the characters bounced off the page, and suddenly, boom – you were intoxicated. As you read, something intangible grabbed you, hooked you, and soon you were both sinking and flying into a kaleidoscopic joy that you somehow knew was going to rearrange your bones forever. Nicky was that book for me. He was just that good.

Most of the time I wasn't stupid enough to mistake our moments of private closeness with him wanting to be open with me out in the world, though. Once when we were biking, I lost my brain and got up right next to him, and we rode in tandem for a minute, locked in heaven. Then we rode up to a bar where some of his friends were supposed to be.

"Don't," he whispered apologetically but tersely, unable to meet my eyes. It made me feel like the smallest person in the world. Forget about *Honey, We Shrunk the Kids* – this was *Honey, We Shrunk Coley Furman.* I was nothing.

"Oh, yeah," I said, finding a safer distance. He was just a few feet away, but in that moment he felt further away than New York.

The next day, the distance between us widened even more.

"Cole?" Nicky asked on the way to lunch. He was the most careless and absent-minded driver in the world, so I was already alert when I responded.

"Yeah?"

"I've been having a lot of fun with you and everything, but...I had a dream."

Ugh, I thought again. Here it was: the flight. I was still in awe of how he could just fly away and leave, even when he was sitting right there in front of me.

"Okay? And?"

"...And my dad walked in us when we were hanging out. In the dream, I mean."

"...Why is that bad?"

"It wasn't *that*, necessarily. It's what we were doing."

I waited for him to finish. He didn't.

"And?"

"Well, you were on your knees."

My chest exploded. Inside I was all supernovas, waterfalls, booming canons. But I tried not to let any of that rise to my face. "You…you had a sex dream about me?"

He scooted away a little. "Dudes have sex dreams about each other, okay? It's totally normal. Happens all the time."

Sure, I thought, trying to force my smile back down my throat. "Okay, well, it was still just a dream. What's the big deal?"

He cut his eyes away. "It's not only that. Remember Dylan? The dude who can pump two forty in a high muscle snatch, easy?"

I blinked. "You must've forgotten who you're talking to. I don't speak 'straight guy.'"

"Okay, whatever. Anyway…Dylan asked me why I was at Target with you the other night. Remember when we rented that war movie and watched it at my place?"

Of course I remembered. Nicky had tried to keep me in the car, but I came inside anyway. That night I'd fallen asleep on his floor after fifteen minutes. Stupid war movie – I couldn't even pretend to like it. Why did people pretend, anyway? I was growing less and less patient with the concept every day.

"What about it?" I asked.

"Well, my friend saw me there. At Target. The next day he asked why I was being so 'chummy' with another guy."

I sighed, stared out the window. I wanted to rage, to punch the glass and ask Nicky if he was as sick of this shit as I was, but I just sighed instead. "Well that's just great, then. Awesome! I don't even want to know what you told him."

He winced a little – he didn't want me to know, either.

"We're moving too fast, Cole," he said after we stopped at a light. "Our…friendship is, I mean. The vultures are everywhere. If the guys start talking…I might as well move back home to Savannah. If they ditch me, if I lose that, I don't know what I'd have."

You'd have me, I wanted to say, but I didn't. *If you ever have nobody, I'll be everything to you.* "So what? They're all ignorant garbage receptacles," I said instead, "and you know it."

He shrugged. "We've been over this. The situation is what it is."

"Oh, okay. Why not just ditch me, then? Just get it over with a little early?"

He looked over at me with such genuine emotion in his eyes, I wanted to hug something, anything. "Why would you say that? Is that what you want?"

"Geez," I said. "I didn't think you'd mind. It was just a joke."

He sighed with that masculine cool I didn't have, had spent my life coveting. "Okay. Thank God."

"Why do you say it like that?"

"I don't know. I like having you around. You're cool, Cole. You're different. You're a pretty weird kid, actually, but I like it."

I looked away, my mind spinning like a dradle. That was the first time he'd ever said he liked me. "Weird?" I asked, egging this on.

"Can't put it into words, really. All the others – you're not like them. You fell from somewhere else, with your big blue eyes and crazy blonde hair and everything. You're just an alien."

And I fell deep, but it didn't last long. Soon I looked over and noticed he was shaking with nerves. "Nicky…are you okay?"

"I mean…yeah. The thing is, I wanted to go to my favorite little café, but…I don't know. My mom is coming in town, and I don't want her to see…us. Together. After the dream, and Target, and all. I don't know…"

I looked out the window at a town that suddenly seemed to shimmer less. "Oh. Okay." I was so ashamed, and more than that, I was borderline disgusted with myself for putting up with this again and again. He was always going to hide me, lie about me. I was always going to be the tagalong.

He shook his head. "I still want to hangout, though. Let's go to a library."

Instantly I knew why he was asking me to go to a library: nobody went to libraries anymore. Nobody *he* knew, at least. We would be isolated, hidden. And so I said yes. Because at this point I still halfway wanted to hide, too. I didn't know anything else.

At the library I took Nicky to my usual area in the corner, hidden by great love stories of the past. I found myself being pulled into him, and as I stood about an inch away from him in the magazine section, a librarian's eyes landed on us for a second longer than was necessary. Something like disapproval shaded her eyes before she looked away again. Or was I imagining it? In any case, being in my happy place with him felt like a rare triumph, like a shooting star in the corner of the sky that you'd just barely noticed at the last possible second.

I took a deep, nervous breath. "Do you read?" I asked him.

"I do. Not as much as I'd like, but I definitely do. Books give me tickets to worlds that are so much better than this shitty one *we* have to live in. And you?"

"Of course," I said. "It's like dancing with the world without ever leaving your own mind."

It was like I'd dreamed him into reality. I wanted to play it cool, but I couldn't. I was a book nerd: playing it cool just wasn't in my wheelhouse.

"You can't be real," I said.

"I certainly was last time I checked."

My face smiled without my permission. I couldn't believe how quickly my world had turned on its side.

"I know what you mean, though," he said. "This is so crazy, and nice, having someone to talk about this stuff with. *Books*, I mean."

"What, Ryan and the guys aren't in any book clubs? I'm shocked."

"Touché. I kind of dug my own grave with that one."

I laughed. I was beginning to realize I laughed at every single thing he said, actually, and I probably sounded like a maniac.

"What's funny?"

I just shrugged, as I couldn't really put it into words. Describing him with words was like taking a picture of the moon: no matter how good your angle may have seemed at the time, in the end it'd still turn out looking stupid and faded and terrible and just like every *other* picture of the moon ever taken. You just couldn't capture him – he was a specific kind of magic that refused to be bottled.

"It's just weird," I said, and I brushed my arm against his before I could stop myself. "You-"

I felt eyes on me again, and I snapped my head over and met someone's gaze. It was my father's best friend, Robert. He glanced from the way I way standing totally oriented to Nicky's body, then to Nicky's face, and finally to me. I wanted to get up and scream at him, tell him to mind his business, but I just stared back. Then he turned away, his nose high in the air, with a look on his face like someone had just served him a plate of dirty diapers. And I had no doubt in my mind that he was going to call my father about this.

"What is it?" Nicky asked.

"Nothing! Just don't feel that well. Let's walk somewhere else."

We passed some photography books. "Your job is really cool," he said.

"Thanks, but it's not, just, like, 'a job' for me. I'd be taking photos even if I never got a dime off it." I took out my phone. "See here – I take pictures of people all the time, even when I'm not doing the *Honesty* thing. I'm a professional creeper, basically."

I started scrolling through my pictures of my subjects, praying I wouldn't come across any porn-y ones in the mix. There were old women sitting beside dumpsters, little babies in fancy strollers, teenaged girls on bicycles. His eyes turned into bigger and bigger planets as he watched. "What is it? What's with the face?"

90

"These are just amazing," he said. "You can really *see* people in these pictures, as dumb as that sounds."

"Nah," I said.

"Yes!"

As he spoke, he reached over and sort of clutched my shoulder, like a teacher did when they explained something to you. It made me feel like the government had raised the terrorism threat level. "Look at their eyes – you can see what they want, what they need, and the fight between the two. This is amazing, Coley. What you're doing, it's brave."

I felt like I was floating, but still, I frowned. I'd never understood the argument that artists were "brave." Soldiers were brave. Firefighters were brave. The dudes and dudettes in Doctors Without Borders were brave. I wasn't brave, sitting on my phone, doing my job. What was courageous about trying to pay my rent?

"Stop," I said. "It's just...it's nothing."

He looked at me, and I felt like I was disintegrating. "Coley. Really. I admire this. You're telling stories for people who are too afraid to tell their own. Lots of people can't express themselves-" he paused for a moment, but only for a moment- "be it because they're scared, they're inarticulate, whatever. You're doing it for them. Nobody says what they feel anymore, but you do. What's braver than honesty?"

I had to look away then. He was the sun, and I was burning up.

"How do you do this? How do you...read people so well?"

"I've gotten it down to a science, I guess," I said. "It's not easy. Especially with some people..."

"Well, Mr. Artiste, I want the juicy stuff. What's your technique?"

"I don't know. I never talk about this."

"Tell me!"

"Well, for one, I like finding either very young people or very old people."

"Why?"

91

"Well, little kids speak truth, because the world hasn't taught them to lie yet. And old people – they've lived more and seen more and had their hearts broken, and part of me doesn't care about the opinions of any adult who has never known devastation." I swallowed. "And crazy people, too. They give great quotes. The best people usually have something *not-quite-right* shining in their eyes."

He was silent.

"Enough about this," I said. "Don't *you* have a special talent? There must be something you can do?"

His face turned into a bomb. He licked his lip and it made my stomach feel like it wasn't a stomach anymore. "I can tie a cherry stem together with my tongue."

Something that won't make me spontaneously combust, I thought to myself. I didn't even know how to touch that one, so I pushed through.

"Well, back to my pictures – one thing is, I watch people. You have to get to know them first sometimes. I study them before I ask them for their secrets, to see if anything is behind their eyes, I guess."

The air went from tense to electric to aflame. "Do you watch *me*?" he asked soon, sounding afraid of the answer. I swallowed. I usually saw the world in muted tones, but the colors exploded around him. The room filled with blues and greens and oranges, all neon. How could I possibly admit any of this?

"No. Not really. Not for *Honesty*, anyway. But I've seen your house," I whispered, but of course I didn't tell him I knew he lived at 22053 First Street North. "Or, I mean, before you'd ever invited me over, I knew where it was."

He inhaled. "Okay. How?"

"A check-in on an Instagram map. And Google Maps."

I waited for him to hit me, to run away, because I was crazy. We were two kids running from the world, and this wasn't supposed to happen. We were friends. Just friends.

"Is it crazy that I'm flattered?" he finally asked.

"I don't know. Maybe. Yes. But I'm still crazy."

He turned, and I followed. And together we walked, into an even more deserted row of books.

"When did you first know?" I asked him, tossing it out like a fishing line. I'd been skipping closer and closer to the gay subject, but he hadn't taken the bait yet. Would today be the day?

"Know *what*?"

"You know what." He looked off at something, but I persisted, my voice barely a whisper. "Come on, Nicky. You can talk about this now. Nobody cares. Okay, fine, some people care, but…you know what I mean. You don't have to pretend when we're alone."

He looked at me. The silence crackled, fizzed, burned with everything we couldn't say. "Why do you want to know?"

"Because I've never had anyone to talk about this stuff with."

"Well, then." He gulped some air with what looked like some difficulty, and even this was beautiful. Everything he did was beautiful. Too beautiful for me to hold, probably. "It was the day the towers fell, actually," he whispered, and I perked up. Here they were: the parts of him he'd been hiding. "Our teacher gathered us up by the TV, and then everyone's parents started coming to pick up their kids, one by one. My friend Tyler and I were the last ones left in class, and obviously we were little and we had no idea what any of it meant. When our teacher stepped out, Tyler found a doll in the toy box and dared me to kiss her on the boobs. It grossed me out, but I did it anyway, and I didn't really feel much. But God, did I *try* to feel something. Because that's what little boys were supposed to do, right? Love girls. Kiss girls. Date girls. Never was there a Disney movie or Nickelodeon show that showed anything different. Anyway, yeah, I just remember sensing that something about me was…different." He looked over at me. "What about you?"

I bit my lip. I'd never been asked that before. The truth was, I'd always known, I'd just never been able to admit it. In the beginning I'd lied to myself, told myself I was just

93

different from the other children because I was unusually smart. And so the games began. If I was watching a movie with friends or family and someone onscreen cracked a gay joke, I'd kill myself trying to laugh the exactly appropriate amount, not howling like a try-hard and looking suspicious, and not staying too quiet and looking suspect, either. If a girl ever liked me, I would tell *everyone*, as if it was proof that I liked the correct gender. If I was good at something on the sporting field, or I ever beat another guy at a game, I'd never let it die. Although I was very interested in fashion, I was careful not to dress too well – I'd buy a Polo shirt instead of a tight European top, watering myself down so nobody would know. But I knew. Who I loved was as much a part of me as my hair color or the fact that I was right-handed at everything except taking photos. Boys were in my DNA.

"I remember when I was in first grade, my mom got this chandelier installed in my living room," I said as my eyes filled with sparkling lights and my ears with the faraway sound of crystals clinking together. "My dad didn't give two shits, but I remember sitting there and staring up at the lights and the crystals for hours, totally obsessed, and that's the first time I remember being…different. My friends and cousins built forts and played football and watched war movies, but all I cared about were pretty things. I wanted everything to be beautiful, and I didn't care about anything else. For a while I thought I could stop it, change myself, quit thinking about boys and style and chandeliers, like some people just stopped smoking or drinking or something…obviously that didn't work out very well." I glanced at his biceps and laughed to myself.

"Well just for the record, I support your obsession," he smiled. "There's nothing wrong with chandeliers."

I laughed. "Thanks. That's *also* when I redecorated my room with antiques from my grandparents' storage facility, and let me tell you – it was like Richard Simmons had vomited all over my bedroom. Nate Berkus would've blushed at the seating areas I arranged in that room with my grandma's fancy little lamps and side tables. I don't think anyone in my family had a doubt about me after that – but my parents still swept it under the rug, as usual. But at least it was a designer rug." I laughed.

"Who in your family knows?" he asked. "Dad?"

"Nah. We've never spoken about it. Ever. But I think he knows something. I mean, I was a boy who had a set of Barbies. How could you not know? And he heard the rumors. It was sort of this unspoken thing, the biggest, ugliest, pinkest elephant in the corner. He doesn't like me, and I can only imagine that's the reason, since I've never done anything bad in my life." I sighed, then paused. "But it's still so messed up, though. Even if I was…what he suspects I am, it's like, *what kind of messed up garbage human doesn't like their own kids,* regardless of who they are, you know? I've seen mothers of convicted murderers sit under oath and testify about their kids and talk about them with more love than my dad talks about me. That's kind of part of the deal: you pop out a kid, and then you love it through thick and thin, and maybe even through gay and gayer. But my dad just…disengaged, wiped his hands of me. He didn't even know about my new job for six months, because he never talks to me. The last time he came to see me, I could see my breath in the air – it was that cold outside."

I stopped. I was starting to fear I was being a huge Debbie Downer, so I switched it up. "But whatever – I don't care much, anyway. I'm not surprised that he sucks. I mean, my dad went to segregated elementary school, for shit's sake. He remembers the busing, the riots, everything. That's what I'm dealing with here – these people are from different worlds, different cultures, different everything. Gay marriage is suddenly legal? Well, great, my uncles in South Carolina are sixty and don't give a shit. You cannot change people, and minds, as quickly as the world is trying to change them, you know?"

"Ain't that the truth," he laughed. "Guess we'll just have to wait for everyone to die, then."

"Honestly, it doesn't sound half bad." My lack of remorse horrified me.

I sighed. The truth was, I didn't even like thinking about my family issues, much less talking about it. I didn't want to believe that someone's past defined them. I wanted to believe that we were not what happened to us, we were what we did about it. Because where would my life leave me? Two disastrous parents, a crippling sense of inferiority…by those standards, I was dead in the water. The past shaded everything I did – every time I tried to make a big decision, strike out on my own, I was pulled backwards into the nightmares. When would I bloom into the adult I'd always imagined? When would none of this matter anymore?

He stared down at his hand, which was fidgeting. "Preaching to the choir, Coley. I could write ten thousand books about people who won't leave. And people who *do* leave when you don't want them to, and people who were never really there at all…"

He tracked his eyes to me. "Coley?"

"Yeah?"

"Do you ever wonder why you never became the person you thought you'd become? Why you won't just wake up one day and be…fixed?"

"Every day," I sort of laughed, really quietly, getting lost in his galaxy eyes. "If my life had a story, that would be the title."

He met my eyes as something seemed to bloom within my chest. This time, though, he didn't look away.

"Geez!" I finally said, looking at the time on my phone. What was it about him that made want to unlock all my gates? "It's getting late, and I've done ninety percent of the talking."

"So?"

"So, tell me something I'd be surprised to hear about you. Just one thing, before we leave. Friends do that. Friends get to know each other." Please. *So I won't go home feel like such an over-sharing psycho.*

His lips smiled, but his eyes smiled harder. "Okay. You know your hobby is taking pictures? Mine is writing.

96

Only letters, though. I write breakup letters to everyone I've ever dated. With my hand."

"Why?"

"I don't know. I like the idea of leaving before I am left, so I dump the person prematurely. When things get deep, I usually leave. But there will always be a note on their doorstep."

Gee, thanks, I wanted to say. But I let it slide.

"Have you ever had a boyfriend before?" I whispered.

He looked around. Nobody was remotely within earshot, but he was still terrified. "Hell no. I've never dated a guy. Well, I had a hookup buddy before, but it was nothing. We'd just do stuff."

I sat up. "What kind of stuff?"

"Well, we'd…make out. Jack off. Mostly those sorts of things."

"Mostly?"

"We tried something else, but he was awful, so we stopped."

"Who?" I wanted to kill this person immediately, but I didn't say that. He looked away again. "Okay, you *gotta* tell me now – you're the one who mentioned it."

"Dave Saul," he said, and I felt my jaw fall open – David Saul was one of Ryan's best friends, a card-carrying member of the goon squad. He'd never really actively participated in their life-ruining nonsense, but he always laughed and pointed just like the rest of them.

"No!" I said, and he laughed.

"I know. He's very…macho. But he came onto me one night at a party after everybody else had taken bong rips and passed out, and next thing I knew, he was on his knees, and I couldn't say no."

I wish I didn't find this so delicious. But I did. It didn't surprise me at all, either. In high school, the popular straight guys had been flirtier with *each other* in the locker room than they ever were with any girl. I also found it infuriating, too, though. "Screw that!" I said. "And *screw him.*"

"Why?"

"You know why. He's awful! Once, when I was at the water fountain and he was behind me, he told someone I had a 'gay voice.' As if there was one voice all gays were allowed to have, and they all had to fight over it or something." I pictured a bunch of lisping men feuding over a voice while wearing halter tops. I laughed, and he looked at me funny. "Do the other guys know?"

"Are you kidding me? Hell no, and if they ever do find out, Davey would run me over with his truck. He would pay someone to kill me and dump my body in some ditch somewhere. Literally."

"Did you ever like him?"

"No. Never. I only liked…what we did. It was just a hookup thing. He was a douchebag. No amount of dimple smiles can make up for a shitty soul, unfortunately."

I balled up my fists and balled them into my pockets. "Oh, that hypocrite…I should just-"

"You won't do or say *anything*," he told me. "It's none of your business, and I shouldn't have even said anything."

"Well, still – that kid and his friends gave me hell. And all while he was doing the same thing!"

He shrugged. "Whatever. And why are you giggling? What could be funny right now?"

"Oh, nothing, it's just that…*Dave's a fag*! I am never letting this go."

He blew out some air. His mouth was a little too small for him to as mad as he was trying to act. "It's *not* funny, Cole. It's not. It's sad. His dad was a crazy alcoholic who beat the shit out of him in middle school after he got caught with an issue of *Playgirl* behind the shed. He told me. Dave is just part of a cycle – that's all he is. Someone made him hate himself, and then he saw himself in you. So he hated you."

I nodded. "Yeah. You're right. Totally sad. Big gay bully who tortures local closeted kids turns out to be a homo. *A homo you hooked up with*. Not ironic, nor hilarious, at all. And I should've known he was gay – why else would he have been so fixated on hating me? Jesus, I'm dumb."

Finally I lost it and started cackling into the silence. After a few minutes, I heard his voice again, and he was trying *so hard* not to laugh.

"Okay. Fine. It's kinda funny."

When I'd finally stopped giggling, he smiled at me. "Come over after this," he murmured, and I lost it.

"...To do what?"

He inhaled, and I got so overwhelmed I had to look away. "Whatever's clever."

"You didn't even have to ask," I whispered. "But Nicky? Promise me I'll never get any breakup letters?"

He didn't say anything, just laughed quietly.

"Oh," he said, turning to the shelves, "and before we go, I'm actually looking for a book."

"Which book?"

"Oh, you know – white girl meets white boy, white couple overcomes white people problems to finally pose together on a beach at sunset, inspiring the book cover chronicling their very white love affair. I'm sure you've heard it a million times. It's actually for my mom for when she comes in town, I just figure this'll be a lot cheaper than having to buy it."

He shuffled through the shelves to find a book for his mother. As I watched him, something dropped in me, sank in my chest like a stone plummeting through the water of a cold lake, and that's when I knew the million different times I'd told myself I didn't love this boy had simply been a million different lies.

7

We didn't leave the library until eight, when the librarians started passive-aggressively ushering everyone out with their stage whispers and waving arms. He said he wanted to eat at home before he drove me to my house, but I almost sensed he wasn't done with me yet. Which was good, because I'd never be done with him. As we headed to his house, a huge black mass of clouds loomed on one side of the road, but I didn't care. My life was becoming something it had never been before: exciting.

I looked over at him, his faraway galaxy eyes, his body that was angled as far away from mine as possible, and it really got me thinking. You know, maybe forever wasn't in the cards for us. Maybe hiding in the library would have to do. But with the way his eyes were drilling into mine, the library would be enough. And maybe it *wasn't* going to work out. Maybe we just weren't in the stars, or even in the same galaxy, and this was going to be another letdown, another disappointment, another case of me retreating to my room for a week and telling myself I wasn't lonely, I wasn't heartbroken, I wasn't doomed to sleep in a cold empty bed forever. But I was starting to sense that getting to our ending, whatever it held, had the potential to be the adventure of my small and boring life.

His house was dark and quiet and perfect. As soon as we walked in, the air took on some strange quality, like it expected something from us. "Let's drink," I said. "I have some vodka in my freezer back home. Should I run and get it?"

He stared at me from under his eyelashes, so long and lush, his eyes playing tricks with the light. Then he inhaled, and it was sharp and perhaps pained. "No need. I've got some champagne."

"What's the occasion?"

"Us," he said as he walked away. "Being good friends."

A few minutes later we clinked glasses and both chugged. *Everything*. I knew this was dangerous, drinking alone with him while my father was out there, probably aware of his existence now, thanks to Robert. But I couldn't stop. Even if it meant getting drunk and uninhibited and letting out our inside selves, unleashing all the things we kept in the dark.

"More," I said. "Please."

He stepped over to refill my glass. When he bent forward, his face graced the side of mine in an awkward and electric way, and my vision blurred and my skin took flight from my body.

"Ah, sorry." He stepped back and refilled his own glass. And we drank again. The bubbles spread over me, comforting me, warming me. Nothing disturbed the sound of our breathing until his mom called a minute later.

"Hello?" he asked after a quick, apologetic glance at me.

"Nickicito!" a woman fawned in a very strong accent. "We just wanted to say thanks for having us again, and say sorry for Cha Cha peeing on the new rug! Here, she wants to talk to you, *un memento*…"

A little dog started yipping in the background. Honestly, I couldn't understand a lot of what his mom said – she had one of the strongest Hispanic accents I'd ever heard. Soon they lapsed out of English and Nicky spoke with her in Spanish, and it made me so horny I had to control myself from grabbing him right there. I wanted so badly to know his dynamic with her. Moms were the original "fag hags," for lack of a better term, and they were usually a boy's best friend until he inevitably branched out into befriending the sassy girls of his grade. But I knew Nicky wasn't like that. Still I yearned for a relationship with his mother. I wanted to do all the things the girlfriends got to do: I wanted to attend family dinners and go shopping with her and sit and drink coffee with her while he rolled his eyes at our friendship. And the fact that I would probably never do any of that made me ache inside. I was losing something I'd never even had, but it still hurt.

I used the opportunity to grab his eReader, which thankfully didn't have a passcode, and stalk his reading selections. Ugh, he was so smart…he read historical fiction, nonfiction about the wars, gorgeous and literary YA novels about dying teens – all of it. Actually, his tastes were a little more masculine than mine, but I tried not to think about it too much.

"Sorry," he said when he came back and tossed the phone down. His back was to me, but I didn't mind – the back view was just as good as the front one. He *was* Puerto Rican, after all. "Sorry for making you pretend like you weren't here. But I know you get it."

I sniffed. "Not really."

"What do you mean?"

I didn't know how to say this. I wasn't even really allowed to say that I liked him. "I don't know. I wouldn't really give a shit at this point. We're just *friends*, aren't we? Why wouldn't you be able to at least introduce me as a friend? It's not like she would know."

"Because she *would* know," he said, his head hanging low with shame. "My mom knows me better than anyone. I'm sorry. I can't…I don't know how to broach it. She thinks I'm interested in my sister's best friend, and I don't wanna crush that dream for her. And there's a lot you still don't know."

"Like what?"

He gulped. "If she knew about certain things, there's a chance I'd lose everything. *Everything*. My mom goes to church twice a day."

"Oh," I said. If a corpse had a voice, it would sound like me in that moment. "Yeah. It's fine, *Nickicito*." He blushed, but I waved him off. "Don't be embarrassed, it was the cutest thing I've heard in a while."

"Thanks. My dad is Nicholas, too, so my family's always called me that – it means Little Nick, basically."

"What's your mom like, anyway?" I asked, and he smiled. His eyes looked like they did when he looked at *me*, whatever that meant.

"She's a mess. But she's my favorite mess."

102

He laid himself out on the couch. He was so graceful, so fluid, while I moved like all of the bones in my body hated each other. Soon he changed the channel and paused on something. It was *Flashdate*, on MTV. Two gay guys were out on a blind date, and they had to decide whether they wanted to meet again. Nicky froze up very quickly and changed it to a rerun of SNL. I reached over and changed it back. I knew this was perhaps a step too far, but I couldn't stop.

The date heated up, and the guys got a lot closer. Nicky tried to resist, but soon he was into the show. *Very* into it. Until he realized I'd noticed.

"Enough," he said, changing the channel again.

"But-"

"But *nothing*," he said. "Enough of all this. I like girls anyway, you know. A lot."

He turned away, indignant. I filled with fire and stared out the window. I was three feet away from him and yet we were a galaxy apart. I puffed up my cheeks, then blew the air angrily out. I liked him, and I thought he liked me, too, and yet here we were, playing "friends" in a dark, deserted living room. We'd been blown so far off course, I didn't even recognize the map anymore. The world was not going to let us be together. *Never was there a tale of more woe,* I thought. We weren't Romeo and Juliet, we were Romeo and Julio.

"The thing you have to remember is…I like pussy," he said, his voice low. "It's not, like, some excuse, or some ruse or something. I really like it…in my face, on my dick, everything. So I don't think I'm totally…you know, *that* thing, that you want to say I am." His eyes track out the window. "But then, obviously, you know, other things happen…and I can't be open about it, because no girl would ever touch me if they knew." He sighed. "Everyone looks at people who like both sexes as being dirty, soiled, damaged goods…one girl on Twitter said she would never date a bisexual because he would get AIDS and die. Not even to mention the unspoken gender code of society, in general. *No homo, yo!* What does every leading man in every movie act and look like? Tall, muscular, athletic, deep voice, aggressive demeanor, 'straight'

103

characteristics. Nobody makes a place for softer, artsier kids who don't necessarily give off the lady killer vibe…and if you can't stand it, you've got to take it."

I winced. Then I wondered if he was being honest, about the thing with girls. I was occasionally attracted to women, myself, just not as much as I hoped to be. I'd certainly rubbed one out to lesbian porn. A lot of times, really. I'd hooked up with four girls in the past, and I'd enjoyed it, and I'd had orgasms, too. I just enjoyed watching men on the Internet a lot more. Nothing had ever compared to how I'd felt for guys.

And honestly, there was a lot about the gay community that made me uneasy. Most of the gay men in my town were not exactly living my dream. They maintained cheesy gym bodies far later in life than any man should ever maintain cheesy gym bodies, and they lived in cold, soulless, immaculate condos that were spotlessly clean and completely devoid of love, maybe save for a few pictures of a niece they barely saw. They cheated on their partners relentlessly, they drove age-inappropriate sports cars well into their sixties, and every weekend they left town to attend corny Miami-area nightclub parties with theme names like *Wet-N-Wild Foam Night* or *Naughty in South Beach (Day-Glo Edition)*. I didn't know what I wanted out of this life, but I knew it looked nothing like that. I wanted a *real* life, not a loveless day-glo one. Also, a lot of gays acted like being gay was the best and most important and most definitive thing about them. One guy on the news had even said that being gay was the best thing he'd ever been, and ever would be. Um, no! I wanted to be a lot of other things, and *also* gay, all at the same time. I just didn't know how to say any of this without sounding like an asshole.

Nicky twitched once, then twice. And finally he turned it back to *Flashdate,* despite it all. As the show went on, the rumbling of the thunder got closer, and soon the sky started dumping so hard we couldn't ignore it anymore. It was a real Florida storm, the kind that shook the windows and lit up the room in grey scale like an X-ray. I wrapped up in a blanket and looked over at him as the TV lights danced on his face. This was what I'd always wanted. Since I was a kid, I'd wanted this.

At the end of the date, one of the guys got drunk and started crying and confessed that his father had disowned him and hadn't spoken to him in three years. I inched away. We listened to the wind outside, and it seemed to carry all the things we couldn't say, everything we couldn't fix. It was a funny thing, when you let someone into the little world you'd created for yourself and then realized you'd suddenly become incapable of imagining it without them.

"Why not just...*tell* everyone?" I whispered soon. "This is so dumb. Aren't you sick of it all? Aren't you sick of believing you have to hide from them? Even if you're just bisexual?"

"You don't *get it*," he said, his eyes becoming suddenly interested on something in his lap. "And you never will. Not really." He took a breath. "I hate myself because of all this. And sometimes it makes me hate everyone else, too."

I didn't know whether to grab his hand or turn away. "You're wrong," I said. "I do get it. I hate myself just like you. Always have, pretty much."

He said nothing. The date on the show wound down with both of the guys drunkenly making out on a dirty little back porch. The whole show was a sad cliché, and it made me feel sort of icky. As the credits rolled, Nicky seemed to snap out of whatever evil gay trance that had allowed him to watch a homosexual dating show on a couch at night with another boy. He got up and stretched, but it looked more forced than anything. "Damn, it's getting late. Your bike is here, right? I've got so much stuff to do in the morning..."

I looked at the ground. I could take a hint. I was being dismissed. "Okay. Yeah. I'll go."

Lightning exploded above and beyond us, sending out white feathery tendrils into the sky. He stared out the window, his galaxy eyes seeming to see nothing at all. "Oh, damn, I forgot it's raining."

"Yeah, but it's fine. I'll survive. Probably..."

105

"Okay, cool. Feel free to wait a minute for it to calm down out there."

He grabbed the remote and started flipping channels again. I hated him for being so casual, for brushing me off so easily, like I was nothing to him. Soon he got to *Fox News*, which was showing an infomercial about a service for old people to get cheaper dentures – but then it segued into a breaking news report. A group of guys had been caught on a department store's security camera beating down two gay dudes on the sidewalk, calling them *fags* and *cock suckers* while they kicked them down an alley and stole the cash from their wallets. The attackers had been identified and tracked down on social media and had finally been arrested earlier in the evening. Of course this had happened in Rhode Island and nowhere near here, as the police probably wouldn't have cared enough to find the perpetrators down here. The evening news was full of stories about gay-bashing cases that had gone cold with mysterious swiftness, cases of transsexuals being gunned down in their own driveways on sunny mornings only to have the police simply stop investigating after a few weeks.

I stopped breathing, but I wasn't surprised. I should've known. On one channel was an unabashedly gay dating show, and on the other, a report about hate crimes. Everything was colliding, old and new, and didn't make any sense.

Nicky changed it as quickly as he could, but it wasn't fast enough. That story was still the only thing in the room. Besides the thunder, which boomed from over the ocean with more ferocity than ever. And my heart...

He turned a little closer to me. "Okay, sorry. Maybe you can't get home right now. I'm not thinking straight."

"Neither am I," I whispered. "I've never been able to do *anything* straight. That's the problem..."

He laughed. For real this time. Gallows humor was still humor, I guessed. "So," I said. "What should we do?"

He didn't answer. I knew exactly what I wanted to do. I'd wanted it all my life. I took a sip of champagne, and then I reached my hand closer and rested it beside him. He stared down at me, both of our hearts pounding. He was hard now. It made me hard, too. But he didn't say anything. I just looked at his hand for a second, but soon I couldn't control myself. The alcohol hit me in shimmery waves, and soon my insides were storming harder than the skies.

"Nicky," I said, "what are we? What is *this*? You say you just want to be friends, then you spend all your time with me, touch me, tell me all your secrets, pay for my food…"

He scooted away, leaning over his lap to hide what was going on down there.

"This is happening," I said. "You know it's happening. I feel you in the pit of my stomach, all day, every day. Stop turning your back on that."

"I'm not changing my rules," he whispered. "No matter how I feel. You don't understand what's at stake. My whole stupid life would come crashing down."

"Shh," I said. "It's okay." All I wanted was to roll forward in a world that was pulling us back. But Nicky wouldn't let me.

He got up, looking disgusted. "No, no, no. Ugh, look at us, Coley. It's not okay. We don't know what the hell we're doing." He started for his room. I knew he'd closed the window, and this thing was done. "I'm over this – I'm going to sleep. You can crash on the floor, I guess."

"The floor?"

He paused, looked down and to the side. "My dad has a key, and if he came over…"

"Doesn't he live, like, hours away?"

He didn't respond.

"Fine." I got up and started gathering pillows and a throw blanket from the couch, since I knew he wouldn't have anything in a closet for me. All his closets were full. "Fine fine fine. The floor it is."

I followed him into his room, admiring his walk all the while, despite myself. I'd never been allowed in here before, and I drank it in like a frozen margarita. It was what I expected – straight. *Ish.* He had all kinds of sports equipment in the corner, and it was messy and smelled like sweaty clothes. All kinds of academic plaques and certificates from

107

high school decorated the top of his dresser, and it didn't surprise me when I saw that he'd been in the accelerated program. An enormous pile of grooming products in the bathroom was the only thing out of place for someone so "hetero." And also…

"Is that my shirt?" I asked, pointing at the yellow shirt bearing the logo of my high school on the table by his bed. I'd left it on his porch after a beach session and had never even realized it.

He looked away. "Oh. Yeah. It is."

"…Why is it there?"

I heard him swallow. "Because I was gonna give it back to you. …And because it smells like you."

And everything in me stopped moving.

"Ready for bed?" he asked. That boy glanced at me one last time, guilt in his eyes at my sleeping situation, then got into his bed. I looked at his glorious ass one final time and then laid myself out on the floor. His carpet was surprisingly soft and clean, and knowing he stepped on it every day made me want to sink into it and never come out. Did this stupid carpet know how lucky it was to get stepped on by Nicholas Flores every single day? Ugh. "I sleep in my underwear and no shirt," he said. "Is that okay?"

I was too choked by lust to respond – *oh, sure, strip in front of me, it's not like I'm horny enough already!* – but he didn't wait for an answer anyway. I could hear him kicking off his clothes, and it made me want to die.

We lay in the darkness. I was hard, and I had to twist on my side to avoid crushing myself. I tried as hard as I could to ignore the fact that I was a few feet away from Nicky Flores, but he was the only thing in my brain. As the rain sloshed against the windows, the silence turned neon, electric. I could feel some force splintering into the air from his body and reaching out to me, pulling me in, begging me to touch him. I even felt my body realigning to be more in line with his. There was no getting around it: this thing was gravitational.

Lightning cracked, just like it did in the movies and the books, and I looked up and saw the Madonna above his bed. And not the gay Madonna, either, Our Lady of Refusing to Age Gracefully. It was the religious Madonna – the Holy Mother, with the baby and the manger and everything. Ugh, *seriously*? He'd been telling the truth about his family's religious crap. He was *so* Catholic, and he would never let me in with shit like this surrounding him. Intolerance literally stared him in the face every night while he slept. Maybe this thing was useless.

"Cole?" he said into the blackness, and I self-destructed, because that was the first time he'd called me Cole, just like my mother used to.

I propped myself up a little so I could see him. He was staring at Mother Mary.

"Yeah?"

"I just want you to know I'm sorry."

I lay down again, too overwhelmed to function. I thought I would break his resolve and open him up, not push him further into the closet. I wrapped my legs around a pillow at the knee and squeezed hard, staring at his dust ruffle. Then I thought about the word "sorry." A word could hold so much in it. There were so many things wrapped up in his version of "sorry:" *I'm sorry we are who we are. I'm sorry the world is like this. I'm sorry we have to pretend to be friends. I'm sorry we'll never work out. I'm sorry you have to love me in the dark.* And I knew he was sorry. Because I was sorry, too. But that didn't change it, didn't help it, didn't fix it.

I swallowed, the dread plummeting into me. I was so ashamed of how he treated me, and of how I *let* him treat me, like I was those built-in apps that your phone wouldn't let you delete, so you piled them into a single folder and shoved it to the corner of your screen. Nothing in me wanted to leave this and walk away, but maybe I needed to. I was out-of-control infatuated with a boy who made me sleep on the floor.

"Nicky?" I said.

"Hmm?"

I wanted to tell him so much. I wanted to tell him he was the brightest part of my dreams, that I'd stop breathing for him, that he was a human photo filter who'd made my moon

109

shine brighter and my waves crash louder. But this was a language I could feel but not yet speak, and I was dealing with an alphabet I could grasp but not yet fully comprehend. So I sighed instead. "It's not okay, but…I get it. I understand."

Even though I didn't. What was happening between us wasn't wrong, and he needed to stop acting like it was.

A pause followed, a pause that seemed to give new meaning to the term "pregnant." It was the Octomom of pregnant pauses. Finally I heard ruffling on the bed, followed by his face, beautiful and luminous and sexy as hell in the rainglow, hanging over mine. "Why do you like me so much?" he finally asked. "If I was someone else looking at me, I'd probably drive me crazy."

"I don't like you," I breathed, then my eyes tracked to his figurine. "The thing is…I think you might be my Madonna."

Another pause. Then he smiled. "Actually, you know what? Screw it. Get up here. No funny business, though. Promise me I won't wake up to a finger up my butt, or anything?"

As everything inside me heated up, I nodded and crawled up off the floor, slinking myself onto the bed, totally unsure of how to act. *I was in bed with Nicky Flores and the Madonna – holy shit.* He moved all the way over, staring at me, as I made my way under the covers with him. This was it. Or was it?

I faced him. His eyes were so big I could see myself in them, and he was lit from within like a movie star on a film poster or an angel in an oil painting. I pulled the covers all the way up, concealing myself up to the neck, and finally he calmed. And suddenly I could see past the campus hottie, the gym freak, the alpha he wanted the world to see, and saw the boy within, the boy inside all that, the boy he'd tried to erase. He was running, he was scared, but he wanted it all to stop. He just wanted to be happy, to feel love from someone that didn't need anything in return.

And I realized that I understood him then – it was like he'd come from my own bones. All he wanted was to feel safe. I studied his beautiful, sad, alive face and only now noticed his cheeks were covered with light acne scarring, the little pockmarks sort of like the craters on the surface of the moon. His galaxy eyes glittered, too, and it was all so beautiful. He was a space kid, my boy on the moon. Liking him was so impossible, so easy. And I never wanted to stop. Being with him just felt warm somehow – not hot or sexy or slutty or anything, just…warm. Warm like fresh socks, warm like getting one last hug from my Nana, warm like barricading myself in bed on a rainy night and opening up *Harry Potter* to hangout with the Weasleys again and feel like the person I'd been before adulthood happened.

"Coley?" he whispered one last time, watching me, planting dreams with his eyes.

"Yeah?"

"You're my best friend."

Something grabbed me, took custody of me, pulled me under. I moved my arm from beneath the covers and held out my hand. He took it – slowly, hesitantly, but still, he took it. Then he closed his eyes, smiled, and started to breathe slower and deeper. The thunder rumbled from somewhere over the sea, calling to me, and that's when I knew for sure that I was free.

8

I slept like a baby that night – and by that I mean horribly. (I'd babysat my little cousins enough times to know what a load of bullshit that cliché actually was.) I tossed and kicked and sighed, fully aware that I was annoying him, but I couldn't stop, or calm myself down. I finally passed out at four, and when I rose into the light at what felt like nine-ish, I stopped breathing. Nicky's arm was around me again.

I froze, nearly choking on my tongue. Then I felt around a little. He must've kicked off his underwear sometime overnight, as well, because his bare dick was against my back. He was hard. And in his sleep, he was rubbing me with it.

I stared straight ahead, out the window, as my heart pounded in my throat. I'd never felt desire like this before. Ever. Having him this close to me swamped me in feelings I could only describe as red, and I wanted to stay right there forever. As we lay there I pictured him waking up, digging his face into the back of my hair as he cracked up with the morning giggles, then turning me around and getting to work…

No. That wasn't going to happen. I knew he would be furious if he snapped awake and found us like this. Would he blame me? Would he accuse me of arranging us in some sexual position, of stripping him in his sleep? I had no idea what to do, so I swallowed too hard, and it made a sound. I felt his eyelids open against my neck.

"The *hell*?"

He jumped out of bed, and as he kicked off the covers and walked to the bathroom naked, I fell into the deep end. I didn't know whether I wanted to masturbate or kill myself – he was out-of-this-world gorgeous.

Once I could feel my face again, I turned over and huffed. So we were back to this – he wouldn't even look at me.

"Bro," he said a minute later, sticking his head out of the bathroom as the shower steamed up the space behind him. He'd put up a gate in front of his face, but still, something about him looked curious. I sort of took a detour into his eyes for a minute and envisioned padding into the shower while he lathered off, stepping into the steam as the water slipped down our bodies, placing a kiss on the back of his neck before tracing my tongue up his jaw, then doing other things I'd spent my life dreaming about...

His closed-off voice snapped me back to reality. "I'm taking a shower, but there's coffee in the cupboard above the stove, if you want it. I'll be out in a minute, help yourself."

He turned back into the bathroom, and the door closed. And it was that simple: I'd been banished.

But then he opened it again.

"Coley," he murmured from behind the door, and everything in me stopped moving. "Wait."

"Yeah?"

Our only guest was the white noise of the shower as steam poured out of the doorway. He inched into the light from the bedroom, and I saw that he was holding himself. No...he was *rubbing* himself.

I stopped breathing.

"Do you want to...come in? With me?"

My throat closed. "Oh, um...I..."

I finally got my muscles to work and started for the bathroom, but he held up a hand. Then he rubbed himself, up and down, around in a circle. "Coley," he whispered...

I closed my eyes for a second. I reached down and took myself in my hand, then opened them again.

But I was too late: something was already dripping from the door handle, and he was retreating into his shower as fast as his body would take him.

~

True to form, my dad called as soon as I got home that afternoon. The "awkward small talk" phase of the conversation was alarmingly short, so I knew he had a whammy to get to. And a whammy it was:

"So…we heard you were at the library the other day…with someone?"

I winced, because after recent events I didn't even know if I had the energy to lie. "Um…yeah. And?"

"Relax, big guy, we think it's amazing. You're finally making some male friends."

"I, um…I am? You do?"

"Hell yes! It's about time. How about we go on a hunting weekend to the Gatling's hunting camp down in Live Oak in a few weeks? You, me, and your friend? I'll make some turkey chili – it'll be awesome. Just us boys, how does that sound?"

I shivered a little. I felt so dirty whenever my dad tried to shove his Normal, Masculine Son Dreams onto my unwilling shoulders, and I couldn't really explain why. I almost felt bad for him, too. This was a fantasy that was never going to happen. I would never be the son he wanted me to be. Not to mention the fact that I wanted to reach my hand into Nicky's pants and hunt for dick, not sit in a tree stand and hunt for animals to randomly kill…

"Yeah, Dad, sounds great," I finally said. "What else did you call for?"

He inhaled a little more sharply than usual. I got a weird, uneasy sense then. He knew I'd always sealed off part of my life from him, but in that moment I think he sensed I was hiding more than ever before. It made me feel further from him than I ever had, which really said a lot. "Well, you know the divorce has gone through, right?" he asked after a minute.

"Wh…you what? You were fighting about money, like, a month ago. That divorce was nuclear. What happened?"

He sighed, drawing out the drama. "Well, your mother says she wants to move on with her personal life, and I do, too, and so we rushed some documents through the system."

"Okay?"

"Which brings me to the condo issue. We might just sell it if we need to. The extra money can't hurt, with all the lawyers' fees. I guess it all just depends…"

Of course – here it was. He was dangling it over my head – he owned the floor I was standing on, and he decided the rules. My parents could barely afford the upkeep on this place, their former weekend home, but since it was still cheaper than campus housing, I'd been allowed to stay temporarily until they worked out the last of their divorce-y type money issues. I thought I'd heard a threat there, an ultimatum, but I wasn't sure. What did he really know? Was he watching me? It sounded like he was saying *mess with a guy, and you'll be homeless* – or was I just imagining it? Whatever the case, I knew he wouldn't drop this for long, and I had absolutely no idea what to do about it.

I hung up the phone and screwed up my face a little. I tried to get into this book I'd been reading, but I couldn't concentrate. All I wanted to talk about was Nicky and how he was making my life burn brighter, and soon I realized I had nobody to talk to about him with. Nobody even knew I liked guys. My female friends didn't know about me, dad would castrate me, my few male friends would nod and then quietly excuse themselves from my life.

Actually, I suspected that many of my female friends knew about me, but I avoided this subject like I avoided Wal-Mart on Black Friday. Whenever someone came out to most girls, they immediately threw their hands up in the air and squealed "OMG, let's go shopping!" as if gay guys deliberately chose difficult and persecuted lives simply for the sake of becoming prototypical gay BFFs who would tell them they were pretty and hold their shopping bags for them in some Victoria's Secret while they tried on bustiers. My gayness didn't make me want to be some girl's sassy sidekick any more than any other guy's straightness did. *Or* they'd tell me that they had another gay friend they wanted me to meet, like I had anything to do with anyone else just because I was gay, as if there was some law that said all of us were obligated to meet…

That night I did the lonely heart thing, buried myself in pillows and tried to get into some Netflix show. But none of it meant anything, because all my thoughts belonged to Mr. Nicholas Flores. It somehow hurt me to know how much I needed him. He could slap someone's grandma while reciting misogynistic chants at a puppy killing party, and I'd probably still come running. How sad.

Waiting for him the next day felt like purgatory. But he never texted me. He didn't the *next* day, either, or the next, and by day four I was in a panic. What had happened? Had I gained weight overnight? Was he retreating into the closet again? Had I asked for too much, gotten too close, scared him off? The line went dead, the wifi stopped connecting. And soon I knew it: I'd scared him off, done too much too soon, and he was done.

On the fifth night I dreamt of Jonathan, the one and only boy I'd ever liked before. Even thinking about him these days made me collapse inside, made me mourn the love he'd never let himself give me. I met him on the second day of seventh grade. (He was the new kid, of course, and he'd skipped the first day out of boredom.) There was a stir around school the second he walked in, because he was inhumanly beautiful and wore a necklace and a tight-fitting sweater. It was like my eyes were made for him, and all I ever did was stare at him. I was small, but I was already all grown up inside because of my problems at home. I had seen misery, and that made me wise. So when I looked at him and knew that I could love him, and that he was capable of loving me back, I knew it was true.

I set up the opportunities for us to become friends, and we did, even though he was a stratosphere above me, socially speaking. Kids like us weren't supposed to come together, but in the halls of my middle school a miracle bloomed. He invited me over for a sleepover one weekend, and our friendship only picked up from there. Whenever I was with him I was breathless and dazed and overwhelmed, like when you finished your new favorite book for the first time and felt like you were experiencing every emotion in the world at once – it was almost like I was full of shooting stars or something. But he could never admit he liked me back. Soon I became

116

desperately infatuated with a coward, and we embarked on some sick, parasitic pseudo-relationship. It was so messed up: I would do his homework and fill out his study cards and clean his room for him while he just sat and watched. He would dangle affection in my face, talking about girls or guys he liked while resting his hand on my leg, before yanking it all away again and watching my death throes. But I was a moth drawn to his misery and his perfectly-gelled hair, and I could not leave him alone. Every time we hung out was just another chance for him to insert the knife, twist it and watch me suffer. It was sick, but I needed the pain like water. I fell into the worst kind of love, and it broke me. I gave away too much of myself to someone who'd never even asked for it, and I knew I would never get it back. I wanted to leave, but there was nothing to take. He had all of me.

I never told him a word. He knew, and he liked me back – we could both feel it in the air. Being with him was like settling into a warm bath and turning off the world. But he would never acknowledge it. He was much better at "playing straight" than I was, that pathetic whole song and dance, and as our friendship started to fall apart I'd see him out at birthday parties or pizza places with his baseball friends, and I would be like vapor to him. Having my best friend in the world look past me, through me…it made me feel like I was nothing. He was ashamed of me, and I never got over it. Afterward I could do nothing but sit and watch our times together over and over again in my mind, hoping for a different ending like when you catch *Titanic* for the eightieth time on Netflix and pray that Rose would let Jack onto the floating board and let him live. But she never did. She never scooted over, and the ending never changed.

Gradually Jonathan and I lost touch. As time went on I became even quieter and more withdrawn and, let's face it, *gayer*, while he doubled down on the illusion of who he wanted to become, and morphed into a jock times a million. By the time we started high school, he wouldn't even look at me in the halls when we crossed paths. We never spoke again after all this. *Ever*. Our strange "relationship" was something neither of us would admit, and would probably *ever* admit, out loud at least. It was puppy love, but he still broke my heart, and for years I was lightly depressed. Not living, but drifting. On the lowest days I'd tell myself I'd imagined it all, and that the memories of our "relationship" were all as one-sided as duct tape. But he liked me too – my soul knew what my brain was too weak to admit.

I'd found some solace since then, of course. I still had a chance at happiness, and he didn't. While I was tiptoeing closer to the truth of who I really was, he was miles away, and running further every day. I knew he would never live in his truth, never look into the eyes of a boy he loved and smell his hair and savor what their love felt like. He was too arrogant, too weak, to admit he was different, and that made me feel a little better, warmed my cool insides like the sick asshole I was. He would never be happy, and I was happy and sad about it. But the memories would still hit me sometimes like a rogue taxi in the night. Jonathan wore Cool Water by Davidoff in middle school, and every time I smelled it on a passing stranger it would hit me like a summer storm. I'd close my eyes and let it take me back, back to what I'd lost, back to what I'd never really had at all. I hoped I never smelled that boy again.

These days he was "straight," refusing to hook up with his girlfriends until marriage because he was "staying pure for God," or so I'd heard from a few of his frustrated exes. Just seeing him now, at the gas station or at random birthday parties or whatever, felt like being stabbed in the stomach. The worst thing I ever did was let him let go of me, let him fall out of infatuation with me. I would do anything in the world to never feel like that again – I would not survive another Jonathan-sized heartbreak. I was sure of it.

So why was I perhaps running towards another Jonathan all over again?

None of this changed the fact that without Nicky, my life was crumbling. So when the text came Thursday evening saying simply **Hey, come over,** it felt like a fantasy. When I got there

118

he opened his door and just smiled at me. His eyelids were crinkling in the corner, and his eyes brought me home. God – so there really *was* magic left to find out here in the world. And here I thought I'd turned over every stone.

"Well," he smiled. "It's you."

"Wow, that's a warm welcome, I thought you were still mad about…hey, have you been crying?" I asked when I noticed his nose was runny and his eyes were a little red. He turned around and led me in. I didn't care about any of the past few days – I only cared that I was back in his orbit.

"Maybe. I don't know. I just got off the phone with my mom."

I sat down, staring up at him, my happiness crashing. "And?"

"*And* my dad came into the room while we were talking, and she put down the phone, and she didn't know I could hear their conversation."

"Do I even want to know what he said?"

He stomped over to his laptop and swiveled it around to show me a project he'd been working on – it was a beautifully rendered version of his living room, but it was decorated with what looked like professional eyes. It was chic, trendy, and very gay. It looked like some plunge into impossibility – the house he could be living in, if his life was what he wanted it to be.

"I'm doing an interior design project for an art class," he said bashfully. "My dad was snooping around in my mom's email and found the file."

"And?"

He sniffled. "He said it was 'too good.' He said at this stage I might as well throw in the towel and become a hairdresser or a fashion designer. And it just makes me feel…"

His knuckles shook with all the frustration of someone who just couldn't handle it anymore. For one white-hot moment he cracked. One seismic wave of angst, hatred, loathing, exploded upward from somewhere deep, rolled over him like Old Faithful. He turned away and let it hit, holding his face tight like it was going to break apart, and then with one quick jolt of a breath he swallowed it back down again. And that was it – it was over. It was almost admirable, how good he'd gotten at living in this world that wasn't built for him. So he built other worlds. I did, too. We were all pretenders, actors, shape-shifters, and we were the best.

"Sunday School got our parents good, didn't it?" I asked. I wanted to hug him so badly, but I knew I couldn't. Even my grandpa, whom I'd loved more than anyone in the world, had kept an old newspaper article on his bedside table that called homosexuality a "deviation" and said gays should be banned from the military.

"*Shit*," he finally said, sitting taller and wiping his eye, as if noticing where he was for the first time. "Just when you think you're having a good day, your mother calls."

"I'm sorry, Nicky," I said. "I really am. It shouldn't be like this."

"I know it shouldn't." He reached over and took me by the shoulder. "I'm really glad I met you," he said.

"Why's that?"

"You know why. Even if I can't say it."

I smiled out at the room around us. Just because *he* was too scared to live in something as beautiful as his dreams didn't mean *I* couldn't do the work for him. "You know what? This room *could* use some gay. It needs to get gay'd up ASAP, actually."

I jumped up and got to work. First I took a floor-length mirror from behind his refrigerator and set it next to a window. It made the room look twice its size immediately. Then I took a chic, colorful blanket that was wadded up in his entry hall and laid it across a love seat. After that I took some paintings from his kitchen and moved them to the living room, hanging them from tiny nails I found above the sink and banged into the wall using a big spoon.

"There," I said, dropping back down next to him. "Next time your dad walks in here and makes a remark about anything 'gay,' take that sculpture I just put in your foyer and insert it into his anal cavity."

He stared at me, and I stared back. "Wow, Coley."

"What?"

"You're just, like, redoing my whole life."

I smiled. How I'd ever survived without him, I had no idea. His glory was breathable – just being around him made you feel like a different human, want to live a better life.

Before our fight we'd had this secret game where we'd just look at each other, not saying anything, just staring. Because I loved the way he looked at me. More than anything I'd ever loved, really. His eyes got all big and warm and soft and crackly and I just felt myself soar into them. The best part was that I knew he felt it, too – I could just sense it. Sure, the world could hate us and God could disapprove of us and everyone could be after us, but when he made those magic eyes at me...

"It hurt when you stopped talking to me, you know," I said.

"Really?"

"Yes. Every time we get closer, you bump away. And I don't understand why. Was it hard for you?"

He grabbed a string of my hair, his fingers shaking, then sighed. "Every day I don't talk to you, I feel like I'm not me." He smiled, and it looked like victory. "Thank you for letting me hangout with you again, by the way. I know I'm not much. But with you, I'm...more."

I smiled. For the first time ever, I was being seen. He was the beginning and the end – everything went back to him. "You're so wrong, though."

"Really? What do you like about me?"

"How long do we have?" He laughed, and I gulped. "...And, what do you like about *me*?"

He sighed as the galaxies swirled in his eyes. "I can't count that high."

"Okay, what do you *not* like?"

"I'm still looking for something. But as of right now, zilch." His eyes changed. "By the way," he said, and I could suddenly see that he was semi-hard, "the other morning was...great."

I stopped breathing again. "It was?"

121

"Yes. Sometimes I think about you…doing things to me…and it makes me…well, you can see how it makes me…"

I licked my lip as he leaned forward.

"Coley?" he asked, eyes bright.

"Yeah?"

"I think we should-"

His phone vibrated, and he turned away. "Ugh. *Damn it.*"

"What?"

"This totally slipped my mind. The boys'll be here in, like, ten minutes. Schultz just Snapchatted from his bike from, like, three blocks away."

"Oh. My cue to leave, I guess."

He breathed. "I mean, not necessarily. Can you just…stay, and play along?"

"Why are you asking me that?"

"I'm asking you because I…because I want you to stay, I guess."

"And…and meet your friends?"

"Yeah. But just, you know, like, as a buddy. Obviously."

"A *buddy*," I said, my voice sounding disgusted even to me.

"Don't worry, though, it's not the same dudes from FitTrax."

How many friends did one person need? I thought. "Thank God. And obviously I'll stay," I said instead, trying not to think about how risky this was – for both of us, not just him.

"Hey everybody," he said ten minutes later, to some assorted jocks. They were all hot, and I was trying very hard not to notice. I recognized Zack Frederickson, one of the nicer guys from the gym, but the rest were strangers. "This is my buddy, Cole, by the way."

I stared at everyone, frozen, as they did the same. "Um…*yo*?" I said, and the room went silent. A few people grunted and then returned their eyes to the television. This was mostly a different crowd from the FitTrax goons, and (thank god) Ryan wasn't there. One or two guys stared at me, confused and mildly irritated by my presence, but most ignored me, blissfully. So I sat in the corner and did my best to disappear into the couch cushions.

I was here…in Nicky's house…with his friends…this was happening. I did my best impression of a "bro," staring at the football on TV, but nothing clicked. Me watching sports was like how I imagined a Chinese-speaking person felt watching American movies: the colors moved and the sounds come out, but nothing registered. It was like I looked at the world through different eyes than these guys did. From time to time I felt that great sadness wash over me, that melancholy that told me I'd never be accepted into situations or fit in with crowds like this, not really. I felt pathetic for wanting the guys' acceptance, but I still wanted it for some stupid reason, and I didn't know how to earn it. With my own guy friends who suspected something was up with me, their approval felt conditional. *Act like a bro or get kicked out, because I'm not doing that faggot shit.* Something I'd noticed over the years was that the general sense of male-ness of a straight guy was *way* more fragile than any gay guy's.

But Nicky was good. So good that he had everyone fooled. I couldn't believe how thoroughly *I'd* been fooled, too. This person he'd let me get to know – that person wasn't real. This sort of bro-ish behavior had always made me a bit nervous and uncomfortable, mostly because of how frequently the act of spotting a group of fratty-looking dudes approaching me in the hall at school had usually ended in stares and whispers and laughs and maybe even insults. By nature, straight guys were always trying to one-up each other and become top dog, and whenever they were safely within their little mob, whoever picked on me the hardest became automatic alpha of the day. I was a deer, and they were the hunters the only thing that kept them from pulling the trigger sometimes was happenstance.

During a break, one of the goons finally noticed I existed. "So…what's your name, again, kid?"

123

I blew out some air. Alpha guys were always calling me "kid" or "big guy" or condescendingly petting me on the shoulder, even when we were the same age. I think they noticed my inherent different-ness and wanted to assert the upper hand, just in case I ever forgot. Ever since freshman year of high school it had been the same: I was not taken seriously because of who I was. Even the smart, progressive girls at school had treated me like some kind of disposable pet. I was tossed aside as soon as they found a guy they liked, and then I was sent out to pasture to roam the halls alone, glaring at any other boy with suspiciously-good dress sense who knew my plight, too. The masculine football jocks, they were the *real* guys, and I was a flawed model, a monkey meant for dancing in the corner and not much else. My few guy friends ignored me at school and then called me to come over when they were bored, or feeling homoerotic and wanted to dance around the gay subject with me while their boners showed through their pants, or whatever.

"I'm Cole," I told Nicky's friend. He looked at Nicky as his face lit up.

"Oh, dude, you've told me about this kid before. A lot, actually."

Nicky's eyes became large and terrified as I sank into the deepest and warmest ocean in the world. *Nicky talks about me.* It made me feel like everything in my life was going to be okay somehow.

"Um, I have?"

"Yeah." He turned to me again. "You do *Honesty*, right? That's so legit. My sisters follow you. You're, like, famous. I'm Trevor, by the way. People call me TJ. How do you guys know each other, anyway?"

My eyes caught Nicky's from across the way as paranoia seeped into the room, cold and hot. I'd never expected being asked this. What could I possibly say? *Oh, you know, just on a gay sex app. Would you like some Doritos?*

"Fit, um, *FitTrax*," Nicky finally stuttered, and the dude shot a weird, confused look at him. Thankfully, nobody else seemed to notice or care, and so he rolled his eyes a little and returned his attention to the game. I could feel Nicky's relief from twelve feet away.

I sat for another hour pretending to like craft beer and know about line violation rules. Near the end of the game, a PSA-type commercial came on featuring a female reality star who had coincidentally identified as male the year before. "*Faggot,*" TJ said. "That queer should walk into this room right now wearing that dress and see what happens."

And I stopped breathing.

At around eleven, the last person see-ya'd his way out of the living room, and Nicky and I were alone. I just stared at the carpet for a minute, unsure, but soon I felt our little world opening up. And like a magnet to a magnet, Nicky rushed over to me. Instantly all the fear, all the panic of the evening *whooshed* out of me, and all that was left was him.

We fell on the couch together. "God," he smiled, the light dancing in his galaxy eyes. "Sitting there all night – having to stay away from you, was…hard."

I smiled at him. I was trying so hard not to fall for him, and I was failing *so* massively. *Touch me,* I wanted to say, but instead it came out as "yeah." Plain old yeah. If only he knew how much I wanted to run to bed with him and never leave. I know he felt it too, because he pulled his eyes away with what looked like more than a little effort.

He smiled. "Let's continue question time."

"Yeah?" I asked. He was like Bill Nye: I didn't even know him that well, but I trusted him wholly.

He motioned at the air around us, then looked at me. The spirit hit, and I was alive. How could he not know that he was to be treasured? "Well, can this possibly…I don't know. Can you really feel around me, like I feel around you?"

I didn't know what to say. Being around him was usually like driving down a highway too quickly and being unable to see anything at all – he blurred the world, and it terrified me. I didn't know you could like a boy like this. I didn't know you could like *anyone* like this. And I know I was late. I know I was already supposed to have felt these things,

125

this shimmery, teenagery love thing. But I'd never been *allowed* to have this. My whole life, my love had been kept from blooming by church and society and fathers who disapproved. But for the first time, I was letting it happen. For the first time in my life I was allowing myself to be young and in lust with someone, and it felt so warm. I wanted to pour water on possibilities and watch love grow, and I was starting to get there. Around him I felt, for the first time in my life, that I was enough.

And that was also the underlying problem, I suspected: we had no idea what we were doing. We were two boys, two *children*, unable to reconcile with the truth cresting around us. He wanted to stay closeted, and I had a father who would kill me if they knew about this, who would stop speaking midsentence if they saw this scene right here. So I took a photograph with my eyes. I scanned the room and took in his redecorated living room, his pile of dirty clothes in the foyer, this boy next to me who made me feel like my shitty little life was finally paying off. I remembered it all, just in case.

"What does it feel like to *you*?" I asked him. I sensed that he didn't want to answer, but he still did.

"Fireworks are coming to mind. And explosions. And Paris. And all that stuff…"

"I know," I said. "Paris doesn't sound so stupid anymore."

He shook his head. "But it's not just that. Whenever I'm with you, I don't really have to wonder about who I am. I just *know*. And who I am feels okay. Sometimes."

I sank into myself. Nicky liked me. This was happening. "You don't have to tell me. I know it all. I feel it. And I thought it was so cute that you…well, that you told your friend about me."

He blushed, smiling at the coffee table. "Whatever," he said softly. "And why wouldn't I tell people about you? Something about you just makes me want to shout things. You're like a book I want the whole world to read."

126

My body stopped working. He looked away, his hair dancing in the air as his head moved. "But still…will we ever be out of the woods?"

"The woods?"

"The woods," he said, pointing around us. "Friends. Religion. My parents."

I winced. He was already trying to push me off, send me away because I made him feel dirty.

"Nicky. It's the twenty-first century," I said. "Who cares about them? It doesn't have to be like this. We don't have to sit ten feet away from each other in a room full of people, staring straight ahead all night. You know we have…options now, right, Nicky? Choices?"

For a moment he seemed to let the possibilities bloom in his eyes. Then he killed them. "No we don't."

I started to talk. He shut me down. "You're living in a fantasy, Coley. The world pretends it's accepting now – it's not. We'd be outcasts. Jokes."

"We're not those things here," I said, hating myself for being so desperate. "We're safe here. Why not kiss me while we're alone? What's stopping you?"

He sort of smiled with his eyes in the way I suspected only he could. "Kiss you, huh?"

"The idea isn't as crazy as you're acting like it is."

"Yes it is. You know you shouldn't kiss your friends, right?" he whispered, assaulting me with his sexy smell. "I hear it's a slippery slope."

"But we're not friends."

He smiled that victory smile. "Is that so?"

"Yeah, you-"

"Shh," he said.

"What?"

"I don't want to talk about it anymore. I don't want to talk about how we have to hide."

I closed my eyes for just a moment. "Kiss me, Nicky. Just kiss me. I…I need you. I need you all the time, and you don't even know how much."

127

He looked down at my chest. "But I don't know how to…I can't…"

His words were leaving his mouth limply, as if they were being taken back before they could even escape. He wanted this. I knew he wanted this. I wanted it too. And we were going to get this.

I stood up. He stood up, too. I had no idea what I was doing, but I couldn't stop. This thing was relentless. I pushed him against the wall by the window and forced my way into his mouth, daring him to pull back, and soon it was almost like we were fighting. I was punching above my weight like a reality singing show contestant attempting a Whitney Houston song, and I knew it. He wriggled a bit and then just stood there for a second, stiff and stupefied, as I licked my way from his ear down to his collarbone, which tasted salty and perfect. Holy Christ, I had never wanted anything like this before. For one triumphant moment his body crumpled and he gave into me, but then he froze, pushing back in a movement so overpowering, I almost fell.

"What the *hell* do you think you're doing?"

"Redecorating."

And then it happened: he opened his eyes, and something glimmered and caught fire. There was something beneath what he showed the world – something else was there – and for the first time, he let me into that something. His eyes caved in, and everything he'd been hiding on his face showed itself.

"Ugh, Coley…"

He leaned in and kissed me hard, and the lights went out. I had never kissed a boy before, and it was…everything, really. His soft lips and coarse stubble felt like a poisoned daisy, just the wrong kind of right. Part of it felt so bad, worse than anything I'd ever done, but that badness felt beautiful, imperial even.

Suddenly I remembered I hadn't brushed my teeth in twelve hours. "But I-"

"Shut up," he grunted, and then he sort of pushed me up against the wall, and I gave in to him.

128

Lots of people have described what it feels like to be kissed for the first time by the person you dream about. Millions, probably. To me it felt something like soaring, and also stopping, falling from the sun like Icarus into cold air, undoing damage. Nicky made contact with my face again and moved his tongue into my mouth, and it felt stubbly and good and right. We both wrapped our arms around each other like there would never be enough of us to touch, and I felt like I was flying, or falling, tumbling into something I'd never known before. And right then and there I knew with certainty that this, whatever *this* was, I would never be able to walk away from it.

I leaned into his ear. "Did you hear that?" I asked, brushing his lobe with my lips.

"Hear what?"

"The last lingering shred of my heterosexuality, leaving the building."

We stumbled for the bedroom, discarding a shirt here, a sock there, a pair of underwear over by the bathroom wall. I pushed him down and then crawled on top of him, and even though every inch of me was touching him, it wasn't enough. I wanted more. I needed it all.

And maybe we really were built to fall apart. Maybe we needed each other more than we actually liked each other, and we were clinging to a sinking ship to avoid jumping and taking our chances in the open water. Maybe it was a done deal, and I was just chasing beautiful pipe dreams. But he was worth every minute of that stupid chase. The fire in my chest told me that much.

He kissed me again, and then we started doing things I'd never done before. Things that made me regret every day of my life before he'd entered it. I was making sounds I'd never heard before and he was saying words I'd only heard in videos. We weren't perfect, but we were eager – we were exploring, breaking new ground. And the way I moved with him, so in sync, made me swear I'd known him forever.

He grunted, leaned closer, and licked my ear, and that's when someone knocked on his door.

129

We both stopped.
Someone was here. In his house.
With us.

9

Nicky jumped away, *literally* jumped, like someone from a
Jackie Chan movie. I heard a big, booming voice that was big
and dumb in the same exact way all of the FitTrax meat heads
sounded big and dumb. Telling them apart was like taking a
two-second glance at the sky and closing your eyes trying to
remember what each cloud looked like. There was no point.

Nicky stopped and stared at me, eyes and hair wild. I
stared back – I had no idea what to do, either. Finally he crept
over to the door and opened it just an inch. "Yeah?"

"Yo, I forgot my wallet. Any ideas?" The guy paused.
"And what's up? You're all messy-haired and shit. You got a
girl in there, boss?"

I could practically hear Nicky's heart pounding. "I've
um…yeah. Got someone. A girl."

He tried to walk past. Nicky held tight. He looked over
Nicky's shoulder. "Ah, really? Lemme watch."

More heart pounding. Why were straight guys so much
gayer with each other than gay guys were? "Nah, you sicko.
Go away."

"Who is it?" the guy asked. "Stephanie, the bitch with
the big titties from Sunday? You guys were all over each
other."

Now *my* heart was pounding. So *that's* why he'd
stepped away and stopped texting me. The realization made
my face feel like it was melting off and my chest was caving
in on itself. I hated everything, starting with him.

"Yeah, it's her. I haven't seen your wallet, maybe try
the floor of your golf cart?"

A minute later the guy had finally left. After locking
the door behind him, Nicky padded back into bedroom where I
was waiting, looking like a dog who'd been caught tearing
apart the kitchen trash.

"Well that's just great," I said once we were safe and
sound and alone. "We can't even do anything without flipping
the hell out when someone gets close. That really speaks well

for the future of…whatever this is. And Stephanie? Something you need to tell me? *Bro*?"

He wrapped his towel tighter as his eyes left me. "Yeah…yeah. I made out with someone. But before you get mad, I only did it to shut down my friends' suspicions or whatever, and it felt like kissing porridge, and I hated it, and they basically *made* me do it."

I was staring at him and I didn't know what to say, because this was it: the moment I realized he'd fully taken control of my mood. And I hated him for it. He was remaking everything about my world. I never knew what it was like to wake up in the morning and feel giddy about living, and if that ever stopped…if I ever lost him and had to go back to that…I didn't even know how to finish that sentence. I'd rather die, probably.

"Are you dating someone?" I asked. He looked at the window. "Is that why you've been so absent? Nicky, *are you dating someone*?" The thought of him kissing and loving and screwing someone else already made me want to end myself.

"No, I'm not dating anyone. I just told you I liked you. I just *kissed* her."

"Well, whatever. Same thing. *Stephanie* – what a whorish name. And why are their girls' shoes in your house? And yogurt and granola bars and other girl foods?"

"You think I have a *girlfriend*? Coley, all that stuff is my sister's. She comes down here all the time."

"What? Why didn't you just say that, then?"

He looked away.

"Tell me."

"I just didn't want you to know about her…I didn't want you to ask to meet her."

I closed my eyes for a split second, but still I saw him. And that was the problem. I would probably always see him. I wasn't mad at that, just heartbroken.

I looked at him. Something strange flashed in his eyes, something almost malicious. But then it went away. "Well, whatever. I did what I did. And you don't get what it's like, to hangout with them. They're ruthless. They circled around me and egged me on. One of them even said, 'What's up with you, you don't like chicks anymore?' People are talking, Coley. I'm with you all day, every day. I thought maybe they'd seen me with you, so I panicked. I was just trying to protect…this. Us. The longer they don't know about this, the better." He stared at me. "Coley, *say something*."

The truth was, I had nothing *to* say. I only knew a few things for sure about this, and they were different and absolute. I hated the way he treated me. I hated the way I *let* him treat me. I loved the way I felt around him. I hated the way I felt when I wasn't around him. I hated the way I could never walk away from him when I knew I needed to. And all those facts flew at each other and collided and exploded in my mind like nothing I'd ever faced before. I had no idea how to like him any less. Maybe I didn't want to.

He stepped forward and kissed me – but this time it was soft, like a promise, or an apology. Someone walked by outside, though, some stranger that could not see us or even hear us, and their faint shadow passing the window doomed my fantasy a premature death. He pulled away a little and wiped his lip, chastened, chastised by the world like a mother with a wagging finger. As he loosened his grip around me I closed my eyes and bid farewell to the moment, knowing his heart had closed, and no sex would transpire between us tonight. And I tried to remember how this felt, for the sake of posterity, to be wrapped in the sinewy arms of someone I'd never even expected to touch me.

"I want to hangout with you, as…as whatever we are," he said, and a jolt shot through me. "And pursue this. And do what we just did, like, every single day, basically."

"Pursue what?"

"What we both feel right now. But under one condition. You can't tell anyone. Seriously. Not ever. You saw how bad that was, and he didn't even see anything. There's still stuff you don't know…the stakes are so high with me…"

And then things were falling in a way that didn't feel breathless at all. Just shitty. He pulled his hand away, and I could see how deeply he was hurting about this. He was me, a year ago.

He closed his eyes. "God, I'm horny again. Ugh. Drama turns me on, apparently."

My entire body jolted a little. "Let me do stuff, then. I promise I won't kiss you."

He breathed, and I thought again that we shouldn't do this. This could get us both beaten.

Or this could remake both of our worlds.

"Okay," he said. "Just wash me, then..."

And so I did. He turned off the lights, and I followed him back into the shower. I took the rag hanging on his rack and rubbed it slowly over his chest after it was wet, never making direct contact with his skin. He tensed up, but let me proceed. As I continued, letting my hands go further south, he angled away a few times, but I kept going. Slowly he gave over to what he was trying to resist. I never touched his skin directly, but I didn't need to. He felt me all the same.

"*Harder*," he moaned in that sexy voice of his, detonating me. It was the hardest thing I'd ever done not to touch him, not to kiss him, not to love him. But I did it. When we were done he grabbed a towel, hiding himself, and ran into his darkened bedroom. But as I turned back and washed myself in the water, I knew there would be no running from this. We would never be cleansed of each other.

10

Nicky and I didn't question many things after that night in the shower. Or *I* didn't, at least. We would hangout as friends, cloaked in secrecy all the while, but I was hopelessly infatuated with him and wasn't really trying to hide it anymore. I'd laid it all out there, and he knew. He didn't mention that day we'd hooked up, but I didn't care. Out in public, the "friend" thing was the rule, but as soon as that boy closed my door and entered the safety of my house, that all ended, and he would rush to me, and the little world we were creating together would open up. Soon I no longer recognized my own life, in the best way possible. I never knew I could feel so alive and aroused and on fire, and I never knew there were so many places on a human body you could love. To my shock, I didn't feel dirty or guilty or wrong or sinful about them. I couldn't change, and for the first time, I didn't want to anymore. We didn't talk about it, didn't even acknowledge it, but he blew my life open.

For the first time ever I wasn't waking up sad. This secret world bloomed inside my life, a world I was forced to keep separate from the rest of the areas of that life, and the effect was both comforting and bizarre. It was like having a raucous party in one unit of an apartment building late into the night, and trying to tamper the lights and sounds and happiness so the party wouldn't bleed over into any other units. Every time I saw an old friend and busted at the seams wanting to tell them about what a thrilling carnival my life had become, and then remembered our "secret" status and shut my mouth, I started to realize more and more just how dangerous it could be to live your life in compartments. He made me keep my giddiness a secret, and what was kept in the shadows could not flourish – wasn't that an Aristotle quote or something? We were strapped into a jolty, panicky, start-stop nightmare of a fantasy, and most of the time I didn't even care whether we ended up in clouds or in flames, just as long as we ended up there together.

We read magazines together, we watched Netflix on my bed, we screwed on my coffee table. At night, the real fun would come – we'd break onto my neighbor's roof deck and eat oranges from his potted trees, we'd skinny dip in the ocean, we'd get on his golf cart and raise hell in the neighborhood. When we were apart, I could not think about anything or anyone but him. I would count down the moments until I could see him, and then I saw him, I'd dreadfully count down the seconds until we had to part ways, and I'd have to go back to dreaming. I didn't even care *what* we did, just as long as we did it together. Mostly he would lead me straight to a bedroom – mine, or his. I longed to go on dinner dates, maybe go to the movies or the park or do whatever the hell normal couples did, but our activities usually only involved Netflix and mattresses. Our world existed in dark rooms and quiet cars and deserted movie theaters. If anything, the near-miss with his wallet-losing friend had pushed him further into paranoia.

I still didn't really know how to date, or whatever this was. Even secretly. Sometimes I'd do the stuff I'd seen in movies – hold open the door for him, write him little notes and stuff, maybe steal a kiss when he wasn't looking – but all of it felt weird and forced and "too much." But that's not to say I didn't like that boy. I grew to protect him above all else, put him before anyone or anything in my life. I grew attuned to the slightest change in his emotions – if he was in a bad mood, I was inconsolable. If he was happy, I was flying a million miles above him. I knew I was a fool, but I didn't really care just as long as I was *his* fool, as dumb as that sounded.

A sticky Florida summer marched on. As our love exploded, he retreated further into the closet while simultaneously appearing to fall in love with me. The public hangouts became increasingly rare. He steered us clear of anyone he knew, to the point where he was dragging us across the place whenever a girl looked at him. I tried not to notice it. There were a lot of things I was trying not to notice. On the rare occasions that we *did* go out on "dates," he'd only take me to deserted restaurants at completely crazy hours – a pizza place at eleven in the morning, a Mexican place at midnight, etcetera. He said he was claustrophobic and hated crowds, and I tried to believe him at first. He'd rush me through the restaurant to the corner, never making eye contact with a single soul, and then he'd scoot across the booth and barricade himself against the wall and immediately order a beer with his fake ID to calm himself.

We still got looks everywhere we went, especially from older people. One time when we were crossing the street, an old man stopped his motorized scooter and gaped at us open-mouthed like we'd killed his firstborn child. It made me feel icky and dirty and less than human, and I knew Nicky felt the same. Most people were more polite and surreptitious, but they were still gawking. What right did these people have to assert their opinions on us, anyway? Two guys hanging out at the gym or a bar was expected – normal, even. But two guys sitting at a dark table in a restaurant or walking through a mall together on a shopping trip sometimes elicited open stares. Some people would assume we were gay and go out of their way trying to act like they didn't care and weren't paying attention, but their deliberate avoidance of us just made things even *more* awkward. And one night, as Nicky forced us to scoot to the very end of a bar that had a grand total of two people sitting at it, I knew I couldn't ignore it anymore. He wasn't avoiding crowds, he was just ashamed of being seen in public with me. *Still* – after all this time. We existed in a bubble, and any threat of intrusion of the real world into that bubble scared the living shit out of him. He kept entire rooms of his life off-limits from me – he hated talking about his family, he refused to talk about his past dating life, his eyes glazed over when I asked about his friends. He gave me a truncated version of himself, the fun-sized version, and I wasn't breaking him down fast enough. I knew I had to change this, to figure out how to pivot this from "friends" to whatever was beyond friends. I had to make him love me – I just didn't know how.

But this is what kept us going: as soon as we came together, he'd sort of collapse next to me and then hold me close, and the affection that flowed through us would shock me every time. He understood every cell of me, and that's the only way I knew how to explain it to myself. The sex was sometimes painful, occasionally gross, but always explosive. Being able to touch and adore my dream boy, even in the dark, felt too beautiful to be true. Afterward he'd hold me almost desperately, flesh to burning flesh, and the current was almost electrical. This world between us would open up, ColeyAndNickyVille, and we'd disappear into it, *whoosh* into the void and not come up for air until we had to. I could sense that he felt it, too – I'd never met someone who understood all of my fears without me even having to say them, felt all my pain without me even have to tell him where it hurt. When we lay together, even in the austere darkness, the world and all its complications just didn't matter. Everything could still be spinning apart out there, and uncles could be bigots and women could stare at us in shops and "homosexual activities" could still be labeled as criminal in nine states, but in Nicky's messy bed, his galaxy eyes kept me together. Those eyes could save anyone, after all. The person he saw when he looked at me – that's who I wanted to be, always. I always wanted to be the boy he adored. And if he couldn't adore me in the right way all the time, I would wait. Because I knew the hard way that burying your feelings was like burying a lit match in a pile of gas cans – something had to blow eventually.

It just killed me a thousand times that every time we had to go out into the light again, our little world would disappear, and I'd be his "bro" again.

One day when I was feeling low and alone, plagued by some vague anxiety I couldn't quite trace or pinpoint, he texted me:

I miss you

The message felt like sitting down next to a hot fireplace on a cold day. All the fear, all the heartache, just melted away. He could be so sweet when he wanted to, like when I'd caught him staring at me and asked him what was wrong. "Nothing," he'd said. "You're just making me live." He could set my day on fire with just a sentence.

You do? I asked. **Why do you miss a friend?**

Shut up. I'm coming over.

An hour later he brought over a pan of cinnamon rolls. He'd made a heart shape with the icing.

"Ah, my favorite!" I said as I took the plate with wide eyes. "Ugh, and calories were the last thing I needed, too. Why'd you do this?"

"Because I, um…my mom left some groceries at my house last time she came, and I just wanted to make them. For you."

"Aw. Why?"

He smiled. "Because you're you, and you're my favorite You that has ever existed."

I breathed him in, wanting to preserve the memory. It was the first time anyone had ever given me anything. Even my parents, really. He didn't have the tools to love me, but he was *trying*, and that meant everything. "Thank you, Nicky. Thanks for this."

"No problem."

"Touch me now," I said, swept away by something foreign and strange.

"What?"

"Hug me," I said, my voice low. "Touch me…like you do at night."

His eyes dropped to the floor. "But I can't…"

I closed my eyes and winced, but only for a moment. We settled on my couch and put on this Netflix documentary about murderers, and he spent at least an hour kissing my arms and hands while I lay there, happier than I'd ever been in nineteen years.

"Have you been thinking about me today?" he asked soon. "We didn't speak much."

139

I didn't want him to know just how much I really *did* think about him, so I looked away. Sometimes he seemed to relish how much I obviously liked him, and then hold it over my head in a weird way whenever he got mad at me.

"Nope," I said.

"Well, you should have. I'm pretty alright."

"So I've heard."

He leaned in, tapped me on the forehead. "Hey, grumpy. What's the issue?"

"It's just…can we do something that *isn't* in a bedroom or living room?" I asked. "Or, like, something in public that *doesn't* take place ten minutes before closing time?"

He looked stumped. It made me really sad. "Like what?"

The fact that he had to ask me that was troubling. I pushed the subject from my mind, or tried to. Because I wasn't upset enough to stop seeing him. This whole thing felt like a jig that was about to be up. Every time he texted me, I was terrified that he'd come to his senses and realized how subpar I was, how below him I was. So I leaned into him and let it go. Lately being around him just felt like…being around myself, even despite all our problems. I couldn't explain it: we just felt like we were flesh and blood sometimes. But at least he kept me on my toes. He was magnificent some nights, wordless others. He'd take me so high, and just when I thought we were about to scrape the clouds, he'd drop me. But I enjoyed it somehow, because I never knew what to expect. Were we perfect? No. I wished I could be strong enough to demand the love I knew I deserved, but I wasn't. I was too afraid that without him, I'd be nothing at all.

Soon it got late, and sleep started to get close to us. My mouth twitched once, then twice, and before long I knew I couldn't hold it in anymore. Finally, I asked the question I'd been obsessing over for weeks.

"Are you my boyfriend?" I whispered, my voice like a little child's. He was half-asleep, too, and I felt him kiss the back of my hand one last time.

140

"I don't know," he mumbled. "But I do know you're the only person I wanna be alive with."

The next morning I brought him on an *Honesty* mission. I'd been abandoning my life with a shocking casualness since meeting him, and I knew I was going to get a passive-aggressive email from my editor any day now if I didn't start posting more entries. I found an older man sitting outside a café who said he wrote for a local magazine and gave me some fascinating advice about his job.

"To write is to access all the parts of yourself that others avoid," he said, holding his notebook. "A book is like a rose that blooms from the most barren corner of your soul."

"That'll do," I smiled as I wrote down his quote. "That'll *certainly* do."

"So what's with the whole *Honesty* thing?" Nicky asked as we walked down the sidewalk after I'd taken the man's photo and bid him adieu.

"What about it? It's going well. It seems like the bigger it gets, the faster it grows. I just posted something about a little girl who missed her dead dad, and it was my first picture to reach three thousand likes. There's even a whole community of fans now that chat in the comments section and share their own stories – it's getting so big that it's weird to think about sometimes."

"No, like…on a deeper level," he said. "Do you think you're so obsessed with getting the truth from other people because you…well, because you run from your own truth, yourself?"

I frowned. He could sink deeper into me than *I* could. And not only in the sexual sense. "Um…I've never thought about that."

He smirked. "Yeah. Not trying to pry, but…it's just funny that you're so open and honest about everything else in your life, except this. And it's ironic that the operator of the famous blog about people being honest is…well, *closeted*."

My breath left me. I'd never looked at it like that. "I mean, I don't know. It's not…me. It's not about me. It's about the subjects. I have nothing to do with it."

"Sorry," he laughed, "but *no*. That's like the head of PETA being an African big-game hunter. Doesn't mesh. Or the head of the Lung Cancer Council of America being a pack-a-day smoker…"

"Okay, you've made your point," I said, my cheeks warming. "Drop the shovel, I'm already dead."

"Sorry! Just saying – you can't broadcast truth when you're living in a lie."

I'd been thinking about this lately, too, but Nicky was a huge hypocrite to be preaching bravery when he was…well, Nicky. "Hold on, Mr. Honest, let's look at your-"

"Okay, okay, let's drop it. I'm not the famous one, here."

I waited for my temper to recede.

"I just do what I do," I said soon, "because I want to. I grew up with a camera in my hand. I guess that when I'm looking at the world through a lens, I don't really have to deal with reality. Trust me, there were a *lot* of things in my childhood that I didn't want to see, so I saw them through a camera instead."

"What do you see when you look at *me*?" he asked, and I closed my eyes and swallowed some air and thought about how when I was with him, one plus one equaled three.

"You don't want to know."

"Okay then."

"And what about *you*?" I asked him, glancing his way. "What do you see in me? You're so hard to read."

"Freedom," he said. My eyes gleamed, and his eyes ran away with my fears.

"Let's come out together, then," I whispered through a cringe. "Let's just do it. Let's be…well, free. Like how you see when you close your eyes. Like you just said – I should be more open about this. It's a new century – who cares?"

He laughed, and it was an insane sort of cackle that made my stomach jump a little. "Oh, sure!" he said, smiling this wild smile. "Great idea! I'll just march right into my parents' house and tell them I'm a homo. I don't need tuition money, or money for my apartment, or my car payment, or my phone bill, or, you know, the love and support of a family, even if it's fake, and comes with quid pro quos. You're right!" he shouted, looking around at the empty lot next to us. "Come on out, queers! There's nothing to worry about! The world will love you! Yay!"

"Okay, gotcha," I said. "Coming out doesn't make sense for you. I understand."

Finally, he calmed. "Ugh. You don't, though. And if you're waiting for some dramatic 'coming-out' moment from me, anyway, some party where I thank all my friends for their support and start crying and kiss a guy on the lips, it's never gonna happen. That whole concept in general is a lie the world needs to stop believing. The world forces people to go into hiding, and then gawks at them when they come out of that hiding. But it's all a false concept. We don't owe the world anything because of who we are."

"Huh?"

"Think about it," he said, and he got this passionate look on his face I'd never really seen outside our bedrooms. I almost wanted to photograph the moment and use him on the blog: this was what people looked like when they drudged up their deepest passions, when they touched on what they *really* cared about. "When's the last time a straight person was asked to 'come out?' When's the last time a straight person had to make a rambling Facebook status to announce they were heterosexual, or have a melodramatic sit-down meeting with their parents and confess that they liked the opposite sex? Never. The world has claimed gay peoples' personal lives, co-opted their private lives and told them they've gotta offer everything up to be accepted, with every gory detail included. But forget that. My life is mine." He sighed. "And even if I *did* come out, which would never happen, I still don't want to play that game, and deal with that aftermath. These days, coming out is more about straight people flaunting their acceptance than about the people coming out themselves. *'Oh,*

143

you're gay? Come here and let me show you how tolerant I am!' I don't want someone to come up and be amazing at me and pat me on the back and treat me like I'm a wounded kindergartner for being gay. Nobody has ever been asked to 'accept' a straight person for being straight, and that shouldn't be any different for me. I don't even *want* the world's acceptance, really. I just want them to leave me alone and treat me like they would anyone else."

I stared at him. "I've never looked at it all like that. You are so…insightful."

He sighed. "So, yeah, there they are – my thoughts on all this." Then his eyes flashed. "You've got me all hot and bothered now. I can't come out, but I *can* do other things, though…maybe with my tongue…"

I shivered a little. That look – he set me on fire with his eyes. I wanted to feel like that for the rest of my life, even when it burned.

I knew he wanted to go home and hook up, so I hit the brakes. "Wait. Let's do this more often. Maybe along with tongue stuff sometime. But this, too."

"What?"

"Hangout. In public. During the day. Just me and you. We've been getting better, but I want to do it…more."

"…Just us?"

I nodded. "No alcohol, no late nights, no hiding. Just this."

He nodded back, fear bright like a torch in his eyes. "Okay. I'll try."

This only led to more problems, though. Being around Nicky was almost like being with a child – his lack of experience showed everywhere. Or was it *just* a lack of experience? Sometimes it seemed like he picked fights for the hell of it. A little argument here or there turned into more regular bickering, and then the drama started roaring at full throttle. We'd start going at it over the timing of a text message, an unanswered phone call. Soon we were volcanic together, two kids on a Coney Island rollercoaster. I'd catch him checking out a girl and delete his number. He'd catch a

144

male friend texting me and tell me he hated me and say he was never going to speak to me again. But every time I said goodbye, it would tear me apart, and I'd want to run back the second I could. I needed him so badly, but sometimes I hated him just as much. When he was mad at me, I could not function – I was restless and distracted and felt like one of my organs had been removed.

As August opened up we fell into this dysfunctional little routine: we'd grow closer than two people had ever been, then fight about something stupid and bump away like magnets meeting on the wrong sides, then meet again. I didn't want to live without him, but I couldn't live with him, either. School was starting soon, time was running out, and we both felt the stress. We'd share a beautiful set of days together, then get into some dumb blowout and stop talking for an afternoon. He made me feel emotion on a scale I'd never experienced before. Every heartbreak was a hurricane, every ignored text message felt like a breakdown. He knew exactly which buttons to push, which things to say to make me explode. His temper was an absolute livewire, too, and in his rages he'd block me from every single social media platform possible. But then I'd find a way back in and message him that I missed him. After that, we'd slowly start talking again, and then have an explosive hookup on my bedroom floor.

One night he caught me checking out a basketball player while waiting in line for a late-night movie, and he hit the roof. I couldn't help it – I guess I was getting more open about those things now that I knew how beautiful the touch of a guy felt. Nicky saw, though, and as the theater girl handed us our tickets, he whispered to me that he hated me and never wanted to see me again. I stood at the ticket stand, stunned, as he disappeared into the lobby. He sat alone in the theater, glaring at me on and off the whole movie. We didn't talk for a day after that, and it was miserable – not only was I without the boy I loved, I was out of a best friend. That afternoon I went on my balcony and watched a lady fall flat on her face into the sand as she attempted to take a selfie while jogging, and as I laughed I realized I had nobody to tell – I would've texted Nicky about it immediately, but I couldn't. That was the worst part, the little gaps in my life that were already showing in his absence. He'd already sifted in and rearranged things, and I felt incomplete without him. And in that moment I knew I never wanted to feel that lonely again – I wanted him around me, always.

He relented and unblocked me and invited me over the next night, of course, and the fight was never even mentioned, but something told me the drama was only going to get worse. And it did. Over the span of one week, we broke up four times. *Four*! Sometimes I felt like I was standing in a dark room, screaming at the top of my lungs, with nobody around to hear me. But why did I keep running back into the flames?

I know it was all crazyballs, but at the same time I was starting to learn that love was a pacific insanity. I was inching closer to the edge than ever before, but strangely I loved every minute of it. He was becoming the other half of my world, and that world was blown off its own axis all the time. Without him I felt blue desolation. With him I often felt red fury. On top of him I felt white heat. When he left, it was all black. That's what that boy brought me: for the first time ever, I was living in color. Those deep, previously unexplored feelings and instincts I'd spent my life hiding and burying and denying – he pulled them all to the surface in one dizzying, intoxicating whoosh of Technicolor madness. Sometimes I found myself enjoying the pain, too – he opened up a sublime rage in me that I didn't even know existed. Hurting him felt like heaven, and I hated myself for how much I wanted to hate him sometimes. He was like a book, one of the really good ones where you had to slip away and press your face close to the page and disappear into the world that was slowly blooming between the two of you. I'd see him, he'd see me, and poof – we'd be gone. Our love existed in an empire that no one knew about but us.

"Beautiful," he whispered one night in the midst of the craziness, as the empire crumbled. He was in an unusually happy mood for a moment, and I remember wanting to savor it, wrap my hands around it like it was a warm mug of coffee on a cold morning and never let it go.

"What's beautiful?" I asked, as he bled at the edges like a November sunset. We'd just watched a gorgeous documentary called *Living Earth*, and I guess he had some things on his mind.

"So many things. You right now, mostly."

"Okayyy, what else?" I asked, stretching the moment, since he gave me so few of them. I felt an eyebrow twitch. He smiled and breathed, half-asleep. But this wasn't one of our jokes – this was real. This was ours.

"What else is beautiful? God, so much – right now, at least. I think it's beautiful that we're alive on this blue planet. I think it's beautiful that airplanes are taking off and landing all over that planet right now, so many of them, and that children are looking out of the windows of those planes and falling in love with their lives. I think it's beautiful that my grandpa nursed my grandma through Alzheimer's and held her hand while she was a vegetable and told her how lucky he was to have had her. But mostly I just think you're beautiful."

A tear fell out of my eye, and I hated it.

"I like you so much, Richard Cole Furman IV, I can barely take it. You're making my world go mud."

The next morning he was as cold and distant as ever, though, and I couldn't shake the feeling that something was about to blow. The great baking sun was doing something to us, making us lose our minds. His eyes were getting more paranoid than ever, and it could only be so long before his fear broke out for good. He was struggling – with *exactly* what, I wasn't sure – but I knew things were starting to spin out of control.

A few days later he took me to the library – *our* library. He'd been reluctant to so much as walk down the sidewalk with me lately, and so he was already in a black mood when the librarian appeared.

"Would you guys like the computers next?" she asked. "I'm taking reservations."

147

"Oh, I'm good," Nicky said. She kept her eyes on him, but pointed at me.

"Okay, and what about your…?"

She let the question hang. She didn't know what he was, and she didn't want to say the wrong thing and offend us. For a moment I wanted to say it – I wanted to blurt it all out. *What am I? I'm his secret boyfriend. He's all I care about and I want to spend forever with him and God, even sitting here right now, I want to rub his face and kiss his forehead because he's the cutest thing I've ever seen.*

"Brother. He's my brother," Nicky said. "And no, he's fine, too." The librarian nodded and left.

Ashamed, I looked over at Nicky, the boy I was falling in love with who couldn't even acknowledge me to a stranger. He stared back. And then the sadness of the South rolled over us, filling the room, saying everything we couldn't. I looked around at the books on the shelves, antiquated artifacts in a world that had moved past them. Just like us.

I got up.

"Don't go," he said. "I didn't mean it."

"The hell you didn't," I scream-whispered.

"Oh really, Mr. Perfect? What about when you sat so far away from me at that fro-yo place the other night, you fell off your chair? Do you think I don't notice these things, too?"

I didn't respond. He grabbed at my hand, and I pulled away and turned around, my eyes wide caverns of anger. "Screw you, Nicky. Screw. *You.*"

"No," he said. "I'll explain. It wasn't-"

"I'm trying, Nicky," I said as something in me sort of broke. "I'm trying so hard, every day. And it won't work. We barely go out, at least not when the sun's up. We don't touch. We don't even stand next to each other. And here we are, hiding between rows of stories, as 'brothers,' and this is all we have to show for the past two, three months. All we've *ever* had, really. How long are you going to keep me locked in your library?"

He just stared at me, and that was all confirmation I needed to turn and get the hell out of there.

I walked home and spent the next day cold and alone, loneliness descending on me like a snow cloud. My dad forwarded me an article about a Mississippi judge denying a marriage license to a lesbian couple, along with the subject line *SERVES THOSE BULLDYKES RIGHT!!!* Aside from being gross, this email made me mildly panic – what had my dad seen *now*? What did he know?

I drank some wine to chill myself out. That night I was watching TV and thinking about what a good *Real Housewife* I'd be when he showed up unexpectedly at my door, sweaty and blotchy-skinned and endlessly beautiful. Even his eyes swirled. How could I resist this galaxy boy? I looked down the hall to see if anyone was around and then grabbed him by the elbow, pulling him in. Then I kissed him. Hard. He kept his mouth closed, though. I opened my eyes and stared at him. He moved away far too quickly, and it made everything in my eyesight turn red.

"Chris knows," Nicky said, wiping his mouth of my spit. "It happened."

"What?" I asked, getting myself together and backing away. "Who?"

"Chris. My friend. He knows. About us."

A sound came from the back of my throat that did not mean anything. I stared at the ground as the ceiling fell in. "Okay. Rewind. Chris…is that the religious one? The one who said gays should be lined up and shot?"

"Ding, ding! That's the guy."

I reached up and rubbed my temples in the silence. "Okay. Okay…okay. Okay. What happened, exactly?"

He looked off towards the ocean, his mouth a horizon on the globe of his face, looking like someone who'd been awakened from a nap too early in the afternoon, right in the middle of a really good dream. "He saw me with you. At the gas station." He made a face like was swallowing a tree branch. "He said he saw us…he saw us being…*flirty*." He said the last word like it'd been poisoned. Because it had been. By God and religion and the South and friends named Chris and

149

so much more. As everything started spinning, I braced myself against the counter. Honestly, I'd been waiting for this moment. I knew someone had to see, something had to give, something had to fall apart. I didn't really care that much, but he clearly did. And here it was: the fall.

So I stood taller and started yanking excuses out of my head. "Okay, well, two guys hang out all the time! He wasn't there that day I got gay-bashed, so he doesn't know who I am, or that I like...yeah. Just say we were on the way to the batting cage, or we were going kayaking, and that we-"

"It's not that," he said. "Chris said he saw me kiss you."

I clutched my head harder. "What."

"And I remember it, too," he whispered, almost wistfully. "Last week, at the gas pump. I leaned in and kissed you when we were waiting for the receipt to print. It was almost dark and I had no idea anybody was around." He buried his face in his hands. "What were we *doing*? God damn it, how could we have been so stupid?"

My heart broke for him. His voice was bathing in hatred – for himself, for me, for this whole situation. But I wasn't surprised. The world was built to embarrass me. If I ever did anything bad, the universe would produce an onlooker immediately.

But this *wasn't* bad, I reminded myself. This was love. Love was never bad. That was something I felt in my bones every time I looked into the eyes of the beautiful boy standing in front of me.

"How could we have been so dumb?" he repeated, and he was crying now.

"Lie!" I said, desperate. "Try to lie. Say he imagined it."

He looked away, shame in his eyes. "I did. I said I was just bending over to look for my phone charger. I swore I had a girlfriend...."

I winced and closed my eyes. Just picturing this exchange made me want to die. He'd denied me to his own friend. I could see it so clearly because I'd done it, too. We've all been confronted before, and we all acted the same. Hell, I'd been attacked and accused by my own father a hundred times. You slipped on the camouflage and you stood taller and you spoke with a deeper voice and you looked them in the eye even though it burned. *"I'm no queer!"* you might say. *"You don't think I'm a queer, right?"* Because it was the South and homosexuality destroyed lives and nothing was freaking changing.

"Did he believe you?" I asked. Nicky looked away, answering me without words.

"He said he's noticed a lot of things that are different about me. He said I've been dressing 'gay' and doing my hair 'like a girl.' He said he's gonna tell people what I'm doing, because it's not okay."

Now I was getting mad. Really mad. "What does he have to do with any of this?"

"I don't know, but he said I should be careful."

His voice was becoming softer, further away. I could already sense it: he was flying away from me. This was too much for him.

So I reached for his shoulder. "Okay, Nicky, it's okay. We'll figure it out. I promise. It'll all be fine, and-"

"No!" he said, pulling away. "It's not okay. Don't you see? It's *not* okay. We shouldn't have to be hiding like this. But we are, Coley, we *are*. We've been hiding our whole lives, and it's not getting any better, any easier. Don't you see the way people look at us?"

I stared off at nothing. Of course I noticed.

"The whole world is trapped," he said. "Trapped inside their dogma, trapped inside their fear, trapped inside their own minds…we're two kids who don't even pay our own rent or buy our own cars. I can't lose my family yet – I would be nothing, and *have* nothing, without them. I'm not ready to be on my own any more than you are. How the hell are we supposed to find our way through this?"

I stared at him. We both knew I was answerless. "…By loving each other?"

151

He didn't say anything. I was so sick of him not saying anything. Underneath it all, I was the same as anyone else: I was dreaming for the love of someone who wouldn't give it to me.

He turned away again, maybe for good this time. "Yeah, um, I'm gonna need some time alone. I've been thinking, and I just don't know if all this is for me."

"What?"

"You heard me."

"So…so this is why you came here? To dump me?"

He was silent. This wasn't about his stupid friend – this was about Nicky. He liked me, and it terrified him so much he was walking away. Unhinged, I punched him on the shoulder. "Do it, then. Do it, you idiot. I hate you. Dump me and walk out of here and never come back. I dare you."

His body language deadened, and the lights in his eyes blew out. Then he smiled, and it looked so empty and cruel, I wanted to vomit. "Nah. I'm not dumping you, bro. How could I dump a *friend*?"

And he was right. He wasn't dumping me. It was worse: he was dismissing me, denying everything that had ever happened between us, sending me back to the bro zone, back to the beginning.

"Don't you dare call me your *bro*," I breathed. "I forbid it."

He looked away, and some of my resolve slipped. In the beginning, before all the complications, he'd looked at me like I was a Ferris Wheel on a Sunday afternoon. Oh, God, I could remember just how sweet that felt, how warm it made me, to be wanted like that. Lately he was just looking past me, and it broke me apart.

Now, I didn't know much about the boy standing in front of me, who seemed to be spinning apart at the seams just as quickly and as thoroughly as I was. All I knew was that I would like him, very much, to be the rest of my whole life. So I tried to make him stay. Because everything up to this point had been fake. Everyone else had been…well, someone else.

Everyone had been less than Nicky. And I couldn't let go of this magic yet.

"Don't do this," I whispered. "We'll figure this out, Nicky. I don't want to live alone in this place, with no you around."

"Why?"

I breathed and looked down at the floor. "I don't know. Maybe because you made everything matter again. Like, you're cute and funny and you're so close with your mother and it's adorable and God, you look so good in basketball shorts that it makes me want to kill myself sometimes. I like you more then I've ever liked anyone or anything." I blinked. "You've kind of redecorated my world, and sometimes I'm sure that's a bad thing, because now I'll never be able to go back. So...don't do it. Don't make me go back to that. I don't think I would survive my life BN."

"BN?"

"Before Nicky."

After the longest silence of my life he looked right at me, his eyes opening like shutters. "Cole, you're right. I like you. I really like you, and that is so rare."

"You do?"

Tears fell silently down his face. "Yeah, I do, and I have a sickness, and that sickness is called being unable to think about anything but Coley Furman, and you're smart and funny and interesting and you make me feel excited about going to sleep because that means I get to wake up again and see you again the next day, and I don't know how to do this anymore."

He turned to leave, and I heard my voice rise from my throat uninvited. Everything I'd worked for, everything I'd experienced over the past few months, was about to walk out the door.

"Wait."

He stopped.

"Please stay. Don't go. I never had a home until you, Nicky."

He reached for the door, and out it came: the honesty.

"I wish you were a book, and I'd never read you," I said as the tears started flowing.

"What?"

I started talking, but I didn't even know who I was talking to – the ground, mostly. "When I was thirteen I picked up *Harry Potter* and it fixed my life. I was a little gay kid with two absent parents and zero friends, and when I found that book I realized there were other worlds out there, worlds where it didn't matter what I was, even if they weren't real. It named unnamable feelings in me and pointed out things in me that I didn't even know existed – I felt those words to my bones. It described the act of being me better than I could. I had the time of my life inside those stupid books, and then I turned the last page and it was done, and when I looked around at my life again, everything else was so subpar in comparison. So…yeah. I wish I could unmeet you, unread you, unknow you, unarrange my life around you. That way I'd be okay with a downgraded life without you."

"Coley," he said. Then he kissed me like the world was on fire and walked out of my house.

11

On Sunday morning I opened my eyes on white light and felt
an instant dread smothering me like a nasty woolen blanket.
When I squirmed around, I felt a ball of something heavy in
my stomach. The light in my room was muted, and the air felt
stale and old. I lay there for a long time, not even feeling the
need to get out of bed, and that's when I realized the problem:
it was my first time waking up without Nicky in my life.

Except it was real this time. And he wasn't coming
back.

~

That afternoon I drank a bottle of wine and then threw myself
into *Honesty*, more out of desperation than anything else. The
first guy I approached waved me off, and another lady literally
ran across a parking lot to avoid me after I tried to flag her
down. After twenty minutes or so I found a homeless woman
named Kimberly of about sixty years old sitting on a bench by
the lifeguard stand, and she opened up a can of worms I didn't
even want to touch.

"Okay. I'll give you something. I should've chosen
love," she said, her eyes misting over like a cold fog rolling
over the ocean in February. Her face had a mean quality in it,
but something in her eyes told me she had been beautiful once.

"W…what do you mean?" I asked, dropping my
Polaroid camera for a second.

"Wait. Are you a Baptist?" she asked suspiciously.

"No."

"Methodist?"

"Uh, no."

"Not even Presbyterian?"

I shook my head.

"What, then?"

"Well, nothing, really. Not right now, at least."

She nodded and relaxed a little. "Okay, good, then –
you're unoffendable." She sighed, then looked around. "Her

name was Abigail. She lived next door to me. We were not quite twenty-five, I believe. She'd come around smiling at me, telling jokes, dropping by with a bottle of wine after dinner. By the time I realized I was in love with her, it was too late. She loved me, too, but I was engaged to a man, and I was scared. She had a serious boyfriend as well. So I denied her, cut her out like a tumor. My fiancé found out we'd been talking at night, anyway, and kicked me out. That's about when I started in on the old drink, here." She leaned back, smiled, and breathed, and in that moment, she looked free as fifteen. "I still see Abbie's brown hair every time I close my eyes."

She shook the PBR in her hand, turned her head. Some kind of sadness floated up in her eyes, dark leaves in a murky pond, and it looked older than anything I'd ever seen before. I wanted to stop, to say thanks and dismiss myself, but I couldn't.

"What ended up happening? Are they all dead now?"

She laughed, threw up a hand. I studied her closer. She had clear, open brown eyes and a habit of speaking out of the corner of her mouth. "Heavens, no. I'm not *that* old. She married a man, of course, and had her children. Lived out my dreams with someone else, basically. They've retired over in Ortega, but it's only a bus ride away. I stand on the sidewalk outside and watch them sometimes. She saw me once, looked right at me. And it was like no time had passed at all. We were back. And I could still smell her perfume."

This was hitting too close to home, but I couldn't leave, or even look away. I was inside her memory: I could smell the grass, see the bushes, picture the look in the woman's eyes. "Did you talk to her? What happened?"

Her eyes clouded over again. "*Nothing* happened. She turned away and got back to the life she'd chosen, and I got on a bus and came back here, to…this. It's okay, though. Pain will never be your friend. But with luck and time, you *can* learn to make it your acquaintance."

Jesus, I thought, looking back down at my phone. I tapped out an overview of her story and then bit my lip.

"Okay, um…could I get your contact information, for when I post the, the thing?"

"Kiddo. Do I look like I can afford a phone to you?"

I rocked back on my heels. "Oh, um…address, then?"

Pointedly, she looked down at the sidewalk under her.

"Oh, um, of course. No address. Well, thanks. I'll get back to you when-"

"What about you?" she asked, and I stopped.

"What?"

"I said, what about you? You're puttin' me on the hot seat here, and I wanna see you drink the same medicine. What are you running from? What makes you drink at night?"

She smirked, and I knew she wanted my truth now. The words wanted to tumble out so badly. *I'm in love with a boy, a boy who makes nothing else matter, a boy who makes me feel like I'm painting with all the colors in the sky for the first time in my life, a boy who won't even make space for me in his world, a boy who shuts me out and makes me sleep on the floor…*

"Um, I really miss my grandpa," I said instead. "That's all I can think of right now."

Her eyes glittered. She didn't say anything, but she knew. She knew my words were hollow and false.

"Thanks, bye," I said. And then the *Honesty* boy ran from his honesty.

As I walked away to find my bike, I buried the woman's story in a Notes draft and hated myself. *Haaaaaated myself*, full stop, like when you wake up from an out-of-control night out and realize you're in for a full day of being disgustingly hungover. Here I was, digging into peoples' souls to get at their most basic truths, while running from mine with everything in me. I couldn't go on like this. I couldn't hide. I needed to let out my inside self before it suffocated. I just didn't know how.

Nine days. For nine days after the kitchen blowout, Nicky would not talk to me, would not text me, would not breathe in my general direction. I was lost, and lazy, and my general everyday look soon went from "sexless bookworm" to "homeless elderly woman with two ratty bathrobes to her name." The late summer rains set in with a gross, muddy vengeance, and after the ride of a lifetime, I was slammed back into the friend zone. Or somewhere below the friend zone, if that place even existed. I wasn't even acknowledged by Nicky half the time in gym, on the off chance that he actually came. He was pulling away and I knew it. One day I handed an exercise band to him, the boy who had held me with all the tenderness in the world just days before, and he thanked me and called me "buddy." *Buddy*! He might as well have punched me in the face. And the sickest thing was that he knew the pain he was inflicting. He stared at me after that, almost taunting me, and I lit up with a rage I'd never felt in my life. Ever. For a second I considered going public with it. Touching him or kissing him or doing something to blow his cover. Instead I just walked away. But that night I felt like crying and jumping off my balcony. I would've just landed in the pool, but still, I was in the mood for theatrics. What did you live for when the person you *wanted* to live for wanted nothing to do with you?

The politics of all of it were explosive, so confusing. There were so many buttons I couldn't push, so many silent truths I could never convert to words. I looked for him on the Mixr app with a sick, obsessive zeal, certain he was trying to hook up with other dudes again, but I did not find him. Dating someone I'd met on a sex app horrified me in general, because if he'd met *me* there, what wasn't to say he'd been meeting other people there the whole time, too? Because it was a new century and sex was always just an app away and, oh God, we were all gonna die in a pit of flames and syphilis! But one night, after I'd abandoned reading two different books and exited out of half a dozen different Netflix shows due to anxiety, I realized something: this went beyond my typical issues. Basically, I did not want to be alive without Nicky anymore. I never had a clue how deeply my feelings had run for him until he'd stepped away. This was something I'd never experienced before, something I'd never even known was possible. I felt like someone had reached into me, taken one of my ribs, and walked away. His name called from inside me, getting louder and louder, until it was not so much a chant, but an anthem. It felt like the sun would not turn on. What was wrong with me? I'd been fine on my own my whole life, and now I didn't even know what to do with myself.

Outwardly, I went about my life like the independent kidult I was trying to become, but deep inside, I was torn apart. Nobody had ever liked anyone like I'd liked that boy. And he wouldn't let me in.

Hey.

The text came while I was watching some home decorating show and trying to follow some Pinterest roast beef recipe. The mixture in the pot looked more like a pile of horse turds, though, and I was halfway to giving up. Looking down at my phone and seeing his name on the screen felt like drinking water after a week in the Sahara. It felt like validation.

It also made me see the homeless woman's eyes, two little haunted houses inside a human skull…

Hi, I said, but then I deleted it. What did I say? That I didn't know how to live without him anymore? That my world had stopped happening? This hadn't felt like a breakup. This had felt like someone taking away all my oxygen and then telling me to sing the national anthem. I did not want to live without this boy's music in the air.

So I called him. He didn't answer. I called again, and he picked up on the fifth (!) ring.

"Hiii," he said, and his voice was smiling. "Hi, Coley. Sorry, I got tangled up in my mom's worthless little dog's leash and couldn't answer."

I stared at my ceiling. What was I doing, besides pressing my finger on a hot stove and expecting not to be burned? "Hi. Where have you been?"

"Oh, you know, sorry. I've always been a bad texter."

What a load of shit, I thought. People who said "I'm not good at texting" might as well have just announced "I'm an asshole who saw your text and chose to ignore it" and saved everyone the charade. He just didn't want to talk to me.

"Whatever. So…how goes it?" I asked him.

"Um, it's going. You?"

"Oh, I'm spectacular." Silence filled the space on the line. "So are we going to talk about things?"

"What things?"

I didn't respond. He knew.

"…Yeah?" he asked, still playing dumb.

"Maybe about you leaving my house? Or ditching me? Or publicly ignoring me?"

"Hold on," he said, his tone lower.

"What?"

"I need to find some privacy."

I heard some shuffling around, then a door slamming. The background air seemed to close in, like he was in a closet or something. "My mom is visiting again. I can't hangout this second."

I felt smaller somehow, younger, and old at the same time. "Okay…okay. I guess we can hang out some other time. There's this dinner delivery app I wanted to try out tonight, anyway, and that show on Netflix I've been neglecting…"

"Coley Furman, are you crazy, or just stupid? We're hanging out as soon as she leaves. Why did you think I texted you?"

"Um, I don't know," I said. "Why did you?"

He hesitated, but only for a moment. "Because my lungs won't work without you anymore, Coley. This has been the worst week of my life. I missed you, and I never want to miss you like that again. No matter what I do, I just can't leave this thing alone."

"Why not?"

He sighed. "I don't know. But whenever I close my eyes and picture what I want from this life…well, lately all I see is you."

"Oh," I breathed as my chest lit up with something that felt like the sun. "Okay. Be there soon."

The sex that night was the hottest and most explosive I'd ever experienced. He was TNT and I was a mountainside – he moved me. He let me sleep over after that, and then we spent one gorgeous day on the beach. I was so glad to be back by his side, despite everything. I know most Floridians would murder me for saying this, but I'd never been crazy about the whole beach thing – I hated sand, and being wet was my own personal purgatory – but I'd be happy anywhere he was. He brought a blanket and his iPhone's music player, and I got some pink wine with my fake ID.

It was the last weekend of summer, and we were both trying desperately not to think about it. I could feel everything changing around me, and I hated it. Summers in my part of Florida were hot and muggy and temperamental, pleasantly sunny one hour and lashing rain the next. Today was sort of hazy and in-between. He put his leg next to mine at around three, just staring down at our skin, and that's when I knew what he wanted. So I grabbed his shirt and led him toward his house, never stopping to check who saw. And that's when I decided to do whatever I had to do to keep him from leaving again. Because people always left me, but Nicky wouldn't. And this became my mission: I would not let the Jonathan situation happen again to me. If Nicky drove me away, I'd drag him back harder. If he'd get bored, I'd offer him sex whenever he wanted it, even when it hurt. I would not let this slip through my fingers again.

We didn't come up for air until after dinnertime. When we did, we just lay there in bed for a few minutes, hating different things while we stared at each other's faces. I didn't know much about the world, but everything I really *needed* to know was being answered in his eyes.

Finally I sighed. "Wow. Today was…interesting," I said, and he laughed a little.

"Yeah. *Especially* when that old guy from the donut shop saw us sitting together under the pier. I swear he was going to shoot us down, right there."

"Tell me about it." I stared at the ceiling, and something in me changed, shifted. We could barely be together for five minutes without letting the fear drive us apart again, and I was so over it. "Ugh. Sometimes I just wish we could…leave. Get away from this shit. I'm so sick of this."

"I'd run away with you," he smiled.

"You would?"

"Indeed. I don't know how to quit you. You're like a drug made just for me." I groaned. "What?" he asked. But what could I say? How could I put all this into words? *You're too perfect, and nobody's ever said anything to me like that, and this all built to fall apart, and why can't I walk away from this?*

I just said, "I enjoy you, that's all. And the fact that this might not work out…well, sometimes it makes me want to not exist anymore. That's why I want to leave."

He reached over and wrapped his hand around my leg, above the knee. He didn't have to say I was treasure to him. In that moment, I knew it. So I just studied him. Looking at him was like staring at autumn leaves and banishing the thought of winter. Nothing that came after mattered, not while you had such vivid reds and oranges and yellows to enjoy.

Then he sat up, his veins popping. "You know what? Screw this place. Let's do it. Let's run, like you said. Screw all these stupid, ignorant, provincial assholes. Let's go."

I hesitated. "Nicky," I said calmly, "I was half joking about that. We're nineteen. We have no money. Where would we go?"

"Savannah."

I sat up, too. "As in your hometown?"

"As in, my hometown. I would love to show you Savannah." He paused, his shoulders falling a bit. "But wait. We need rules. We *gotta* have rules. No touching in public, for one. My family could be anywhere."

"I can live with that," I said, even though I couldn't.

"Okay. And…no gay bars. No gay movies. No gay clothes. No gay jokes. No gay *anything*."

"Okay. Anything else?"

My beautiful boy didn't say anything. Instead he just reached over and tightened his arm around me and sort of smirked up at the fan in a dangerous way that told me he was in the business of killing the lights in peoples' eyes. "Nah. But we're going to Savannah! We're really going! For real!"

"Yay!" I said. This was insane, but I didn't want to pop his bubble. We were all allowed to have our bubbles. "But, you know, what if they…"

"Realize I like penis?"

"I mean…yes."

"They won't. They would never suspect…this, if I'm careful. I think."

The doubt in his voice was obvious. "And if they do?"

"We'll just have to deal with it, won't we? But I'm not letting go of you again – that's all I know. I've never been able to be this honest with anyone in my life."

I just swallowed. I wanted to be excited, but I was *so* scared for him. This thing was going off the rails, and I had no idea how we were going to keep it hidden now, especially in the same town as his family. The closer we got, the harder this was to hide – and we just couldn't help how we looked at each other anymore.

12

And so we set out under a cloudless sky the next morning, clunking along in his ugly old hand-me-down Pontiac from his dad. But I didn't care. For weeks I'd been forced to adore him in his bedroom, my living room, my shower – places that didn't move. But when I fell into his car and smiled as he took a deep, freeing breath and pulled out of his driveway, I felt my whole body opening up. Our world started moving, and the whole weekend rolled itself out before us.

As we passed the Georgia state line, I fell asleep. When I woke, we were pulling out of a gas station and his hand was on mine. I'd never been so comfortable. At a stoplight we paused next to a straight teenaged couple, and I looked into their car, their life, their world. They looked so…easy. They sat talking and laughing, and even their silent stretches seemed weirdly non-awkward. They were good at dating, and it made them look like adults.

Then I looked over at Nicky. He was buried in his cell phone as he drove, his body language miles away, save for his hand. I looked at his wavy hair, his green eyes, the way he seemed strong like the sun and delicate like sunrays. How did people date?

"So…what are you thinking?" I asked, figuring that was a good place to start.

"About my snails. And how lucky they are to have shells to disappear into."

"Oh, come on. Man up," I smiled, but his face turned acid.

"Don't say that phrase."

"Why?"

"Because it pisses me off and, reminds me of how homophobia is rooted in our language, and shit."

"Excuse me?"

His lips disappeared into his mouth. "It's just that you sound like my father. Phrases like 'man up,' 'get some balls,' 'grow a pair' – these are all meant to further the idea that males need to be strong and aggressive, aka straight-seeming, and any male who doesn't fall under that category is somehow less than other males. Just the word 'gay' – do you know where that word comes from? It meant silly, happy, jovial before it was applied to dudes. Why do gays have to be sillier, and therefore taken less seriously, than everyone else?"

"You've thought a lot about this," I said after a second. I guessed the idea of seeing his father was making him angry already. "More than I ever expected you to."

"Lord knows I've had a lot of time to think." He bit his tongue, then held his breath. Soon he exploded. "Okay, you know what? I like guys, but I've liked girls, too, and the whole damn situation pisses me off. The world gives people three choices: straight, gay, or lying. And I'm sick of acting like it's okay, like I'm not mad, like it's not messed up that nobody will ever acknowledge…what I am. Nobody will ever make space for me out there."

I didn't say anything. Finally we were getting somewhere, even if it'd taken digging. I didn't really believe he was bisexual, but then again, what did I know? Maybe I just didn't *want* to believe it. My world would go black if he ever found some girl and started dating her. And besides, self-acceptance was a different road for everyone, and if this was all he was willing to admit, I would let him stand in that truth, even if it was halfway a lie.

"What do you mean?" I asked. "About not making space."

"*What do I mean*? Okay, question time. Do you eat vanilla ice cream?"

"Um, sure."

"And do you eat strawberry ice cream?"

"Yeah, sometimes."

"And do you like both?" he asked.

"Sure."

"No you don't," he said.

"What?"

"You're lying to yourself. A person is only ever allowed to like one flavor of something, one type of something, and if you say you like both types, you're delusional and wrong and lying and a coward."

I paused.

"You see how ridiculous it is?" he asked. "A girl who makes out with another girl at a party is applauded. She's the hot girl, the fun girl. It's a phase, a flirtation, a passing curiosity, and a *sexy* one at that. Two guys making out a party would clear the room, and then get beaten into the dirt, too. If guys claim they're bisexual, they're worse than hated: they're just a joke, right? They're too weak to admit the big gay truth, and they're just one drunken night and one train station away from Gay Town. *No.* Sexuality is not mutually exclusive. What ice cream store clerk ever said, 'nope, you can't have a scoop of each, you have to choose. One. Forever?' Sexuality is a preference, a taste, a proclivity, just like anything else." He paused, his veins throbbing. "And how could I 'identify' as something that the world tells me does not exist? *'Funny joke, gay boy, but you like dick, so give up the charade and move to Brooklyn or San Francisco and call it a day.'* No. I've loved both sexes, and been attracted to both sexes, and nobody can take that away from me with their small minds and their grabby little stupid hands."

I just stared at him as the world passed us by.

"It's not changing," he finally said. "They act like it is, but it's not. LGBT people, or whatever you want to call them, couldn't be in the military until a few years ago. They still can't give blood. In the Middle East, they're being thrown off cliffs while crowds cheer. In Alabama, homosexuality is still listed as a criminal act under state law. North Carolina's law book officially says gay sex is unhealthy and dangerous. Actually, every day I see another story about some state's governor trying to block the new laws that are passing in favor of gay rights. All the people who turn a blind eye to hatred and homophobia and say we've moved on – they're lying. Where's the freedom? Where is it?" He stopped, tried to breathe. "It's just that, when I read history books, something like slavery – that doesn't even seem real to me. How could society have been so messed up to have let that happen, you know? How could the act of legally *owning* other humans ever be considered normal and okay? It just seems bizarre and surreal. But you know what? *Our* kids are going to be *just* as confused when they open up their books and learn that it took until 2015 for the most advanced empire in the history of the world to say, *Oops, my bad – two humans who love each other CAN legally get married. Sorry for the mix-up!*"

He looked over at me. "Well?" he asked, a little nervous. "Are you gonna say something? Why are you staring at me like that?"

I shook my head. I had never in my life heard someone speak a truth so succinctly into existence. This was me, distilled.

"Whatever. My point is, the others get to choose who they are," he continued. "But we don't. In every article ever, a gay actor is referred to as 'openly gay actor so-and-so,' but if they're married to a chick, they're just described as 'actor.' And not only do they list the gay person's sexual preferences, they list them *before* whatever the person has done with their lives." He picked up a scandal magazine on his floorboard, which was his mom's, I assumed. He scanned the articles showing the straight celebrities (or the ones who claimed to be, at least). "Here, let's see what they're calling the straighties these days." He took on the voice of an NBA announcer. "*The legendary bachelor, who is currently riding the top of the box office with his WWII drama, Crow's Nest...Hollywood's sweetheart, country singer so-and-so...the award-winning actor...the platinum-selling singer...the reality superstar...*"

He looked up at me. "Now, here, let's look for the freaks." He adopted the deep voice again. "*The controversial reality star, who recently came out as transgender...the openly lesbian golfer...the celebrity chef, who is gay...the disgraced bisexual actor, who lost his marriage to his TV star wife after admitting to an affair with his male personal trainer last fall...*"

Anger flickered in his glassy eyes. "We don't even get to choose who we are, and what we're known for, Coley. *They*

167

do. The normal ones do. 'Gay' is all you can ever be. How will we ever be able to rise above this shit and become who we're supposed to be, when the world has already decided who we are *for* us? They're killing us and they don't even know it. When an athlete or a rapper has an affair with a woman, they all say the same thing about it. *Oh, that's natural, he has groupies throwing himself at him, he's only human, the wife needs to accept the diamond apology gifts and get over it.* But if he sleeps with a man or a transsexual, he's a trending laughing stock, he loses millions in endorsements, he's a punch line on your aunt's Facebook wall." He shook his head. "None of this is even to mention the shit I've dealt with from being Hispanic in the Deep South – but that's a whole different story."

I looked over at him. "Shit. I've never even really though about that. I mean, yeah, a lot of people may hate me, but I'm still an upper-middle-class white boy from the suburbs. I can't even pretend to understand what you've gone through in that area."

"Hatred is hatred," he said through bared teeth, shrugging a little. "No matter what you call it. Homophobia, racism – it all comes from the same place: *fear*. They've arranged the world in the way they want it arranged, and any threat to that order needs to be taken out."

It was awkwardly quiet for a minute or two. I checked my phone, then rechecked it. Then checked it again.

"Question," he said.

"Yeah?"

"You talk about being 'out' and all that so much, but you never do anything about it. You don't even know what you're talking about, really. Say you did…come out, or whatever. Tomorrow. Hypothetically. What would happen?"

"Well, I-"

"And be honest," he said. "No sugarcoating."

I sighed. "I don't know. I'd probably lose my house, first of all. My dad would tell me he loved me, and then tell me he didn't want what I did happening under his roof, and tell me to leave. And my mom…I don't think she'd care *that* much, actually. She had an inkling about me, and once I heard her tell her friend that she'd be afraid to ever have a gay kid, since that kid would automatically be hated by half the world because of the Bible and everything."

"Ugh," he groaned. "Don't even get me started on the hypocrisy of all that. The Bible denounces gays? Well, great, but what about all the *other* verses they don't teach you about in Vacation Bible School? That Bible also instructs people to kill their own children, gives you tips on how to treat your slaves, and even tells women not to speak out of line or else they'll be disowned by their husbands. Not to mention how it refers to mixed-race marriages as being 'evil' and 'impure.' Oh, and in one particularly cute passage, it says that if a girl loses her virginity before marriage, she deserves to be publicly murdered. So why do people just follow the rules about hating gays? How can they pick and choose the lines they let dictate their lives? Don't stop there – by all means, embrace *all* the rules in that wonderful book, and see what happens!"

"Tell that to my mother," I said quietly, probably sounding sadder than I'd meant to.

"Why don't you ever talk about your mom, by the way?"

"Because I don't talk *to* her.

"Huh? Why not?"

I bit down on my tongue. How could I explain this? What would I say? *Maybe I can't talk to her anymore. Maybe she made it impossible. Maybe I'm better off without her. Maybe she ended my childhood by forcing me into the adult position while she acted like a kid. Maybe I'd spent so much time helping everyone else, I was nineteen and a stranger inside my own skin...*

"Because of reasons," I said. "When I was fifteen, my mom went on a vacation to her best friends' second home in the Turks and Caicos. She was an absolute mess because of how she and my dad had been drifting apart, and everyone thought it would be good for her to get away and be alone for a while. But she called me two days into the trip from the Miami airport, and I remember all she said when I answered was 'put your father on the phone.' Her voice sounded like a corpse's or something. And that's when I knew."

"Oh, shit."

"Yeah. The first night there, she got wasted and cheated on my dad. She was so embarrassed, she left the next day and told my dad everything."

"What'd he do?"

"Divorce her. That day. She tried to beg and plead and everything, but everyone knew it was over. My life was already a mess, but that shook everything up even more. My parents were all I had, and to lose that, to lose what they had together...it really did feel like the proverbial death everyone describes divorce as." I paused and realized I'd never told this to anyone in my life before. I didn't tell him the last thing, though. The day of the Miami call was also the day I'd promised myself to never to cry over love – all love did was end, and so I wasn't going to be some fool caught in the crossfire. Or so I'd thought...

Still, I let out a breath that felt a million years in the making. "It's all better now, anyway. They're better off apart. But the weirdest thing is that my mom didn't even want to come back. She wasn't ever a bad mom or anything, maybe a bit distant, but yeah...she just left after the divorce. She almost seemed relieved that she had a fresh start. But now she wants back into my life now that I'm older, and it's kinda like...*where the hell were you when I was an injured little teenager and I needed you around*, you know?" I swallowed, paused. My temper was running away from me, and I was revealing too much.

"What do your parents do, anyway?"

"Nothing," I said. "My dad was old money, but trust me, the money ended with him – he's already squandered his inheritance. His ancestors were huge landowners or something – my dad likes to brag that they once had more slaves than any other family in the Carolinas."

He looked like he'd eaten a rotten banana. "Who the fuck would ever want to brag about that?"

"Exactly. He's not exactly a gem. And it was just us two after my mom left, which was about as pleasant as it sounds."

"Geez. But at least he stayed, right?"

I blew out some air and shook my shoulders in a shruggy sort of way. "I mean, yeah, technically. He was still gone, though. People don't have to pack a bag and slip into the night to abandon you. They can disappear and check out of their own lives from right in front of you, go lights out, and they're as good as gone. My dad abandoned me from six feet away. And holy shit, sorry for unloading on you."

"You didn't," he breathed. "I'm kinda glad you told me all that."

"Why?"

"Don't know. It just makes me feel closer to you. Whenever I'm with you, I can just…*be*. What I am. And I've never had that before. Not even close, really."

I didn't know what to say. I felt the same way, and I sensed that he understood that this was our golden common ground, this ease we felt, this weird sense of understanding. It made me feel so free, just to have someone look into the parts of me the world had always ignored.

But then he blinked and pulled away, in so many more ways than one. When he was at his best, he could disarm a Navy Seal with his eyes. He made me feel glory, true human glory, like, opening-credits-of-Star-Wars glory or babies-giggling-themselves-awake-beside-you-on-a-Sunday-morning glory. But now it was like I didn't even know him. And maybe I never would, no matter what came out of his mouth. He was still locked inside himself, and it wasn't really getting any better, no matter what I told myself.

Suddenly he pulled off the road so hard, it jerked my neck back. "I can't do this."

"What?"

"See my family," he said. "With you. Talking about this gay stuff…it's freaking me out. I can't do it yet. I'm scared."

171

I looked at the big green road sign ahead. "...But we're twenty minutes from Savannah..."

"My parents' friends have a hotel where I can stay almost for free," he said. "We can go there. And still have a vacation." He stared out the window, into the trees, the woods.

"Fine," I said. "Fine. Hide me again. Put me away like a sweater in a drawer..."

"Oh, stop. Don't you think this hard for me, too? The stakes are so much higher for me. Your parents suck, but at least they're not religious fanatics. They didn't walk in on you watching gay porn as a kid and send you to some bible camp in the mountains for six weeks where they told you that you were worse than a cocaine addict for being gay..."

I swallowed. He'd never mentioned that. Maybe I'd been underestimating his family's fanaticism.

"Look," he said. "You don't get it. It's just harder for me. And sometimes I..."

"Yeah?"

He sighed. "Sometimes feel so out of control that I...I don't trust myself. I'm scared I might do something...something to make it all easier, I guess. There's a smudge inside me I can't scrub out." His eyes were like small volcanoes of misery. "Coley, sometimes I get so mad about all of this that I...I don't want to be alive anymore."

I didn't know what to say. I bumped my arm against his. "Nicky. I don't believe that. You would never do that. ...Right?"

"I've wanted to. Maybe. In the past. It gets so hard being in my brain sometimes."

I felt like crying. "Well do you ever feel those...suicidal type of thoughts anymore?"

His eyes grew. "Don't talk to me like I'm crazy, Coley. Are you telling me *you* haven't felt like this sometimes?"

I bit my tongue, because I couldn't deny that I had, occasionally, envied dead people. Sometimes when I was younger and my preacher was spitting fire from the pulpit and Mrs. Combs across the street was talking about how all gays should be sent away on a train and I was getting really tired of feeling like I was crazy, I could remember thinking death would be a better option than what I was feeling. But lately I'd felt better. The world was moving forward, slowly, but still, progress was all around. Just not in the South, perhaps.

"Nicky," I said. "The thought of you ever doing that makes me want to…fall into hell."

"Well sometimes when I think about who I am, how much I hate myself…I can't see anything else." He clenched his fists. "And the way I treat *you* because of all of it…I don't want to be like this, and I hate it."

My mouth opened a little. I didn't know why he wouldn't understand. Death wouldn't set him free from this. He was locked inside his hate for himself until he stopped giving a shit. Sentence: life.

And suddenly so much made sense to me: he didn't even *want* to love me. Loving me mortified him. Every time he'd walked away from me this summer, he'd been trying to dump me, get rid of me, become "straight" again. But he couldn't stay away any more than I could. He was just as dependent on ColeyAndNickyVille.

"Don't ever say that," I said, looking away. "Nicky, if you did something like that, I wouldn't be me anymore."

He just sighed again.

"Okay, we're gonna stop talking about this now. This isn't Instagram," I sort of laughed, trying not to cry. "I will never be able to unlike you."

"I know." The way he said it, like it was a bad thing, broke my whole heart. He stared down at his phone, his brow and nose the only parts of him visible in the techglow.

"Nicky, do you…do you *want* me to stop liking you?"

"I don't know what I want," he said. "I thought that was clear enough already. I don't know what to do about this either. Trust me – I hate myself for hiding you sometimes. All I want is…well, the light…"

I turned my head so he couldn't see my face while I spoke. Sometimes I hated how completely Me I was with him, because that meant it dragged up all the bad parts, too. I

173

contained multitudes, and most of them sucked. "And I hate the world for making you feel like you have to hide," I said.

He considered this, then looked away. When I thought of the trip's magic already being over I got that sinking feeling again, that dread that reinforced just how much I didn't want to reenter the real world, the world without him. This thing sucked, and it was so draining, but I was addicted. He was like a good book that sucked me in so thoroughly, I had serious trouble returning to my life again after turning the last page. I could remember this quote my English teacher had used once, and it had always struck me as so idiotic: "man is free the instance he decides to be." That was just so untrue. We were trapped in ten thousand different ways, and there was nothing we could do about it.

"Okay," he finally said. "We need to lighten up. The hotel is right on the water. You'll love it. But the thing is…"

"Yes?"

He breathed. "You can't come in. With me, I mean. They would notice. I'll get us booked and then text you the room number."

"Okay, whatever."

He took off down the road again, but it felt like we weren't moving at all.

"And Coley?"

"Hm?"

"Don't tell anyone that you know me if they ask, okay?"

At the hotel, it took fifty minutes for him to text me. When he finally did, I speed-walked through the modern, hipster-y lobby and found him in a giant, sleek room on the third floor.

"Sorry," he said after I threw down my bag and tossed him a look, "they wouldn't let me get a room first, they said I was too young, so I had to get them to call the owners."

"Doesn't that defeat the whole purpose? Won't they tell your parents?"

"Ehh, doubt it. The owners didn't really care."

He looked back at his phone. He was in one of "his moods" and it made me want to punch him.

"Should I sleep on the floor again?" I asked after I brushed my teeth. How was it that I liked him more than anything I'd ever liked, and yet he could still make me feel like I was so small, I disappeared? Being next to him sometimes made me feel more alone than I ever had in my life.

"Are you kidding? Get over here, kid."

I came over, and what followed was a kiss – a kiss that made the previous day melt away. *What's a kiss?* I thought as our lips combined into one entity. Why did humans feel the need to press their faces together and swap spit with someone they felt feelings for? A kiss was....

An explosion of forces you never knew existed inside of you, a deep dive into possibilities you never knew to be on the table, a burst of light and color and sound mixed and amplified in ways you'd never experienced, one brave and final step into the breathless and terrifying and undeniable unknown...

A kiss was a kiss. But a ColeyAndNickyVille kiss was something else altogether.

We fell asleep with his legs wrapped all the way around me.

The next day started off strong and only got better. It was one of the best of my life, actually. I kept trying to slow time down, grab it and hold it, but the happier I was, the faster it rushed by. Before we left, though, we hooked up in the shower, and then I found him struggling to get on these chic, buckled boots I'd gotten him at a clearance store. Soon I realized he just couldn't do it – he couldn't bring himself to put them on. He didn't want to.

"Here, let me help-"

"I can't," he said after I knelt at his feet. "I can't do it. They'll see...they'll know..."

"It's okay," I said, looking up at him. "It's *okay*, Nicky."

175

I wrapped my arms around his waist and just held him until his breathing slowed.

"What are we *doing*?" he whispered soon, and he was crying and smiling. I could feel it then, ColeyAndNickyVille, our world, closing in around us, whispering into history. "We'll never come back from this. Everyone knows now. We're exploding each other's lives, that's what we're doing." He kind of smiled. "And the weird thing is…I think I kind of like it."

"Me too," I told his shoes. "I think this could save me."

I just held him like that until the morning opened out.

At noonish we left the hotel and walked down a street lined with brick townhouses, oak branches splintering out above, protecting us from the Southern sun. I got a few *Honesty* shots here and there, but mostly I just let Nicky tell me about his hometown. He knew so much local history, and he spoke about it as people did when they had passion in their veins, quickly and loudly and without stopping. Soon we hit the shops on the main street. I really did love the South, despite it all – the sweet tea, the slowness, the smiling old ladies, the great gnarled oaks standing guard at every corner. The town was so bizarre to me, because with all its brick storefronts and general stores it looked straight out of the 1950s, but it was so full of bohemian college kids from the local art school, it almost felt like a constant pride parade. I saw Nicky looking at two boys holding hands, and as they approached he literally crossed the street to avoid them.

In a district filled with antique shops, one little store was waving a rainbow flag, and the one across the street had a Confederate flag shirt in its window. And it made me think of my life, this senseless collision of old and new, with so many factors rushing me out of the closet and yet so many more pushing me back inside and nailing the door shut. I thought of a news report I'd seen the other day about a cafe that was suing the government to protect their right to deny service to gay couples. The owners said their religious views needed to

176

be "protected from discrimination." The restaurant was doing everything they could to discriminate against gays, and yet *they* needed protection? Bigotry didn't deserve protection.

But still, I'd never been to a place like Savannah, where everyone was so…open. You could see every kind of love here, not just the accepted kind. It almost seemed like it wasn't even in the South, and I *almost* felt free. So did Nicky. One time he even let down his guard and took my hand. It only lasted for half a second, but still: he'd never done that in public before. He smiled like a little kid, and there were not words for how badly I wanted to put him in my pocket and keep him there forever, for how badly I wanted to disappear into his galaxy eyes and remain there always.

Later in the afternoon I used the last of my birthday money to buy him some chic (and, let's face it, pretty gay) clothes from a little boutique, which he reluctantly accepted. Then we tried to get into this pub he liked, but we got turned down for having bad IDs. We ended up hanging out in this park, not really doing much at all, and soon I got all nostalgic, and it struck me: *I'm gonna miss this.* All of it. The way his eyes were flashing, the way my heart felt too big for my body, the way the sun was skittering off the awning of the pub, even the way a squirrel was trying to sneak food from a lady's picnic blanket – from galaxy eyes right down to the laces on my shoes, I knew I was going to miss the fleeting blessing of being young and alive and slipping into love beneath an oak tree. I couldn't have dreamed this into reality any more beautifully than it already existed, and so I took a photograph with my eyes and tucked it away forever.

We were back in our bed by seven PM, staring at each other's faces from six inches away. He grabbed some mini vodka bottles from the fridge and we went to town on them. I'd never felt so content, so safe, so guarded. I ran my finger from his shoulder up past his ear to his forehead and then down to his nose. His skin was oily, but I still shivered at the contact. I would never get used to him. He made a crazy face and I laughed so loud I got worried the neighbors would hear, which only made me laugh harder. I was always laughing when I was around him – he was an umbilical cord to happiness, my own personal connection to the sun.

"Why do you wear that ring?" he asked, playing with my hand. He touched the old, scratched golden band on my right ring finger that I sometimes wore.

"It's my grandpa's," I smiled. "It was his older brother's wedding band that he inherited. He said he wanted me to use it when I proposed. He told me to find a 'nice little gal' and give it to her…I didn't have the heart to tell him the truth."

"And you shouldn't have," he said. "Sounds like it would've just stressed him out."

"True, probably. But ever since then I've just worn it sort of to…punish myself, in a weird way."

"Huh?"

"Well, I'm obviously never going to get married, like he wanted me to, so it became sort of an inside joke. It just represented…everything I thought I'd never have, I guess. Some dreams were for normal people, accepted people. Which was kinda sick for me to wear, now that I think about it…"

I slid it off and started thinking.

"Why won't you get married?" he asked.

"…Um, because Republicans exist?"

He stared at the ring, and I swore I saw something like hope in his eyes.

"Is that…is *marriage* something you want one day?" I asked him. He just shrugged.

"I don't know. That's all a million miles away. But I doubt it. What's the point of starting a family if the world wouldn't accept it? The Supreme Court allowing gay marriage is great, sure, yeah, whatever. But what about *after* marriage? If we tried to buy a house and the owners said no because of who we were, we'd have no legal rights to challenge that. And if we tried to adopt? Bingo, you guessed it, still banned in many states."

"Well…what if we came *here*?" I asked, not meeting his eyes. I realized I'd never even really considered any of this. "Like, together? What if we moved, and tried to be together that way? You'd be into that, right? It's so different here."

He sighed, and I looked at the drapes and started imagining a future, a life, that I'd never let myself imagine before.

"It could be just you and me, you know," I said soon. "We could do it. We could get a place in that garden district you like. I was looking at a magazine when you went to the bathroom, and the apartments here are so cheap and cool. Brick walls, wooden floors, ten-foot ceilings…I could do my blog and you could transfer to Savannah College of Art and Design. Nobody would care about us. You saw how everyone looked at the gay couples today – or should I say, *didn't* look, actually. Nobody even cared."

He kept his eyes away. I would do all this in a nanosecond. It hurt my heart to imagine being that happy.

"That would be nice," he finally said. "But it's not realistic. My family is here."

"What about – in a perfect world? Would you be interested in all of it then, if none of that other stuff existed?"

"Of course. I'd husband the shit out of you," he said, and I smiled. "I've never been as high as I am with you."

I didn't know how to respond, because I felt the same way. But for the first time in my overly-emotional life, I could sense that he was flying even higher than I was. It was then that I sort of realized love could actually feel good. I didn't have to be the Me of the past, the little boy hiding in the closet listening to his parents rage and holler. Love could be nice.

"Ugh, but you could never like me as much as I like you," I sighed. "I'm sure of it. I like you so much it makes me cringe. I overflow for you. It's all too much, really."

"Then you don't see what I see. I don't even know how to explain it."

"Try, then."

He bit that beautiful lip. "You just feel like home, and you make my eyes burn. You're all of the good in me, and none of the bad. I like you so much it makes me feel like someone else." He swallowed. "And I kind of admire you."

"*What?*"

"I do. It's almost like you're the person I'd be if I was a little…braver. You just are who you are, and you don't really try to hide it – well, not nearly as hard as I do, at least. You wear what you want to wear, you do what you want to do, you act just as nerdy and…well, *soft*, as you want to act. I never had that courage. And still don't." He swallowed. "Which brings me to another question – why do you deal with me? We both know I treat you like garbage sometimes. Why are you still here?"

Suddenly my brain filled in what my lips couldn't say. *Because I see galaxies in your eyes, and I want to get old and wrinkly with you, and my life wasn't a life before I met you, and the thought of ever losing you and having to go back to that makes me wanna die, and you're my whole world and I just wanna be alive with you.*

"Because I don't want you to become a what if," I said instead.

"Huh?"

"I just don't want to look back and regret you. This could be so much better than it is now, only if…if you could be open about certain…" I sighed. "If the world wasn't such a shitty place that was so against kids like us."

"Your legs," he said.

"What?"

"You are lying as far from me as you can, with your legs pointing away, because you're embarrassed deep inside. Don't preach to me when you're two miles deep in the closet, yourself. You keep acting like everything's changing, but it's not. You're still just as afraid as you were in the beginning. I see it on and off, every day."

I set my jaw. "No, *you* don't preach to *me*. I hid a raging dick addiction for nineteen years and counting, *in the South*, no less. Don't talk to me about hiding shit. My whole life has been carried out in hiding. Just like yours has."

He sighed again, and I reached over and pulled him closer as my temper receded. "Thank God we just had some alcohol," I laughed, and then I stared at him and thought about forever. The human brain wasn't even built to understand the concept of forever, in my opinion. Things like eternity and infinity boggled our minds and let us know how small we really were. But in this moment, I understood forever, or a glimpse of it at least. Because I knew with certainty that I would have happily spent my forever with him, the version of him he was right then. Even with everything that came along with it.

He drank another vodka bottle, and I did too. We rolled closer, so close I could smell his every breath.

"Do you...do you *love* me, Coley?" he asked out of nowhere. Suddenly the Atlantic Ocean sloshed around in my brain, mixing in with all of the stars in the Georgia sky. I was full and confused and dizzy and I was in love. But I couldn't say it. Society had conditioned me not to. And besides, I wasn't even really sure if I knew what "love" even *meant*. All I knew for sure was that I didn't feel like me anymore – I felt like *us* – and that seemed like a good enough definition for now.

"I think you know what I love," I said, giddiness making my voice all weird and shaky, like it could escape from me if I didn't hold it tightly enough. "It's obvious enough already."

"That's not an answer."

"Hmm. I could say yes, but that wouldn't do. This thing feels like...more than yes."

"Well tell me what this thing is, then," Nicky said, sounding almost nervous. "And I don't want the Hallmark answers, either. Hallmark was never us. Don't give me the clichés. Don't tell me I mean the world to you."

"Okay," I said, a smile exploding onto my face. "You mean the moon to me, then."

For a few seconds there was just silence. "Okay," Nicky finally said. "I'll take the moon."

I clutched his chest, listening to – and feeling – his chest rise, fall. Fall, rise. Soon his fingers were exploring places they'd still never explored before. I sighed, moaned, and let the moonlight take me somewhere else...

181

When we were done, he grabbed a pillow, locked the door, and got in bed again. "This is so weird," he said as he wrapped his body around mine, even through the bed was tiny. "I've never even liked being touched, much less being in the same bed as someone. But now I never wanna sleep alone again."

"Agreed," I smiled. "I've never felt so… easy. With *anyone*."

He looked at me then, unleashed everything within those galaxy eyes, and I wanted to curse him for the power he held on me. I liked him so much, and it made me feel like I was nothing. For some reason he smiled. His eyes fully locked with mine, and I drowned in them. That was odd. I always thought you could only drown in water, never humans.

With some effort, I finally tore my eyes away from his stupefying perfection.

"For the record, I like you, Coley," he said. "Very much. I like the way your eyes explode when you look at me and I like the way you bite your pinkie when you're scared and I like the way your hair is the color of honey set on fire. More than anything I like this little world that happens around us whenever we're alone. Sometimes I think I could live in that world forever." I fell to pieces. "But I still don't know how to do this, either…I keep looking down, wondering what would happen if we fell, if-"

"Don't look down, then," I said. "Nothing down there matters." I inched closer. He backed up. "Nicky, come on. Don't go into your faraway mood again. Stay here, with me. I've been by myself for way too long, and…"

He turned his head, but he was still so beautiful in the winterglow. "Why do you always say my name when you talk to me? Nobody does that."

"I do, Nicky. Nicky, Nicky, Nicky." I laughed a little, lovedrunk. "Sorry, Nicky, for happening to love your name, Nicky. I'll have to thank your mother for choosing it. *Nicky*."

And that wasn't all I loved. But that was *crazy*, I reminded myself as my shoulders slipped a little. He'd already said it: we would never work out, even if he made me feel all

182

colorful and dreamy. And we both knew I'd probably never get to sit and talk to his mom, or go around with him in public, and be with him in a real, genuine way. He'd never let me into his life, his family, that world he kept inside his eyes. That just wasn't in the cards for me. For us...

I felt his eyes on me as the truth hit. I knew he wanted to take me in his arms, but he couldn't. I stared at his hair, kissed by the sun, and suddenly I didn't care about the fact that his body was totally pointed away from me again. There were worse things in the world. I'd dealt with so many shitty things before, and now none of them mattered. Because now I came to Nicky, a boy remade. I didn't have to hide here in this hidden room at the end of the world. Now that my newly-lightened life contained him, music sounded better. The breeze smelled fresher. Food tasted better. My skull felt lighter. Babies in strollers were things I noticed instead of glancing past. Everything had changed, and it was that simple, that groundbreaking.

I heard a sniffle. "Why are you crying?" I asked him, and he hid his face.

"Because I don't...I don't know how to love," he said. "My father has never told me he loved me, not once. Ever. I don't even know why that's coming to mind, but it is, and..."

"Oh, God, come here."

I hugged my boy, and I knew I couldn't deny it then: I loved this person. More than anything, really. I loved him because he'd opened up a new world for me and because his face looked like a song and his hands moved like the movies and his eyes were sad like violins and victorious like saxophones. I loved him because he saw all the brightest part of me and noticed things in me I couldn't admit to myself and actually believed I might be somebody in this life. But I couldn't say it. Up to this point, this thing had been all about sneaking around the truth, hiding the facts and tiptoeing around everything so we could carry on with our whole sad charade of being "straight." The weird thing about words was that once released, you could never get them back. This was the point of no return, and if I spoke now, pivoted now, there would be no coming back. But I had never known anything in his neighborhood, and a love like this deserved words.

"You were totally right earlier – it *shouldn't* be like this. I just don't want to put you through this," he said, "and maybe we should just-"

"I love you, Nicky."

He looked at me, eyes wide, as my body spun in his warm love. "Coley?"

Sometimes you couldn't pinpoint the exact moment you realized you were in love with someone. Your feelings gradually deepened and changed and transformed and took root until one day you turned around and realized your life has bent itself around someone, and you'd never even noticed it. But this was different. This was no slow burn. Right there, right then, in Savannah, Georgia, I knew. No eureka moment needed: I was in love with Nicky Flores. Maybe I always had been, ever since the moment my mortal eyes had first made contact with his galaxy ones.

"I love you," I said, as something in me seemed to speed up, "and I know the world is stacked against us and everything, and I knew we'd probably get written off by a lot of society if we walked down the street hand-in-hand right now, and I know this is gonna be the hardest thing either of us have ever done, and I love you, and I just…"

He opened his mouth. Closed it. Then he stood up. So did I. He smiled. He was glowing, shimmering, incandescent. And he was mine. This boy was mine.

Tomorrow, today would be yesterday. We were all stories in the end, and one day soon we would be in the past to somebody from the future. All of these things would go away and we would merely be memories that people told stories about. But before that happened, I wanted to make us a memory worth sharing, not hiding. So I got closer to him, swept by something I couldn't quite place, and put a hand on his chest. He looked down, terror in his galaxy eyes, but he didn't flinch this time. I moved it slowly up past his nipples and then to his neck, and he still didn't wince. I heard guitars, pianos, orchestras, screaming choirs, angels, all those things that are supposed to accompany love. Every cliché in the world suddenly made sense to me now – clichés were made for this. Even if they ripped me apart.

What's in a label? I thought as I leaned closer to his mouth. Gay, bi, lesbian, closeted, out: all of it was garbage in the end, all meant to slap names on us and box into corners and limit us. I knew the world would toss many of those labels at us, including many other ones, like *fag* and *queer* and *cock licker* and so many more, but I didn't want to waste any more time wondering if those people were right. Because this right here, *this* was right, even if it couldn't leave the four walls around us. I loved Nicky Flores and I wanted to build my life around him, and a love like that was never wrong. It was just magnificent.

I wrapped him up in me and kissed him. Life could be so beautiful if you let it be. He didn't fight this time. He relaxed, and soon I was supporting his weight. Together we just stood. The world had always moved past people like us – it had always rushed by, busy and hurried and self-important like so many rude New Yorkers, bumping us out of the way to remind us we did not belong, that we were on the outside. But for the first time, all that didn't matter. We were islands in the stream of a humanity that had shunned us. Suddenly, beautifully, we were standing still. Together.

"So what now?" he asked as I held him. Shivering, I locked my hands around his back and held him even tighter. I'd never wanted to touch so much of the same person at one time before – all my flesh screamed to be pressed against his, for every second, every minute, maybe always. I had no idea two humans could have so much affection flow through them – my skin was breathing into his, two as one. I'd been right all along. We were twins.

"Now," I said, "we-"

Nicky's phone suddenly lit up, and he reached down and inhaled.

It was sister.

Her friend had seen us.

And she was demanding to know why he'd come to Savannah without telling her.

13

Next day. We slept until noon. Then it was all gross hotel coffee. Semi-awkward silences. Sex after the silence got old. After he fell back asleep, I walked into his bathroom and knew again that I loved him, because his clothes were all over the floor and his body wash was expensive. I knew I loved him not because of these things, but because I *wondered* about these things, noticed these things. I noticed everything. I was like an overweight kid who'd been dieting for six months and had just stumbled into a donut shop for the first time. And I wanted to know so much more. Everything, really.

Lazily, we walked to a candy store on the river, and I took a picture of him on one of Savannah's famously-steep stone staircases leading down to the river walk. In the store, he was so cute – he got as excited as any child as he stared at the chocolate machines and candied apples and rows and rows of pralines, Savannah's specialty, a mouth-watering food made of melted sugar and pecans. Then we visited *my* heaven, a cool old bookshop with brick walls and a huge fireplace.

"Do you think we were supposed to meet?" he asked out of nowhere on the walk back to the hotel. Then he looked at me like I was a secret and nobody in the world knew the answer but him. It made me smile a smile that felt too big to be contained by one face.

"I don't know," I said. "But I do think I was meant to love you."

And then…then the other thing. When I finished showering that evening, I found him on the phone with his sister, watching me. When he stared at me like that I felt naked, stripped, like nobody had ever seen so much of me at one time, not even close. I was always trying to present him with the best version of me, as if he might realize at any second what a dud I was and run for Montana. When he hung up, he came over to me. He took the boy who was glared at, stared at, snickered at, and swallowed him into his arms, made him his own. He was into me, and it was a revolution.

"Is she still insisting?" I asked.

"Yep."

"And we have no choice?"

"Nope. Not really. Her best friend saw us walking by that restaurant, and she's saying I have to bring you. She doesn't understand why I didn't want to."

"And why are you *this* worried?" I asked. "I still don't get it."

I felt him tense up against me. "Because she's my father's daughter, and she makes him look like the Dalai Lama."

I spent an hour or two dressing him up in some of the clothes I'd gotten him, and for some reason I had more fun doing it than I'd ever had doing anything in my life. He was my fantasy – my own personal male model to style (and boss around.) I'd never even *told* anyone about my love of fashion before, much less messed with clothes in their presence. And the best thing was that he didn't care – he just acted like fashion was a detail about me, which it was, I was learning more and more every day. He looked hot as shit in anything I put him in, too, which was the best part of all. I could remember crying in my bed alone as a little kid, praying for a friend I could share all this stuff with. Now I got to share it with my *best* friend, whose body I also got to touch in the shower sometimes, too. Life was a dream.

After I dressed Nicky, I threw on some random outfit. Then I remarked that I was going to throw away an ugly old T-shirt that'd fallen on the floor, since I had no more space in my suitcase.

"Don't," he said, throwing up a hand, genuine concern in his eyes. I paused, holding the shirt.

"Um…why?"

He bit his lip. "Because it's what you were wearing the day I met you."

Just before nine, we finally met Nicky's sister and her friends in the back garden of a restaurant downtown – and Victoria

Elizabeth Yarelis Santos Flores was awful. (I peeped her ID on the table just to creep on her.) I didn't know what I'd been expecting, but it wasn't this. Judging by the family pictures I'd seen, she had all of Mrs. Flores' imperiousness and none of her warmth. I knew her type the second I put eyes on her: she was one of the popular girls, the tennis girls, with hair the color of champagne and eyes like galaxies. She'd had her life handed to her on a tray, and she had the posture to show for it. She was *almost* beautiful, in a way that was all sharp edges and icy glares, and when she looked at me, I could tell she expected an introduction. Because who *wouldn't* want to be introduced to her? I saw her take in my tight-ish jeans and then flicker over to her brother for a second, but only a second. She recovered immediately, but it was *too* quick.

It was then that I suspected she knew about us.

He looked away, the overhead Christmas lights shining in his eyes. He was a coward, and still I loved this coward of mine. "Hey, Toria. This is…my friend," he said, and then went silent again. *Ouch.* I'd never expected how bad it made me feel to be his secret. This felt different from all the other times – this was *family*. Here Victoria was, the closest person in the world to him, probably, and I was being kept hidden right in front of her. It made me feel like less than nothing, a negative integer. But I swallowed it down.

Victoria stared me down with those luxurious snake eyes. "Okay, Friend. Hi, Friend. Tell me, what were your parents smoking when they decided to name you Friend? This was the 90s, so I'm gonna guess crack rocks?"

I didn't even know what to say, but thankfully Nicky smoothed things over for me. She did glance at me several times while I made accidental magic eyes at him, but after a while I just stopped caring. She knew. She had to, right?

But seeing him through the eyes of his sister was still a revelation. Here, he wasn't a wounded, beautiful, autonomous head case – he was someone's little brother. She was so proud of him, so fussy with him, and seeing him through her eyes was the cutest thing I'd ever known. It made me want to grab hold of him and hold on for a long time – forever, probably. It also reminded me of how young he was. He acted totally different around her, and even his body language changed – his shoulders dropped a bit, his head lowered, and he deferred to her in every way. How had I forgotten that he was only a teenager?

All this also made me sad, partly because I had never had that "family" thing for myself. I felt so guilty sometimes for banishing my mom, but I still couldn't let her in. I was embarrassed of everything she'd done, but at the end of the day…I still *wanted* to love her. I wanted to forgive her. I just didn't know how.

Eventually Victoria fell in with her other friends at the next table. Nicky and I ordered another round of shots, and soon we were somewhere between drunk and wasted. Alcohol was the only thing that ever cooled the hot anxiety of our being seen in public together, but this was too much. Sober Me knew we were getting too public, but Drunk Me didn't give a shit.

A straight couple in the corner in the back was being totally over the top, making out and whispering loudly about their love, and Nicky and I kept sharing disgusted glances about it. Then we started this game where we'd try to out-cheese each other, just to make fun of them. We'd always done it, on and off, actually, because that's what this generation was about, wasn't it? Surpassing the Joneses?

"The Earth is four billion years old, and yet I was lucky enough to be alive at the same time as you," I said in a dramatic but quiet voice, so nobody would hear. "Everything you do amazes me."

"No I don't!" he said with mock theatricality. "I amaze nobody!"

"Bet me."

He leaned closer. "My turn. I can't feel my face when I come across your smell."

Suddenly it didn't feel like a game anymore. "Well I can't feel my body when I see you."

"Good, then. I don't have a face, you don't have a body. Even Stevens. We're like a cubist painting – a regular

190

Picasso. Your turn," he said, and I scooted closer, too. This wasn't hard, as I was drawn into him naturally all the time, anyway.

"You're like my favorite book. I wish I could go back to the first page and read you all over again, just to enjoy you twice."

"Not bad," he said. "Very meta. A book-related quote about love, and books, coming from a book lover who is in love."

"Hey, who said I was in love?"

He leaned forward, took a breath, bit his lip. "Your eyes did."

I just stared at him, my shoulders rising. It was the strangest thing – he just made me feel like there was more of me.

"I really like you," I heard myself say, and I sort of swayed in my seat a bit, caught off guard by the intensity of the emotions bursting up within me. "You made me like my life, and that is so weird."

"Prove it," he smiled, but I was sick of the words, I was sick of the declarations – they would never be able to convey how much I liked him, how proud I was of him, how much it turned me on just to *freaking call this beautiful creature mine.* So I just stared at him again. I didn't know how to say what I needed to say, that he was everything and more to me, that he shined like nothing else did, that if the world was sinking into the Atlantic I would still believe in him. I had not seen enough of the world, nor accessed enough of myself, to be able to really put all that into words, not again. So I just reached over and rubbed him through his pants instead.

"God, I want you," he whispered, not even caring if Victoria was looking anymore.

"Same here," I whispered, the alcohol hitting me in shimmery waves. "It's all so crazy. Your eyes look like disco balls and you make me feel insane."

He smiled that smile of his that burned my stomach, overloading me with longing. He scooted even closer so nobody would see, then traced a line down my body. "First, I'll go here, and then I'll go…"

And that's when I looked over and realized his sister was staring right at us.

I lurched my eyes away like they'd landed on a hot plate. I tried to stay calm, like I *hadn't* just accidentally outed the boy I was starting to love, but my face felt hot and red and twitchy. The next time I glanced over, she was glaring at me like I'd killed a puppy. And she wouldn't stop.

Shit shit *shit*. I'd blown it. The one chance to impress his family, to fall into the fray – that was done. I just couldn't win in this game of grace. Never could.

I fled to the bathroom, splashing cold water on my face to punish myself. On the way back, Victoria passed me in the hallway, making me absolutely panic. First she just stared at me, not so much daggers in her eyes as heavy artillery. Then she walked closer.

"Be careful with this," she said, shoving me in the shoulder a little. I stopped moving. She was wasted, and it terrified me.

"With…*what*?"

"You know what. You like him, don't you?" she asked, and I was shocked into silence. "What's going on? Why does he look so different? Why is he so happy and smiley and stuff? And why aren't I allowed to tell my mom that he's here?"

I stared down at her shoulder, which was bony like Nicky's. "This really isn't my issue to talk about, but I don't think he wants her to know," I finally said. "That he's here, I mean. He's his own person…"

She sniffled and then started crying right there in the hall. I felt her breath on my face, and it smelled like cinnamon whiskey. This was bad. Really bad. I had to protect Nicky, but I didn't know how.

"I knew it," she said to nobody as she wiped her smudged eyes. "I knew it I knew it I knew it…you're doing something with him," she accused, throwing me another hateful glance.

192

"No," I said. "No. He's…he's my friend." Then my temper took me away again. "And even if we were…doing *that*, which we're not, I don't know if that'd be any of your business."

She composed herself and then looked me up and down like a bad girl out of some '80s movie. Something was flimsy in it, though – more than anything, she just looked scared. Desperate. Nicky was the showpiece of her family, and he was messing around with guys. And that's when I realized I was afraid of this girl, truly scared of her. Because she wasn't necessarily evil or out for blood or anything, she was worse: she was just a misguided girl trying to protect someone she loved. Some of the worst things of my life had come from uninformed people thinking they were trying to do the right thing and help me. Nicky was clearly the pride and joy of the Flores name, and if Victoria knew about us and thought ending us would be in her little brother's best interests, she could do anything…she could tell his parents, she could tell his friends, she could hold it over his head and use it to drive me away and take away everything I wanted…

"He's my baby brother," she said very softly. "His business is mine."

And then she did the scariest thing of all: she walked away.

14

I was silent for the rest of the night, and I knew Nicky could tell something had gone wrong. I'd been so stupid to think we could do this. We were horrified of ourselves, of each other, of the world, of our love. As soon as we got back to the hotel I broke down and told him everything. His eyes filled up with something between panic and sadness, just like I knew they would, and then he left.

"Where are you going?"

"Ubering to her townhouse," he said over his shoulder as he disappeared.

I slept alone that night. It was cold and lonely like January or heartbreak. And soon my dreams took me back…

After my parents' marriage fell apart when I was a teenager, a concerned family friend brought me to Miss Irene, a hippy-dippy therapist from my church who smelled like cheap incense and whose suburban home was filled with tacky travel paintings from moderately expensive home-décor stores. What she told me struck fear into my heart forever.

"So, there's one thing I want you to remember," she'd said after our awkward introductions, a terrible print of a Venice sunset lording from over her left shoulder. "You have witnessed dysfunction all your life, and when you grow up, you are going to chase after it. You won't even know it, not on the surface at least, but you will. You'll search for people to fix, because that's what you know – you thrive on chaos, even if you don't know it yet, and you're going to try to replicate your childhood. So find a sane person with no issues and stick with them. If you run after destroyed people, all you'll do is destroy yourself in the process, too. You'll undo each other. And I know you think I don't know what I'm talking about," she said after a minute. "I know your family, though, and beyond that, I've seen all this myself. My first husband, Todd? Bipolar and borderline personality disorder. Crazier than a bat straight out of Satan's asshole. And one day, I was hiding under the kitchen table while he threw various kitchen utensils at me, one after the other, including a Panini maker, and it hit me: my life didn't have to be like this."

"So you left?"

She lit a Virginia Slim and shook her head. "No. I wish. I stayed with him for three more years until I found him hanging from a laundry pipe in the attic. He killed himself during a low in his mania cycle." Her eyes filled up with ghosts. "I could've gotten out of there earlier, though. I could've listened to the bells and whistles before they became Panini makers flying at my face and then bodies hanging in my house. But I didn't. I didn't love myself enough to remove myself from the pain I was still chasing from my childhood. Everyone thinks they can find a broken person and love them back together, when in the end, both are usually casualties of the broken one's implosion."

Then she fidgeted for a minute and then told me never to confuse the two, to confuse love with pain. She said that *dependence* was seeking out something from someone, while *love*, on the other hand, was offering someone something because you were already full. "In the end," she'd told me, her cigarette burning low, "the best gift you can ever give the people around you is your own happiness, because you can never be there for anyone else if you're gone, yourself. So take care of yourself. Make sure you find some good love, and not the bad stuff. Or else you'll be caught up in this cycle for the rest of your life."

Looking back, I recognized Nicky in this situation immediately. We were both empty and broken, and our assault on each other was just sinking us deeper into misery and dependency. We were suffering together and we didn't know why. But maybe this was it. Maybe he was the pain I was chasing.

When I woke up I thought of Nicky, beautiful and essentially broken. He was supposed to be the big, strong man, the hero, the dream boy. But this was the truth: he was terrified, running, hiding, desperate to conceal himself from a punishing world, all because he was scared. He was a coward, and I understood that cowardice better than he would ever know. Because I was just as scared. We weren't up against the world, we were just up against the worst ten percent of it, the ten percent that wouldn't change, and that ten percent was so loud and hateful and effective, they'd maybe already won.

But still, I knew I didn't want the sanity anyway. Sanity bored me. Here was Nicky, my Panini maker, telling me at every turn that he was broken, that he was crazy, and it just made me want to love him harder. And I guessed that was the problem, wasn't it? I wanted to run to him, to have him take me in with open arms, hold me until my world wasn't broken open anymore. Even though he was the one breaking it.

And this was when I knew I loved Nicky Flores, really *loved* him: because he was awful for me, poison in my veins. I guess I officially couldn't tell the difference between love and pain anymore. I'd probably always looked for poisoned love – I'd always been drawn to the ones with the empty eyes and the aggressive attitudes and the vacant hearts. I was always just chasing heartbreak. My family had made my bed with their chaos and now I was forcing myself to sleep in it forever. My childhood was over and now I'd become my destiny. I was already Me, incurably.

Or was I? Could I still change? Did I really love Nicky, or did I just *need* to love him? Could I still walk away from this toxic shit-storm of a relationship, if I got strong enough? And did I even *want* to?

I guessed it all came down to this: was Nicky Flores really a tortured, damaged creature doing everything he could to overcome his issues and love me in the way I deserved, or was he just a dickhead?

My Panini maker showed up at around ten in the morning.

"So how was it?" I asked him as he started gathering his things. He was blank, moodless, all grey. And I knew what it meant: he'd shut down. He was a million miles away again, and maybe he wasn't coming back this time.

"Eh. Could've been worse. Could've been better. I think I contained it, though. For now."

196

"What does that mean? Tell me."

He stopped. "Well, I denied it all."

"*Everything*?

I watched him. He looked dead.

"Everything," he nodded. "I'm sorry, but I had to. It was basically an ultimatum-type situation."

I just stared at him.

"Stop whatever this is," he said in an approximation of Victoria's cut-glass voice, "or I tell Mom and Dad what I suspect, and all hell breaks loose."

"She…she *blackmailed* you?"

His eyes revealed nothing. He turned and headed for the bathroom.

"No," I said, following him. "*No*. Don't just walk away from this. All you do is walk away. Why do you keep walking?"

"I think we should take a break," he said, so casually I wanted to die. "This is moving too fast. I'm not sure I'm okay with it."

I wanted to cry right there. In the beginning I'd wanted an epic love story out of this. I'd wanted epic love, in epic settings, under epic conditions. Because that was the crazy thing about Nicky – he made the epic seem possible. But this was all *so* not epic, and it was all *so* far below the grand scale I'd wanted us to love on. We weren't on the Golden Gate Bridge at sunset, or atop the Empire State Building, or in any other place I used to read about in my books. This was our ending: we were alone, in the dark, in a stupid hotel room.

"Don't you say that," I said. "Stop. When are you going to let me into your life? When is this going to stop? The breakups, the hiding…I can't take it. Your family doesn't own you!" I stopped and swallowed, my voice falling into my throat. "How can you hold back the one thing you know I want? How are you so…*cruel*?"

He stopped, staring at nothing. "The world made me like this, Coley. It messed me up real good."

"No it didn't, it made you a coward."

He turned around. "*I'm* the coward?"

197

"We both are, okay? Go out and be a bro and deny me in public again. You're living inside a pile of lies and you don't even realize it." I looked at the boy I wanted to grow into a man with. "You're never gonna love me like I love you, are you? I just wanna be close to you. But I can't. You won't let me."

He stared blankly at me, and that's when I knew he was lying about something. "Nicky," I said, "tell me the story, the *whole* story, right now."

He sighed. "Ugh. I guess it's time." He tossed his wallet down on the bed. "If I date you, this wallet will be useless."

"Excuse me?"

"When my dad caught me watching gay porn when I was younger, he gave me an ultimatum, in a way. Get over this 'problem,' as he called it, train yourself to change your thinking so you can be accepted at church and in society, and you can keep your trust fund. But if I ended up 'becoming' gay, as he put it, he'd keep every last cent of my inheritance from me."

I didn't even know what to say. "What the hell kind of ultimatum is that?"

He shrugged. "So I had no choice. I never did. I can't plunge myself into student loan debt for the rest of my life just because of this."

He turned, considered me. Opened his mouth. Closed it again. And I knew what it meant. Nicky was gone. He had flown away.

But I still didn't want to accept it. We were two boys who liked each other with our whole lives opening out in front of us. There was no reason to shut that down.

The seal broke inside me, and I punched the dresser. "You know what? Screw you, then. Screw this. I'm the addict and you're the pipe and I can't put you down. But I hate you. I'm done living in your nightmare. I need you like I need water in my lungs."

I knew we were childish. I knew we were melodramatic. But I couldn't turn this off. Falling in love with

198

him was the stupidest thing I'd ever done, and I never wanted to go back.

I went to the bathroom, splashed water on my face. When I walked back in, his eyes were glassy. I just sighed.

"I'm sorry," I said soon. "I am. I like you too much, Nicky. If you were a book, I would read every chapter twice and then tuck you into bed next to me. And the thing is...I'm afraid you wouldn't even pick me up if you passed me in a bookstore. If you ever knew how much I really needed you, you'd delete me like a typo. And now it's too late."

"Don't think like that," he said, avoiding my eyes. "And I feel the same way. You're so hard to read – half the time I don't even know how you feel."

"What?"

"You disappear all the time. Into your eyes. Like your dad used to."

I stared at him, unable to comprehend how he thought things like this. "Nicky, why don't you get it? Every time I go dark, every time my eyes glaze over, I'm not mad at you – I'm mad at *me*. I'm looking at you and thinking, shit, this boy is perfect, and my face is asymmetrical and my teeth aren't totally straight and I do this weird thing with my arm when I laugh and, oh God, I will never measure up to this boy in any way, shape or form. But that's on *me*. It's my past's fault that I hate myself, not yours." And that was the funny thing, wasn't it? The more I worried about him losing interest, the more I pushed him away.

"Stop," he said. "Don't be stupid. I need you, too. No matter what happens."

"Not like this."

We listened to nothing. It was starting to dawn on me that this would never change – he would always be too afraid. "Hasn't it ever occurred to you to be alive?" I asked him.

"We can't go on like this," he responded, and the worst thing was that I knew it, too. He was still that scared little boy, rattled senseless from the vision of his gay neighbor's body. Whenever he looked at me, that dead body was probably all he saw. "It's not working. I'm just no good. I'm gonna break one day, just collapse like a building, and you don't deserve to get injured by the shards. And it's not just me. Savannah has been great," he said, in a formal, faraway voice that sounded nothing like the Nicky I knew from ColeyAndNickyVille, "but it's not reality. Tomorrow we're going back home, to the real world, the same one we started out in, and what then? We thought Victoria was bad, we thought my friend seeing us at the gas station was bad – it's just going to get worse. Next week it'll be something, and then next month it'll be something else, something worse. We can't run and hide forever. I would do anything in the world to change all this, but I can't. I'm just one person."

I looked out of the window at a world that already seemed darker. "Oh, stop blaming it on all that. I'm perfectly happy with you exactly how you are. Stop blaming it on anything other than your fear. Look at what we're up against. Walk outside with me."

He fidgeted, his eyes darting around like balls on a pool table. "Well, it's kinda bright outside, and my friend's grandma lives close by, and-"

"Exactly. We can't walk down the street, Nicky. *We literally can't walk down the street.* You'll only ever love me with the lights off."

He stayed silent, and in that moment I realized I knew he would never turn the lights on. So I closed my eyes and started to imagine a world without him. I had to accept it and get it into my head: he was too weak for this. Maybe we weren't meant to collide: maybe we were meant to explode. Maybe we were fundamentally incompatible, and by staying together we were just delaying heartbreak. I couldn't deal with this, but I was going to have to *pretend* to, and then save all the falling apart for later. Because if I was going to have to give him up, I wanted to do it now. I had to. Heaven contained him, and if I couldn't have this forever, I didn't want it at all. I was at a high water mark, and I would not be strong enough to do this in the future, not after I'd rolled even deeper into him. I just needed five more beautiful minutes of this.

The most terrifying thing about love was that it ended. My parents' pathetic marriage had proved that. Maybe everything beautiful fell to pieces. My parents had been consumed by each other in the beginning – you could see their love in the pictures, so young and rosy-cheeked – and all it did was burn them up. Maybe we'd been kidding ourselves all this time. Death was in the stars for us. He wouldn't accept me, so no point in running from it now. We would never be out of the woods, and there would always be monsters around every corner. There would forever be bigoted Southerners and frowning parents and a society that told us we were dirty and sinful and doomed to hell, even while it dangled its flimsy "acceptance" in front of us like carrots to a horse. This "relationship" was falling apart, dead on arrival, and maybe I just needed to escape this burning house before the roof caved in.

"I'm sorry," he said again. "But we're getting older…the deeper I get with you, the more I see the other route fading away. The normal route, or whatever. It's starting to become an either/or thing. And I know Victoria knew that."

For some reason I laughed. "Wait…*what*? Are you saying you're actually listening to them, and you think you'll become…*straight*?"

He shrugged again. "I see two roads. One is you. But the other is…normality. Acceptance. My parents were right – no girl wants a guy who's been with guys, and if we get any more serious, if any more people find out, I'd be done. And there's more, too. I see two roles for gay guys in this country – one is the tank-top-wearing fairy, the glitter-covered queen hopping around on a Pride float and throwing rainbow-colored condoms at passing children or something. You know, the kind that takes out their anger on the world by forcing everyone to accept them at gunpoint. *'Whoever doesn't stand and applaud for my tutu is a bigot who deserves jail!'* Yeah, that's not me. The 'other gay guy' they want you to be is the one who doesn't even acknowledge his gayness – the strapping dude in the business suit who's forced to keep his personal life private to gain acceptance. That's not me, either.

I'm just…me, a dude with a touch of gay. But the world hasn't made space for that person yet. White American society says to either be the freak on the fringes and flaunt it, or if you want to come sit at our table and have a piece of our pie, act like us and dress like us and become like us. You have to choose, and I don't want to choose."

"Nicky," I said, in shock, "you're so wrong. How can you be so wrong? You can be whoever you want to be. Fuck the world's perception."

"Well what if I end up wanting to marry a woman and not a man?"

"Um, I don't see that happening. You've never once showed a sign of wanting that."

"Well, what if I wake up one day and that changes?"

Anger spiked in me again. "Okay, and how do you think you're going to make this change? Jesus camp?"

"A lot of people pray about a lot of things," he said as his eyes got faraway again. "My grandma has stomach cancer, and she started praying every night about it. Pretty soon the tumors shrank and she was as healthy as a-"

"This isn't your grandma, Nicky," I scoffed. "I mean, have you lost your *mind*? You really believe you're going to…pray away your gay, or something?"

He sort of nodded, true belief shining in his eyes, and that's when my anger sifted out of me and became replaced by something else: pity. This boy was so desperate, he was chasing any lie he could find.

"You're scared," I said, quieter. "Of this. Of love. Of happiness. Of what could happen if you let go of the fear. But it's understandable. Just stop listening to them. They don't matter. We matter. So much…"

He shrugged and cried and pretended to be interested in putting shirts into his suitcase. "I'm gonna try the other road, Coley. I hate the way my life is, and I just want things to be easy."

"Oh, Nicky."

Now the erratic past few weeks made total sense – he'd been pulling himself away, in *every* way, slowly but surely. In his eyes, I'd brought him over to the dark side, and he resented me for it. Suddenly I felt like such a pathetic fool – how could I have missed the signs? Even I couldn't deny that things hadn't been working out for us – the only thing we had in common in the world was love – but still, I'd had no idea he'd been creating an exit strategy all along. All this Jesus stuff was insane, though. How could he pray to these bad relics? How could he willingly drink this poison? "Can I hug you?" I asked him. He looked away, tears falling from his cheek.

"Why? And prolong the inevitable? This isn't easy for me either. It's the hardest thing I've ever done, actually. I love you too much and it scares me."

I turned and took the deepest breath of my life. "Okay," I said. "It's over. Okay."

"Okay?"

"Yeah. But I don't want anyone after this, ever. If I can't have this, I don't want anyone."

"Coley?" he asked as the silence closed in.

"Yeah?"

"Will you just lay with me? In our little world? Until we have to go back to the real one?"

I closed my eyes as the tears came. "You don't even have to ask."

He stopped packing for good. We lay down together, holding hands, passing a bottle of pink wine back and forth one last time. He'd made his decision and I had to live with it, but that didn't mean I couldn't enjoy him for these last few minutes. I looked at him, even though he made me want to close my eyes and sigh. If he ever fell out of love with me, it would prove my father right, bring up all my oldest and most feared monsters, and I would not recover. So this was a pre-breakup. If he wasn't going to love me forever, I didn't want to love him at all. We were a ship in a bottle, and I was going to put us up on a shelf before we broke, freeze the memories in place for the long haul. Now we would be beautiful and young and in love in my memory forever. There was no other option for us. Just ask Nicky.

"So it's over," I said into his shoulder. "Wow." I didn't even want to breathe, I was so scared of ruining the last lingering magic. And that's what Nicky was – that's what this world we'd created was. Our beautiful magical little secret. Again, he reminded me of my books. When I loved a book, I wanted to tell the whole world about it. But when I LOVED a book, when a book got into my bones and rearranged them, I wanted to hide it and keep it my own little secret forever. And he was my new favorite book. My secret.

"Will you remember me?" he asked, sounding so heartbroken it broke mine too. How could I be mad at this? He was delusional.

"Ugh, Nicky. Of course I will." I swallowed. "I was living in literature before you. It's like you…stepped off a page and showed me love didn't just exist in books. Shit, you yanked the dreams right out of my skull and made them real – I'm grateful, even if you've ruined books forever." I smiled. I may have let go of tomorrow, but that didn't mean I couldn't hold onto today with everything in me. "Things'll change, obviously. They've got to. That's how this place works, I think. But I won't forget you. Even when we're vintage."

This stupid perfect boy. We loved each other too much, so much that the love had been interconnected with the need irreparably. Now that we couldn't tell what was what, I guessed it had to end. I knew there were so many more things I could do to try to keep him – throw myself at his feet, cry and beg and plead, but part of me knew it'd be worthless. His mind had been pushed along to a destination by his family and friends and culture. I just hoped he would survive the cold nights that were probably about to come.

Someone walked by with their dog outside, and even though they could not see us, could not even hear us over the rustle of the wind in the oaks outside, he pulled away a little. So did I. Some battles were unbeatable.

"Just for the record," he asked soon, "how did you really feel, all along?"

I stared at the generic TV stand, so ashamed I could die. "I think you might be the love of my life," I said. "You grew me up."

"Same," he nodded. "If my world caught on fire, you're probably the only thing I would reach for."

"I think I love you beyond reason," I said, and he just nodded again.

"And that's the problem," he said. "This is the truth. When I picture the rest of my life and think about you not being in it, I wanna die. But...I don't know how to fit you into that life, even though I want to build it around you."

I nodded, then swallowed. "I was born to meet you," I said simply, as I rested my hand around the inside of his thigh.

"Why are you crying like that?" he asked, brushing my face with his stubble. People talked about the big bang, but he was so much bigger than the bang. "All smiley and stuff? It's weird."

"Because I just saw the kid I was when I met you," I said, my voice cracking around the edges like a boulder left in the wind and the sun, sacrificed to the elements and the stupid world. "I can see him now. Remember? He was so scared, but he looked at you and he saw...safety, I guess. He saw his only shot. He saw something worth waking up for, you know?" I wiped my eyes, but it didn't help. "What if I could go back in time and tell him everything that would happen with that boy with the galaxy eyes? That I'd go to Savannah with that boy and I'd meet that boy's sister and fall in love with that boy? I'd be so proud of everything, but mostly I'd just be proud that I tried. That I was brave enough to put myself on the line and get my heart broken. That I let you become the best part of my life."

He didn't say anything, just focused all the beauty of those galaxy eyes on me.

"Oh, and Nicky?" I asked quietly. "Before I forget, take these. I want you to keep them."

I rolled over, reached into my bag, and then gave him the first picture I'd ever taken of him at the gym, along with a Polaroid I'd taken the previous morning of a chandelier in a hipsterrific furniture store. On the bottom of the second one, I'd written what he'd told me in our hidden library that day. *There's nothing wrong with chandeliers,* it said in black Sharpie, even though there apparently was.

He started to reach out, then stopped. "But someone might see your name," he said, and then left them on the bed without further comment.

15

We drove home holding hands. The way we'd left Savannah was so sloppy and haphazard, I ended up losing or forgetting half the clothes I'd brought, along with my cologne and my grandpa's ring. I didn't even want to think about any of that yet, though. He dropped me off and cried openly when I got out, and then he just stared at me. When you loved someone they became better looking – their molecules aligned perfectly, their pores closed up, their crooked noses straightened. So he was beautiful even when he cried, and that's how I remembered him. And then he drove away and it was over. Just like that.

The next day, I woke up and checked his Facebook. His account didn't come up. He'd blocked me. So I tried to Snapchat him. He'd deleted me. Then I brought up his Instagram, or tried to. He'd unfollowed me and turned his profile private. Just as we'd met – digitally – so he removed me from his world. He'd ghosted me. It was almost like he'd never existed at all. And so I did the same thing to him – I scrubbed him from digital existence. I deleted his email address, every photo of him, every photo of *us*. And soon he was gone from my life, too. He vanished.

Since my life had a tendency to fall to pieces when I was awake, I went to bed for a few days. Those first few nights without him were so hard – all I did was clutch my pillows and stare at the dark windows feeling nothing and everything. I was a different person now. It was that simple. What could you do when you grew into someone else's soul and then they stepped away? Half of me felt gone. I didn't want to live in a world after Nicky. (And because he'd told me about his habit of sending breakup letters to all his exes, I avoided my mailbox like a disease for a few weeks. I hated myself enough already, and I'd rather stab myself than possibly have to face all the reasons he'd found me undesirable and dumped me.) To distract myself I started trying to read one of those teen novels set in a ruined version of the future where some down-on-her-luck girl was somehow destined to save whatever was left of her nation, but I didn't need some author to imagine a wrecked world for me. This place was already a nightmare, so hateful and scornful it had made two boys flee from true love and tell themselves they were content with existing in a silent hell. This world was already a dystopia, and I lived it every day. No author needed.

We'd already broken up multiple times, of course, so I knew the drill. The boy who'd survived a chaotic childhood and countless schoolyard insults and a borderline-abusive father would *not* be felled by a simple breakup. Kicking-and-screamingly, I went back to my stupid routine, my stupid life as I'd known it Before Nicky. I watched Netflix, I walked the beach, I read books that meant nothing to me, I took a few pictures. But no matter what I did, I just couldn't think straight – my thoughts circled back on themselves in an endless loop of sameness. When school started up after Labor Day, it was as bland and unfulfilling as ever. All of it felt useless and pointless, like I was living someone's else's life in someone else's body. I halfway waited for Nicky to text me, call me, message me, like he would before. Sometimes the things I'd said in that hotel room seemed a thousand years old. We loved each other – why not be together? Why run from something like that? And we'd broken up a million times – surely he'd come back, right? He had to.

But he didn't. Even though I somehow felt with everything in me that he wanted to.

At night I would turn it all over and over in my mind, dipping into the memories like they were a warm tub, and that gave me *some* comfort. At least enough to numb the pain in my bones. I knew I had to let go of these memories – I'd never get them back and I knew it – I just didn't want to. So I held on. I kept remembering. And I tried harder to keep going. I took pictures of strangers. I reached the end of an amazing Netflix show and went into mourning before picking a different one to start. And still that boy wouldn't leave. I was learning the hard way that love would not just go away. It would not exit in the night like the last guest at some party. It slithered around in your soul, demanding to make its presence known, and denying it only made it more desperate to be seen. The faster you ran, the tighter it choked you. Because love was a tree root growing under a sidewalk; a vein of lava simmering under a mountain range. Put something in love's path and it will crack stone, conceal love and it will break through and move mountains. Deny love and it will explode, run from love and it will overtake you. Kill love and watch love's revenant, imprison love and watch it break free and sing. Soon I accepted that no headphones would drown out his noise, no book would snuff out his magic, no crowded bar would blot out the black silence inside me: I was suffocating at the absent hands of Nicky Flores.

Everywhere I looked, there he was. Beneath an underpass as I rushed by, staring at me from the shadows, those galaxy-green eyes like spark plugs in the dark. Watching over me as I settled into my bed for another sleepless night, his smirk just south of a smile. And on the rare nights when I did find sleep, I'd sink into the vanished vividness of him, the boy who had loved me so much, he'd disappeared. Wherever I went, whatever I did, I felt the loss of him. But what was the point in wishing for something that was gone forever?

Whenever I finished a really good book, I'd hug it. I'd turn the last page and think about the story and the characters and all the places they went and all the things they saw and all the lessons they did or didn't learn, and I would hold that book close and think that somehow they belonged to me now. All those little characters had walked into my chest and carved out a piece of my soul to call home, and they'd never leave. So that's how I tried to look at our relationship. He belonged to me now, all of it did, the summer and the light and the wind and the love, even if he'd walked away and written our ending.

As the weather cooled down I finally picked myself up and got lost in *Honesty*, taking better and better photos, trying to make new contacts in the blogging world, trying to reach the widest audience possible. The distraction proved to be my savior. The misery made me work obsessively hard, weirdly enough, and soon I found that the more I worked, the less I thought about him. I hit forty thousand fans, then fifty. One day I stopped to talk to a man who looked a bit nuts, and he gave me a quote that pushed me even further into viral territory. He explained that he'd been released from prison three years before, but was still struggling to adjust to life again – in some ways, he felt like he was still locked up.

"Why?" I asked as politely as I could. "What's stopping you from being free again?"

"Chains come in all shapes and sizes, squirt. Some of them we even make for ourselves." He looked down at me, something unknowable in his eyes. "None of us get to choose our own paths for ourselves, anyway, not really. I came from a long line of screw-ups, and my son is likely pegged for the same fate. We never got out. That's the thing about destiny – most of the time, the world decides it for you."

Soon people were even sending me their own admissions, and I started using them on rainy days when I couldn't go out and do my interviews. "I'm fat and I hate myself," one message in my inbox read, along with a selfie of an overweight teenaged boy from the neck down. "My parents liked my little sister Marlee more than me because she was skinny and pretty, so every day, I would give her tubs of peanut butter and ice cream while they went to work. She got diagnosed with diabetes last month. I hate myself even more now."

The post got four thousand likes, and for a few hours I felt fulfilled. Another message came from a teenaged girl who'd kissed her female neighbor and said she wasn't ashamed about it in the slightest. "Why do we do what the world tells us to do, and shut out what the heart wants us to do?" she asked in her message, and it brought tears to my eyes – but I declined it. I still couldn't touch the gay issue. And one day late in September, an *Honesty* mission that had started out in disaster – the first man I approached had whispered *"fuck you!"* before walking away – I got the single most beautiful quote I'd ever heard, from a woman on a Vespa with a rough-looking face telling me about her history of chasing the wrong men:

"Whoever's reading this out there – you deserve to have someone's hands be glued to you, for their eyes to be stuck on you. You deserve for their face to catch on fire when they look at you, for them to lay eyes on you and devote the rest of their day to you. Don't ever let yourself settle for anything less than magic from Dumbledore's freakin' wand. That feeling – you know, that crazy, irrational, my-brain-won't-work-without-you, I'd-make-you-eggs-every-morning-for-the-rest-of-my-life kind of feeling – that feeling is the most important thing you will ever find. No matter what happens in this life, that feeling – that love – will keep you warm, and carry you through. So find that magic feeling and never let anything take it away from you."

The post got eight thousand likes and was mentioned in a national newspaper. Even though it hurt to read her words, I was still so high. This was the most surprising thing, the pockets of happiness that could be found within my misery. Falling so low could kick you back up for a moment, it seemed. But those bursts only lasted until the sun went down, of course. Then I would go home, close the blinds, and feel Nicky slide into my soul like fog. And that boy wouldn't leave. All this world did was kill dreams, blow out flames, burn holes in your soul. How did anyone live here?

From time to time I would log into friends' profiles and stalk him from afar, even though it felt like emotional cutting. And he was doing well. I wanted him to crash and burn, but he wasn't. I was watching the renaissance he was undergoing without me. The further he rose, the more it hurt, and the deeper I fell. Because sometimes breakups destroyed one person and made the other person fly. I'd wanted so badly to believe love was a thing that could exist for me out there, but I'd been a fool. That's all I was. A fool who'd believed in lies and galaxy eyes. And now I had nothing except my stupid blog.

Nicky seemed to get rid of all the clothes I'd gotten him in Savannah, went back to gym shorts and athletic-type shirts. His hair got messier. He looked tan and gorgeous and perhaps a little more muscular, but I could not tell if he was truly happy. It could've gone either way, really. And soon I realized he was trying to look straight. He was going backwards, and I felt so sorry for him.

It was at that bar called the Pier where I first saw him. When our eyes pulled together from across the room, everything else fell away, time included, and it was almost the summer again. He just stared at me, biting his lip and brushing back that sun-touched hair. And then he was gone.

Before I fell asleep that night, I broke down and texted him for the first time. **I think we made the biggest mistake ever,** I said. **I spent the best days of my life with you. Please talk to me.**

I had a feeling he'd unblocked my number after seeing me, and I was right. He began typing, then stopped.

He never did send what he'd started.

One day in November I went into the office to tell my "boss" about my progress. *Honesty* was exploding and he wanted updates, I guess, just to make sure I was aware that he owned me. Facebook had just "verified" me with a blue check, and I supposed he just wanted to assert himself on me, as all stud ducks did. Nicky'd had me thinking about love lately, so I told my boss the story about the gay homeless woman. Being adored by Nicky, being touched by him, being loved by him, in his own little repressed way, had made me realize that being gay wasn't such a bad, shocking, taboo thing, and I wanted to maybe post something a little different from the norm. Because after Nicky, the world seemed so much bigger now. Bigger than it ever had before, really.

"Cute, but no gay stuff," my boss said abruptly as he stared down at the magazine he was reading, as offhandedly as if he'd told me to take out the trash in the break room. I stopped breathing.

"*Gay* stuff?" I asked. He looked up at me, the whir of his hard drive the only sound in the room. I noticed his rotten, decaying teeth and tried not to wince.

"Ehh, no offense to anyone, but two guys together, two girls together – I have nothing against it, it's just not my thing. Not into it. Never have been."

My eyes narrowed – I couldn't believe he was talking like this. If someone were to turn up their nose at a movie poster featuring only, say, Hispanic actors and say "ehh, Hispanic people *just aren't my thing*," that person would rightfully be treated like a bigot. But why was it okay to discriminate against gays in the same way? Why was it completely accepted to write *gays* off, and nobody else? This was one of the last frontiers, as far as I was concerned, and nothing was being done to help. The more I thought about it, the more pissed off I became.

"I'm sorry," I told him, "but I don't see what you're saying."

"You don't? Gay people represent ten percent of the population, kid. It's a niche market, not meant for the mainstream, and nobody else outside of that market cares. It's-"

"Redheads," I interrupted as something in me popped. And suddenly I didn't feel so accepting anymore.

"Redheads?"

"Redheads," I repeated, my voice rising. "Two percent of humanity has red hair, which is *far* less than the gay population, and so that should be a 'niche' thing, too, right? Wrong – you see redheads *everywhere*. Every other book stars an auburn-haired heroine, every other commercial features the quirky redheaded girl with freckles, every other movie has the redheaded best friend sidekick. Now you sit here and tell me why 'gay' deserves to be a niche market, shoved into the corner and kept separate and hidden and segregated from everything else, while 'redhead' is as mainstream as can be. No, seriously, tell me. I'll wait. I've got time."

He opened his mouth and then closed it. For the first time I'd ever seen, my boss was speechless.

"Kid," he finally said. "Look. This is Northeast Florida, not Brooklyn. We're trying to appeal to families and advertisers, not the *fun little boys* down at the gay bar who

213

prance around in their little outfits and wave flags in the air. We're covering human interest here, not furthering the gay agenda."

"Agenda?" I asked, incredulous. "But I'm just a kid with a phone."

"Exactly, and who do you think is changing the world today? Kids with phones. It's scary."

It's not scary, I thought as I sat back and fingered my phone in my pocket. *It's a whole new world.*

The next morning I woke up to a body bag. My neighbor Naomi's partner Ruth had died in the night, and watching them cart the body away while Naomi stared blankly in the direction of the ambulance was one of the strangest and most surreal things I'd ever seen. Nicky had introduced me to a new world, even if he'd stepped away – but Ruth would never be able to live in that world now. She was dead. Nobody would ever show Ruth what it was like to not have to close off the universe from all the love in her life – she'd kept her curtains drawn until the end, and now no curly-haired person with galaxy eyes would ever open them for her. She was done.

But *I* wasn't done, I thought as I made some coffee, some weird adrenaline pooling somewhere near my throat. Lately I just hadn't been feeling so compliant anymore, and the body bag – along with my boss – had sort of kicked that into overdrive. Women like Naomi and Ruth and the lady with the PBR were being made to live and die in hiding because of people like my boss and his fear, his hatred, his ignorance, his confusion. And I knew I was part of the problem, too, because the silent ones were just as guilty as the loud ones. People thought they needed to be at the front of some Westboro Baptist Church picket line with a *GOD HATES FAGS* sign to be keeping the world a shitty place, but they didn't. Everyone who stood aside silently while someone was mocked, everyone who'd ever turned their noses from the hatred and told themselves we'd moved forward – their hands were bloody, too. Maybe bloodier, because they were the ones with the power to change things. If I looked down at humanity as it existed today, I wouldn't recognize us. Naomi's pain deserved to felt by the world, but nobody would ever know. She needed a witness. Obviously I didn't know her and couldn't tell her story, I did have *other* pain to publish…

I thought of the *Honesty* story saved on my phone, the desperate masterpiece of the old woman who had loved another female and let it destroy her. More and more, I was realizing I had a responsibility. Not just as a semi-famous blogger, but as a human, a human who didn't want to be a worthless piece of shit. I'd been noticing things lately – things I'd never noticed before. Upon glancing at the romance novel section at Target I'd noted that out of the twenty books displayed, all twenty portrayed straight couples, while only two of those couples were non-white. The state of Michigan had just passed a law making sodomy a felony, and various other states under Republican rule were also passing similarly heinous bills. The world just wasn't improving. Every time I went to the grocery store or the movie theater and saw a little effeminate boy being dragged around by a parent who hated him, his deadened eyes trapped in his own skull like dogs in a kill shelter, I could feel every action I wasn't doing to help, notice every hug I wasn't offering. My lungs were starting to ache with the words I wasn't saying, and I wanted to give those boys hope that you could be gay *and* happy – I wanted them to know there was a chance that one day they might stop hating themselves enough to let a boy stare at them with galaxy eyes and make them feel put back together.

But I was doing nothing on purpose. I'd always picked my subjects and stories very carefully, desperate not to let anyone even tiptoe near the truth about me. I knew eyebrows would lift to the sky if I ever started to feature gay stories and became some mouthpiece of the gay community or something, so I'd made sure to steer clear of any of that. If someone even *looked* gay, I wouldn't interview them, as gross as that sounded, and if one of my subjects did start sliding somewhere close to the gay subject, I'd rush the interview to a close and find someone else. But lately my stories and posts had been getting stale, shallow, and maybe there was a reason for that. I

215

was disregarding my own truth. What depths could I plumb if I opened up one of the deepest wells of all? What was a blog called *Honesty* without a little honesty?

It was so risky, though, and not just because of the Nicky factor. I was starting to think life was all about figuring out who you were, and then deciding how much of that person to show to the world. I had so much riding on how much I revealed. I was lost, and *Honesty* was my only road, my only plan. It had to work out because it couldn't *not* work out – success was my only option. There'd been a few articles about me in magazines here or there, calling me the wunderkind tech boy of Florida or whatever, and I had fangirls who would comment my pictures with shockingly direct come-ons about my smile or my eyes or my body, even when the post had nothing to do with me. At this point my identity was just as wrapped up in the blog as the blog itself, and I was being such a hypocrite by indirectly preaching the virtues of truth while living my life behind closed, locked doors. But the fans had this ideal of me as some hetero dreamboat, the artsy boy next door. What would I do if it all fell apart and the pigeons flew the coop, onto some straight guy onto whom they could project their sexy fantasies? I could ruin my whole life. This could torpedo it all…

But on the other hand, art should transform. That's what art should do. Nicky told me I was good at what I did, and being good gave me power. Could I set aside my own interests and try to transform people with that power and that art? The possibilities were intriguing in the least…

I touched my phone again and heard the words of my high school art teacher, Mrs. Hargrove: "go to where your passions flow." For some reason it made me think of the bitter, acid, almost supercharged tone Nicky's voice took on whenever he talked about society's treatment of gays. And then his breakdown about not wanting to be gay anymore…every time I thought about that, it made me furious. I wanted to rid our culture of this poison, or at least try to. The things he believed, the things he let the world tell him…maybe I should try to help erase some of that nonsense, scrub it from the world. Or maybe it would end my career before I even started it. Then again, *maybe* the followers would embrace me – maybe they would appreciate the honesty. It couldn't hurt to try, right?

And beyond that, maybe I could do the most noble thing: maybe I could help a little kid just like me a few years ago, a kid who thought he was trapped, a kid who thought he'd never get to wake up in the morning and get to be who he was. Gay guys just weren't being represented or put on display out there – every Hollywood movie starred the same "brave" superhero chasing down the helpless blonde heroine, every television show featured the same slick womanizer, every commercial had the brawny muscle man selling deodorant on horseback or whatever. And since I wasn't seeing myself anywhere, maybe I could become my own mirror. There was no seat at the table for me, so why not build my own chair and force my way in? God knows I'd needed it as a child, to see someone like myself and know there was a place for me out there in the world...

And that did it. The vision of me in elementary school, lost and lonely and confused and in love with boys who could never love me back, made the decision for me. It was getting harder and harder to wake up every day and see the world as being a beautiful place, and I wanted to try to change that. So I walked out onto my porch to get a better signal, then took a breath. And then a kid with a phone pressed publish and tried to change the world.

~

An interesting thing happened the next day: not much. The post got one of the highest reaction rates I'd ever seen, of course, with dozens of teary-eyed emojis and sympathetic comments, but beyond that, nothing much happened. The post didn't spark a forest fire of outrage, but it didn't go viral as some case for equality and compassion, either. People just didn't really care about the lesbian thing – they were more touched by the love itself. It seemed that when confronted by *this* bit of honesty, most people had responded with a shrug. One woman did comment something like "I like this level of honesty – keep going in this direction," though, and I printed it out and put it on my desk.

The biggest shock came from Naomi herself, Ruth's partner. She knew about *Honesty* – I'd told her about it once or twice during random chats on the back lawn – and when she passed me, she met my eyes for the first time ever. Then she nodded slowly and respectfully, telling me she'd seen the post. All she did was nod, but her eyes said all the words in the world. I knew I'd never be able to tell her how good that made me feel, and so I turned and walked away, left it all unsaid. But I felt that she understood, just like I understood her. Posting about things I actually cared about, things I believed in, had suddenly opened up a whole new world for me.

That night, just as I got ready to toss and turn for another endless set of Nicky-less hours, a new message came into my Facebook page. "I cried for hours after reading the thing about the old lady," a kid in middle school named James said. This surprised me, because my experience with children was that they were meaner than any other age group – kids were fearless and guileless enough to say exactly what they felt, and what a lot of them felt seemed to be hatred. "The honesty in the piece was sort of staggering to me. I just want you to know that it gave me hope and made me feel…cleaner, somehow," the message continued. "I might even tell my mom I'm gay tomorrow. I don't even know why I'm telling you this, but…yeah. Just felt the urge to share. Thank you for existing."

I fell asleep sobbing into my pillow for that little boy.

I coasted into the holidays feeling like a gladiator, and on Christmas Eve I stopped by Walgreens for some odds and ends. I first sensed Nicky when I was in the food aisle, looking for something to bring to my dad's house. (I had nowhere else to go, even though my dad's wife hated me for no reason and would probably cut me down the whole night.) Nicky was standing in the beverage aisle staring blankly into the wine fridge when my eyes found him.

Shit. I felt like someone had thrown hot coals into my chest. I turned and melted against the side of a Triscuits display, but then I heard him start walking closer, and I knew I had nowhere to go. He'd cornered me without knowing it.

I felt him, physically *felt him*, getting closer. I had never in my life been so desperate for anyone or anything. I *needed* his love all of the sudden, craved it with everything in me. When he came into my line of vision, he stopped to look at some Cheetos and then jumped a little and stared right at me. I stared back as *White Christmas* played over the intercom. Fate was such an evil bitch. I hated her. But soon something in me twitched, and since I couldn't escape, I figured I'd might as well talk to him.

"Hey."

"Hi," he said. Even when caught off guard, he was still so cool, so presidential. He held his head like a crown needed to be on top of it.

"Are you alone? On Christmas?" I asked him. "Why aren't you in Savannah with your family?"

His eyes left me. He seemed dazed for some reason. "Oh, um…well, I thought things were too fresh, actually. I didn't want to deal with the whole Victoria thing yet. Wanted to let things die down, I guess…"

"Oh," I said, heartbroken for him. "Well, do you want to come with me? My family would be totally cool with a…a *friend* tagging along…"

"Uh, thanks, but I've got a buddy who invited me over."

I looked away, and I felt so sad. For both of us. It was Christmas and we were keeping ourselves alone in a dead-end Walgreens in a town at the end of the world, because that world told us we had to. It was all so effing stupid.

I turned to him. "So you're back to that?" I asked quietly, thinking about how first cuts dug deepest. "We're back to this? *Really*? Strangers in a grocery store?"

His nostrils flared a little. "For the millionth time, Cole, *I don't see any other options*. We tried. We gave it a shot. A good one."

"Love is an option," I whispered, but he looked off at the magazine aisle. Then I laughed sort of incredulously. He asked me what was funny. "What's funny? You broke my freaking *heart*," I said, my eyes on the floor. He glanced around, then touched my chin for one white-hot second. I could swear my body disappeared.

"So what, Coley? That means nothing. I'm always gonna love you. On Christmas, on Valentine's Day, on every day and every holiday. You know that. Nothing will ever change that."

I screwed up my face. What the hell was love if it was felt alone? What was any of this but a futile wish in a cruel world? We were two boys on the edge of nineteen, climbing out of something we neither understood nor were equipped to deal with.

"This isn't you, Nicky," I said, motioning up and down at his gym gear and his buffed-up body. "I know you. This is a wish…it's back to the beginning."

"It *is* me," he said, with a certainty that looked so fake I wanted to both hug him and punch him. "It is. I'm different now. I've been going to this Bible class every week, and they're giving me these 'tools' to be straight, as they call them. I'm gonna be alright, I can feel it."

I stared at him. What could I even say to that level of delusion? *I hate you for every time you take yourself away from me,* I wanted to say. *You're a beautiful maniac who hurts me more beautifully than I've ever been hurt before and makes me think cheesy, insane thoughts like the ones I'm thinking right now. My days feel like centuries without you.*

Instead I touched his collar real quick so nobody would see, then looked into his galaxy eyes. "Nicky. Stop. Seriously, stop. This is madness. You don't know what you're doing." I pointed at his heart. "I don't know much, but I know this. That thing you feel inside your chest – your soul – that thing's going to shut down if you deny yourself for too long, and

220

you're going to die. Maybe not now, maybe not in a year, but one day I'm going to wake up and read somewhere that you're dead, all because you let yourself go dark inside. You've got to stop this craziness."

He turned his head and dropped his hand in a way that displayed his phone screen, which was showing some Christian-type podcast called *How to be Happy*. How could I break into this fantasyland? How could *anyone* do that?

"Don't you need me?" I asked. "Don't you miss me?"

He tried to play it cool, but his eyes were like a crop top: they revealed too much. Catching this, he glanced away again, leaving me singed and smoldering, burning alone, without him. Why was hating him so freaking exquisite?

"Okay. Fine. I need you so much it hurts," he said, watching the tile floor as he licked his lip. "I miss you something terrible. I keep thinking about last summer, trying to imagine how I felt." His voice dropped even lower, and he shook his head, disgusted. "I was alive then. I haven't been since you."

I breathed.

"And why would you even *want* me?" he asked, studying his forearms with pure hatred in his eyes. "Why don't you find someone else, someone who would treat you better? Someone normal? Sometimes I miss all the love I'm not giving you, and it makes me feel so bad, so guilty…"

"Is that what you want?" I asked quietly. "For me to…find someone else?"

He shook his head and slumped even further. "The only thing worse than envisioning *me* with you is envisioning *someone else* with you. It makes me want to stop breathing."

An old man passed, giving us a politely curious look and killing the moment. I grimaced at him – nosy bastard. He blushed and kept walking.

We both straightened up and tried to chill out. When we were alone once more, I looked down at his shoes.

"No, you *don't* miss me," I sighed. "If you missed me, you'd talk to me. If you needed me, you wouldn't have left.

You're still so clueless, aren't you? I hope you never have to love anything as much as I love you."

He said nothing. I swallowed, and it hurt like strep throat. "God, I wish I had wine right now. Every time I try to be alive without you, I can't. I don't know how. Shit, Nicky. What are we gonna do?"

He threw my sigh back at me. "This is all we *can* do. It was gonna end eventually, anyway. It had an expiration date, Coley. You were gonna get sick of me. You were gonna be around me too much and realize I scratched my balls too often or something else gross like that, and you would've gotten tired of me because I'm not good enough, and you wouldn't want to be around me anymore."

I winced. It broke me to pieces to know he didn't see "enough" in himself, in me, in us. How was this not enough? We were two kids who loved each other. It was more than enough. It was everything.

"*Enough*?" I asked. "I know you're not enough. You'll never be enough. And that's the best thing."

"You certainly never acted like it," he said. Suddenly I could remember what I'd thought about him the first time I'd ever really looked at him: *the good kind of trouble*. It was an insane how accurate I'd been.

He looked up at me, mystified. "I mean, what's wrong with you? If you're telling the truth, then I don't get it. *How could you love me so much*?"

And my heart broke yet again.

"Nicky – none of this was your fault," I said. "I'm mad, Nicky. I've had a shitty life and it makes me hate almost everything. And I'm scared, too. My dad left me and my mom left me and all anyone ever does is leave me and, God, that must mean there's something fundamentally leave-able about me, right? If I was exceptional, wouldn't they have been compelled to stick around? But please try this with me again. I don't wanna let the fear keep me from the possibilities of you, of us, of…this. Of…ColeyAndNickyVille."

He bit his lip, his eyes wild.

"So this is it?" I asked, trying not to laugh at the insanity of all this. "Again? Another ending?"

He closed his eyes. "You know it has to be. Let's just keep it like it was. Save the good, so it can never go bad. Keep it golden."

I stepped forward. I smelled him, packaged him, took in the memory of this boy who'd made me a different person, who was so committed to being trapped in his own shell he kept snails as pets. "Okay. But what now?"

"We keep doing what we're doing. I'll date…girls, I guess. Or try to. You'll…"

I glared at this boy who had remade my life. "I'll…*what*?"

"I read all of your posts," he said, watching me. "Every last one. The one about the old lady was…gorgeous, really. It's all growing so fast. I know people make fun of you and try not to take you seriously because you post about love and romance and stuff – which humans shy away from because they're terrified of their own emotions – but anyway, you're gonna blow. Something's gonna go viral, and one day the whole world will know your name. Why would you want me hanging around for all that?"

How could he not understand that he was the *only* thing I wanted around? I was so stupid to think I could fix him. But I still wanted to try.

"I'm *tired*, Nicky," I said, and my voice sounded a million miles away. "I'm so tired. We're getting older. My little cousin just posted on Facebook that she's pregnant, and my dad told me that my mom just got a face-lift. Everyone's getting so damn old. What if we wake up one day and life has just…left us behind? What if it already has?"

He bit his lip, then turned away again. "Don't act like I don't want this, Coley. That was never the problem. I want it more than anything. I lived you, I breathed you…and it scared me so much…"

Nicky started to leave. I couldn't do this anymore – I needed him in my life. So my voice came out small and desperate, but firm.

223

"We're gonna die, Nicky."

He stopped and turned around. The summer came rushing back to me, the summer I'd first felt love, palms and waves and sand and grace and fire, and I threw my Hail Mary pass. "We're gonna die. All of us. The clock app on my phone is ticking, and we're all gonna be dead one day. Maybe it'll happen tomorrow and maybe it'll happen in seventy years, but one day we're gonna be in the ground, and it's killing me already, and I want to do everything I can to spend every possible moment with you before then." I stared at the floor, ashamed of my own words. "You're the closest thing I've ever found to heaven, and I want to live in that heaven while I'm still on Earth."

I looked up. His galaxy eyes slammed into mine, filling up the stale December air, stiffening it and hardening it and electrifying it with all the things beyond our comprehension, all the things beyond what we could accept or even admit, all the things we felt but couldn't put to words, would probably *never* be able to put to words.

"Nicky," I said, his name poisonous on my lips like cigarette smoke. He was narcotic, illicit, and I would never get enough. "Look at us. It's so sad that we like each other this much. We're undoing each other." *Just like that therapist had predicted...*

He bit his lip again, eyes shining. "Take care of yourself, okay?"

"Trust me, I'm a wreck," I told my hands. Then I met his eyes one last time, hoping for a miracle. "Can you hug me?"

He fidgeted. "Why?"

"…So I can remember it when I'm eighty and alone and without a boy to hug in a deserted Walgreens aisle on Christmas Eve?"

"Merry Christmas, Coley," he finally said, January in his eyes, and then he turned and took his wine to the cash register alone.

16

And that was it. I spent Christmas alone. And then New Year's. And then all of January. As winter hit I tried to go back to books, to fly back into the pages that had kept me warm and safe as a child, because books would never leave me. When people failed me, books always stepped in. They would never rearrange my bones and change me, then leave me standing there, different and alone. And if books *did* tear up my soul, I could always turn the last page and be reminded I was only daydreaming. But I couldn't turn this page. *His* page. The Christmas run-in had just reminded me of what I'd lost, and still the whole world whispered his name. What was in the cards for us? For *me,* now that I was officially gay and officially single? Would I become the sad old shut-in, the proverbial gay uncle? The peculiar man who gardened for fun and never left his house? Or would I perhaps fall in love with a woman like I used to pray I would when I was a boy and have a happily easy after?

January gave way to February. My life was becoming so dreary and dull – winter just wasn't my season. One chilly night when I was walking home from the grocery store, I passed what I realized was the gay bar my boss had mentioned. In the past I would've turned my face and rushed off into the darkness, but on this night I stopped and peered into the window. I saw lights, smoke, smiling faces; I heard loud, vibrant music and the sound of laughter   everything was whirling together in a show of color and light and joy. For some reason I was blown away that everyone was so happy and carefree – it looked *way* more fun than any straight bar I'd ever seen, come to think of it. Who knew that being gay could actually be *fun*? I'd had no idea a secret gay community had existed right under my nose all along. Well, they weren't *exactly* secret, but it told me a lot when one couple left the bar, stepped into the light, and let go of each other's hands and started acting like "friends" as they walked to their car. They couldn't exist in public, but still, *they existed in the first place,* and this was a revelation to me.

For some reason I couldn't stop watching this one kid who looked about my age. He was on the dance floor, dancing and laughing and flirting, looking freer than anyone I'd ever seen before. Soon my arms started aching as I held my grocery bags, and I realized I'd been standing there for a full twenty minutes – but still I could not take my eyes off that boy as he danced.

Two days before Nicky's twentieth birthday – and yes, I still measured time in relation to him – I woke up with the weirdest feeling. I saw flashing, troubling images in my head of car crashes and police lights and shooting guns, like when you watched some chaotic horror movie and then spent the rest of the night staring at the ceiling in a cold panic. And I knew it was about Nicky. He needed me out there – I could feel it. I just didn't know how he was strong enough to overcome the missing – God knows I couldn't. We were new people now, but still all I wanted in the world was to wake up and find his warm body filling my bed, see his galaxy eyes exploding at me.

And that evening, so long after we'd first met, I got a text that confirmed everything I'd been feeling:

My grandma just died. I need you

~

I slapped pavement to his house, back to what had broken me, heart pounding and hands sweating, and screeched under the weeping willow before running to his door at full speed. He opened it and fell into me and kissed me like he was underwater and I was an oxygen source, and then something strange happened. Something like magic.

I felt like a different person than he'd fallen in love with. So did he. Before this we'd been play-acting, dancing around our deepening love like the kids we were, terrified by each other. But tonight the concrete had dried and we were set into ourselves, grown up in love, if only for the moment. There was no arguing, no fighting. We moved against the wall as one and kissed without even looking over our shoulders to see who was watching. We were past that. We were meeting in the middle of our problems as if suspended underwater, floating, sliding side-by-side into a love we couldn't run from anymore, here on this night when we were both teenagers for the last time.

"I couldn't tell her," he sobbed in between gulps of air as we kissed. "My grandma…she said she regretted that she'd never seen me with someone I loved, and I wanted so badly to tell her I loved you, because you are the moon to me, and I couldn't say it…even as she lay there dying with her tongue out, I couldn't tell her…I don't know what's wrong with me…I'm ruined…"

"I'm sorry, Nicky, I'm so sorry."

And I was. For so much more than this, but I didn't have to say it. He knew. He started screaming and crying louder, and then he fully collapsed into me, his legs no longer strong enough to support him. I held him as the earthquake hit, and right then and there I made the decision, or rather, the decision made me: *tonight I'm gonna forget about the past. Tonight I'm gonna forget about the future. Tonight I'm gonna love him.*

He looked awful compared to December. His face was covered in acne, from stress probably, and he'd lost some weight. He was also at war with himself, muttering senselessly one minute and sobbing the next. He was a wreck, falling apart in my hands. And really it just made me love him more. He still had his galaxy eyes, though. Those lights were unkillable.

"And I'm so sorry, too," he said, "for everything. *Everything.* I don't know what the hell I was thinking. I guess I happened to myself again. I'm such a coward. I was scared, but I'm not anymore. You taught me how to be an adult, Cole – you taught me how to love someone besides myself. I'm gonna love you forever…"

He kissed me deeper, and it was almost like he'd never left me at all. He could break me and then put me back together again just like that. And in that moment I realized just how much I loved him, with every coil in my pink brain. I was almost ashamed of it, actually. I hated the power he held over me with just a smirk or a scowl or a withheld text message. But that still didn't change the fact that with him, happiness hit me. Years of covering my tracks and telling half-truths and hiding and killing the wishes of my deepest soul were wiped away, and I just fell into this thing. Joy slammed into me, hit me square in the chest and swept me breathlessly away, and yesterday just wouldn't cut it anymore. This was so much better than any life I had ever known. Life wasn't life before him – not even close. I was going to love him into our bright eyes turned grey and cloudy. Forever.

I let Nicky Flores give it to me hard that night. I wanted it, I wanted *him*, in whatever way he was willing to give himself to me, no matter how pathetic it made me feel. He cried while he did it, and I cried a few times, too, in between kissing him for all he had. And in his own language, he *was* loving me – he just had the toolbox of a man-boy with a broken past. We both did. Whatever we were running from, we were running together. Everyone loved differently, and I just had to accept that Nicky sucked at love. When we were done he stuck his mouth on mine like we were underwater again. Kiss of death, breath of life – it didn't matter. It was keeping both of us alive anyway.

"We're gonna make this happen," he said out of nowhere, in between the kisses. "It's gonna work out, and I can't freaking wait. We'll figure it out…they won't make us stop loving each other…they will have to kill us first, so help me God…"

Afterward we crawled into his bed, still wet from the shower, and I just lay there and savored the way his sheets smelled like him, just in case this was the last time.

"Coley?" he said soon, his voice hoarse. "I need to tell you something."

"Yeah?"

He rolled over a bit. "The first time I ever saw you, I loved you," he said plainly. "I fell in love with you, and I still am in love with you. The way you laughed at something outside the gym, the way your hair stuck up in the front, the way your heart broke when those guys made fun of you – I loved you more than I could bear, from the very first second. That's why I downloaded the app – I was desperate to find you. But I was terrified of that love. I didn't want to admit it to myself because it would've confirmed everything I hated most about myself, and so I fought it as hard as I could, for way too long. But I am so sorry for every second I let my fear keep me away from you."

I kissed his forehead and cried. As he smiled and started to drift away I clutched him with the clawing, desperate knowledge that no matter what he told me, our world would never understand our love, not really. It would do anything to stamp it out, actually. As his breathing slowed I held him with this visceral realization sinking into me, this *wham-bam* feeling that this could kill us, this thing we both felt between our living electric bodies, right down to our marrow. This love could absolutely kill us. There were people out there who would relish the feeling of our blood on their hands, figuratively at least. It was us against the world, and nobody would ever understand how close that brought us but us.

As he fell asleep I hugged him harder and breathed in the scent of his bony, hairless shoulder, and right there within that lovely moment, I knew our love would live forever.

"There's nothing wrong with chandeliers," I whispered, but he was already gone.

17

I went home alone at dawn. That afternoon I woke up with hazy memories of sex and wine and tears and happiness, blissful happiness that had asked nothing of me, just made its presence known like a cat on your floor. My phone pinged with a text, and I grabbed it and smiled. All he'd written was "see you soon," but to me it was the most gorgeous set of words that had ever been assembled. He was back. My boy on the moon was back. He made the ordinary beautiful, elevating normality like when you got lost in a dreary edge of town and turned a corner to find a brick wall blooming with graffiti. Red, yellow, lilac: all the colors were there. He had everything.

I waited and waited and waited. I knew he would come, I just didn't know when. Five PM passed, cruel and lonely. Then six. Soon it was nine, and I was yawning, and it became clear I'd been stood the hell up. Oh well. I'd been lied to again, led along again. Should've known. I could always try again, though, I figured.

Nicky did not open my Snapchat the next day. I fluffed my hair and found the perfect lighting in the corner of my room by my bedside table and even sucked in my cheeks to look like a Balmain model. I was thrilled to have him see me looking so hot – why wouldn't he open it?

I added him on all my profiles a million times, of course, but he never accepted me. It didn't make any sense to me. Every other time he'd come to his senses, come crawling back. How much time did he need? I made new Snapchat and Instagram profiles, but he refused to accept my friend requests. And that night, after an incredibly passive-aggressive phone conversation with my dad, I got drunk. Very drunk. All the goodwill I'd ever felt for Nicky instantly dried up. He'd dropped me again, and I wanted him to feel every inch of my misery. I knew I couldn't keep doing this – I couldn't keep allowing him to treat my heart like the cold green beans at the bottom of the sink after dinner, all because I was too afraid to imagine a future without him, too cowardly to envision a world alone. I hated him, and it made me hate myself. So just before the blackness closed in and took me, I texted him the worst thing I could dream up:

I hate you forever, you stupid faggot. Happy effing birthday.

He never responded, but he didn't have to. When I woke up the next morning, vomity and trembling, I already knew I'd ruined everything. And as I lay there in a fetal position I decided that letting him fall out of love with me had been the worst thing I'd ever done. Since Jonathan, at least. I should've tried harder, I should've been anyone but me. Every cruel word from my father, every time someone had called me a faggot or a loser or a freak – all of those words had been confirmed by his departure. I felt lower than dirt. I felt like a worm.

It was probably the hardest thing I'd ever done, but soon I tried to accept that my crazy text had probably been the final nail in the coffin for Nicky Flores and Coley Furman, *whatever* we'd been. He was done with me, and it made me crumple into myself every time I thought about it. I'd been discarded like an old phone after an upgrade. And that was that.

And so that day I did something crazy: I took a breath and told myself to let him go.

~

After a few brutally chilly and windy weeks, winter finally surrendered to spring. Our break lasted longer than any other break, until it wasn't a break, really, but a break*up*. The full Monty. Time started to glide on without him – I didn't touch the ground, but I wasn't flying, either. I was just drifting, existing. It was all grey. Soon almost a year had passed since our first meeting, that humid day in the gym when I'd faced hatred and he'd temporarily rescued me from my own mind. By now we were settling into new lives that had nothing to do

232

with each other. Nicky even moved away. Where, I had no idea, but one day late in February I happened to bike by his house (translation: shamelessly stalked him) and saw moving trucks at the entrance to his unit. As the spring heated up I avoided everything having to do with him. Our separate worlds had never really overlapped before anyway – we had no mutual friends, and beyond that, he was One of Them, a Normal Guy, and I was not – but I made extra precautions to avoid him. I knew that if I saw him I would fall apart, so I stayed away. I still could not escape the cloud of him, the hole his absence had left in myself, my life. I'd sooner swallow curdled milk than go to a bar on a Thursday and see him flirting with some guy – or worse, a girl. A girl who could offer him everything I couldn't, like ovaries and boobs and a normal relationship that wouldn't turn them both into pariahs…

I couldn't believe the school year was coming to a close. The older I got, the faster time seemed to fly. The kids I'd grown up with were, well, growing up. Girls who'd been posting party pictures just a few years before were now loading pictures of their babies, or their new townhouses with their fiancés. Guys who'd been posting gym selfies last fall were now posting photos of their cubicles. My relationship with my dad was the same as ever – he'd call me, use me as his punching bag, and then I'd hang up and feel black and depressed for the rest of the day – and I did not speak to my mother more than once or twice, ignoring most of her calls in between. At least I was starting to think about Nicky less and less. He was always there, obviously, but soon he was a whisper instead of a deluge. Sometimes I still got weak and waited for him to come to his senses. I waited for a text. I waited for a message. I waited to wake up to a drunken voicemail left from the garden of some bar at one thirty in the morning where he'd pour out his soul into the line and tell me how much he missed me and needed me. None of that ever came. When I was the worst version of myself, the version that was tired or hung-over or starving in the line at KFC while the lady in front of me took forever on her order, I would think of Nicky out there in the world and I would wish he was miserable. I would wish he was standing on some pier, choked with nostalgia for me, staring blankly at a sunset he could no longer find beauty in. I would wish he was in bed, crying alone, sunken in and broken down and hating himself for letting me go. But those wishes never lasted long, because I'd loved Nicky Flores once and I would love him forever. So even through the good and the bad, even through the worst and the best of me, I still had one wish for him: wherever he was, whoever he was with, whatever he was doing, I hoped that boy was free. Just as free as he'd been with me. Even if I hated him.

The thought of him lying with someone else, touching them, kissing them where he'd kissed me, made me want to erase myself from the world. But the only thing that scared me more than his happiness was his misery. Because once you loved someone, you could never truly unlove them. If my beautiful daydreamer was hurting out there, crying on a back porch somewhere in the rain, I didn't even know what I would do with myself...

One thing I started to learn was that Nicky had done me a solid. He'd set me free, and I could become anyone with that freedom. I hadn't been good enough to keep him around, so I became better. Soon I was reading more books and jogging all the time. A boy looked right at me in front of Dunkin Donuts one warm morning, and instead of looking away, I stared back for a second. I felt breathless and dazzling and only a little horrifying, like my throat had simultaneously caught fire and shrunken three sizes. He ended up walking away and exiting my life, but still, it was starting to occur to me that I could be whoever the hell I wanted to be. I was in a sea of strangers, free to pretend to be whoever I pleased. So I went to Target that day and got some shirts in size small instead of medium, some shorts in bright blue instead of khaki. I bought a crystal lamp instead of a black one, then I stocked up on grooming supplies in the beauty section, and only looked over my shoulder once instead of constantly. And for the first time, I did not disgust myself on the drive home.

What was I going to do with this small bit of freedom? Who was I going to become? Who was I going to love?

I stayed away from the hookup apps – for now, at least – for a few reasons. I was still a little scared of having someone who knew my family see me on there, but also, the idea of having sex with someone who wasn't Nicky made me feel like dying. Deep down I still wanted to be *his*, and to have someone else make me their own, well…that concept was still unfathomable. But still I knew I would honor the mess we'd made together that summer. Because the thing about people was, they changed. I was changing every day. As the years went on, I knew I would get older and look different and rethink the way I thought about some things, and pretty soon I wouldn't be me anymore. Not the Me I'd been with him, at least. And Nicky would change, too. Eventually we would become other people, and other *peoples'* people, and we would fall in love with other souls who would lay claim on our hearts, and those two kids that had existed in ColeyAndNickyVille would be completely washed away by Ye Ole Tides of Time. They would get married and forget the other one existed and they would disappear. But as I lay there one night, I committed us to memory, set us in amber, and told myself we would always live inside those scenes. The person I'd been that summer was Nicky's, and he always would be. Those kids would exist forever together, even after they didn't anymore.

One day when it was really starting to get warm outside, just like it'd been the day I met Nicky, I passed myself in the mirror, and for a sliver of a second I did not recognize the person looking back at me. I was like a peacock that had just discovered its colors. My skin was a lot better because of all the products I'd bought, my depression-related weight loss had evaporated any remaining baby fat in my face, and my clothes were getting tighter and more stylish with every new shopping trip I took. The lovesick doormat I'd been the previous summer and autumn seemed a million miles away. And the biggest change was this: the kid in the mirror appeared to actually like himself. It almost made me gasp.

And speaking of the summer: across the mall atrium I saw a boy who looked like Nicky with the volume turned down, and I felt something final sink into me – it was done. I had to let go for good. I'd found myself in the loss of him, and we were two different people now. I was still hanging onto his texts, a few of his shirts – I'd even kept his sandals on my floor, right where he'd left them – but I had to stop. He wasn't coming back. Ever. And I had to accept that he didn't want me anymore. So I kept walking and told myself that he was with me forever. He was a sunburst, and when he broke it off, he'd exploded all over me. Maybe I'd never wash him off, not really – he was with me still. Even if I would never again feel his peace, revel in his chaos, let him screw me numb and then kiss me back to life again – he was still there.

The thing was, I already knew the road was going to be bumpy for me, whoever I became. I knew the sun was never going to shine into many corners of my life. I knew I was an effeminate beta male living in the South who liked men and had daddy issues, and I knew I'd probably be a bit of a joke forever. And if not a joke, then at least forever nipping at the periphery, desperate to get into the Circle of Normal but never really allowed in. And it wouldn't be the smoothest of sailing for Nicky, either – he hated every inch of himself. But we still had the memories of that summer, we still had Savannah, we still had those glory days when he'd opened himself to me, even if we were still languishing under the glare of the South. Maybe those days would glide in the clouds forever, somewhere only I knew, and maybe I'd be able to pick myself up sometimes and grab hold of them for a minute, revisit the old happy time when we'd been together at the top of the world.

As I headed back to my car, though, I realized I needed closure. *Real* closure. I needed to say goodbye, if only silently, even if it was only a whisper into outer space. I needed to see his face on my screen one last time…

First I had to figure out how to reach him, since I was blocked from everything. Where was he out there? All his profiles were hidden. It was like he didn't even exist anymore.

So first I looked at his Instagram. Even though I was blocked from seeing his photos, I could still see that his account had gone dead. There was no other way to put it. It looked the same as always – same profile icon, same two hundred and ninety five photos. He was probably off somewhere making new memories with someone else, letting someone else leave their mark on him, too busy to leave photo evidence of this new chapter. All this and more was on my mind when I pulled out into traffic, typing away, and almost missed seeing the van coming for me until it was too late.

I noticed a silvery blur in my peripheral vision at the last second and looked up just in time to swerve out of the way. I missed a collision by inches, but coincidentally at the time of swerving I was also on the edge of a man-made ravine next to a drainage lake. I hit the edge, felt my stomach plummet, and down I went.

My car hurdled down the grass embankment, rolling terrifyingly close to toppling over as it went, as suddenly everything got silent, calm, peaceful, shimmering. *I could die in a few seconds – this could be it.* I saw glimpses of faraway memories like shards of broken crystal – I saw my father holding me on his lap on the way to the hospital after he'd accidentally shut my fingers in the car door, I saw the time I'd jumped off a too-tall cliff at summer camp and almost been knocked unconscious at hitting the lake's surface, I saw the morning I'd stood by a hospital bed and watched my grandfather's last breaths. And then I saw Nicky. He was on my couch. And he was smiling that victory smile.

As quickly as it'd started, it was over. After one last shudder to the right, my car lurched to a stop beside a lake, and another road was in clear view. I was okay. I was safe. I was alive. And suddenly, for the first time in months, the world truly felt like something worth exploring, instead of hiding from.

On the muddy, breathless drive home, I found my thoughts wandering back to Nicky. I needed to find him. I needed to feel alive as I had just now, for the rest of my life. So I took out my phone as I turned onto my street. I needed to see who he'd been talking to, who he'd added, who'd been tagging him in pictures. Just to dig in the knife, I guess, and savor the pain I deserved. So I texted my friend and demanded her Facebook email and password so I could view Nicky's profile from her account, since it was open to everyone but me. After a few minutes she responded, and that's when I logged into her profile, searched for Nicholas J. Flores, and then read the sentence that imploded my world in a microsecond:

RIP, buddy. It's been 4 months today, but we'll still never forget u down here

18

On Venus, a day lasts longer than a year does. I knew this because I was once assigned a group project on the planet and this is the only fact I remembered, as I'd picked my fingernails the whole time and made a band geek named Megan do the whole thing. But a day on Venus lasts longer than a year: the planet takes two hundred and twenty-five days to circle the sun, but two hundred and forty-three days to rotate once on its axis. June 16 was the day my world stopped spinning, the day my sun stopped shining, the day I realized time meant nothing at all.

June 16 was the day my world became not my world anymore. It was the day a hole opened up inside me and I fell all the way into it.

~

I drove the rest of the way home in a daze and vomited into a recycle bin. Then I sort of collapsed in my foyer, and after that I just remember clouds. Vicious clouds rolling in, suffocating me….for the first time in my life, I understood the relativity of time. A second became an hour, an evening became an eternity. I was being raked over the coals, and there was nothing I could do to stop it. No helping it, no saving myself from this pain. As the waves hit me over and over, I told myself it couldn't be true, it couldn't be real…I had to find out it wasn't real. It couldn't have happened. Nicky couldn't have left me here, in this world, without him. It wasn't a possibility.

I didn't know how long I lay there on the carpet. When I could move without shaking too much, I took a steamy shower to clear my clogged nostrils and then crawled back into my dank, sweaty sheets. I opened my laptop as the world closed in around me. And soon I had gathered enough details to discover I knew nothing except that Nicky was dead. He was really dead. Nicky Flores wasn't alive anymore. And I'd had no idea for four months. He hadn't dumped me – he'd died. Nicky….my love…my life…my Nicky…was dead. The words would form in my brain, but they would not make sense.

On his Facebook, and all over Google News, were the details of a death I'd never known about. Comments, pictures, news articles, interviews with his family about their new foundation in his name, all of which had been posted months before, completely unbeknownst to me. I'd stood quietly aside during the biggest event of my life, and I'd had no clue.

Nicky Flores died on his twentieth birthday, one day after he'd come over. At 8:45 AM, Nicky's car underwent an unexplained increase in velocity and collided with an oak tree at forty miles per hour. Basically, he'd been sitting at a stoplight when he'd sped up for no reason and driven into a tree. By the time the Jaws of Life pried him from the Pontiac, he was dead. From the tone of the articles, there was a good chance he'd killed himself, but the worst thing was that they never found out for sure. They still had no idea, really.

I dropped the computer on the floor as it all took hold of me. What could've possibly changed between the time he'd made love to me, triumphant, and then died? I screamed, cried, moaned, shook until I couldn't feel myself anymore. Sickened wasn't the word for what I felt. I didn't even know the word. How could he do this? How could he take himself away? I had never known a feeling like this. Ever. For months I'd been pining over a dead boy. A boy who was in the ground. I was disgusted, broken, infuriated, and almost a little embarrassed. And soon I started to panic for some reason. What was wrong with me? I'd been waiting for a dead boy to text me. I'd been having pretend arguments in my head with a dead boy. I'd been stalking a dead boy. I'd been daydreaming about spending forever with a dead boy. I'd been in love with a dead boy. I'd been casually going about my life for months while he'd been below the ground. He hadn't been ghosting me – he'd been an actual ghost.

I kept seeing him asleep that cold morning in February, beautiful and silent, the last time I'd ever seen him alive. I could've stopped him…I could've done so much more…I could've helped him love himself…

Nickicito was dead, and it was all on me.

I fell into the blackness for an hour, but I wasn't asleep, I was just a prisoner in my own body, watching my mind play out imagined scenes of his final minutes. I saw flashing lights, heard screeching tires, heard bumpers ramming into things. But I couldn't see him. He never materialized. And that was the thing I could not live with, the fact that I wasn't there for him at the end, when he'd needed me. When he'd been all alone.

I woke up at midnight, and I still felt like I was in some screwed up fever dream. I reached for my laptop again, and the more I read about him, the more I realized nothing in the story made any sense. He'd crashed directly into a tree on a clear, sunny, windless morning. His car had seemed to be in good shape before the crash, but there was also a malfunction on that specific model that could've been a factor – but there was no way to say for sure. There was no suicide note, no evidence that he'd had a heart attack or seizure or anything else that would've caused an accident. He'd mentioned nothing to anyone. Nobody had had any inkling that anything was coming. They didn't know about *me*, though…

Humans were animals, and before they died they prepared for it. When my family dog, Harper, died of obesity and old age when I was in the fifth grade, he dragged himself across the house, kissing everyone in my family, making sure to gather all of his favorite toys on the way, and then laid down in his favorite corner under a side table and died. Nicky had done none of that. He'd just…*died*. Was it a sudden deathwish that had come out of nowhere? Had he planned it all to look accidental, to save his parents from driving themselves crazy with questions? Or did he just stop paying attention for a second and *crash*?

The not knowing was the awful thing, the worst thing. What had he even been doing? Where was he trying to go? It was a real possibility that he could've just died senselessly – he could've just pressed the gas instead of the brake in an absent-minded moment. That theory made something inside

241

me lurch, though, because that would've meant he was happy…he perhaps wanted a future for himself…for us…

But I could also see him killing himself. Or I thought I could, at least. And *that* was the most horrific thing, to know he could've sank so low, become so desperate and hopeless, he'd seen death as his only escape. Thinking about it made me feel like such a failure. I could remember the moment when he'd told me he didn't want to be himself anymore – at the time, I'd tried to write it off as his typical histrionics. Looking back, though, I could just *sense* that he wanted to die. I'd just run from the realization with everything in me. And now it didn't matter.

When all the realness became too real to deny, I got so mad at him. Not just for dying, but for creating this whole crazy situation, a situation where he could die and leave me with no way to find out about it. For building his world so far from mine, for keeping me a hundred miles away. Overcome with the need to talk to someone, I picked up my phone and went to my address book, and then I realized I'd been subconsciously trying to call him. I had nobody else to talk to. I needed someone to comfort me, tell me everything would be okay, and for some reason my thoughts traveled to my mother – but that idea made no sense. My mom didn't know about Nicky. She didn't even know I liked guys. I was still too afraid to tell her. What in the world would I say to her? My family never knew about us, and the awful thing was that I *still* couldn't bring myself to tell anyone. Even after all this, I couldn't tell them. What could I possibly say? *Hey there, I've been living a secret life and I'm in pieces because of the death of a stranger whose name you've never heard, can I come over and fall apart?* It just felt too late. Not to mention the whole "my family being huge bigots" thing. My father would shun me, and beyond that, Nicky's friends either hated me or had no clue I existed. I had nobody to turn to, nobody to grieve with, nowhere to go. Except backwards, into a past I'd never get back…

This was so unfair. I didn't just not get to say goodbye – I didn't even know I *needed* to say goodbye. Holy God. If I

242

was a girl he'd been dating, I would've already been accepted into his family long ago, and I probably would've been one of the first phone calls after the accident. But I had nothing. I'd been kept clear out of his life. I didn't even have a picture with him – after our fight I'd gone into a blind rage and deleted the few he'd ever let me take of us together, and now whatever was on his phone was probably gone forever, too. We didn't even exist in the cloud anymore. It was so goddamned unfair.

So I went to bed. Every tear I'd never shed every time he'd denied me, every time he'd turned away from me in public, every time he'd kept his love apart from me…I cried all of those tears that night. Every last one.

The next night, my mom called. I answered her calls occasionally, and on this night I just picked up and listened to her silence. Suddenly something just burst open in me. I had never, in my life, wanted anything more than I wanted to unlock the gates and unleash on her, sob into the phone and share my pain and tell her all about the boy who had changed me, the boy with glitter in his eyes. Every bone in me ached to have her listen to me, comfort me, come over and hold me, tell me she was sorry, that it was okay.

"Coley?" she said soon. "Helloooo? You there? You're acting weird…is something wrong?"

I swallowed, winced, and hung up. After all this time, I was still too afraid. I still couldn't do it. And it made me hate myself on a level unlike anything I'd ever imagined.

When I was nine, I went to Hawaii with my parents and grandparents, and the most vivid memory I have is of visiting all the battleships that had been lost in the Pearl Harbor attacks. The water was so clear, you could still see all these underwater boats that'd been there for the better part of a century – it was so weird. But what I remember most was the oil. For decades, a ship called the *Arizona* had leaked the very oil that'd been pumped into its tanks on its day of sinking in 1941, sending up its sadness from the ocean floor to bloom on the surface in the form of strangely beautiful bursts of blue and green and copper. And now I was the Arizona, I guess. I would leak for Nicky forever.

Soon I retreated from the world. I lost my laptop in the mess in my room, stopped answering my phone, let my mail pile up unopened. I fell away and let the fury take me to some horrible place nobody knew but me. I never expected how painful this would be, to fall apart in secret. Every time a grandparent had died or something had gone wrong in my life, I'd had family there to hold me. But now I had nobody, and it was all my fault.

To get the memories back, I'd look to my past and hug my ghosts, hoping they'd give me something to hold. I'd try to remember how he made my feet feel, like the ground wasn't so solid anymore. I'd try to remember how his eyes made my skin feel, like I'd never looked at anything before in my life – like I was a newborn baby and he was the doctor, first sight. I'd try to remember how my whole body felt whenever I thought of him: light and heavy, lovestruck, full. But there in the cold of night, alone, mostly I just remembered the way he made my soul feel:

It was something like flying.

One night in the midst of my empty misery my mind took me back again, and there was nothing I could do but watch. My memory tied me to the posts and got out the whip. This scene was from near the end, after we'd torn each other up, just before the war had come. His mood had slipped up some kind of slope for the night, though, and momentarily he was the boy I'd fallen down the hill for, the boy for whom I'd joyfully thrown away my life.

"I like you so freaking much," he'd whispered, holding my eye contact for once. We were finding heaven between the red lights and the stop signs, too in love to let it go.

"Stop," I'd said. "The game is over. You don't have to play anymore."

"I do," he'd smiled. "It's so funny. And weird. I used to be made of stone, but I don't even recognize me anymore. You make me want to listen to fuzzy '80s love songs in the rain and you make me see neon lights even when the room is dark and you make me feel like the world isn't such a bad and scary and shitty place anymore. You make me so happy, and I never thought my life would be like this. You're my best friend."

And I realized why my memory was showing me this moment: it was the first time I'd ever *truly* admitted to myself that liking guys wasn't wrong. For the first time, I didn't believe the world was right in its belief that this was sinful. I could remember staring at him that night and just luxuriating in him, feeling the pain fade away. Because two humans with brown hair falling in love was okay. Two humans with blue eyes falling in love was okay. And two humans with two penises falling in love was also okay. The *world* was messed up, not us. This, what we shared, was beautiful and right and pure. They were so dirty out there, so tainted in their hatred. And I hated them for hating me. It wasn't Nicky's fault that he'd had to hide, that he'd maybe chosen to die instead of live in his truth. They were the problem. My boy wasn't...

But as the memory faded, I got so mad again. He was so annoying. He was so frustrating. He was so perfect. I would give anything to get annoyed by him again. Just one more time. Now that I'd ruined everything and lost him, I wanted to undo everything I'd ever done, remake all the decisions I've ever decided, go back to square one and do it all again.

Except Nicky. He could stay.

The next week was a cold, furious purgatory unlike anything I'd ever known before. The Year of Nicky was over, and I'd been tossed back into the blackness. Every morning when I woke up, it did not feel real. I would delay the realization until *boom*, it would hit, and I'd come apart again. I was imprisoned by him, just like I had *always* been imprisoned by him. Friends texted several times. Most of them looked something like: **Dude, your mom said you're not normal, or more "not normal" than usual. What's going on? Plz text me!!!** I never did, though. I didn't want to talk to any of these people.

245

Where were they before? Where had they been when I was happy?

I couldn't shake my obsession with the case, with his death. I wanted answers. Why had he done it *then*? Why *that* morning? What had set all this into motion? It wasn't enough. I didn't really believe my psycho text had sent him over the edge, because we'd fought all the time and insulted each other constantly – it wasn't that out of the ordinary for us. I wanted to ask his family every last detail, try to learn everything I could so I could form my own opinion, make all the pieces fit together, but I couldn't. His parents didn't even know about me, and there was a one hundred percent chance his sister wanted nothing to do with me. But I couldn't leave his death in my mind like this. Because at least the loved ones of suicide victims *knew* it was suicide. At least they had that much. At least they knew their loved ones had gotten so miserable, they'd chosen to take themselves out of the equation. But I didn't even have *that* knowledge. I had nothing. And where did I go from nothing?

After about ten days I had one good evening where I finally got the motivation to make myself some food and tidy up the disaster area that was my kitchen, and the next morning I bit the bullet and went to the hospital. I had no real plan in my head, I just figured I'd sniff around and see where the wind took me. I went to the information desk posing as Nicky's cousin, and thankfully I had his Puerto Rican ID card – he'd left it at my house and totally forgotten about it. The lady at the desk, Phyllis, was suspicious, but she still sent me to another waiting room on the third floor, which I guessed was where he'd been treated. The fact that his body had seen these same walls seemed to pound against my skull as I waited for a new receptionist to help me. The plan fell apart as soon as I failed to produce any real details about the case, though. In the end, they sent Dr. Martin, a kind-eyed man of about fifty who took me into a break area that smelled of cheap coffee and industrial cleaning fluid.

"Coffee?" he asked, and I shook my head, faint from the fumes and the fury. "Okay, well, Mr. Furman. I'm afraid we're not permitted to give any visitors any information which may inform them of any patient's case." He paused, breathed, looked down at me. It was then that I noticed his shirt was a beautiful salmon color, and that he was far more chic than any doctor had the right to be. "That's why I'm legally required to verbally confirm that you are the victim's...*stepbrother*? That's why your names are different?"

"Yes," I said after a minute. I knew I would never be able to repay him for this. Ever. "His...stepbrother. Yeah, yes. That's me."

He sort of smirked. "Okay, well, I will tell you everything I recall. I was the doctor assigned to break the news to the immediate family, and that is not something you forget easily, no matter how many years you've done this. Please, let's sit."

We sat. He spoke. "Nick Flores died of blunt force trauma after an auto accident. The accident itself is still somewhat of a mystery. I've never seen anything like it, really. It was very...open-ended. So many variables. *Sooo* many things to consider..."

Thanks, I wanted to say. *You're really helping me out here.* "I know," I told him. "And I know what some people suspect. But there were so many things it could've been besides suicide. He had two mild seizures in middle school, so maybe-"

"That's a possibility," he allowed. "But because of the nature of the...accident, and how long it took to get him here...it was impossible to say with any certainty that it was seizure, or even the beginning of one."

He grabbed my shoulder, but it felt empty and awkward. I could tell he didn't have any children – parents knew how to touch you better than he did. Most of them, at least. Not mine.

"I also heard of a car issue," Martin said, "a recall of his specific make and model that he never knew about. Three similar cars were tracked accelerating, but none like this, none were ever so deliberate, or so quick out of the gate."

I swallowed. This wasn't solving anything – it was deepening the pit of questions. So I looked for anything to grab and cling onto. "Well he had really bad mood swings, he must've-"

He raised a hand. "There is no way to know his mood that morning, or anything that was happening with…the mental situation at all, since there was never a diagnosis."

I tried to keep it together, but the gates broke. I'd wasted so much of my life hiding, and I had nothing at all to show for it.

"We were in love," I finally said in a voice that was not so much resigned as already gone. But the words still felt hot and scary and exhilarating as they rushed out of my mouth like that, like a beaver dam finally breaking apart. "God, it feels so weird to say that. Anyway…yeah, I loved him the first day I met him, and I love him today. I guess we were both sort of immature, and we'd date for a little while and then break up again and not talk for a few days, and then a few weeks, and then…yeah. We'd have no contact during our breaks, either. He kept me totally out of his life because he was scared, and so I didn't even know about this until last week. I had no way to find out. His family didn't know about me, his friends didn't know about me, his own sister didn't even really know about me…and so when this happened, I just figured it was another breakup, another dry spell…I had *no idea* he was…*dead*."

The last word made a world of horror bloom inside me all over again. I looked away a little, but he didn't. His eyes were leaking onto his white coat. "I'm…God, I'm truly sorry to hear that, Cole. I don't even know what to say. I've probably never heard a story that tragic. And I work in a hospital…"

I wiped my face. "What do *you* think happened?"

He hesitated. "Well. I didn't know Mr. Flores, and I'm a doctor of the body, not the soul, so I'm afraid I'm not the one you should discuss that with. However, I do think the answer to that question will eat you alive if you don't give it up. Not to sound like a fascist, but it happened, and you've got

248

to deal with it. There's nothing else you can do." He swallowed, his eyes pained and his resolve cracking, and that's when I knew he'd lost someone, too.

"What happened?" I asked.

He glanced at me. "I can still remember it – the day my...*best friend*, Neil, disappeared on this white-water-rafting weekend in North Carolina." He fidgeted, and I knew exactly what type of "friend" this had been. "He was last seen at a campsite by the creek, drinking a beer, and to this day they have never found a body. Anything could've happened. He was in and out of rehab and everything, but the strange thing was, before that weekend, he'd been doing so well. He found a job and started gardening again, and we all thought he'd turned a corner, and then it was just...*poof*. Gone. And I will sit here today and tell you that I wasted almost five years of my life despairing over what sent him into that river."

He faltered, but only for a moment. Then he put a hand on my leg, and I tried not to flinch. "I'm sorry, Cole. I really am. For...everything. I don't like this world any more than you do. All we can do is deal with where we find ourselves, you know? And hope we don't disappear into the river, too..."

I met his eyes. "And what if we find ourselves in that river?"

"Just keep swimming," he said. "Swim against the current until the current changes. That's bravery." Something in his eye sparkled, and I didn't really know what it meant. "And again, I'm truly sorry. If I can do anything else – with *honesty*, I mean that – here's my card."

He handed me a business card and got up to leave.

"Wait," I said, and he turned around. "Can you tell me where he's buried? I don't even know his family."

He shook his head one sad, final time, said sorry again, and started down the hall. Ugh. I was so sick of being sorried, of being apologized to. Why was everyone always Sorrying me, anyway? What did I have to be sorry about?

"Oh, and Cole?" he asked, and I looked up. His face softened. "What you just told me wasn't easy. Hell, I'm fifty-

four years old and I *still* can't say it. So I admire you. I truly
admire you. I just want you to know that."

He turned and left before he could say anything else.

Back in the car I wiped my eyes and took out my phone and
wanted to Google and Facebook stalk the case again until my
sight went bad and my fingers broke. Something twisted and
lurched in me, though, and I knew I had to stop. Dr. Martin
was right: I would never find out what really happened that
day. I would never find out why he never came back, and
whether he still loved me at the end or not. It was all just stuff
I'd have to live with, because if I didn't jettison this, or at least
try to jettison it, it would burn me alive.

I slipped into traffic thinking of how much I'd give up
for one final hug. I knew I would probably forget a lot about
Nicky Flores, too. He was a rain that would never stop falling,
but soon those droplets would all look the same. I'd lost three
grandparents already, and I knew how this all worked. I knew
a day would come when I would no longer be able to breathe
in a quick burst of future air and use it to synthesize his crisp,
clean scent, and I knew there would come a night when I
would try to picture him saying something and realize I'd
forgotten what his voice had sounded like. He'd be gone. I
would probably forget the way he moved, the way he laughed,
the exact proportions of his jaw, the way his face looked in the
light of July. I would wear his clothes until they fell apart and
keep his things until I lost them, and soon I would have
nothing left to remember him by. But I knew I would never
forget how that boy made me feel – like I was in the company
of clouds, like the sun had found a home inside my throat, like
I wasn't me anymore. Those feelings were mine forever.

I thought of his smile then, and how it made me want
to melt into the sun. I thought of his dark/bright galaxy eyes,
and how I could sunbathe in them. Mostly I thought of how he
made me feel, like John Hughes soundtracks and warn tomato
soup and watching fireworks pop over water. That boy had
taught me what glory tasted like: metallic, electric, like when
you bite down on tinfoil and feel that surge in your jaw. That

sweet little world we'd created, away from the watching eyes and the prejudices and the word "faggot," where he was kind to me and he acknowledged our love – I missed that world. All my little inside jokes, all our little things we'd ever seen or shared or laughed about – all of it. It didn't matter that he'd deny me as soon as he left that world, and that our heaven was shattered time and time again – it had existed once, and it was real, and nothing and nobody could ever take that away from me. That's what I had to tell myself, at least.

When I really loved a book and bonded with its characters, I loved to stop in with them in my mind here and there over the years, envision where their futures would've taken them, where they'd be, who they were becoming, who they slept beside every night, whether it had all worked out for them. And maybe the fantasy versions of us were still out there somewhere. Maybe ColeyAndNickyVille would live forever – maybe that little universe we'd created together would stretch on and never die, just like I'd told myself after the breakup. Maybe somewhere, Coley and Nicky were talking and laughing and roaming the cobblestoned streets of Savannah together. Maybe, maybe not. But I'd hold onto that hope with everything in me. God knows I had nothing else to grasp.

I wanted to be left alone forever, but right on cue, my dad came over to "drop off some mail" that evening. Immediately I knew his mind was somewhere else, though. My family had known something was wrong with me, they just didn't know what it was. But all at once, I knew my dad had an idea.

"Shitty weather, eh, kid?"

I glared at the window, my esophagus tightening around itself. I didn't want to talk about the weather with him. Or anything at all, really. He made a little throat-clearing sound, and I looked at him. "You didn't come here to talk about the weather, did you, Dad?"

He inhaled. "No. Here's the thing. A few months ago – or more than a few, maybe – I saw you at the movie theater. And I can't get it out of my head."

251

I turned my face and buried it in the covers. My stomach clenched up and my already-sweaty body started pouring. *Oh, God,* I thought as this dizzy sort of nausea rolled over me in waves. *He knows. Not now. This cannot be happening right now. Today. Can he not do this right now? Like, literally any other time but today?*

"You were with...someone I didn't expect you to be with. Doing things I'd never expected you to be doing." He swallowed. "And the worst thing was...the boy looked like...he looked like...some kind of *Hispanic*...and, hey, what do you say, isn't that his picture by your bed?"

I flipped over the *Honesty* Polaroid from that first day at the gym as my entire body bloomed with rage. So now my dad was being a racist, along with all the *other* shitty things he already was? Really? *Really?* Had he not been enough of a shit-bucket before? In all my angst over the gay issue, I'd never even stopped to think about the fact that Nicky had spent his life with a whole different set of prejudices, prejudices I could never even begin to imagine, all because of the tone of his skin. Oh, my poor boy. I'd been so caught up in my own struggles – being gay in a world that largely wanted to erase me and make me go away – I'd never even realized I'd been enjoying a privilege I didn't even know I'd had, which was being white in America. Just as I'd envied the clueless freedom that straight guys took for granted, people of darker pigments probably looked at me and envied *my* freedom...

And how could my dad have said he didn't know about all this? He knew, and he'd been rubbing the suspicion in my face for years like I was a dog who'd shit in the dining room. He'd held this over my head forever, and everyone knew it. Ugh, I was *so* fed up with living by this stupid man's outdated rules. I'd never been sicker of anything, and I'd had severe asthma as a boy. My father had seen me loving the person I was born to love, a boy who was dead, and he was horrified. Why would I ever feel bad about that?

I *almost* wanted this to be some shitty after-school special. I almost wanted him to sit on my bed beside me and

252

tell me he loved me no matter what, that I was still a treasure to him. But he never would. My father was a real person, with real prejudices, real hatred in his spirit, and there would never be some softly-lit, come-to-Jesus, sitcom moment with him. He would never take me in his arms and rock me, wipe away my tears and say "it's okay, son. It's okay." That just wasn't going to happen.

"So," my dad said, "whatever this is, if it's some breakup or something, I just want you to know that your stepmother and I are monitoring you, and-"

"Richard," I interrupted, calling him by his first name because he was no longer a father to me, "you cannot come into my house and stand at my bed and tell me these things. You just can't. It's not in the cards for you. You're a bad father, and that's the worst thing anything could ever be. You hated me because I...because I wasn't who you wanted me to be. You always did. You treated me like a pile of hot garbage my whole life."

"I didn't hate you because of all that," he snapped, and I winced. I guessed it was too much for me to want him to say he didn't hate me at all. "Well...that factored into it, maybe. You know how I feel about the gay issue. I don't support what they do, and I'm perfectly within my rights to feel that way."

I leaned back. "Your wife," I said plainly.

"My wife?"

"Yep, your wife. She's Asian, and she didn't choose to be Asian. She was born that way, just like other people happen to be born gay – she didn't choose her race any more than anyone else chose their sexuality. So you saying that you 'don't support gays' would be just like saying you don't support Asians, and that would sound racist as hell, right? Gay people are born gay, and you don't have the right to 'disagree' with that any more than you have the right to 'disagree' with race or eye color or anything else that people don't choose about themselves. Bigotry is bigotry, and will be treated as such."

He stuttered, then tried again. "Cole, I..."

When he finally realized he was speechless, he reset his shoulders and glared at me. "Whatever. Never mind all that. Mostly I just hated you because you were arrogant."

"*Arrogant*?"

"You'd shut yourself up in your little world back in your bedroom with your camera and your music and your books, totally oblivious to the rest of us, to the fact that I was hurting too, I'd lost my wife…you never cared about me. You never cared about the son I wanted you to be."

And my voice evacuated my throat for a moment. "But you're talking about a – I was a freaking *child*!"

The Coley that had existed before Nicky would've never talked to his father like this. He would've crossed his arms, lips trembling, and taken it on the chin. But if I could survive Nicky Flores, I could survive anything.

My dad looked away, and for probably the first time ever, I saw a glimpse into his mind. All I'd ever done was deny him his dreams. He wanted the football-star son he could play catch with – that was his dream. He didn't want me. I was a defected product to him. Sure, it was a hateful and homophobic dream, but that wasn't his fault. People dreamed about all different things, for all kinds of crazy reasons. And maybe this was adulthood: seeing your dreams fall away, and then walking on. Looking for new dreams…

But that still didn't mean I had to give a shit.

"You were the *parent* in this situation," I said, "and you were supposed to-"

He started to say something, but I interrupted him and told him to shut the hell up. He stared at me and then I smiled a little, because when I was really mad, like really *REALLY* mad, I got nice. (Hell hath no fury like me with a smile on my face.)

I stared down at my hands, marveling at this new universe. My dad knew I liked dudes – holy shit. What a crazy new world we lived in. I waited to feel panic, self-loathing, all the things that would've come before. But nothing came, not really. I knew I was gonna have to deal with the fact that Nicky had left me, abandoned me, found death more attractive

254

than a life with me, but right now…I knew he'd be laughing like hell with me at the look on my father's face.

I knew my dad was probably about to kick me out, but the crazy thing was, I didn't even need him anymore. I was the boy Nicky Flores had loved once, and I would carry that strength with me forever, whip it out whenever I needed and let it unfurl in the breathless wind, triumphant like the stars and stripes. I was also free from my father for other, more monetary reasons. I could still hear the book agent's voice, in rapidfire New York, speaking to me yesterday, after I'd finally picked up the phone for the first time in what felt like forever.

"Is this Cole Furman? Sheesh, kid, we've been trying to reach you for *weeks*, we thought you might've disappeared – anyway, I specialize in turning blogs into books, and I've got editors at four different publishing houses barking up my tree, asking how me to reach you…are you interested in doing a book with me, Mr. Furman? We think it could be massive, spectacular, a real treat for your fans. My office especially liked that post about the old gay women – geez, talk about ripping your heart out…"

I talked to her for a few minutes, real hesitant, and finally I admitted I was scared to go from my own little Instagram account and jump to a stage that big.

"So what, kid?" she'd asked, as the chaotic background noise told me she was doing ten things at once. "I've been afraid, too. How do you think I graduated from some second-rate school with a worthless degree and then moved to the city on my own when I was twenty-two with eight hundred dollars in my pocket? Follow your fear. If it doesn't scare the living turds out of you, it's not worth your time."

I'd kind of wanted to say no. I'd almost wanted to tell them I wasn't a gimmick, that I couldn't be bought. But then she made me a huge offer, and obviously I said yes. It was funny, the doors that opened just when you thought life had pushed you down a dead-end hallway. I already had a sixty thousand dollar contract on the table with a publisher for a hardcover version of *Honesty,* with more offers on the way.

255

The publisher I eventually chose would turn my blog into a book, which they'd then market to my fans and sell in bookstores across the country. One publisher even had a beautiful and incredibly ironic subtitle for the book: *change the world by being yourself.* Whenever I accepted an offer, ten percent would be taken by agents and graphic designers, and countless more thousands would be swallowed up by taxes and other expenses, but I didn't care. I would still have enough money for an apartment. My *own* apartment, where I could be who I wanted to be, love who I wanted to love. Maybe here, maybe in Savannah, maybe on Jupiter. But the thought alone made me happy for the first time since I could remember. I was free from my family's control for definitely a little while, and hopefully forever. I couldn't believe it: a *book*, those beloved pieces of trees that we stared at in hopes of hallucinating vividly, was going to have my name on the cover. If only I could tell the twelve-year-old version of me about all this, and watch the joy spread over his face…

I looked up at my father. I told him all of this, including how unbelievably hard my life had been up to this point because of the world's persecution of my sexuality, and then I asked him to accept me. Or demanded it, really, as I stared at his sky-blue eyes and silver-blonde hair. And deep down, I guess I really *did* want his acceptance, even if I was starting to learn I didn't necessarily *need* it. Somewhere deep within the boy I still was, I really did want my daddy to be proud of me. I would always be somebody's kid, no matter how old I thought I was getting.

And at the end, my father simply glanced at me and then skipped his eyes over to the blinds. "Come on, pull yourself together," he said through a clenched jaw. "Boys don't cry."

I stared at him as an atomic bomb detonated inside me. "Boys do whatever the *fuck* they want to do."

He jerked his head over to me. Here in the South, land of SEC football and hunting trips and camouflage baseball caps, boys were expected to play ball with their fathers, not play with *actual* balls. Although there were notable exceptions, almost every father I knew detested their gay sons, and if they didn't, they were still confused and terrified by them. Nobody wanted a freak for a kid, and that was the saddest truth I'd ever known.

Sitting here in my new truth, though, I almost felt bad for my dad. Something else I was learning was that people were never going to be who you wanted them to be – humans were themselves, incurably. Just look at Nicky. And me. So maybe I could accept him, flaws and all. Or maybe I could, you know, *not*. Because here I was, revealing the horror world I'd called home all my life, and he didn't even care. But I didn't *need* him to care, I reminded myself. And all at once, I realized that my own happiness had never even occurred to me. *I could be happy,* without strings attached. I deserved that happiness, too. I didn't have to live inside a lie anymore. I never did at all. I didn't have to force myself into the shadows and spend my life in some dull state of misery anymore – I could get dressed in the morning in exactly the clothes I wanted and not have to worry about what people thought when they looked at me; I could go on a dating app and act like myself instead of somebody else. I could watch the gay-ass shows I wanted to watch without jumping up whenever someone walked in and pretending I'd been searching for the remote all along. I could be happy, and that happiness did not require my father at all. I felt as good as I had when I'd posted the old woman's love story and had Ruth's widow nod at me from across the sidewalk. The fact that I could turn out okay had never occurred to me, *ever*, as stupid as that sounded. Happiness – what a concept!

Suddenly every insult my father had ever thrown at me, every time he'd ever looked at me with hatred in his eyes, every time he'd scowled down at my tight jeans and told me to turn around and change, lit into me and made me know for sure that I was still alive, on my own, as Coley Furman and nobody else. Of course, my father had every right to have these views – I also had every right to tell him to get the hell out of my life until he changed them. Because now I knew the truth, and it was a taste so bitter I could spit. I would never be

257

free. Not at all. Not until I could wake up in the morning and make my own decisions, walk down the street holding hands with the person I loved. Too much fear and hatred in this world was holding me back. It was holding us *all* back. We were so far back, we were behind ourselves, actually. We could do so much better.

"I like guys," I told Richard Cole Furman III, "and you don't like it, and you don't like *me*, and right now this is still my house, so please get the hell out of it. I'll have Mom come over tomorrow and help me pack, but from this day forward, I want nothing to do with you."

He laughed a little, incredulous. "Really? *Really?* You're going to choose *Diane* over *me*?"

"Mom may be a disaster," I said, "and she may have ruined my childhood, but at least I always knew she loved me. You are a sad, scared little man, and I feel sorry for you. Now get the hell out of my house before I call the cops."

He just stared at me. He was an idiot, and I no longer respected his opinion nor required his approval.

"Oh, and Richard? Nicky *was* Hispanic, fresh from Puerto Rico, you racist shitbag. He spoke Spanish to me sometimes when we kissed, too. It was really hot. Anyway, call me when you're not a bigot. Love ya!"

My father turned on his heel and left my sights for what we both knew would be the last time for a long time.

After Richard left I scrolled through my newsfeed. I saw a photo of Jonathan, the beautiful repressed boy I'd fallen in love with back in middle school, and it made me clinch up inside. I felt so bad for him – oh, how the mighty had fallen. The arm of his "girlfriend" was tossed over his shoulder, but he looked absolutely dead in the eyes. And as I listened to the cars driving down the road outside I realized I would never again have to sit through that game. I would never have to play along and live against my own grain and pretend to be a human I was not, in front of my father or FitTrax jocks or anyone else. Nicky had blown the doors off that life, and I had him to thank for it, even if he was gone. As I sat there I imagined what my life would be like now, had I never met Nicky and fallen in love with him.

This morning I would've woken up sad, then gone to a FitTrax class I didn't want to be at, then maybe come home to watch Netflix alone and listen to my dad berate me and lacerate me on the phone while I sat there and said nothing. Maybe I'd zip over to Target to run from the loneliness, where I would've watched a mom catch her little boy in the *Barbie* section and yank him away by the arm, or maybe listened to a bunch of teenaged boys jokingly call each other faggots and cocksuckers. During each of these hypothetical scenarios I would've bit my tongue and walked away. Finally I would've cooked dinner by myself before watching a few *Bravo* shows and going to sleep in a cold bed, and then I would wake up the next day and do it all over again. I would be comfortable, safe, bored, fed-up, and miserable. Everything was different now, and also new and scary, but still, I was free. This was what Nicky had given me: freedom.

I owed that boy everything.

~

That night I dreamt about him for the first real, tangible time. What I wanted to see in my dreams were the simple little nights I craved more than anything in the world for some reason, when he'd show up at my door, red-faced and excited, and we'd walk down into the dunes and sit on the edge of the sand. We'd love each other under the stars, not doing much of anything at all, just being. But my actual dream was different, not to say it was awful. He wasn't the Nicky of our last few weeks together, the dark and damaged and paranoid version of him, the runner. In my dream he was the Nicky of July, that smiling triumphant boy with the galaxy eyes and the world opening out in front of him, the boy who would sometimes talk about a future with me like it was an inevitability instead of an impossibility, the boy who wasn't afraid. We were on his golf cart together on a random evening, in the only town we'd ever known, the *last* town he'd ever know, the town that had killed him, laughing about something or the other. His hair shined, his eyes gleamed, and he was free. As the light faded from bright to gold and finally to amber, we rode into a burning sunset together, back during the only few months I'd ever truly been alive.

My dream slipped and stumbled and spun forward, and suddenly we were thirty-ish, lying on a bed on a Sunday morning with a galaxy-eyed baby boy between us. Nicky was older and thinner-haired and wrinklier, and I loved him even more. We weren't hiding, we weren't running, we were just happy. And this, I suspected, was the life I could've had if the world had allowed Nickicito to let himself love me.

I woke up gasping into a pillow as wet as a rainstorm.

19

The next day I woke up pretty early, craving Waffle House breakfast. I couldn't really find anything clean to wear, so I threw on a beigey-pink Lady Gaga tee from Urban Outfitters I'd gotten in the midst of my post-Nicky revival. When I walked into the restaurant I felt eyes on me, and I made awkward contact with Miss Velma, my bigoted old neighbor. She was staring at me, disgusted, and suddenly I just didn't want to deal with it anymore. *"Screw you, Miss Velma,"* I whispered as I slid into a booth, middle fingers held high. She turned the color of the maroon jukebox and buried her face in her menu.

Would this last, though? Had I officially stopped caring for good, was this a whole new me, or was I doomed to go back to my old ways in a few weeks? I didn't really know. But for the first time, the mystery of it all excited me instead of scaring me. This really was a whole new world, and I was gonna dare it to be kind. And if not kind, then at least a hell of a lot less douche-y.

When I left, I knew I didn't want to go home. Not yet. There was one more person to try to contact. She was the last person on Earth I wanted to talk to, actually, but I needed to do this. So I pulled into Dairy Queen, shaking off the vivid memories of Nicky and I getting dipped cones there one rainy day in the summer, when the roof was leaking and the employee lady yelled at us for walking through the puddle on the tile. I parked the car and took out my phone with trembling hands. First I looked at the last text Nicky ever sent me before everything went to hell – it was a perfectly normal snapshot of a perfectly normal conversation. **Ok, see you later, loser,** he'd said, since "loser" was something he'd call me as a term of endearment whenever he was in a mushy mood. I cried for a moment, then I brought up the profile of the person I needed to talk to. She probably wanted nothing to do with me in this life and a million more, but I had to try.

I added her on Facebook, and to my complete shock, she accepted me immediately. Not one to wait around anymore, I tried to type her a message, but my app told me she was already typing. I sat back, speechless, and waited for her message to come in:

I remember you, she said. **I know you.**

You do?

I knew she knew of me, of course, I just had no idea she'd actually admit it.

I do. I'm running errands soon, so meet me at the Starbucks in downtown Savannah.

Okay...when?

As soon as you can, she said as I took a terrified breath and put the car in reverse.

~

Two hours later I sat in a corner of the massive Starbucks in downtown Savannah, both reveling in and repelled by the presence of Nicky Flores' sister. She'd aged five years in a matter of months, but her eyes were still alive and all-knowing. I felt like I'd seen her a million years ago and five seconds before, all at once. She still looked so much like Nicky that it was almost like seeing him again, which felt horrible and awkward and weird and gorgeous. And again I thought of all the things the world did to love, and sighed. *Mr. Brightside* by The Killers played in the background, a lovelorn old rock song about a man despairing over his lover moving on with her life, and I realized that for the first time, I understand every lyric. It had all been senseless nonsense to me before, but suddenly every word hit me like a gust of cold air. Love had taught me a whole new language.

"So…" she said. She sounded pissed, and her body couldn't have been angled further away from me. Which reminded me of a Flores I'd once known…

"Yeah…*so*." For some weird reason I laughed a little. The disappeared quickly, though. "This is kinda awkward."

"I know. The thing is…I, um, wanted to talk to you about…everything. I'd been thinking about you a little, ever since that night, and then when you added me, I knew exactly who you were…"

She trailed off. I hated this girl on a cellular level, but I tried to hide it. So she'd known exactly who I was, and what I'd meant to her dead brother. She could've done more to find me. I would've given anything to have been there with them, to grieve with them, to sit with them and talk about him. But I'd lost that chance forever.

"I'm sorry about everything," I said to move things along, and she looked away. "How's your family?"

"Uh. Not good. Their only son is gone. My mom's a mess and my dad is worse." She looked out the window. "*Anyway*. How are *you*?" she asked, her eyes so far away from me, in so many ways.

"I am…well, nothing," I said. "I've been…nowhere, mostly."

"Okay. When did you know? *How* did you know?"

"It took…*a while*," I swallowed. "Too long, actually. It's only been about a week or so. We weren't speaking, and so…I didn't know."

"Oh, God," she said with wide eyes. I didn't know what to tell her. I was sitting there, half alive, because of her brother. And she knew. She could've tracked me down and included me in it all. But she didn't.

"Yeah. It hasn't been fun," I said. This was so awkward. "So…let's get to why I added you today."

"Yes?"

"If there's one thing I know, but *don't* want to know, but feel like I *have* to know…it's about…that day. I feel like that was taken away from me. I should've been there," I said, and then I looked away, because I didn't want to get her mad before I could get the details out of her.

"Yeah, I know, and I'm sorry about that," she said, except she didn't look sorry at all. "You know, my parents, they have their views and their opinions and everything…" She trailed off again, unwilling or unable to finish. I understood. I had spent my life understanding. "Okay," she sniffled. "Okay, I get it. Details: you deserve that much." She leaned her body back, but put her head forward. "I talked to him the night before it happened. He was maybe a little quiet, but there was no absolutely no hint that something would happen so suddenly – he was always a little low, you know? He asked me when I was coming down, mentioned his pet snail, said something senseless about how he missed chandeliers-" I choked up at this, but kept listening- "but yeah, everything seemed normal." She swallowed. "And then…*and then*. The next day. I saw him, first of all. When he was…dead." We both winced at the word. "I didn't even mean to, and I'll probably regret it forever, but I saw him. I was at a bachelorette in St. Simon's Island when I got the call, and I drove down as soon as I heard. They were still getting…getting him out, of the thing. The car. He was…"

She trailed off again in a way that was beyond mortified, then shook her head, meeting my eyes for the first time. I'd never known what the word "horror" meant until that moment. Neither of us knew what to say for a minute, because suddenly the distance between me and the event seemed to disappear. Suddenly I was right there in the car with him, and I wanted *not* to be. It was the hardest thing I'd ever had to envision. I wanted to erase that image forever, and that just made me feel worse.

"But he was still beautiful. He'll always be beautiful," she said in a defeated way that told me she was perfectly aware that her little brother was now a rotting corpse and was not beautiful at all. It made me shudder. Sitting with her, knowing we both cried about the same person every night, was massively uncomfortable in a way I could not describe. And we were all rotting, really. All of us. This futureworld was breaking apart and headed to hell and we were all passengers, burning together.

"Looking back, do you think he did it on purpose?" I asked. She shook her head, and it looked as empty as a cup of water in a cupboard. Because how did you even face a question? A question that basically meant *"do you think we made him miserable enough to make him want to die?"*

"We don't think he…we don't think it was suicide. It was so out of nowhere, you know? There were no big declarations, no arrangements. And there was no sign of a seizure. He just…died." She pulled her eyes to me, with some effort. "But then again, we have no idea. He did take my grandma's death pretty hard. But I wasn't in the car with him. Nobody was...and also, my parents don't know what I know, about was going on…with you…" She cleared her throat. "Did *you* see any signs that…that something like this would…come?"

I played with my straw. She had no idea how much I'd loved her brother, and I didn't know how much I should give away about this. "No. Or, I mean, obviously his moods were…up and down. All the time. And he'd mentioned a few times how hard it was for him to be…alive," I said, editing carefully, "and so I wouldn't put it past him. But I can't really imagine him doing it like this – no letters, no Facebook status, nothing. It makes no sense. But then again, I wouldn't have known, anyway. We'd stopped….hanging out before then."

"Oh. I see." She sighed loudly. "When did you meet him?"

For some reason I didn't want to talk about any of this with her. Our story was Nicky's, and I wanted it to stay that way. So I just shrugged and then shook my head.

"Okay then. I guess I deserve that," she said.

"Yeah. Yeah, you do."

She did a double take, but I didn't care. Something I'd learned in my time in bed was that you could choose what to be ashamed of. And I didn't want to be ashamed of things I didn't choose anymore. I didn't choose to have a father who turned the other way and checked out of his own life while I grew up. I didn't choose to wake up one summer day and fall in love with a dude. What was out of my hands would no longer be a burden on my back. And that decision felt final. Maybe we couldn't decide to be free – but we *could* decide to be free of the world's opinions of us. And perhaps that was the same thing. Maybe finding freedom didn't mean being set free – maybe it meant setting *yourself* free. From your own dogma, from the ideas and expectations and fears that kept you down, from the hatred you felt for yourself. From everything.

And then I felt bad for her, total pity, because she didn't know how to deal with Nicky any better than Nicky had. She didn't disapprove of him personally, she was just trying to help him conceal something about himself that horrified them both – she was being a sister, helplessly.

"Why did you call me here?" I asked.

If her face had looked pained before, it looked excruciated now. "You know why."

"Um…I'm not sure I do?"

"To say thank you," she swallowed.

"For?"

She stared at me, her eyes shining with tears. "For freeing my brother," she said, her voice cracking and breaking mid-sentence, and I still didn't really get it. He didn't feel free. He just felt dead. "Cole," she said, and her eyes easily held onto mine in a way that told me she got whenever she wanted in this life. "Come on. He was more himself around you than any time I'd ever seen him. That night at Mellow Mushroom – God, I've never seen him happier, lighter. You gave Nicky his first-ever chance to be…Nicky." Her eyes overflowed with the tears, and I looked away. "*And I'd never seen him be Nicky before,*" she sobbed, quietly so nobody would stare. "Never never never. He was nobody's secret when he was with you, and I'll never be able to repay you for that. You were a gift to him, in a weird little way. Don't you know that? He needed you. You gave him honesty…"

I covered my face as the tears came. Nothing she could offer me would ever be enough. She was really, truly crying now, too, but she still couldn't touch me, and it hurt like an ice

266

bath. "He was in love with you," she said, tears slopping in her shirt. "He really was. And I know you were, too. I saw it in your eyes. His, too. I could just…feel it that night, in the weirdest way. The air around you two just…exploded. It was the strangest, prettiest thing. Part of me is so sad I'll never see it again…"

Shit. I looked up and stared out of the window as she tried to get herself together.

"So, I really do owe you an apology," she said soon. "I was so wrong, in so many ways…"

Finally I cleared my throat. "I don't know what to say. Thanks, I guess. But still, you're only saying all this *now*. Why didn't you tell me about this before? And maybe, you know, *include me in his funeral*?"

She shrugged in a pitiful way, her face twisted up like the roots of a tree. "Nicky kept his cards close. Everyone knew that. You…crossed my mind, but I had no idea how to reach you, how to find you – I didn't even know your last name. All I had was that night, when you guys had all that…love in your eyes."

This made sense, but I still wanted to shank her. Finally I met her eyes again, and they hit me like a bomb. *She has Nicky's eyes,* I thought with a weird choking sound. I would never see Nickicito's galaxy eyes again.

"Oh, God," I sighed a minute later. "This is somehow so much worse than just a suicide. At least suicide victims' families know they wanted to blow their brains out. Why does the knowing make it so much better?"

She exhaled. "I think because we want to know if we failed him, or if we could've helped. But we don't even know that much. We don't have anywhere to start from."

"Who's we?" I asked her.

"*We* as in, his family." There it was again – her attitude. There was ownership in her tone, and it infuriated me. I couldn't do this anymore.

"Yeah. I've gotta go, I've got stuff to do."

She started collecting herself. "Oh, of course, of course."

Then I turned to her. "But first...can you tell me how to find his grave?"

"Oh, *Cole*," she gasped, her eyes glassy like a pond again.

"Yeah?"

"I'm just so sorry that you have to ask me that. That you have to say those words...his...*his grave*. I'm sorry for...everything."

I sort of angled myself away a little. A rich, straight woman was telling me she was sorry that I was gay. As if she had any clue, any idea, any *glimpse* of what she was talking about. I didn't know what to say, because she would never understand a drop of it. I despised her, but I thanked her nonetheless. I really did feel bad for her. "Thanks. And I mean, I'm sorry too," I said. "You're his sister. You've known him forever. You came from the same bones. This must be really awful for you."

She bit her lip, her eyes small planets of horror. "You know what? It is, and it isn't. Nicky was never happy – we all knew that. We didn't really know why, but we knew. So I'd like to think that wherever he is right now, he's...free. Flying. God knows he deserves it."

I sort of smiled down at the table in a way I did not really understand. "Yeah. Me too."

"Did he ever tell you about our uncle who lived next door to us?" she asked soon.

"Next door to you? You mean...the gay guy..."

"I'm guessing that's a yes. Yeah, that was my uncle. And he was a lot like Nicky."

I watched her.

"I'm not an idiot," she said. "I know – or, *knew* – my brother better than anyone, and I've known about this forever. You have to understand that I'm not just some evil bitch. All I was trying to do was keep my family together. My dad hated my uncle and always made comments about how he deserved what he got, and every single time, Nicky would get this look on his face like he'd seen a mass grave or something..."

Her eyes wide, she sighed. "Sometimes I think Nicky saw this as a…death sentence. And I just wanted to help him through that."

I didn't know what to say. So much more was making sense now, even if the big picture was still blurry. "Wow. I guess there's a lot he never told me."

"Yeah. And that's also another thing." She sat up. Something in her face changed, and she wouldn't meet me in the eye anymore. I noticed she was fingering her crucifix bracelet, and that's when I knew something bad was coming. "After today, I am going to have to block your number, and your Facebook, all that," she told the floor. "I won't ever be able to face this again. I need to forget you, and I hope you understand that. This situation was already really close to making me lose my mind, and your whole involvement is just…stress I don't need to think about." She closed her eyes. "I'm really sorry, and everything."

For some reason I nodded. So this was why she'd rushed me here: she wanted to squeeze all the facts out of me she could and then dismiss me, discard me like her brother had. Oh well. Then I pretended my eyes were a phone screen, and tried to screen-shot her, this girl in front of me, exactly as I saw her. I wanted to remember her for everything she was, every detail of Nicky she still contained in her living, breathing body. Their noses were different, but she had his eyes, his hands, the elegant shape of his jaw. I would never see any of this again – outside of my dreams, of course.

Mercifully, her phone rang. "It's my mom," she said, motioning at her phone as she readied to answer it, and it sounded like an apology. "Hey, Mom. Yeah. I don't know, probably six-ish. Where are *you*? Cool. Um, who am *I* with?"

She glanced at me, and I knew that this was it. Now or never. This was probably the last chance for his family to ever find out about me. But her eyes tracked away, and the past closed up. And I understood what it meant. It was time to say goodbye.

She finally looked at me, and for one moment, the purest, most desperate sorrow I had ever seen radiated from

269

her eyes, so similar to my Nicky's. And then she looked away. And that made it official: Nicky's family would never know about me.

She spoke to the woman I both did and did not know, the woman I'd hoped would become my mother-in-law. "Oh. I'm just with Nicky's...*friend*. It's nothing. I'll come by pretty soon."

I walked out to my car and felt nothing at all. *So much for closure*, I thought. That meeting had accomplished nothing. I'd even half-expected Victoria to pause, take out some crumpled paper, and offer it to me. The tragicomic romance books about dead teens always had goodbye letters, tear-stained missives to tie up all the loose ends, soothing messages from beyond...

"Here," she'd say in this book version of my life, battling tears with a smile. "He wrote this for you. We found it in his room. We love you so much, and you're part of our family now. See you at Easter dinner. Also, here's a photo of the funeral you never got to see..."

But this wasn't a trendy book, this was my shitty little life. Shitty things happened all the time, and it was shitty, and that was it. There was no touching violin sound at the heartbreaking parts, there was no big satisfying ending where we'd run for each other in an airport terminal. Nicky was dead.

Just as I reached for my door handle, though, I heard someone running out to me.

"Cole, sorry, wait."

I turned around, and there she was. In real life. "There's something else."

"Yeah?"

She stopped and smoothed her shirt. "I saw him right before it happened. A few nights before, I mean. He'd lost weight and stopped returning our calls, so I came down with Mom, and we found him living in a mess. Ugh, it was awful. There was rotten food on the stove, he was drunk on his couch...anyway, after Mom went to bed, I sat with him on the floor while he got even drunker. He was wearing this shirt, this really cute dark green thing, and he kept saying you bought it for him."

I winced. "Okay? And?"

"...And I just want you to know I made sure he was buried in it. For you. He'll wear that shirt forever."

I shivered and inhaled. So this was my involvement in my great love's funeral. A shirt.

"Anything else?" I asked, and she reached into her bag and took out an envelope. "What's that?"

She frowned. And that was the first time I saw real, true guilt in her eyes. It was old guilt, washed away at full blast, but still, it was there.

"All I did was glance at it when I found it, but...I think it's some kind of breakup letter he never gave you."

20

I drove to the cemetery with the windows rolled down and the breakup note burning a hole in my pocket. I'd always hated these places, and today was no different. Cemeteries were like hospitals – nobody ever came here for a good reason. You came to either prepare for goodbye, or say it. Never anything else. And here it was. Goodbye.

And maybe first love was an inferno that would never be matched. That was probably the case. True love was a temporary promise, a song sung in an empty church in the woods, and I knew the world did not owe me another Nicky Flores, even on the off chance that it could ever again produce a magic that potent. The odds were that no one would ever burn up for me like that again, no soul would ever sift into mine and join it as one, and it was back to the grey, and I was on my own for good. But I wasn't sad, because I was starting to realize that my love for Nicky would always be there. Shit, he'd been dead for four months and it hadn't faded at all. Maybe true soul mates could never be separated by death – maybe one soul just lived inside the other until they could join again in a different world. For as long as I lived I would be able to close my eyes and take a breath and sail back to the brightest parts of my memory, where we'd be happy and young and free. In my dreamworld he would be nineteen and beautiful and beside me forever – I'd always have that, no matter where this place took me. In my mind, he would always be a city on fire – Nickicito was a moveable feast. Even despite all he'd put me through, he'd still given me one little masterpiece of a summer for me to carry in my pocket for the long haul. And now the possibilities of us – the castle in my mind where he'd somehow survived, where we existed together – would always be my favorite place to visit. He was my first, my best, my chaos, my destruction, and the funny thing was, looking back, I would do it all over again. I was so stupid. At least he'd found a temporary home in my eyes, though.

I parked my car. On the way to his grave – oh, God, *his grave* – I tripped a little on the edge of a bench, and I laughed a little. I just couldn't win in this game of grace. Never could. And as the stone came into view, our final frame, I got the cruelest, clearest flashback out of nowhere. It was kind of raining, and we were coming back from that weekend in Savannah, from those few days when he'd finally opened himself to me. I was driving for a minute because he had a headache, and my hand was resting on his leg. I remember feeling not swept away by love or anything dramatic like that, but just feeling *comfortable*, totally comfortable, for probably the first time in my life. Nobody could gawk at us in there in that car, point and laugh at the freaks. Locked in that glass case of emotion, we were comfortable and at ease for maybe the first and last times ever. Even now, I could see my boy sleeping in the soft rainy sunlight beside me. I could feel how my throat wanted to close when I looked at him because he was too beautiful. I could smell the rain and the leather and the gasoline from the slick, shiny highway. And even though all the rest of it had fallen away, I was sure that moment would soar forever.

But it was built to fall apart, of course. When we got closer to Neptune Beach, the traffic thickened. Every time we passed a car that was tall enough to look into our windows, I'd flinch and take my hand away, too afraid to show my love to the world, or even to passing strangers. But that moment still remained the best of my life. I wish I would've known that nothing that perfect could last. And as I looked down at the stone marking his name and day of death, I prayed against hope that wherever he was, he understood. I'd like to think he did, at least. His sister had been kind of right: he *did* feel free, in a weird way. At the very least, he was out of *here*, and that was one small step in the right direction.

I stopped at his patch of Earth, which had been broken by shovels four months ago but had already partly filled in with grass and weeds. No flowers – they'd already rotted away. The world had already started forgetting him – I'd missed out on so many stages of grief. I couldn't believe it was all already over. A little whimpery, chokey sound escaped from the back of my throat when I saw his name and realized I'd never hear his presidential voice again. And as I stood there I got this lurching feeling in my chest and suddenly, for the first time, I knew it – his death had been no accident. He'd chosen to leave this place. I could feel the smoldering loss of him, the departure of him, his white suicidal anger lingering everywhere, grabbing at me like manic little pixies. Maybe I was realizing it now, maybe I'd known since the first day – but he'd probably killed himself. He'd snapped and driven into the tree at full speed. Oh, Nicky.

I sighed and wiped tears from my neck. Here he was, the boy who'd been born and then died on two different February Twelfths, and loved me in between them.

"Hi, galaxy eyes."

I saw that he'd been buried next to his beloved grandma, Roberta, and that gave me some solace. I knew he would've liked that. But then I noticed a word was missing from his headstone. "*Nicholas Jose Flores*," it said. "*Beloved son, brother and grandson.*" So I took my pen, bent down, and wrote the words *(and boyfriend)* on the slick marble under the inscription. You couldn't really read it, and it would soon fade away, but I didn't care. I didn't blame his family for not writing it – they'd never known a thing about us, of course – but that didn't mean I couldn't do a little editing of my own.

I blew my nose as my throat tickled with tears that were begging to rise to my eyes. What do you even say to the dead love of your life? To the boy you'd hoped to turn to dust with? It was the strangest concept to wrap my head around: Nicky didn't exist anymore. What made people talk to dead people, anyway? I had no idea, and yet here I was…

"It's me," I said softly. "I just came to say hi, I guess. And nobody's watching, so don't worry. Nobody cares. There's nothing wrong with chandeliers, anyway…never was at all…"

I swayed a little as I stood, and I knew I could not pretend anymore. It all felt so real now that I was here, only feet away from whatever was left of him. He was the one that

274

got away, the one that could've been. So my soul burst open in the form of liquid from my tear ducts and vicious sobs from somewhere between my throat and my stomach. "Oh, God. I'm sorry I couldn't fix you, Nicky. I'm so sorry…"

And I *was* sorry. For everything. A word could hold so much in it, after all. I was sorry for this terrible world that had made us like this. I was sorry for a culture so vile it made death seem like a more attractive option than openness. But mostly I was just sorry that I had let it all keep me from loving him, that I had let it beat me. This was a level of sorry I had never experienced, though – I was soaked in it, drenched in it, and I knew I would never be able to take back my actions during the last few months of his life. Or my *lack* of action, to be more precise. There were so many things I could've done to save him, but it was over. I wanted to hope that the world going forward would be better and kinder and less sucky than the one we were leaving behind, but I couldn't. I'd always assumed humanity would reach some sort of critical mass – that we'd figure things out and roll on with it – but yeah, no, this definitely didn't feel like that. In this bright future, my best friend was dead because of the shame. The fear. We were trapped, suffocating, and it wasn't getting any better. It was so freaking stupid that he'd had to die for this.

Cruelly, an old woman was crying at her husband's plot a few graves away, her kids next to her, and as I watched them I just thought, *that right there – that's what the world stole from me.* I would never get the validation of the world knowing Nickicito had loved me. The act of grieving meant so much more when you were doing it in the center of a group of people who loved you, or had at least loved the same person as you. What did my lonesome grief mean to the world? Nothing. People had to know about this, but they never would. I had nowhere to run – I was still closeted to my friends, my mom barely wanted anything to do with my life, and my dad was, well, my dad. The world had erased ColeyAndNickyVille.

As I stood there I tried to imagine what his funeral looked like, how his parents must've sounded as their boy was lowered into the Earth, but I couldn't. And that's when I realized I probably wouldn't even have known about it anyway, even if I'd known his family as a "friend." I wouldn't be the grieving girlfriend, suffering glamorously beside the mother. And if I *did* come I'd be a random guy in the back, crying in the back about the love of his life while the second cousin's stepson looked at me weirdly. Then I would've gotten into my car and gone home alone, as always. I was not even in Nicky's orbit – that was probably the saddest thing. Here in this country that had supposedly fixed itself, a country that promised freedom and justice for all, Nicky's family would never know I had loved their son. They would never know that two boys had met on a windy day on the front side of summer and opened up each other's lives, that he brought me cinnamon rolls when he was in a good mood, that he touched my shoulder when he was nervous or said my name when he was happy. They would never know that in a future that kept sliding into the past, two kids had stared at each other in a Pontiac in August and become immortal together. But I knew. I was the only one who would ever know. And that was going to have to be enough forever.

But still, could it have helped his parents to know about *me*? Nicky had hated his father, just as I hated mine, but even *he* was probably broken after all this. His only son was dead. Could it give them some small amount of comfort to know that in their son's final months, he was loved? That he was held by someone who loved him, kissed by someone who adored him, slept in the same bed as someone who wanted to spend forever inside his galaxy eyes? I guess I'd never know. Neither would they. It was all one big train wreck of Not Knowing. But I did know one thing: how messed up the world was when kids were being forced to hide so deep in the shadows, their own *families* didn't even know the slightest thing about them. If only parents knew the damage they were creating by ignoring the realities of their kids' lives…

And maybe I *would* sit with them in a living room sometime years away in a perfect future and tell them that I was the one. The one their son had loved, the one that had held

276

him and comforted him in his final year. Maybe, maybe not. But it was a beautiful thing to hope for.

I looked down at the grave it came rushing back to me: that one rare Morning Glory of a moment when he'd given himself to me, back in Savannah.

"Shit, Coley," he'd said in the car, and I'd looked over at him then, so happy I wanted to cry.

"Yeah?"

"Love me forever, okay?"

I didn't say anything at the time. I couldn't. But I could now.

I bent down and placed the eulogy I'd written for him the night before against his stone. I hadn't spoken for him at his funeral, or even been there, so this was my makeup session. I'd never been much of a writer – the beautiful shapes and colors I saw in my mind usually fell apart whenever I tried to pull them out of my skull – but I liked what I'd come up with nonetheless.

Here lies Nicky Flores, a boy who loved. He loved with every tool he had, in every way he knew how, as hard as his broken heart would let him. He loved in a world that tried to destroy that love, and really there has never been anyone or anything braver. And as we cry for him, let us cry freely, as he is worth every tear.

Under my own message I'd added my favorite quote, from a pop star/poet called Saviour:

Fate is an artist, and every human body contains two souls intertwined like brushstrokes on an artist's canvas – yours, and the soul of the person you were born to meet.

I stood up and dried my eyes. Nobody would ever see this, but there was nothing I could do to change that. Oh, God. This was so hard.

The weird thing was, the happy moments with him had sometimes been *so* rare. In the midst of all the fights and the

277

drama and the cut-off phone calls and the ignored texts and the "breaks," I'd almost forgotten that we were happy. But, so help me God, I had never been happier than that boy made me. He could be so gentle with me, so caring, so soft. If I could only find a way back to him. I would gladly exchange forever with someone else for five more minutes with him, and that was the worst thing, the fear that nobody would ever compare.

"I love you," I said to his grave, and it did not make sense that he was under and inside the dirt in front of me, wearing a shirt I'd bought him. Because people like him just didn't die. He was just too good, too otherworldly, too majestic. I already missed him with a force so strong, it both hurt and shocked me. "And you *are* enough," I said. "Forever and ever. And I'm so proud to have known you, do you hear me? The world was wrong, not you. Nothing you ever did was wrong. God, we were so close to getting to happy…"

Lost in the blind inferno of first love, I'd never told Nicholas Flores a lot of things. I'd never really told him how much I'd loved him – more than anything I'd ever loved before, even myself. I'd never really told him it was okay to love me. I'd never really told him he wasn't dirty or sinful or cursed to hell because of what he felt. Because the truth was, I'd never known it myself. I'd swallowed the lies of the world, too. But being allowed to drift into a love like that with him, and realizing that despite what I'd been told by my pastors and teachers and parents, the love between us was real – just as real as the love any man felt for any woman, as real as any love any soul felt for any other soul – that love had taught me the truth and cleansed me of the lies. Love was never wrong. Love was always right. But now I'd never be able to tell Nicky that.

Now, I knew I loved Nicky for many reasons. I knew I loved him because of the way I psychotically collected useless facts about him, like how he hated any kind of beef and how his favorite morning show was *Today* due to a weird little crush on Kathie Lee Gifford. I knew I loved him because I could still perfectly envision the way he smelled, like lemons and sand and the same body wash he said he'd used since middle school. I knew I loved him because of the way my eyes burned when I tried to look at him, for the way he made me feel more alive, for the way he'd loved the Kings of Leon with all of his damaged heart. But mostly I knew I loved him because for the first time in my short and difficult life, when I was next to him I felt like I could be, wholly and essentially, and without strings attached, myself. That was a comfort I would never get back.

The world was a big place, though, full of crowds of strangers, and although starting over currently looked like the worst thing in the world to me, I knew I wasn't too afraid to look for more love, eventually at least. I guess you needed a near-death experience to bring you back to life. And I was alive. Barely.

Then I opened his breakup letter from all those months ago, when he'd spent a set of perfect days in Savannah with me and then gotten scared and dumped me. Why he'd never given it to me, I guess I'd never know – I was still so proud to have spent the best days of my life with him, though. The letter felt a little weird and unsettling to hold, like it was a message from a ghost or something, because that's kind of what it was. It went like this:

Coley,

It's funny, because as I write this letter, knowing that we're over and everything, I'm not crying. Well, I am a little bit, because I'm effing crazy, but I'm also smiling. Because I know we tried. You made me grow up, kid. I had no idea how to love anyone before you. Just think back: think of the kids we were when we met. Think of how closed we were to the world, how frozen we were, how scared shitless of each other we were. Think of how I watched people attack you and then laughed with them. We are different people now, and that is victory. Almost. Kind of. We both know it's not enough. But whatever happens, never confuse willfully leaving someone with simply being too weak to love them in the way they deserve. I'm still not strong enough to be alive and alone, without you. That's why I had to disappear.

And I lost it.

But that's not the story I'm writing today. You'll always be with me, no matter what I do. I am writing about the future, I think.

The following paragraph had been smudged and crossed out, after which he'd started again. He'd cried on it too much, I guessed. I sort of cleared my throat in a way that sounded weird and flimsy and kept reading:

So, yeah, instead of thinking about what we lost, let's think about what we could've had, in the most perfect of worlds. This isn't a regular breakup letter. Because you're my always, and I want you to imagine this:

　　It's me and you, just us. We're walking down the street, not hiding, just walking. The world is clean and bright and nobody is staring. We don't have to look over our shoulders, we don't have to walk five feet away from each other, we don't have to lie to our own families. We get pralines. I bend down on one knee and ask you to move in with me into that brick-walled hipster apartment you talked about, and nobody gawks, nobody judges, nobody points. They just clap for us.

　　Imagine this place, Coley Furman. No matter what, let's make sure it becomes real. You have no idea how badly I wanted to, and always did. And when we do, we will rob that world of love. I promise.

Another smudge. Another crossed-out sentence. My tears were falling on the page, too, mixing ink with saltwater. And then the thought struck me: what if I never loved again?

So: I am going to love you forever, regardless of whether I am ever strong enough to love you out loud or not. What would you say if I did ask you all this, once we built this perfect world, or it built itself? Would you take me as your real, actual, official boyfriend, once the wreckage and the bullshit cleared? Or at least just live in a brick-walled hipster apartment with me until you got sick of me and moved out?

Write back soon. I'll be waiting. -Nicky

PS – here's the thing I was never able to say in person, for a million reasons and one: I love you, Coley. Someday I hope we can both be free.

I folded up the paper as I cried, but I didn't have to say anything. He knew my answer. Nicky already knew. He belonged to the skies now, and now he was free. And now the lights would take him home.

Time fell away like a set of dominoes again, and then I was back with him on the last night we'd ever spent together. "There's nothing wrong with chandeliers," I'd whispered to him as he'd slipped into his second-to-last sleep. And as I stood there I said a little prayer that wherever he was, whatever he was doing, he'd heard me, and he believed me. Most of all I just wished he knew I didn't blame him for this. What I wouldn't give to hold that poor kid in my arms for just five more minutes and tell him he was loved, he was accepted, he was good and pure and right...

"Hey, kid," a guy with a cleaning crew or something called to me from beyond the willows. "We're closing for maintenance. If you're not waiting on family or anything, try to get outta here pretty soon."

"Fine," I said. "And hey, are there any chandeliers in the funeral home?"

"Huh?"

"Just, yes or no?"

"Um, sure – a few, I think."

I reached into my pocket and left a ten-dollar bill on Nicky's grave. "Clean them, will you? Make sure they shine."

The guy shrugged and nodded and kept working, and I gulped. The family at the next grave turned to leave, and I knew what this meant. I had nobody to wait for, nobody to hide from, and Nicky and I were together, alone, for the first time in four months, and possibly the last time. The world couldn't touch us here. We had nothing to run from. It was just the combined energy of us.

I sort of awkwardly knelt at Nicky's grave, my martyr, lost to the ancient and championless and embarrassing and stupid fight against prejudice. He'd been born into a new world ruled by old gods that just wouldn't accept him, but I did. I hoped he knew it somewhere. Brought to my knees in so many more ways than one, I placed a kiss on the stone, cold and hard, and thought of how nobody would ever know our story. Our love would, quite literally, go to the grave with him. It already had. He was dead, and our relationship was gone, and we had never really told a soul about it. How strange it was, the lengths humans would go to when running from fear. How strange and how awful. More than anything I had ever wished in my life, I suddenly wished I could've been more important to him than the fear that'd taken him out.

I knew I would eventually have to deal with the fact that he perhaps chose to leave me, that he perhaps chose to die instead of face all this. And maybe I could've saved him. Maybe I could've tried harder, or then again, maybe my quest to change him had been fruitless from the start. Maybe you couldn't stop people from being who they were born to be any more than you could reach up and grab the whistling wind. Maybe humans were set in stone, and all you could do was point them in the right direction and pray they didn't fall out of the sky. Nicky had perhaps been born to be weak, born to fall, but still I'd love that kid forever.

I blinked. I wanted to swear to myself that I would Promise To Be My Best Self and Start Over and Leave No Sunset Unwatched and Grab Every Chance I Got and all those other things people promised themselves after events like this, but the truth was that I couldn't. Living was so hard. I didn't know where my life would end up more than anyone else did.

All of those sayings and promises suddenly seemed kind of empty and dumb, anyway. This wasn't going to save me, it was just wrecking me, and how many people got ruined and came back stronger? My life now had a Nicky-shaped hole in it, and it would now be measure in two units – before Nicky, and after him. For the rest of my days, I would walk around with his bright sadness inside me – on and off, I would wake up and see that same Facebook status in my mind again, fall into that same hole, crash into that same wall. How did adults live like this, anyway, go around with all this accumulated horror and tragedy and hurt within themselves? How did anyone withstand growing up? All I could do, I figured, was my best, with what I still had, and try not to dwell on what had been taken away from me. Hope that what I'd learned in the past would shade my future in some way, and that all of this mess hadn't just been a shot in the dark…

So I took out my pen and wrote a letter to nobody.

I'm nineteen and I like guys. That fact has defined and upended my whole life, and only today am I able to say it out loud without totally hating myself. But it's too late. I lost the only person my heart has ever wanted, and it's all my fault. So don't be like me. Don't settle for the fear. Choose the hard thing. Choose the love. Always.

Go redo your life. Redecorate your whole ecosystem. Create a world inside your head that is exactly as colorful as you want it to be, and then make it real. Now. While you still can.

I didn't know what else to say, so I turned the camera on myself and snapped a photo. Then I took the Polaroid selfie and placed it under the one of the chandelier that Nicky had never accepted, along with that photo of him from the first day. I added some mementos I'd brought from home – a shard of pottery we'd found on a walk deep in the woods, a ticket stub from a late movie, a wristband from the fair on a Sunday night – the remains of a love affair carried out in total darkness. Then I put it all in front of Nicky's stone, careful not

283

to step on his patch of dirt. This would never make it to my blog, or the Internet. Nicky deserved this particular bit of truth – the world didn't. Our story had been a secret, for worse and better. We'd met in the shadows and bloomed in the dark. But now he was mine, and I would safeguard him for eternity.

At the last minute I changed my mind and grabbed the chandelier Polaroid, though. An idea had just come to me, and that particular Polaroid was now reserved for the cover of a book. A book called *Honesty*.

I looked at the bleeding sky. It was starting to rain – nothing major, just a fine, swirling mist that covered everything around – and I had to leave. I wiped my nose and smiled a little. I missed him so much already. "I'm gonna love you with the lights on now, Nicky. No more hiding." I stopped to choke on my own spit. Then I smiled a little. "I promise. Remember ColeyAndNickyVille? Remember laying in your bed and just being with each other like we were the first people we'd ever been with in our lives? Remember those mornings when I'd try to make turkey omelets and then burn them and drive us to McDonald's instead? I'll keep that world alive forever. I'll come back to your grave sometime, too. I promise. Bye, Nicky. I'm gonna be so brave for you, just watch." I swallowed. "And if humans go anywhere after this life, I'll do everything I can to meet you again one day, back in ColeyAndNickyVille. So…I guess that's it. I love you beyond reason."

I stuffed his note and the envelope back in my pocket, but a glimmer hijacked my eyes. That's when I noticed the ring, my grandpa's heirloom ring, tumbling onto Nicky's dirt. I got confused for a minute, and then I bent down and stared at it and realized what had happened. Nicky had stolen it and taken it with him, back at the hotel in Savannah. I couldn't believe it. All this time I thought he'd spent all those months hating me, and yet Nicky had kept my wedding ring. It was funny, the things people kept where they thought no one could see…

I just picked it up and set it on his grave, though. He could have it. It was already his, if you asked me. Gay marriage in the United States of America, land of life and liberty and the pursuit of happiness, was still a technicality at best. Judges all over the nation were still fighting over its legality, county clerks were still denying marriage licenses to gay couples, churches were still denying baptisms to children of gay unions. Nicky had never lived to see the day he'd be fully, totally accepted by this great country's law book. But here in a cemetery in Georgia, I gave him my ring, my word, my promise, and that was as good as gold. I knew time was going to change me, but the Me he'd known – the Me that was making this promise right now – would be Nicky's forever.

I stood back and smiled at what I'd left behind. I guess it did give me *some* comfort to know that Nicky had died in his way, on his own terms, in his own style. It was so like him to exit the world just as he'd lived in it: as a giant question mark. He just wasn't going to live under someone else's terms, and that's all there was to it.

In any event, my boy had died free. By God, Nicky Flores had died free.

I left the cemetery with this visceral feeling knocking around in my bones, this thrilling/terrifying/electrifying thing that told me Nicky was dead and I was not and I could still start again and therefore anything in the universe was possible now. I wasn't growing up, but I was growing *somewhere*. I didn't really mind, anyway, because I was forming a theory that adulthood wasn't real. First you thought you knew everything. Then you discovered you knew nothing. Then you learned that knowing nothing was okay. Then you started over from there.

I guessed I was somewhere a few inches into the "starting over" stage. I didn't really know what my specific future contained – I was confused and I was damaged and I was smart and I was hopeful and I was still trying and I was getting there and I never again wanted to love anyone like I'd loved Nicky Flores. That kind of love, that big grand violent malignant chandelier love that made you go insane and made you stalk social media for hours in the privacy of your bedroom and made you spin apart and then stand up and grow again, felt like it was uniquely his, like he'd stamped himself onto my heart that summer, and that spot was his forever now, even if he was nowhere. I would honor that, or at least try to. I would give him his rightful territory, keep it golden, treasure him like the crystal chandelier he was. I'd just have to rebuild in a different direction.

I didn't really know what being a human meant, either, obviously. I was still such a kid in so many ways. I didn't know how exactly to grow up and become an adult who paid his taxes and had a mortgage every month, or what any of that even entailed. I didn't know why I'd been put on a rock spinning in space to be gay and feel something different than ninety percent of other humans felt. But for the first time I was sort of, *almost*, okay with that. I was probably never going to wake up one day and suddenly be an adult – adulting was a journey, not a destination. But I figured loving other humans on my way to finding out the answers to all those things couldn't hurt. Love was never a mistake, regardless of what my Sunday school teachers had told me. To love was the most grown up thing of all. All I knew for sure was that I would try to search for more beautiful sunsety moments and try to live inside more confused, breathless instances where someone I loved looked down at my shirt and took a pause and realized they loved me back. I would try to find more lovely little conversations where a stranger's eyes clouded over and they realized they could not be anything other than honest with me, and I would try to one day fall in love with myself the way I fell in love with strangers on the street. I didn't know if any of this was feasible, or even possible. But I did know I would try.

When I passed the graveyard's sad little business office, I was reminded that business was a death that people profited from, and one day my departure would fill the coffers of a similarly pathetic place of rest, too. This disgusted me in a weird and indescribable way, but I shrugged. I'd be too dead to notice, anyway. Then I saw the UPS guy stuffing a package into the office's brick mailbox, and I remarked to myself how strange it was that all UPS guys looked the same, balding and frazzled and like their eyes were elsewhere. And I thought about how kind of beautiful it was that everyone had a place in this world, even my cleaning lady, even the president, even this UPS guy who was doing his job and carrying out his purpose in the world, dutifully and reluctantly. I hadn't really found *my* place yet, but I still *had* a place, and that was kind of gorgeous and comforting to think about, that one day I would possibly learn to be the hell out of myself. I'd thought my place was by Nicky's side, but clearly not. I'd just keep looking until I found somewhere I fit.

Once again he was like my favorite book: it infuriated me that I couldn't go back to the beginning of us and read him again, meet him with brand new eyes, just so I could live inside every second all over again. Because magic wore off: that was the nature of the magical. It was love's job to strike us like lightning and light us up for one blazing extraterrestrial moment before retreating again and reminding us that we were mortal creatures living on an unspectacular planet. Love was a blessing from the skies, and as soon as we took that for granted, poof – love was gone. But I could, and *would*, write new stories, look for more magic. In any case, that explosion of passion – that moment when someone's face lit up, when their voices shook, when their eyes took on that manic energy that came from somewhere deep, where they held their holiest truths – that's where I wanted to spend the rest of my life. No more sleepwalking – I was going to wake up. Because so many adults were sleeping, frozen, dying, already gone. We told ourselves it was too hard to experience life for the beautiful and unpredictable and frequently damaging sunburst that it was, and we retreated into the shadows of ourselves. Soon we got cold, turned ourselves off to numb the pain of being alive. But I never wanted that for myself. I wanted to look at the forest and see the trees, I wanted to wake up in the morning and look at the day as something to chase instead of something to hide from. Tomorrow was never promised, regret was terrible and easy to avoid, and love was the mother of everything under the sun. That's what I thought, at least.

I hit the interstate smiling through salty tears. I hated the world, even though I kind of loved it, too. All I wanted was what everyone else wanted, which was to love and feel loved in return – and the world wouldn't let me have that. They'd stamped it out like a smoker putting out a cigarette on a smoke break. I would never get over this, not just for what it was, but what it could've been. My soul had been split in half and would always exist in two places: within me, and with him. Wherever he was. In any case, here it was, in the final frame: the resurrection of Coley Furman. Alive and dead, all at once. Torn open. Afraid, but strong enough to limp forward now. Oh, God. Hopefully…

As I drove, I couldn't stop picturing his grave, and the sense of enraged uselessness around it. This shit had to end. A healthy, strong, smart boy was dead, all due to stupid outdated views shoved down society's throats by people who'd supposedly been cleansed by holy water. He was a chandelier in a world of boulders, and he just couldn't survive his own delicacy. I never wanted anyone else to have to feel like this again. They didn't deserve it. Donald Trump didn't even deserve this. People were literally fighting for their lives out there, and maybe getting my story out there could help change minds and prevent this shit-storm of a situation from replicating itself. After all, I'd lived this story, breathed it, fallen to pieces at the hands of it. Maybe now it needed to be told, and I had *every* right to tell it. Maybe I *could* put our story into the book, as some vague type of author's note or something. Hadn't I just been lamenting the lack of gay-themed stories out there? Lots of people would *kill* to have the platform I had, to be listened to in the way I knew I could make people listen to the blog. I shivered a bit, already getting excited. Who knew – maybe I'd been born for this. Maybe this story was my opus. Maybe I'd been put through the ringer to learn these lessons and push this knowledge forward. Maybe this was just the sunrise of my life…

This wasn't exactly what I'd envisioned for myself, but suddenly I was *so* beyond caring. At some point you just had to drop the charade and step into the person you were. Eventually you had to let go of the person you'd never become and accept your life for what it had had never been. Things

288

were going to blow, and you just had to let the shrapnel hit where it was going to, let the casualties fall where they were going to fall. I couldn't be normal if I tried – that just wasn't an option for me – so why was I still chasing a life behind picket fences? People always said "it gets better" – nothing had gotten any better, but *I* was getting better at *dealing* with it, and I figured that was a start in the right direction. I knew a potential "coming out" moment would probably embarrass my family, my cousins, my friends – for nonsense reasons rooted in fear and prejudice, but still, the end effect would be the same. I didn't really care much anymore, though, because for the first time in my life I knew I'd found something I believed in – and that confidence would have to carry me through whatever was about to happen.

There were also other issues, now that I thought about it. I wasn't sure if the gay community needed another gay tragedy, another miserable story about a closet case dying in shame. But then again, our story was so much more complicated and more beautiful than that. There was so much love to be found between the miserable spots. Nicky had been coaxed out of the closet by a world that had flashed acceptance and progress like a shiny lie, then forced back into it after he'd realized it was just the same old world with a glitzy new bow on top. The old world was still underneath, poisoned by the same ugliness. We were all the same in the end, just a bunch of hurt creatures with small galaxies of horror revolving within ourselves that we were too scared to let out. And maybe I could do the brave thing and let it all out...

But it was *my* book, after all, and I could probably do whatever the hell I wanted with it, within reason. I needed a place to put all my rage and fury and grief and despair, and that could be the perfect outlet. What better gift to offer to the world than my pain? Perhaps I'd been born to sing this song, the song of Nicky Flores, and now that he'd taught me how to sing, well...

I knew it wouldn't be easy. The world at large would hijack my story, anyway, rendering it simply "another gay story," glossing over every moment every hug every kiss every tear every triumph every chandelier and paint it as a big gay joke, just like they did with every other story not occurring between two humans of opposite sex. But screw that, and screw them. I wasn't responsible for the world, but I was responsible for all the people under me, all the people to come after me, all the people I could possibly lend a hand to. Maybe I could use the story of NickyAndColeyVille to do that. Our love may have existed inside a snow globe, now and forever, isolated and pristine and shut off from the rest of the world by our collective fear and shame and self-doubt, but I could still shake us up and let the memories fall on my shoulders and cover me like snow. Because snow turned to water, and water cleansed you, purified you, baptized you, remade you…

I also knew from photography that the best photos were taken from the places that were hardest to get to. Climbing a tree or wading out to a sand bar or forcing yourself up a steep sand dune was shitty, yes, but the vantage points you reached after all the difficulty gave you a whole new viewpoint, a whole new perspective. All you had to do was get there. And – so help me God – I wanted to get there.

So I grabbed my phone and found the number, area code 212. The office manager answered, already sounding annoyed and impatient.

"Kate Griscom, please," I said. "I'm…her client, I guess, technically."

"Are you, or aren't you?"

"Yes," I said, sitting taller. "Yes. I am Kate Griscom's client."

She sighed and patched me through. After what felt like twenty minutes, my agent finally answered.

"Kate, hey, yes, it's Cole Furman with *Honesty*. I'm just calling because I…well, I was lying when I said I didn't know what to focus on. With the book, I mean."

"I'm listening."

As I got closer to Jacksonville I told her the basics of my story, my treatment down here, my pain. Then I told her

I'd like to include some LGBT stories, stories that could potentially open some eyes and start changing things. When I finished she took a long breath.

"First of all, I'm sorry," she said. "That is…awful. Jesus, that's just terrible. And second, I'm not surprised. I went to college in Dallas for two years. Some of the things I saw and heard there…it was just beyond belief. One of my roommates Eileen was a lesbian, and although most people were nice enough, she was absolutely miserable sometimes – she's probably still licking her wounds. The things they did to her, I swear…" She paused. I screwed up my face, trying not to think about Nicky. "I must tell you," she said soon. "The gay angle…in the Deep South…it's certainly…*intriguing*. I don't even know if that's even been done before yet, in a book at least. It would definitely get people talking."

"Well that's the thing," I said, swallowing hard. "It would burn up my life, to be honest. And I just don't want…I don't know if I want to make a splash, or cause any trouble or anything…"

"Uh, Cole, I hate to tell you this, but the trouble is already there." I thought I heard her laugh a little. "Hell, this nightmare of a country could use a little disrupting, anyway. You're really good at this whole communicating thing, so put that skill to use. Put yourself on the line – make them feel your heart."

I gripped the wheel. Somehow it made me feel so much stronger to know the world still contained good, kind, open-minded people somewhere. "So…you're saying I should fight it?"

She inhaled, paused. "To the death, Mr. Furman."

So as I drove I wrote my own *Honesty* entry into my phone, the official start of work on my book. I began by writing one true statement and then going from there. The sad thing was, I really wanted to portray Nicky as this knight on a horse, some romantic hero who'd swooped in and rescued me – but I couldn't. Looking back, it almost seemed like I'd forced some ideal of perfection onto his shoulders that he had not only never asked for, but probably didn't even deserve. I'd probably been dating the person I *wanted* him to be, instead of the actual person that lived inside his skin. He was weak, and the crazy thing was, that's why he was so magnificent.

So I wrote and wrote and wrote. I'd already been writing this out in my head, actually, for reasons unknown, so as soon as I put my fingers to the keyboard, things just started flowing out:

THE YEAR OF US

It was the year of abandoning comfort zones
And throwing myself at the world
And seeing what stuck

It was the year of spotting a pair of galaxy eyes
And being swallowed up in them
At light speed

It was the year of finding myself on an overgrown sidewalk at
the golden hour
With the boy of my purest dreams
And realizing I didn't know my own life anymore

It was the year of hung-up phone calls, unreturned text
messages, fights in my backyard
It was the year of cinnamon buns and Sunday morning cuddles
and being loved like crown jewels in between the car crashes

It was the year of hating him in bright red
And feeling his passion in neon green
And loving him in burnished gold

It was the year of rushing through the summer air on a golf
cart, getting to be a kid again
It was the year of growing up alone in the winter cold

It was the year of laughing in sand dunes

And screaming in deserted kitchens
And crying in my bed alone

It was the year of tumbling into blackness
And somehow finding a pulse on the other side

It was the year of looking into the wreckage in me and finding
something worth excavating

It was the year of him.
Until it wasn't

And in the final frame
It became the year of getting to know the soul inside my skin
And realizing that nobody's love was going to save me
But my own

THE END OF US

*It was the last weekend of the summer. There was gold in the
sky and wind in the air when you sat down with tears in your
eyes and dumped me. You said you hated yourself for what
you felt for me, you said you wanted to change your life and
get into heaven. For four months or so, you were my heaven.
Whether you found that place or not, I hope you know you
were the brightest part of my life, the part I held above all
others. I hope you know you weren't dirty or wrong or
unlovable for loving me and being different. I hope you know I
didn't hate you even when I said I did. Mostly I just hope
you're at peace. Remember when we got drunk in that messy
hotel room and blurted out that we loved each other for the
first time? Remember when your grandma died and you came
over and sat on my bed and asked me to hold you? Remember
driving in your car down the beach, running away from a
world that had it out for us? Remember the slate-blue Atlantic
and the way the waves sparkled just for us, the evening winds
that smelled like palms and suntan lotion and sand and
bougainvillea, that canary-yellow shirt of mine that you kept*

in your room? I will hold those memories with me forever,
even after we fade to black and white.

I sat back with misty eyes and thought about what I'd written,
and what I was about to do. Part of me couldn't believe
myself, but another part was exhilarated beyond anything I'd
ever known. Maybe I'd lost my mind, and maybe my sanity
had officially left the building. But at least I was free.

I was so proud of myself, too. For some reason I saw a
vision of my bigoted old childhood preacher, Mr. DeShane,
coming across the letter, his eyes growing wide with disgust
and fury as he read. *What would he think of this,* I wondered?
And then I smiled, because as far as I was concerned, Mr.
DeShane – and everything he stood for – could suck my
sweaty left testicle. I was so stupid to ever think the world
couldn't be changed. All you had to do was be brave enough
to light the first match. I'd found my lighter, and now I was
about to attack the world and fight until it started listening.
And who knew: maybe somewhere, Nicky would be prouder
of me than my father had been.

I turned off the highway to my hometown at sunset.
The sky was the strangest shade of burnished pink, a
bubblegum tangerine. I took the long way back just to avoid a
certain street where I'd always golf carted with Nicky – for
some reason it still felt too hard for me to face that particular
stretch of pavement where I'd run wild with him. Part of the
majesty of youth, I was starting to learn, was the complete
ignorance of it; the cluelessness built into being young and
free and sick with the dreamer's disease. Sitting in a parking
lot on a hot, windy night drinking gas station wine with Nicky
and listening to bad pop music from his golf cart's speakers
was not an inherently magical experience until I looked back
and realized I'd never be able to do it again. That was all I
knew at the time, so I didn't really stop to think about it –
tomorrow didn't matter. By the time you realized moments for
what they were, they were already gone. Only after you grew
older and looked at memories you could never get back could

you realize just how valuable those cheap nights were, and learn you were inside a messy miracle called being alive.

I got stuck behind a city bus in a clogged construction zone, and soon I realized I was right in front of my old FitTrax gym, ground zero of ColeyAndNickyVille. I smiled a little. "Hey," Nicky had called the very first day we'd ever spoken, looking bright and fresh and new as a summer sunrise. "You in the business of staring, or do you do it for free?" I could still hear his voice perfectly in my mind. It made me so sad, and so, so happy.

Across the road I spotted a giant truck pouring greyish concrete into the foundation of a new townhouse, and I got curious. Soon a family would be moving there, mom and dad and little kids, hopefully more whole than mine had been. I got to thinking about this fantastical family of the future. They would never know about me or Nicky or the little world we'd shared, but they would probably know people *like* us, people who were different. What would they think of those people? And what would that family be like? How would the parents raise their children? What would they teach them? What would those kids' ideals be? Would they grow up to hate themselves like me, or be in love with everything they did? Would they be trapped like I was, or would they be brave and free like how America was supposed to be? I didn't know, but I hoped they would be better humans than had existed yesterday, and inherit less bullshit than I had. The world was just going to keep happening no matter how shitty my life became, and I was stuck with me – I had no other choice but to learn how to inhabit this body I'd been given, try to use it to help the rest of us. And as the liquid concrete glooped out of the tube, laying the foundation for tomorrow, I imagined a world with no heaven to aspire to, no hell to avoid. No guilt, no goals. Just love, and all it encompassed. Life could be so beautiful, after all, if you let it be.

So I grabbed my phone again and sent my mother one simple message: *I love you, mom.* Because I did love her, despite everything she was, and everything she wasn't. And suddenly I wanted so badly to give her all the hugs and kisses and love I'd never been able to give Nicky. All I knew how to do going forward was love people with all the love in me for as long as I could, and hope that when they left this place they'd been filled up with love by me, and would be taking more love with them than they'd come in with. It was kind of cool, actually – I was just a tiny little person living in northern Florida who could contribute to humanity's global pool of love. How awesome was *that*? After all, humans were just small, breakable mammals on a largely unspectacular planet in a thoroughly average solar system located in one unimpressive galaxy out of trillions, who were meant to love each other. That's all we were. The rest of it was so useless. All we could do was love…

As I idled, one of the construction dudes caught my eye as he built a new future. I sensed that he was gay, but he wasn't the tutu-wearing spectacle of my childhood nightmares about what my future held, either. I'd been so judgmental my whole life, so quick to assume "gay" meant one thing, when really it meant a million different things, or nothing at all, really. The butt of the joke had been me all along. This construction guy had latte-colored skin and a big, sweet-natured smile as bright as stadium lights, and he couldn't have been much older than I was. His eyes weren't galaxies, but then again, nobody else's would be ever again. It would always be Nicky – in a million neighborhoods, under a million suns, in a million different lives, it would always be him. But then again, here was a new boy, and he was looking at me. Being honest with society was one thing, but could I be honest with *myself*? You didn't get to decide what the world thought about you, but you did get to decide how you thought about the world, and this construction dude wasn't thinking at all. He was just being. And the fact that he was black, and that my father would have a dozen heart attacks if I ever ended up dating him…well, that just made me like him more, honestly.

Another big happy smile shattered his face, and suddenly all the months melted away and I was back in the body of that shy, skittish kid who'd fallen in love with Nicky last summer at the very gym in front of me, terrified of his own gay shadow. *Create your world*, I heard someone say in Nicky's voice deep in my mind. Something cracked open in me, then lit itself on fire, throwing sparks into the darkest parts of me, and I knew I was a boy remade. Every molecule in me buzzed and burned, and suddenly I knew I'd been put on this Earth to live this truth, tell this story, speak this honesty. In that moment a drifting kid, forever lost, took on his destiny and became, for the first time, proud of himself. We were all born for battle into a cruel, shitty world intent on blowing out the fires in our eyes, but the moment we let that world harden us and close up our chests and destroy our ability to love – *that* was the moment the world won the war. And since I had no intentions of losing just yet, I did the second-craziest thing I had ever done in my nineteen years and eleven months of being alive: I pulled off the road and parked my car.

I rolled down my window and leaned into the light. I said one true sentence in a shaking voice, thirteen words long. The boy gave me a startled look, dropped what he was holding, and walked toward me.

THE END
A SPECIAL NOTE FROM SETH KING

On a clear, cold afternoon when I was thirteen, I walked to the top of a mountain and thought about jumping off of it. I was being mistreated by someone very close to me for having "feminine qualities," and so I slipped out of the cabin my family had rented for Christmas, tiptoed to the edge of a cliff, and peered down at the jagged rocks and swaying trees below. I was in love with a golden-eyed boy from my science class and part of me wanted to die for that love, because he couldn't admit he loved me back and I knew it would never work out and the world was built against us. What stopped me was imagining a new world where it wouldn't matter who I dreamed about, where I wouldn't be insulted or belittled for being different, where a boy could love me back and not have to run from it. I didn't want a future where I could scream from the hilltops about my love – that wasn't really my style – I just wanted a world where the news about me would be met with a shrug. What kept me on firm ground was envisioning that place.

Today is December 22, 2015, and I'm back. Back in this town that almost served as the end of me, back in this same struggle I faced a decade ago, but hopefully not for much longer. I lost the love of the boy with the golden eyes, or maybe I never had it all – but still it changed me forever. I had to watch from the sidelines as he flourished and became a famous athlete, but I think I'm finally becoming myself, too. I've loved women and men since then, and I've felt them love me back. All of it has gone into the story of who I am today. I have known I had to write this book ever since that day on the mountaintop, and when I knew I couldn't run from Coley and Nicky anymore, I sat down and took a breath. *Honesty* drifted out of me like an orphan that had looked for a home all its life, flowed out of my fingertips like small galaxies. I am so proud of this book.

At the same time, I'm not stupid. The world is so different now, but much the same. We are closer to the utopia

298

I imagined in some ways, miles away in others. Technically speaking I am one the most prominent young male authors in the country, and the news that my first love was a guy could change everything. I am famous for writing books about men who fall in love with women – which is just as much a part of my past as this book is, to be fair – and I operate in an industry where heterosexual love stories count for over ninety percent of sales. I know I am a canvas which a lot of my readers splash their expectations onto, and I know I have female fans who probably want me to write the same hetero love story ad infinitum. I will be the first to admit that a novel about two male teenagers falling in love one bright, brutal summer might not be what they're looking for from me. I know who it is for, though. It's for all the little kids like Coley and Nicky and me, all the kids who have ever been told by classmates and parents and society that they are dirty and inadequate and tainted, all the kids who have ever climbed something and thought about jumping out of hell. More than that, though, it's for the ones who *did* jump. It's for the lost ones, forever silent, that I remained after. I can still try to be brave enough to change this world I live in – they can't. So as I sail into a new world alone I do it with the wish to both speak for the ones who left before me and improve things for the ones who stand on the edge today, uncertain if the future is something they even want to see. So help me walk them back. We've done so much, but we still have so much more to accomplish. In this gleaming new future we think we've created, people are suffering everywhere. Nobody else needs to die for this, especially children. According to the *Educational Researcher*, forty-four percent of bisexual teens are seriously considering suicide, and that is a statistic our society should not accept in 2016.

This is *Honesty*, my declaration of independence. I was born to write this book. I know it could derail everything, but if one attempt to help humanity ends my career and puts me in the poor house, save a street corner for me. Kids like me are still killing themselves every day, and with visibility comes responsibility. I am committed to writing about subjects that may help some folks out there, and not just pacify my fans and maybe buy me a yacht. History tells me I am naïve to expect this to not be an issue. I dare you to prove me wrong.

To my family: I love you. To my brother's kids: I live for you, and I hope you'll grow up one day and understand this and be proud of me. To everyone else who has ever supported me so far: thanks. And to the boy with the golden eyes: thank you for showing me what love felt like. I won't forget the way we laughed when we stole those oranges from your neighbor's tree, the way you cried when you crashed my dirt bike, the way your leg felt next to mine when we fell asleep on my trampoline under a blanket of stars that just weren't in our favor. Even that morning when I indirectly asked you to admit that you loved me and your eyes filled with tears and you walked away and said you were late for church – every moment of that year we spent together will stay alive in me forever. Even though our story is over and you haven't spoken to me in years, even though those two kids who existed on that trampoline are long gone, you're with me still. You are engraved in me, and I carry you with me everywhere. I even wrote a book about what could've happened if the world had let us love each other. Here it is.

As I write this note and finish this book and close this chapter of my life, I do it looking out of my window at the exact cliff I peered over as a kid, with wind whistling in my ears and dread settling into my stomach and all the fear in the world pulling down at my young bones. Something new is ringing all around me, though. It sounds like freedom.

Seth King
Beech Mountain, NC
December 22, 2015

Seth King is the twenty-six-year-old author of The Summer Remains. He lives in Florida.